Meet Me Under the Clock

Annie Murray

Meet Me Under the Clock

MACMILLAN

First published in Great Britain 2014 by Macmillan
an imprint of Pan Macmillan, a division of Macmillan Publishers Limited
Pan Macmillan, 20 New Wharf Road, London N1 9RR
Basingstoke and Oxford
Associated companies throughout the world
www.panmacmillan.com

ISBN 978-0-230-76993-9

1 3 5 7 9 8 6 4 2

A CIP catalogue record for this book is available from the British Library.

Typeset by Ellipsis Digital Limited, Glasgow
Printed and bound by CPI Group (UK) Ltd, Croydon, CR0 4YY

1940

One

September 1940

Sylvia was helping her mother with the weekly wash when she heard it. She was standing at the kitchen table, hands in a bowl of soapy water, while Mom was feeding clothes through the mangle. Sylvia pushed some dark curls of hair away from her forehead with her arm and tilted her head.

'Ssh, listen – what's that?'

Her mother, Pauline Whitehouse, her thick red hair held back in a flowery turban, stilled the handle of the mangle. They could both hear it then, coming from next door's garden.

'Oh good Lord, it sounds like Marjorie!' Pauline rushed for the back door, wiping her hands on her apron.

It was raining outside. Over the pattering drops Sylvia could clearly hear the sounds of distress. Her heart pounded. Surely those noises weren't coming from cheerful, good-natured Mrs Gould? But already she knew, with a terrible dread: something had happened to one of the boys.

In the distance she heard her mother's soothing tones and Marjorie Gould's terrible, choking cries. Mom led Marjorie through the gap dividing the two gardens and towards the house. Sylvia forced herself to move. She rushed to wipe her hands and put the kettle on.

'Come on, bab, let's get you in the dry,' Pauline was saying. 'That's it, let's sit you down . . .'

There were dark spots of rain on Mom's apron and on Marjorie's dress, which was royal blue, patterned with little white anchors. Sylvia froze again with shock. She had known Marjorie Gould all her life – Marjorie was like a second mother to her – and she had never, ever seen her like this before. Marjorie was a big-boned, normally splendid-looking woman with thick, blonde hair, who favoured bright frocks and lipstick. But today she was hunched over, shaking and weeping, her face contorted. As Mom guided her to the chair by the unlit range, Sylvia saw that Marjorie had no shoes on. She had run out into the wet in her stockinged feet.

'No!' she was sobbing. 'No . . . No . . . !' There was a piece of paper crumpled tightly in her right hand.

'Get the kettle on, Sylv,' Pauline said.

'I already have.' Her eyes met her mother's and Pauline caught hold of Sylvia's arm and pulled her hurriedly down the hall, out of earshot.

'It's Raymond.' They were standing by the coat hooks. An old black mac of Dad's sagged from a peg. 'He's . . . Oh good heavens—' Sylvia saw the awful truth of it hit her mother. Her hands came up to her cheeks. 'His ship's gone down.'

'No!' Sylvia gasped. Raymond was the oldest of Marjorie Gould's three sons: Raymond, Laurie and Paul. 'But does that mean . . . ? Is he . . . ?'

Pauline looked down with a faint nod. 'Must be.'

Sylvia felt sick and shaky, even though her mind could not fully take in the news. Raymond, the boy next door. Raymond, a gentle, dark-haired lad who had gone off and joined the Navy, looking for a new life, a way to escape from his father and to separate himself from the girl he loved, but who did not love him back – Audrey, Sylvia's elder sister.

'If only Laurie hadn't just joined up as well,' Pauline said, anguished. Laurie had not long gone into the RAF. 'This *terrible*, wicked war . . .' She squeezed Sylvia's arm. 'I must go back to her.'

Sylvia sank down onto the stairs as her mother headed back to the kitchen. She heard Mrs Gould break into more gulping sobs. Crouching on the third step up, she gripped her hands together to try and stop them trembling. She had to remind herself to breathe. Raymond – Raymond Gould, aged twenty-one. Sweet, solemn Raymond, just a year older than herself, whom she had known for as long as she could remember. Raymond who would now never be twenty-two, or -three or -four.

She rested her head in her hands, staring, unseeing, at the tiled hall floor.

Raymond was in so many of the family photographs.

Sylvia moved restlessly around the house that afternoon. Mom was next door with Mrs Gould and her youngest son Paul. Dad and Audrey were at work and her brother Jack was at school. Sylvia worked evenings, but it was her day off. She found herself wandering into the front room. They did not light the fire in there very often and the atmosphere was rather cold and stiff compared with the back room, where they all ate every night around the table.

There were three dark-green chairs arranged round the fire with its polished brass fender. On a side-table facing the window Mom kept her carefully dusted

5

collection of framed photographs, arranged on a red chenille cloth. Sylvia and Audrey as little girls smiled out of the most eye-catching one. At least, Sylvia was smiling. She had been six when the picture was taken and Audrey eight. Sylvia, pink-cheeked, with her cloud of black, frizzy hair, was beaming amiably, displaying a selection of teeth and gaps. Audrey looked more solemn, unwilling to smile if she did not feel like it. She did have a full row of teeth, though.

Sylvia always wondered why Mom had gone to the trouble of having her children's pictures done just when they had half their teeth missing. The one of their younger brother Jack, freckly and auburn-haired like Mom, showed him grinning, with black gaps along his gums. There was Mom and Dad's wedding photograph: Dad skinny and happy, Mom with her hair piled magnificently on her head and looking shy. And in the front row there were tiny portraits in ornate pewter frames of each of the three of them as babies, once they could sit up. As they grew older there were lots of pictures, because the two dads, Ted Whitehouse and Stanley Gould, had bought a Beau Brownie camera between them. From all of these photographs the Gould boys smiled out as well. Raymond was in so many of them, dark-eyed and serious, while Laurie was blond like his mother. Paul came along later.

Sylvia chose a picture with all of them in, and sat down to study it. Raymond, about nine in the picture, was standing at the end of the line of children in the back garden where they spent so many hours playing. The picture seemed so real and close. She could hear his piping boy's voice, before it broke into a deep, manly one; and she remembered his skinny legs in baggy shorts, tearing along the garden. Raymond bowling a tennis ball for cricket games, furious when Audrey whacked it over

6

onto the railway line. Raymond intent on his homework, getting more and more nervy as he floundered at the grammar school into which Stanley, his father, had steamrollered him.

She looked closely into Raymond's eyes. He was so familiar, like a brother. She realized then, though, with a pang, that in her whole life she had scarcely ever been alone with Raymond or talked to him on her own. They had always been in a gang. He had just been one of those things she took for granted, like the furniture, or the buses in Kings Heath High Street, or the Market Hall in Birmingham. And now Raymond was gone and the Market Hall had been wrecked by a bombing raid.

All through the long 'phoney war' of last winter Raymond had been on HMS *Esk*, a destroyer, laying mines around the coast of Norway and Holland. The ship had taken part in the evacuation of troops from Dunkirk. Sylvia knew all this must have made Stanley Gould prouder than he would ever be capable of saying. The last time Raymond came home on leave he had been just as serious, but he looked older, and strong and capable. Sylvia had wondered then whether Audrey might change her mind and love Raymond back. She knew Marjorie was hoping – and Mom. But no. Poor Raymond carried his flame for Audrey quietly and stoically. And now . . .

'Oh, Raymond,' she said, smoothing her finger over the glass. How could it be that he was dead, that they would never see him again, ever? Cradling the photograph in her arms, she rocked back and forth as if giving comfort to Raymond and to herself. Gradually the ache in her released into sobs and the tears came.

*

It was all they could think about.

Ted Whitehouse, Sylvia's dad, was a foreman at the Rover in Acocks Green. It was one of Herbert Austin's shadow factories, set up before the war to disguise the whereabouts of armaments production by removing some of it from well-known factory sites. The works were making parts for Bristol Hercules engines.

Since the bombing started Ted had to take his turn at the works, on fire-watch, but it was not his shift tonight. He was able to go round and commiserate with Stanley. Ted, a tall, slender man with dark hair and eyes, looked pale and strained after this experience. He sat down in the kitchen to unlace his boots. Sylvia and Jack, who was twelve, were in there with Pauline already. Pauline had broken the news to Jack when he came in from school. He went up to his room for a bit and now he was silent and withdrawn.

'This is when you really know you're at war,' Ted said, pushing each boot off with the other foot.

'Oh, I think we all know that, love,' his wife said. They had got used to so many things already in this war: gas masks, the shortages, the dark streets and blacked-out houses, the terrible news as the Germans invaded one country after another. But this was the worst so far. This brought the war right up close, into their homes and hearts. Pauline's eyes were red. 'How's Stanley?' she asked.

Ted shook his head, laying the black boots side-by-side. 'As you'd expect.'

They heard the front door open as Audrey came in and they all exchanged looks.

Ted got up. 'You tell her,' he said quietly, moving out of the kitchen, boots in hand. 'I've had all I can stand.'

They heard him say, 'All right, love?' quietly as he

passed Audrey. She came into the kitchen in her office clothes: a dark-blue skirt and white blouse. She worked, without enthusiasm, as a shorthand typist for an insurance company. Crossing the kitchen, she flung herself into the chair next to the range in which Marjorie Gould had howled out her grief earlier.

Audrey was tall and slender, very much like her father with her brown eyes, dark lashes and long, sleek hair, which was pinned back in a fashionable style for work. Though less obviously pretty and pink-cheeked than Sylvia, she had a striking, strong-featured face and a large, well-defined nose. She gave off a fiery kind of energy, which attracted people to her. Among the three children in the family, she was definitely always the boss.

She slid her black court shoes off, crossed one leg over, twitching her foot impatiently up and down. She looked round at everyone.

'What's the matter with you lot?' she asked. 'You've got faces as long as Livery Street.'

In the silence that followed she uncrossed her legs and sat up, really taking in that something was amiss.

'Why are you all in here?' It was rare for Jack to be in the kitchen at this time, as the grammar school gave him so much homework.

Sylvia and her mother looked at each other.

'Audrey, love,' Pauline said, slowly, as if she didn't want to bring the words out. 'There's been some terrible news today.'

Jack made a small sound, as if stifling a sob, and covered his face with his hands. Sylvia felt her chest tighten so that she could hardly breathe.

Audrey's eyes searched their mother's face. 'News? How d'you mean?'

Pauline explained. Sylvia watched Audrey's face as she

tried to make sense of what her mother was saying. Her eyes widened. She curled forward, arms crossed, hugging herself.

'Could he be alive?' She just managed to keep her voice steady. 'He could be . . . I mean, he can swim, can't he?'

'I think it's over,' Pauline said gently. 'There was a telegram from the Navy.'

'Marjorie came in earlier,' Sylvia said. 'She was in a very bad state.'

Pauline went to Audrey to put her arm round her. 'Audrey, bab . . . ?' But at the first touch on her shoulder, Audrey threw her mother off and got up.

'That's terrible news,' she said. 'Poor Mr and Mrs Gould.' She wasn't meeting any of their eyes. 'I can't really take it in. I'm going up to take my things off.'

She walked out of the kitchen, leaving them all watching the space she had left. Her shoes were discarded at untidy angles next to the range.

'Oh dear, oh dear,' Pauline said. She sank down on one of the chairs, looking completely exhausted.

Two

The Whitehouses and the Goulds had lived side by side in Kings Heath in their quiet, terraced neighbourhood for years. First Pauline and Ted moved into their house, with Audrey as a baby. When the house next door came up for rent a few months later, the Goulds moved in when they had just had Raymond.

The children grew up together and rubbed along, as youngsters are expected to, and most of the time it was lovely. But there were always things that were not so nice, that stayed with you – like that one afternoon Sylvia would never forget.

Mr Gould made them all play one of his games. Stanley Gould was forever thinking up pastimes designed to make his sons count or add up. Dad said that Stanley had always been 'a clever bugger', and he pushed his sons into anything he thought would make them grow up to be brilliant engineers. He loved anything to do with counting. One of his favourite hobbies was collecting loco numbers. They often saw him craning over the fence at the Kings and Castles and the other engines rushing along the LMS line. Just beyond the iron railings that bordered their gardens was the cutting, its vegetation scorched by fires from the scattering sparks.

Stanley Gould was a short, restless man, his hair brushed back over his head like two tarry bird's wings. He had a clipped black moustache and, at the left side of his mouth, a metal tooth, which glistened when he spoke. Sylvia found it fascinating. Stanley worked as pattern-maker in a firm that, for the war effort, had gone over to making parts for tanks. He was quick-minded, competent and chirpy and expected everyone else to be the same. On this particular warm summer afternoon, when the children were playing in the Goulds' garden, he started giving orders.

'Come on,' he urged. Sylvia could sense his impatience underneath the jolly tone. Life was for getting on – it was no good idling about, wasting time! She felt a plunge of nervousness in her stomach. 'Line up now, in age order. Raymond first.'

Audrey was never easy to order around at the best of times. She planted herself in front of Mr Gould on her long legs, throwing her dark plait back over her shoulder.

'*I'm* first. I'm the oldest.'

'So you are!' Mr Gould said, flustered at being found in the wrong. 'By a whisker. Right, step up, Audrey.'

They lined up in front of the pile of builder's sand that they called their sandpit.

'Right, give your name and age.'

'Audrey – ten!'

'Surname?'

Audrey rolled her eyes. 'Whitehouse, of course.'

'Right, next. Look lively!' Sylvia's father sometimes said that Stanley Gould should have been in the Army, though up until now he never had been. He'd been too valuable in the factory during the Great War.

'Raymond Gould.' Raymond leapt into position, his pumps spraying gritty sand. 'Nine – nearly ten!'

'Sylvia Whitehouse – eight.' She was always much more biddable than Audrey and plodded into the line-up, happy just to be included with the others.

In the middle of this Marjorie Gould came outside. She stood with her arms folded over a vivid green dress, watching the military line-up of the children.

'Oh, Stan, leave 'em be,' she said in her easy voice. 'Let them come and have some lemonade – I've got it all ready – and a bit of cake.'

'We're in the middle of something, Marjorie,' Stanley said. 'They can have a reward when they've done some work.'

Marjorie went off, shaking her head. 'Work . . . They're only kids, Stanley!'

'Now, next!' Stanley Gould commanded.

Raymond's little brother looked very uncertain and they hustled him into line. Sylvia took pity on him, whispering, 'Say your name, and how old you are.'

'Laurie Gould . . .' He looked at Sylvia with anxious grey eyes and quietly inserted his little hand into hers. 'Seven!'

There were only the four of them then, although Mrs Gould must have been carrying Paul at the time, but they didn't know that. Jack's arrival was a good way off yet.

'Right,' Mr Gould said, hands on his waist. His forearms, below the rolled-up sleeves of his shirt, were covered in dark hair. 'Now, what do I get if I add Raymond and Audrey together?'

Sylvia tensed. Her hands started to feel clammy. This was when Mr Gould's games stopped being fun. She had not the faintest idea what the answer was. In fact, she didn't even realize he was talking about a number. She pictured a strange creature with four arms and four legs, with both Audrey's and Raymond's heads. The same cold dread filled her that she felt at school. She was about to be caught out and punished. She found she was gripping Laurie's hand as tightly as he was hers.

'You get nineteen,' Audrey said straight away. Her handsome face looked back at Mr Gould with something like defiance.

'And what if I take Laurie away from Sylvia?'

'One!' Audrey cried.

Sylvia was beginning to feel thoroughly fed up with Audrey, though at least it meant Mr Gould might not ask her his horrible questions. Although they weren't at school now, and no one would stripe her hand with a ruler until it smarted, like Miss Patchett did, she was already feeling churned up with nerves. Fortunately Audrey had also had enough of Mr Gould and his numbers.

'Can we have some lemonade now?' she asked.

Stanley looked disappointed at their lack of stamina. 'I think you mean: *please may we* . . . Go on then,' he said. 'Boys, we'll carry on with this later.'

No wonder Raymond and Laurie had both won places at the grammar school. When Paul was born, they were told he was a 'mongol'. It was some time before Sylvia had any idea what that meant. When they were at last allowed to see baby Paul – she and Audrey vying to be the first to look into the pram – she could see that his eyes were a bit different, that was all. It didn't seem to be so bad, she thought. But Stanley Gould knew what it meant and saw it as a curse – probably from God, because it was hard to know who else to blame. He seemed to believe that God might be as spiteful as that, and didn't know what to do with a child who wasn't clever. It had taken years for him even to begin to come to terms with it. For a long time he didn't even like Marjorie to take Paul out of the house, which of course upset her.

As she grew up, Sylvia often wondered why Dad and

Stanley were friends. They were forever arguing. For a start, Stanley was a staunch member of the Church of England, while Ted said he wasn't having 'any of that old claptrap'. And that was before you got to their views on politics, the education of girls (which Stanley Gould thought was basically a waste of everybody's time) or the best way to grow carrots. But the two of them drank together, went for long bike rides, played the odd game of cribbage and chewed the fat contentiously over the garden wall while their wives rolled their eyes. Sylvia realized, eventually, that they thrived on their arguments. Maybe that's how she and Audrey had learned to fall out all the time.

Despite pressurizing his sons, Mr Gould had a kindly side to him and could be a tease. It was he who had nick-named Sylvia 'Wizzy' because of her dark, flyaway curls. The name stuck and her own family started calling her 'Wizz' sometimes as well.

But that afternoon stayed painfully pressed into Sylvia's memory and one reason was that Raymond, who was usually quite kind, had been *un*kind. Audrey had managed to stop Mr Gould's number games, but Raymond wanted to carry on after the lemonade and cake.

'What are nine nines?' he demanded. He was good at tables, and so was Audrey.

'Eighty-one,' Audrey answered smartly. She and Sylvia were kneeling, tunnelling their hands into the pile of reddish sand. They gave each other a shove every so often, if one felt the other was too close. 'Get off, that's my bit!' 'No – you get off.'

Sylvia loved playing with the sand and resented Raymond carrying on like this. She kept her head down.

'What about six sevens, Sylvia?' he demanded.

Sylvia pretended she didn't hear him.

'Come on,' Raymond said, standing over her. 'It's easy!'

'Sylvia can't do numbers and things,' Audrey said in her superior voice. 'She can't even *read*.'

Sylvia hid further under her cloud of hair to hide the red heat seeping through her cheeks. She squeezed handfuls of the coarse sand, longing to hit Audrey over the head with something. They knew she was bad at letters and numbers! They were so *mean*. None of them knew what it was like to see a mass of letters merge into a swimming chaos in front of her eyes until she was in such a panic she couldn't think at all. With all her being she hated Raymond at that moment – and Audrey even more. But she felt too small and shamed to fight back.

'Six sevens are forty-two,' Audrey said airily. 'It's no good asking Wizz.'

'Sylvia's *stupid*,' Raymond said. He stood rocking from foot to foot, chorusing, 'Stupid-stupid Sylvia! Sylvia's a du-unce!'

Then Audrey joined in the chant, hopping from foot to foot in time with the words. 'Stupid-stupid Sylvia! Sylvia's a du-unce!'

She thought she even heard Laurie join in, until she was surrounded by their jeering voices. Of course they teased each other often, but not like this. Not with this mean, humiliating nastiness. The words echoed in her head, filling her as if she would never be able to get rid of them.

Sylvia got to her feet, keeping her head down so that she didn't have to look at their mocking, superior faces. All she wanted was to crawl somewhere dark so that she could curl up and never come out. Trying to keep from sobbing out loud, she hurried away, down to the gap where you could walk through between the wall and the railway fence and into their own garden.

'I'm *not* stupid,' she growled in a fierce little voice. 'I'm not, I'm *not*! I hate you . . . *I hate you.*' She ran into the house, hardly able to see where she was going through her tears.

Her teachers never understood that she was willing, but not able. Words and numbers ganged up on her. When they learned about the parts of flowers and fruit, everything went well until Miss Patchett wrote names by the arrows, pointing into the parts, and then Sylvia was lost. She sat staring at her slate in despair. A moment later she realized, to her terror, that Miss Patchett was standing over her.

'What's that?' Miss Patchett pointed her scrawny finger. She was quite a young teacher, with wire spectacles, hollow cheeks and stony eyes.

'It's . . .' The named bits of the flower scrambled in Sylvia's head. There'd been something beginning with S, she was sure. 'It's a staple, Miss.'

Miss Patchett slapped the left side of Sylvia's head so hard that for a moment she couldn't see straight.

'It's a *stamen*. As I have written perfectly clearly on the blackboard.' She pointed witheringly. 'See? *Stamen.*' This brought another slap with it.

The other children sniggered.

'Yes, Miss,' Sylvia murmured. She couldn't see anything now through her tears.

'Thank heavens your sister's not like you!' Miss Patchett said. 'A *staple*,' she went on, witheringly, 'is for attaching one sheet of paper to another. Go on, girl – write the proper label on your flower.'

Almost beside herself with panic, Sylvia leaned towards the slate, her hand so sweaty she could hardly hold the pencil. She breathed in. S. It began with S. She managed to write a wavery S, but then couldn't think for the life of her what came next. There was a twinge in her lower body and she was frightened she might wet herself. Miss Patchett was leaning over her. Sylvia could smell her greasy hair and body odour, blended with the stale tea on her breath. She squeezed her eyes closed, fidgeting to avert the urgent pressure from her bladder, and said 'stamen' to herself over and over again.

'Come *on*, girl,' Miss Patchett insisted, standing tall again. 'Keep still! What comes next?' The class had gone quiet. Sylvia felt as if she was the only person in the world apart from her bony teacher with her nasty, slapping hands.

'I don't know,' Sylvia was about to say when Jane, next to her, dared to breathe, 'T.'

'T,' Sylvia said grasping this like a life raft.

'T! Well, write it down then, girl.'

'A,' Jane sighed next. How Miss Patchett didn't hear her, Sylvia would never know. She was able to sit still now, for the crisis had passed.

With Jane's help she managed to get to the end of the word without another slap. Miss Patchett moved away and Sylvia gave her friend the smile of the rescued.

She could *draw* a flower perfectly. Why could she not do the rest? She didn't know, and no one seemed to understand. She hated school, every part of it except playtime, when she and Jane and some of the other girls played jackstones and skipping in the yard, at the other end from the rowdy boys. When she came home it was like being let out of prison. She tried to shut school right out of her mind so that the thought of it did not pollute the rest of her life.

But the teasing at home was different. The humiliation and unfairness of it bit deeply into her. She felt it as actual pain in her body, an ache that spread all over her. As she ran inside, Mom heard her sobs and came out to see what was going on.

'Oi, where're you off to, Miss?' Pauline asked as her daughter tore up the stairs. She stood in her apron, looking up. 'Have you hurt yourself?'

Sylvia curled up tightly on her bed in the room she then shared with Audrey. Hearing her mother's steps on the staircase, she tensed, afraid this might mean more mockery or punishment.

'Wizzy?'

Sylvia opened one eye. Mom was standing at the door. She looked comforting, with her round pink cheeks and her auburn hair in thick plaits, pinned around her head and crossing over at the front. Sylvia desperately wanted someone to understand. Her reports from school were very poor, and her parents sighed over them in a way that Sylvia took to mean: *Why can't you be like the Goulds? Or at least like Audrey?*

Mom came and sat on the bed. Her pinner was dusted with flour and there was a whiff of onions about her as well.

'What's going on?' she said. 'I thought you were all playing next door?'

Sylvia squeezed her eyes closed and pulled herself into an even tighter coil. Words burst out of her. 'Raymond called me stupid. And Audrey! I *hate* them. Both of them are pigs.'

19

Her mother gave a long sigh and Sylvia felt her hand rest on her skinny shoulder.

'You don't want to take any notice,' Pauline said. 'Your sister should know better than to talk like that – and Raymond. I don't know why you and Audrey can't get on a bit better.'

Sylvia pushed herself up, limbs stiff with outrage. 'I *can't* not take any notice! They're calling me horrible names and . . . And I'm *not* stupid!'

Mom was looking at her with a tender expression. She raised her hand, and Sylvia felt her mother's work rough-ened, oniony thumb rubbing away the tears from her hot cheeks.

'Look at your little face,' her mother said fondly. She dropped her hand again and sighed. 'I know you're not stupid, bab,' she said. 'That's the worst of it. Your father and I've talked about it. You're as bright as a button. So why can't you read and write properly, like the others?'

Sylvia hung her head. 'I don't know. I just can't.'

Pauline had words with Marjorie Gould. Could she please ask Raymond not to be nasty and upset Sylvia? After that, they all kept off the subject. They never got to the bottom of Sylvia's problems. Year by year she struggled on.

The one person she felt at ease with was little Laurie Gould. He was younger than her and left-handed, so he struggled with writing. Stanley did not like having a left-handed son. In his day you would have been made to sit on your left hand and write with your right one – that was his attitude. Under the pretence of Sylvia helping Laurie learn to read, she would help him with his little story books; and he helped her, with Sylvia learning along with him. She did get the hang of reading and writing eventually, but she was slow at it. After Paul was born, even Stanley Gould stopped keeping on about success and 'getting on', now that he had a son who had little prospect of it.

Sylvia dreamed of the wonderful day when she would be able to walk out of school and never come back. At last, when she was fourteen, the day arrived and it was one of the happiest of her life. She took her reference and headed away from the place of shame and humiliation, to a job – any job that did not involve reading or writing. At first she worked in factories and then a laundry. No one made her read or write. The work was boring, but restful. No one went out of their way to make her feel stupid.

Raymond floundered at the grammar school and did not pass his exams with much distinction. He couldn't sit exams without being paralysed by nerves, which Sylvia's dad said was obviously Stanley's fault ('the silly bugger'). Raymond left school when he was sixteen, almost as glad as Sylvia to get away from it.

Only when she was much older did Sylvia realize that Raymond's nastiness that day was in some measure Raymond passing onto her what he felt about himself.

Three

22nd November 1940

Just for once, everyone was at home. Dad had just got in from the Rover works on his bike and they were all eating tea together.

'So, is lover boy coming round tonight then?' Audrey said, with a provocative smirk at Sylvia.

'No, as it happens, Ian's working late,' Sylvia said, determined not to be riled. She knew Audrey didn't like Ian much. But then it was she who was engaged to marry him, not Audrey, so Audrey could put whatever she thought in her pipe and smoke it.

'Ah yes, the great radiologist,' Audrey said.

'Audrey!' Mom warned, hearing her sarcasm. 'If you haven't got anything nice to say, don't say anything.'

'But he *is* a—' Audrey began.

'Wench!' Ted snapped. 'That's enough.'

'I'm not a wench,' Audrey muttered.

'I wish I could join up,' Jack said gloomily, 'and liberate myself from all these squabbling females.'

'They don't want a little squirt like you, After-thought,' Audrey said. Jack had been such an unbearable know-it-all since he got into the grammar school that they were still trying to squash him. Audrey did tend to overdo it, though.

'At least I'm not an embittered harridan like you,' Jack retorted.

'Ooh, swallowed the dictionary, have we?'

'Audrey!' Pauline snapped. 'For heaven's sake—'

The air-raid siren wailed out, abruptly cutting her off. Sylvia's heart immediately began to race.

'Here we go,' Ted said wearily, pushing back his chair, his tea only half-finished. 'Those buggers are at it again. Best get weaving.'

'Oh no!' Pauline said, jumping up from the table. 'We've only just sat down. You'll have to bring your plates out with you.'

'For heaven's sake,' Audrey groaned. 'Not again.'

'Those Krauts don't care about your tea, Pauline,' Ted observed, halfway out through the back door. 'They're not civilized people like us. I'll go and get it opened up.' Ted and Stanley had each put up an Anderson shelter in their gardens, halfway along.

'At least we had last night in our beds,' Sylvia said. 'I'll put the kettle on.'

'There won't be time,' Pauline warned, but Sylvia did it anyway. The thought of a long night without a flask of tea was too much.

'Get your siren suit, Jack!' Audrey called.

'Shut *up*, sis!' Jack shouted, already halfway upstairs to fetch his things. The idea that he would be seen dead in a siren suit at his age was just another thing she liked to tease him about.

They all scurried about as the siren wailed on, collecting up blankets, which could not be left in the damp shelter, torches and flasks and things to do. Sylvia found herself running back and forth in a panic, forgetting where she'd put things. Everything seemed to take forever.

'I've got the torch. We'll have to come in and fill the flasks if there's a lull,' Mom was shouting from the kitchen. 'Where're those rugs, Audrey?'

They hurried into the freezing garden, wrapped in as many clothes as possible, with their plates of stew and rugs thrown over their shoulders. The drone of engines was already close, menacing in the sky. Sylvia felt the cold biting into her cheeks.

'It's so clear tonight,' she said, looking up into the cloudless sky. The full moon had waned, but the sky was full of criss-crossing searchlights.

'Yoo-hoo!' they heard Marjorie, from over the wall. She was helping Paul out to the shelter.

'We're just over here, if you need us, love!' Pauline called to her.

'Stanley's here tonight,' she replied. 'See you after the All Clear!'

'Come on!' Ted was shouting from the shelter. 'It's all ready – and it's dry.'

'Oh my Lord, what about the cats?' Mom cried. Usually they gathered up the two cats, Sherry and Brandy, and brought them into the shelter. 'Here, Sylv, Audrey – take these things. The two of them'll be under the bed, that's where they always go.'

But the planes were dangerously close.

'Mom, leave them,' Audrey said, bossy as usual, but for once Sylvia agreed with her. 'They'll be all right – they've got each other. They'll be under your bed, you know they will.'

Their mother hesitated.

'Look, we leave Mr Piggles out,' Sylvia said. The family's pet rabbit stayed in his hutch during raids. 'He's all right.'

'What the hell are you all playing at?' Ted came

24

charging out of the shelter and grabbed his wife's arm. 'Get in, wench.'

'Oh dear,' Mom was saying. 'I don't like to leave them . . .'

For some reason Sylvia suddenly found the whole situation comical and got the giggles as they all ducked inside the shelter.

'What the hell's the matter with you?' Audrey asked as they bumped about in the dark with only the jittering torchlight, trying to find a space to sit down.

'Nothing.' Sylvia couldn't explain. It was how her nerves came out, wanting to giggle hysterically. But once she stopped laughing, a sober mood came over her. She couldn't help thinking again what a tiny, flimsy thing the shelter was, when you set it against the destructive horror that could fall from the sky. She tried not to think about stories of direct hits on Anderson shelters.

'Come on, budge up,' Pauline said, closing the door. 'Let's get our dinner down us before it's stone cold. I didn't cook a meal for the flaming Hun to spoil it.' In the torchlight she struck a match and lit the oil lamp, switching off the torch so that a different set of shadows patched their faces.

'It's going to be a bad one, I can feel it in my bones,' Audrey said.

'That's it, Aud – look on the bright side,' Jack retorted, through a mouthful of potatoes.

It was hard to think of anything but the noise outside. Sylvia, Audrey and Jack sat squeezed onto the wooden shelf on the left-hand side of the shelter, having to lean forward because there was a top shelf above them as well, for sleeping on. Pauline had a folding chair in the far corner and Ted waited until they were all in and then squeezed in another chair to sit on.

The cold air was knifing up into their nostrils. They all sat in silence for a time. Jack was polishing off his tea regardless, and soon the rest of them did the same. Pauline put her plate down, took Jack's off him and lit a cigarette. Jack leaned against the wall, seeming lost in thought.

There had been a number of heavy raids this month already. Night after night the planes droned over Birmingham, looking to target factories and railways, wreaking huge damage and leaving houses without gas or water, as well as families without any homes. Many of Birmingham's big works, like the BSA, Fort Dunlop and Lucas's, had taken hits. With the lack of sleep and fear they were now experiencing, everyone was living on their nerves. For the moment, all squabbles were forgotten.

'Why aren't you working tonight, anyway, Sylv?' Audrey asked, leaning down to put her empty plate on the floor. 'It's Friday.' Sylvia's latest job was as an usherette at the Theatre Royal in town.

'I swapped with Betty,' Sylvia said. 'She wanted Saturday off, to see her feller. I didn't think Ian would mind if I worked tomorrow.'

'Mustn't upset Ian now, must we?' Audrey said. The barbed tone was back and immediately infuriated Sylvia, but she silenced herself with a last mouthful of stew. 'You're a soft touch, you are,' Audrey tutted, also drawing back from a squabble.

Perhaps, Sylvia thought, Audrey had had the same realization as herself: they might all be dead soon. It'd be terrible to die in the middle of a quarrel. 'Mind you, you wouldn't want to be in town in this. You might have done yourself a big favour.'

'Oh dear,' Sylvia said uneasily. She pictured the lit

stage in the theatre, the frightening determination that everyone showed to keep going, whatever was happening outside 'I hope they'll be all right.'

The planes roared over. The ack-ack guns were pounding from Billesley Common. There were thumps and bangs in the distance. Sylvia was glad to have both Mom and Dad there. If they were all going to go, at least they'd go together. She found the smoke of Mom's cigarette comforting, its tip glowing in the shadows.

'Oh my Lord,' Pauline said at regular intervals, between puffs. After a while she pressed the stub into the ground and stood up to arrange the bedding on the top bunk. She was a bulky figure in the flickering light, in her coat with a shawl wrapped round her head. Her breath came out in ghostly wisps.

'You lie down, Mom, if you like,' Audrey said. 'I'm not sleepy – are you, Sylv?'

'No, not yet.' She blew on her hands. 'I'm too blasted cold to sleep. Oh, let's hope we can go in soon. If it lets up, I'll go in and make some tea.' She felt prepared to risk a lot, just for a hot cuppa.

Pauline swivelled round. 'God, Sylv – did you turn the gas off?'

'Yes, it's okay. Hey, listen.' There was a brief lull outside.

'Come on, Jack,' Pauline patted the top bunk, 'you've got school in the morning.'

'No, I haven't – it's Saturday!' Jack protested.

'All the same, lad,' Ted ordered, looking up from the newspaper he was squinting to read by torchlight. 'Do as your mother says.'

Jack scrambled up, grumbling, and got his book and torch out to read. He was deep into John Buchan's *The Thirty-Nine Steps*.

'Don't go out there, Sylv,' Ted said. They'll be back any minute, sod 'em.'

'Ted!' Pauline protested. 'All this language, in front of Jack!'

'Doesn't matter about the rest of us, of course,' Audrey said. 'Just the delicate little boy.'

'Shut *up*, Audrey!' Jack snapped.

Ted looked up at his wife in his lugubrious way. 'Pauline, there's blokes up there trying to bomb us to smithereens. I don't think the odd *word* is going to be the lad's ruination.'

'Oh, ow – aaagh, I'm ruinated!' Jack cried, acting as if he'd been shot. He made choking noises followed by elaborate death-rattles. 'Dad said "sod". Eeurgh – those are my dying words!' He shone the torch up at himself and made a corpse-face.

'Very amusing,' Pauline said, sinking down onto the chair in a layer of rugs. 'Now, you just settle down, all of you.'

The night seemed endless.

'I hope Ian's all right,' Sylvia said, yawning. She and Audrey were each end of the little bunk, their legs squashed in beside each other.

'Oh, I expect he is,' Audrey said rather tartly.

Sylvia thought Audrey was jealous. Boys were always after Audrey, and at last she, Sylvia, was the one who had an admirer! Ian was rather a catch. He was tall, quite good-looking (at least she thought so, whatever Audrey said), with a good job. He was six years older than Sylvia and was a radiologist at the Queen Elizabeth Hospital, which was a reserved occupation, so he would not be called up. It still felt like a miracle that Ian had fallen in love with her, silly old Sylvia, when they met at a local church fete. She had gone to buy an old rugby ball for Paul, from the White Elephant stall, and Ian came up and told her that it used to be his. He had seemed attracted by her straight away, and she was flattered by this and by his gentlemanly quaintness. He and his family lived a few streets away, in a nice house in Kings Heath, although he more often came to see Sylvia than she went to his family.

'That mother of his is going to be the bane of your life,' Audrey predicted from the other end of the bunk.

Sylvia felt rage flare up in her. She felt like kicking Audrey's legs off the side. But the remark hit home. Try as she might, she couldn't warm to Mrs Westley, Ian's mother. His father was nice enough, in a remote sort of way. He was a doctor and always seemed to have a lot on his mind. But she found Mrs Westley – a neat, brittle woman who had once been a nurse – cold and intimidating. Sylvia was sure that Mrs Westley looked down on her and thought she wasn't good enough for her son. Ian told her she was imagining things.

'You just need time to get used to each other, that's all,' he tried to reassure her. 'She thinks you're delightful – and so pretty! She told me so.'

Sylvia chose to believe him, though she just couldn't imagine Mrs Westley saying anything of the sort.

'Well,' she told Audrey now, 'I don't know how you think *you* know what's going to happen. But since Ian and I are getting married, we'll all have to get used to each other. She's all right, really.'

She heard Audrey say 'Huh' quietly.

It grew late. Jack had put his torch out, but the oil lamp was still burning steadily. It was hard to know how much time had passed: in the shelter, all time felt the same. The girls heard another wave of planes approaching.

'Audrey,' Sylvia hissed, wriggling about to try and get comfortable, 'd'you think Mom and Dad're asleep?'

'I think so,' Audrey said. 'Dad's snoring. He can sleep through anything.'

There was another silence while they listened to the banging, crumping sounds in the distance, and to Dad's snores close up. The cold pressed on their faces. Sylvia found herself thinking, as she often did these days, about Raymond Gould. She imagined the huge ship in the grey, North Sea waters and a shudder passed through her.

'Audrey?'

'Mmm?'

Sylvia hesitated. 'I was thinking about Raymond. Do you . . .' she dared to ask, 'I mean, d'you feel guilty about him?'

'Guilty?' Audrey sounded cagey. 'How d'you mean?'

'Well, he carried a flame for you, didn't he?'

There was a long silence and Sylvia began to regret saying anything. She waited for Audrey's rage to break over her.

In the end all Audrey said was, 'I know.' After another silence she half sat up, leaning on her elbow, and whispered, 'I feel terrible – about what happened. Raymond was all right. Sweet. But I don't feel guilty that I didn't feel the way he did. It'd be like walking out with your kid brother, wouldn't it? Imagine how it would feel, if it was you and Laurie. It's not nice to say it, I know, but I found him a bit boring.' She lay back again. 'He'd have got over it. He wasn't my type at all.'

'I s'pose not,' Sylvia said. She could see Audrey's point. She had never given a thought to Laurie Gould, though he was nice enough. He was just a kid, compared with Ian. The thought of Ian filled her with a moment's warmth. 'Who is your type, d'you think?'

Audrey gave a low chuckle. 'Oh, I don't know. Someone with guts, and dashingly handsome! Nobody I've ever met yet. I just can't see me getting married to anyone. I don't want to spend all my time in a pinner with kids round my ankles.'

Sylvia listened, amazed at her sister, as she often was. It was nice that they were talking for once, but they were so different. The idea of a cosy house and children appealed to Sylvia. A house with Ian and a family, all safe and sound together. She would give Ian children! She might not be very clever, but at least that might be something she could do.

'But what would you *do* all day?' she asked Audrey. 'You don't even like your job. What would you do if you didn't have a family? If you could do anything?'

'Oh,' Audrey said without hesitation. 'I'd be an explorer. I'd go to India and Russia and China and make maps!'

'Don't they already have maps?' Sylvia asked.

Audrey laughed. 'I don't know. I just mean I'd get out of here – see the world. I just think men have a much better life. I don't want to live like women are supposed to. It makes me feel so hemmed in. Sometimes, when I'm sitting in that office with all those sodding typewriters clattering away, I feel as if I'm going to *explode* with boredom.'

'Well, why don't you get another job?' Sylvia suggested.

'It'd just be more of the same thing,' Audrey said, sighing. 'Unless, I suppose—'

She didn't say what she supposed, because the noise outside built up again abruptly. There were planes loud overhead.

'God!' Sylvia whispered. 'They're so close.' Fear built

in her. She envied Jack and their parents, who were fast asleep.

To her surprise, Audrey suddenly said, 'Take my hand, sis.'

'I can't.' There wasn't enough room to sit up, even though they both strained towards each other. 'Here –' She pressed her feet against Audrey's leg and they lay like that instead. Neither of them spoke.

Go over, just keep going . . . She found her lips moving. *Don't stop here, please just keep going.*

There was an almighty series of bangs and long, crunching crashes, horribly close. The ground jerked under the shelter. Both girls instinctively wrapped their arms over their heads.

'Uh! My God, what was that?' Ted and the others woke with a start.

'Oh! What's happening?' Pauline cried. 'Audrey? Sylvia? Jack? You all right?'

'Mom!' Sylvia heard her voice come out like that of a frightened child. Thank goodness Mom was here. There were more explosions, and the ground was shaking again.

'God, that was close,' Audrey said hoarsely as it began to die away. 'It's not ours, is it? D'you think the Goulds are all right?'

Jack jumped down and went to open the door of the shelter.

'Don't, Jack!' his mother ordered. 'For heaven's sake, leave it.'

But he had the door open and they all peered out to see a sky that was orange with the flames of fires. The outside air, full of bitter, burning smells, poured into the shelter, making them all cough.

'Oh, my,' Pauline Whitehouse gasped. 'That's our

street, surely? Oh, Lord save us. Jack, shut it again, please. I can't bear to look.'

Now that they were all awake, they sat in tense silence, listening. Fire-engine bells tinkled in the distance. The raid was the worst they had known in their part of town. Sylvia never knew afterwards how much sleep she had managed. A little perhaps, in quick snatches. But it had started at seven, and it was six the following morning before the All Clear sounded. Now the Germans were in France, they could keep it up for hours, flying back and forth. It was a test of everyone's endurance.

Nauseous from lack of sleep, they all crawled out of the shelter in the morning, commiserating with the Goulds as they walked back to their houses.

'Well, we got through another one!' Marjorie called.

'You all right, love?' Pauline asked.

'Yes – right as rain, ta.' Marjorie waved bravely.

However cold and stiff, though, they were alive! It was a wonderful and exhilarating to be out in the morning light, even though the air was still heavy with burning.

'At last,' Sylvia said, 'we might get that cup of tea.'

'We'd better go and see the damage,' Pauline said.

Sylvia checked on Mr Piggles, who was trembling when she took him out for a cuddle. But the big, lop-eared rabbit seemed happy enough when she let him loose in the garden to nibble the grass. As they walked into the house, the cats fled screeching outside. Mom put the kettle on and they all went to look out at the front.

'Oh, my!' Sylvia gasped. The road was full of rubble and there was a gap further along where two houses had been. An ambulance was parked near the end, unable to get right up to the houses because the road was obstructed.

'Oh dear Lord – that's Mrs James's,' their mother said, hand going to her heart. There were people in shocked huddles along the street. Pauline pulled her shawl back around her and hurried along to speak to them. Sylvia could hear a woman crying.

'I'd better go and see if I can help,' Ted said. He headed off along the street after his wife.

The three of them followed, trying to take in what had happened to their close neighbours, thinking how easily it could have been them. They had to watch where they were walking over the rubble: glass crunched under their feet. Sylvia stared at the ruined shells of the houses, showing the remains of sooty fireplaces and fragments of flower-papered walls. Mixed with the smoke was a horrible musty smell.

'God, look at it,' Audrey said. There was bitter rage in her voice. Arms folded angrily, she stood for some time, taking in the piles of brick and plaster and timber, the mess of ruined possessions amid the rubble; a battered game of Ludo, smashed chairs, a pink dress twisted and filthy in the gutter. 'Right,' she said, furiously. 'That's it. I've decided. I'm not just sitting here any longer. I'm going to join up – today.'

1941

Four

January 1941

When Sylvia stepped out of the dark theatre, Ian was waiting for her. The audience, whom she had ushered into their seats, had already hurried away. They had to file out almost in darkness, the lights dimmed in the foyer so as not to let any glare escape. They had got through tonight's performance without a raid, but the first thing everyone did outside, by instinct, was to look up at the sky. It was bitterly cold and foggy, but so far also blessedly quiet.

'Hey, Wizzy, I'm here!' Even Ian had taken to using the family nickname.

Sylvia stopped, her heart lifting with excitement. He'd come to meet her – that was a rare treat these days!

'Ian?' She could hear his footsteps, crossing over from the bottom of Bennett's Hill and suddenly he was right there, stooping to kiss her cheek.

'Hello, pretty lady,' his said in his quaint way.

'Have you been waiting long?' she said, pushing her arm happily through his. 'You never said you'd be in town.'

'Long enough for a quick one in the Gallery Bar. I came in earlier to meet John Dawson, a chap who was in my form at school. He's off into the Navy, last-night nerves and all that. But I thought it was about time for you to finish, so I waited around. Come on, we've got a few minutes before the bus. Quiet tonight, thank heavens.'

She snuggled up to him. 'Oh, I love it when you're here, waiting.' It meant not having to feel her way, frightened, along blacked-out New Street on her own. In daylight, she knew, there were chalked signs saying, 'BEWARE FALLING DEBRIS'. They could sit cuddled up on the shrouded late bus, talking over the day and snatching kisses.

She took his arm and they felt their way cautiously between the scarred buildings. Ian had a tiny torch, which let out a thread of light, but in the fog it made the visibility worse, so he turned it off. They could hear, rather than see, other people in the street. Sylvia loved walking about with Ian. He was so nice-looking, tall and always sprucely dressed, with neat brown hair and a thin, clever-looking face. In this darkness, however, no one could see anyone at all. And tonight she felt nervous, for more than the usual reasons. Her stomach clenched whenever certain thoughts came to her.

No one knew yet about the interview she'd had yesterday. In two days' time she'd be gone from the theatre into an entirely new job! The idea of it made her thrum with nervous excitement. She still hadn't told anyone – not even Ian. She had felt very emotional tonight, standing as usual, in her dark-red dress and neat black court shoes (her stockings were hardly holding together and she had mended endless numbers of holes in them, but there were no new ones to be had). Outwardly she was guiding the theatre-goers to their seats, polite and helpful, but in her head she kept repeating, *Soon I won't be doing this any more.* As the music struck up from the orchestra pit, she stood at the back in the velvet darkness and felt tearful. She had been there for two years now, and in many ways it was a lovely job. But the restlessness – the feeling that everyone else was moving on and leaving her behind – had grown too much for her.

Audrey had finally received her call-up into the WAAF just before the New Year began. Her letters home were full of a new vocabulary of service life. Jane, Sylvia's best school friend, was now somewhere up north with the ATS. It was all awful and frightening, and not what any of them had planned for their young lives, but it was an adventure as well. As the weeks sped by, Sylvia felt more and more as if life was passing her by. Paul was the only one of the Goulds left at home, and she missed Audrey, even if they did squabble. She wanted to do something new herself. Joining up was unthinkable for her. She didn't want to leave Ian, and she couldn't do it to Mom. Pauline had been upset enough when Audrey went; she didn't like any sort of change. The world was a nasty, dangerous place in her eyes and she wanted them all safe in the nest together.

Sylvia had butterflies in her stomach as they reached the bus stop. Ian should be the first to know. He'd be so proud of her! His own job at the Queen Elizabeth Hospital was recognized as useful, while all she could feel was use*less*. But now she'd answered that advertisement she had seen in the paper, at least she could say she was joining other women in doing *something*.

She was about to speak when Ian said, 'We had a lady in today, fell down her cellar steps in the blackout. I don't think I've ever seen a leg more smashed up. If you only saw the X-ray, you'd think she'd just jumped out of a plane.' He began telling her about various other

39

accidents he'd seen, and then the bus came and there were people sitting so close that Sylvia didn't feel like being overheard saying what she had to say. Ian was in a chatty mood, so she listened, as she often did. It wasn't until they had got off the bus in Kings Heath and he was walking her home that she managed to get a word in.

Once they had turned off the main road she tugged on his arm. 'Stop a minute, Ian. I've got a surprise – some news to tell you.'

'Really, Wizzy?' He had a teasing way of talking sometimes, which made her feel even more the difference in their ages. Obviously Ian was much cleverer than she was, but sometimes it felt as if he was talking to her as if she were a child. Tonight that irked her more than usual. He put his hands on her shoulders and she could just make out the whites of his eyes in the darkness. 'Am I going to like the surprise?'

'Of course you are,' she replied, in an arch way to match his tone. But this didn't feel right for her momentous announcement. It was all turning into a joke.

For a second he bounced her dark curls against the palm of his hand. The cuff of his flannel jacket brushed her cheek. 'Let's hear it then.'

'Well . . .' Her heart was thudding. 'I decided I wanted to do something different. So I've got myself a new job.'

'Oh,' Ian said pleasantly, making as if to start walking again, but she stopped him, gripping his arm. 'Where are you going off to then? The Prince of Wales? Or the Hippodrome? That'd be a change of scene – oops, sorry. Terrible pun.'

Feeling rather put out at his joking, she said firmly, 'No, a bigger change of scene than that. I've been taken on by the railway.'

Ian drew back in surprise. 'Oh! Gosh. That really is a

change of . . . I see!' He was chuckling. 'Yes, well, I suppose they must need a lot of extra staff. Good for you! So what will it be? Filling in forms at New Street? Pouring the tea – I imagine the cafeterias must be rather jolly places to work, even though everything is rationed up to the hilt at the moment.'

'No,' Sylvia said, trying to sound casual. 'I'm going to be working as a goods porter. For Great Western.'

She waited for his gasp of surprise and admiration. She wanted him to be proud, to congratulate her on being selfless and brave. What she heard was an even bigger explosion of laughter. He rocked with it.

'Oh dear, oh dear – that's a good one! A porter, *you*? You are joking, I hope?'

Sylvia withdrew, hurt and annoyed. 'No, Ian, I'm not. I'm glad the thought of me trying to do anything for the war effort seems so flaming *hilarious*. I'm not stupid, you know, whatever you may think!' She moved off along the road, her body stiff with an anger that increased with every step. Why did everyone always think of her as incapable of doing anything?

'Hey, Wizz! Stop!' He was beside her, reaching for her hand. 'Look, I'm sorry. Of course I don't think you're stupid – you're one hell of a girl. I just thought you were joking. I mean, seriously, it's not very feminine, is it? And that's what you are, always. To me, you're just so *womanly*. You're not one of those mannish types in trousers and caps, like those girls in the services. I can't imagine you like that at all – you always look so pretty and nice.'

'Well, I can hardly lump heavy goods around in a frock and heels, can I?' she snapped.

'No, I suppose not . . . Well, *gosh*. I can hardly take this in, to tell you the truth. No, it's marvellous. Well

41

done you.' He tried to pull her to him, but she resisted.

'I just want to *do* something.' She was close to tears suddenly. She wanted to feel understood, and Ian had failed her. 'Your job's useful, and you can feel as if it's important—'

'Well, I'm not so sure,' he interrupted. 'All the other chaps are going off.'

'But I feel . . .' She trailed off. It was hard to put into words what she felt. 'I feel left out. I just thought you'd understand.'

'I do, Sylvia.' He sounded serious now, and careful. No nicknames. 'I really do. It just takes some getting used to, that's all.' He put on a wheedling tone. 'Don't be cross with me.'

'I'm not,' she said. Crossly. She felt like a mutinous little girl.

They were walking on now and had turned into her road. Sometimes, even if it was late, he came in for a cup of tea before walking back to his family home in Cartland Road. Mom and Dad always made him welcome if they were up. But tonight she didn't want to invite him in. She wanted him to know how fed-up she was with him.

'I think I'll head straight for bed tonight,' she said, outside the house. 'I'm feeling done for.'

'That's all right,' Ian said, in a stiff, gentlemanly way. 'And, Wizz, don't be cross. The railway – my goodness, what a girl! When does all this start then?'

'Next week.' She felt suddenly very tired and cold, as if something had been spoiled.

They embraced and kissed, and it was lovely to feel his arms round her, but she couldn't be completely wholehearted tonight.

'One day we'll be together, properly,' Ian whispered,

his lips close to her ear. 'Oh, my darling, you're lovely.'
She heard him take a sharp breath of desire. 'God, I only
have to come near you for a few seconds. If only we
didn't have to wait . . .'

'Well, you do,' she said, the one teasing now. Ian's
desire was always a pressure. 'I'm a respectable girl,
remember?' But she began to relent and snuggled closer
to him. They were engaged, were planning to marry in
July. At least that was something sure. And while everything else was so uncertain, Sylvia told herself, why
waste precious time being angry?

'Not too long now,' she said. 'I'll be Mrs Westley and
an old matron.' She knew this would please him.

Laughter rippled through his body. 'Not you – never.
See you tomorrow?'

'I expect so.' She took out her keys. They'd had a set
cut in case she came in very late.

'I love you, girl.' He was backing away.

Sylvia ran to him and kissed him again. 'I love you
too. Goodnight.'

Five

Sylvia did not sleep well. There was no raid, but even with this golden opportunity for sleep, she lay awake for what seemed the whole night, her mind racing.

She heard the trains moving along the line at the end of the garden and thought of all those people out there, toiling in the night. Her tiff with Ian went round in her mind: *You're just so feminine* . . . It was odd how this didn't feel like a compliment, even though it was meant as one. Why did being *feminine* seem to mean . . . what did it mean? Feminine: soft and weak and not able to do anything very much? Was that what Ian was implying? She knew that if she put that to him, he would argue and say that was not what he meant at all. But that was what it felt like. As if he wanted to keep her locked up, like something decorative, but of no real use.

Heavens, she thought, I'm getting like Audrey.

'As soon as you get married you're tied, like a dog to a post,' Audrey sometimes said, in her scathing way. 'I'm not having someone bossing me about, telling me what I can and can't do. I'm not bothering with all that.' She somehow managed to make Sylvia feel that, in promising to marry Ian, she was giving in to something and was slightly pathetic.

'You don't want to take any notice of her,' Mom would say, even though she found Audrey bewildering as well. 'She'll settle down in the end.'

After what felt like an endless night, Sylvia pulled back the corner of the curtains and saw a hint of light in the sky. Cursing the fact that she felt every bit as queasy and exhausted as she would after a night out in the shelter, she dressed in as many layers of clothes as she could find and went downstairs. In the kitchen, she filled the kettle from the groaning tap and set it on the gas.

The pail for the hens was set ready by the back door. It was so hard to buy eggs that Mom had decided, a couple of months back, that they would keep chickens. Then they'd gone in for rabbits as well. What with them and the enlarged vegetable patch, there was not much left of the garden where she, Audrey, Jack and the Goulds used to play.

Sylvia picked up the pail and went out to the hen coop. Freezing, smoky air stung her nostrils. She unfastened the hatch in the top and tipped in the cooked-up mess of bran, potato peelings and cabbage leaves.

'Here you are, girls. Grub's up – come and get it!'

The five Rhode Island Reds stalked out of the coop: the 'royal ladies' – Isabella, Elizabeth, Victoria, Eleanor and Lady Jane – pecked at their mash with little scurrying noises. The missing one of their number out of the half-dozen they had bought from the Bull Ring at the end of November had turned out to be a cockerel, Henry VIII, who had roasted nicely for Christmas dinner.

Sylvia looked along the garden, hugging her coat round her. To the right, familiar after all these months, was the Anderson shelter with its thick layer of soil on the roof, now draped with strands of dead nasturtiums. Sylvia shuddered, thinking of the cold hours of terror they had spent in there. When did it become so normal, always listening for the sirens and feeling sick with fear?

Hard up against the shelter, and nearer the house, was

the rabbit run. Sylvia went over to the rabbit hutches and let the brown rabbits – the ones she didn't permit herself to grow fond of because they were also destined to feature as dinner – into the run. Then she went to the one solitary hutch nearest the house.

'Hello, Mr Piggles.' Squatting, she unfastened the door and reached in for the big, lop-eared bundle of rabbit that sat complacently on her crouching legs, his nose wiffling. She stroked his velvety ears, then stood up, cuddling him, enjoying his furry warmth and his comforting rabbity smells. The light was rising. She could see the railings at the end of the garden more clearly now, and the hens were tinged with russet.

'I've really gone and done it now,' she murmured. 'I don't wish I hadn't or anything, but I haven't half got collywobbles, Mr P. How am I going to tell Mom? She'll have a fit.'

Faintly, she heard a train coming. In the cutting between their garden and the park ran the LMS line to Bristol and the West Country. Even though they had lived here, backing onto the railway all her life, the sound always made her blood thump harder, the familiar whoomp-whoomp of the engine growing louder as it hurried towards New Street. The loco rushed past and she could just see the top of it, black and dramatic. There was a second's glimpse of the orange glow from the furnace and a thick sleeve of smoke unfurling behind its chimney. Sparks whirled up into the morning gloom, carriages rattled and lurched and then suddenly, with a last rush of sound, it was gone. The noise died as it ran on into Birmingham, leaving them in a sprinkle of cinders and with the smell of smoke in the freezing air. The banks on each side were always charred black. Sylvia loved the trains, although Mom was always cursing that there was no point in hanging out washing, with the state in which it came in again.

'You're up early. I shan't have to dig you out for once.'

Sylvia jumped. With all the racket she hadn't heard her mother come outside. Pauline was in her dressing gown, with a coat over the top, fleece-lined slippers and her shawl wrapped over her head. With her thick auburn hair – her crowning glory – hidden beneath it, she looked more like an old lady than someone in her forties. The cats had followed her out and were stalking across the grass.

'Couldn't sleep,' Sylvia said. It was no good; she was going to have to tell her.

Her mother came close and stroked the rabbit. 'Look at him – loving it . . . Have you fed the girls?' She nodded towards the hens.

'Yes. Mom . . . ?'

'You can help me with some shopping before you go to work. All this endless queuing.'

Cuddling Mr Piggles even closer, Sylvia said, 'Mom. I'm finishing there on Friday. I've got a new job – different hours.'

Pauline turned, frowning. 'What d'you mean?'

Mom wasn't going to like this. She was another one who thought there were all sorts of things girls shouldn't be doing. Or at least, not her girls.

'I've got a job with Great Western.'

Her mother's grey eyes narrowed. 'What're you on about, Sylvia? You've got such a nice job at that theatre. And I thought you were engaged? You're going to marry Ian.'

'Well, yes,' Sylvia laughed. 'But not this week! I don't have to stop work because I'm engaged, do I?'

'Does Ian know about this? What on earth does he think?'

47

'He's right behind me,' she fibbed.

'I should've thought he'd say you've gone mad,' Pauline said, beginning to turn away, arms folded.

Sylvia could feel more frustrated anger boiling up in her. Why was it up to Ian what she did? And why did Mom always walk off when you were trying to talk to her?

'Why should Ian mind?' she said to her mother's back. 'Things are changing, Mom. Girls are doing all sorts, now the war's on. We're not still living in the Stone Age. And anyway, it's not as if Ian and I are married yet.' Why couldn't everyone be pleased and think she was doing something good?

'He ought to have a say, Sylvia.' Her mother turned to her again. 'You can't just do as you like once you're married.'

'But I'm *not* married!' she almost shouted. 'He doesn't own me, Mom.'

'And what d'you mean, working for the Great Western – as a clerk? You know how much trouble you had with writing and sums at school. I don't mean to be unkind, Sylv, but you'd have to admit, it was hopeless.'

As if I need reminding, Sylvia thought.

'No, I just . . .' She hitched up Mr Piggles to her. 'You know when I went to see Auntie Jean, the other week? When I came back in, through Snow Hill, there was a lady there, in uniform, collecting tickets at the gate. And I just thought: I could do that! I don't have to stay put, being so *useless*.' She tried to pour into the words all her feelings of restlessness and frustration. 'After all that's happened, Mom – all the bombing, and the lads all going off, risking their lives.'

'Not Ian, though.'

'No, not Ian – but Raymond and Laurie; and girls like Jane and Audrey.'

Pauline Whitehouse tutted, pulling the ends of her shawl more tightly round her. 'Oh, you're not just trying to keep up with her again? Audrey's just Audrey – she always has to be difficult. Why can't you just ignore her and live your own life? You've always been more of a home bird. Horses for courses.'

Their mother had been frightened and appalled when Audrey joined up. Both of them were puzzled by the force of Pauline's reaction.

'Anything different and she goes round the bend!' Audrey had said.

The girls had spent a long time discussing whether this was to do with their mother's own upbringing. She had grown up in a poor area – a 'slum' she called it – right in the middle of Birmingham. She never wanted to talk about it, and they knew better than to push her to.

'What happened, Mom?' Audrey had plucked up the courage to ask, before she left. 'When you were young?'

'Happened? How d'you mean? Nothing *happened*. No one murdered anyone, if that's what you mean. It was poor and sordid and unpleasant, and there were people I never want to see again in my life – always poking their noses in. And then I met your father and got out of it.' She shrugged. 'I want your lives to be different, that's all.' Now she had made a comfortable nest, she didn't seem to want anyone else to leave it.

'I do think Audrey's doing something important, Mom,' Sylvia said now. 'But it's not just that, anyway. It's *all* of it! Every time there's a raid: what they've done to Coventry, and all the mess in town and the Market Hall . . .' She was almost in tears. Emotions seemed to rise up and startle her these days. And what about Mr and Mrs James?' There had been two couples killed that night when their street was bombed, and Mom had been friends with one of them, Mrs James. 'And we just sit here while everything's breaking up around us. All I'm doing is that *silly* job.' Tears escaped and ran down her cheeks into Mr Piggles's fur. 'Anyway, it's too late now. The GWR have taken me on.'

'To do what, pray? Drive a train?'

'They want me as a porter. I told them I was no good with writing and such.'

'A porter?' Her mother removed the shawl from her head as if to make sure she hadn't misheard. Her hair stood up in a wild coppery mass. 'A little reed of a wench like you, heaving stuff about like a man? They can't want you to do that!'

'They do – and I can!'

Pauline Whitehouse shook her head. In her world, the best thing was never to stand out or make trouble. Girls shouldn't draw attention to themselves.

'I can't see the men putting up with it. They won't want you taking their jobs.'

'Mom, you used to work on a milling machine – like the men!'

'That was only during the war.'

'*This* is during the war, too. There aren't enough men left – you know that.' Sometimes it felt as if her mother lived with her head in a pile of sand.

'But they are bombing the railways . . .'

'They're bombing *everything*. They could bomb the theatre just as easily.'

There was a silence. Both of them stared down towards the railway line. Sylvia knew her fearful mother was torn between not wanting her children to take any risks, to wrap them up and keep them safe forever, and knowing that everyone had to do their best for the war effort. And no one was guaranteed safe. Not anywhere.

Pauline let out a long sigh. 'Well,' she said at last, less frostily, 'I hope you don't live to regret it. But as you've already gone and done it without asking my advice, or your father's, I suppose there's not much left for me to say, is there?' She paused and, to Sylvia's surprise, a smile appeared on her lips. 'Fancy, you'll be at Snow Hill. I used to meet your father there when we were courting – under the clock in the booking hall. Handsome devil he was, in those days.'

'He's not so bad now, Mom,' Sylvia said. Mom was coming round.

Pauline smiled properly now and looked at her. 'No, I s'pose not. Seems a long time ago, though.'

Six

Audrey sat crushed into the canvas-scented darkness of the heavy truck, holding on tightly to the handle of her old suitcase. Though the WAAF driver was speeding along expertly, the winding roads were making her feel sick. Around her was yet another collection of young women, mostly in their late teens and early twenties, a few older, all clad in Air Force blue uniforms and most of whom she had never seen before. Now that she had been in the WAAF a few weeks she was getting used to this: having to keep starting again and adapting.

'Are we nearly there yet, d'you think?' a voice asked above the roar of the engine. 'If we don't get there soon, I think I might lose my breakfast.'

'Well, do try not to,' the woman next to her pleaded. 'I'm somewhat in the firing line.'

Audrey looked round at all these new faces, missing the pals she had met during the intense weeks at the training camp in Harrogate. They had all 'passed out' now and were on their way to their first proper air base.

The truck eventually lurched to a halt and the driver came round and let down the back for them. Audrey had her first proper look at her. She was a creamy, buxom girl with an overgrown, wavy Eton crop and a round, amiable-looking face. Audrey envied her driving job. To her disgust, having hoped for something more active and exciting herself, she was about to start work doing what she had always done – secretarial work.

'Right, here we are, ladies!' the young woman said. She was well spoken, but not in a cut-glass way. Audrey liked her voice. 'Welcome to RAF Cardington.' She stood back with her arms folded as they clambered out, squinting in the bright winter light. 'Heavens!' she added. 'Look what the cat's dragged in.'

It was the latest of a number of such arrivals that Audrey had experienced over the past couple of months. The call-up had arrived just after Christmas. Since then, her experience of the WAAF had been a whirl of activity. After a tearful parting with her mother (Pauline was the tearful one, not Audrey) she went first to Croydon. From there, she had had to travel to Bridgnorth. Four days of initial training and kitting-out later, her vocabulary had expanded to include terms like 'irons' for her eating utensils, 'blackouts' for their far-from-glamorous underwear and 'bumf' for any of the heaps of paper that she might have to deal with.

For those first bewildering days Audrey scarcely had time to think about what she had done in joining up. What she did feel, suddenly, was as small and insignificant as a grain of sand.

'We're just like links in a long chain, aren't we?' one girl said to her as they queued in another line, for a Free From Infection inspection. 'It makes you feel humble.'

It was true. Looking at the great mass of young women in uniform gave Audrey a shrinking, rather sad feeling in the beginning. Here she was, used to being at home where everyone knew her, and to being the oldest, so that she was accustomed to being in charge. Here, she was nobody special. She was suddenly aware of the variety of classes around her. There was what she called the 'roughest of the rough', like Cissy, one girl in her intake who had previously 'worked' at the Liverpool docks, and clearly knew the sailors in ways that involved a good deal more than conversation. At the 'posh' end were the likes of Daphne, who led a society life in London that Audrey could scarcely imagine. Audrey began to see that she would have to fit somewhere in the middle. She had never especially thought of herself in this light before. It seemed important to discover ways of getting along with everyone, as far as possible. She found herself behaving more quietly and less bossily than she would have done at home.

After Bridgnorth they moved to the main training camp in Harrogate. Audrey arrived at their billet in the Queen's Hotel in Harrogate in possession of a whole set of gear, including two royal-blue uniforms with brass buttons, a painfully robust pair of new shoes and a cap with a brass badge. They had to keep polishing the shoes, badge and buttons, so that her fingers smelled perman-ently of polish and Duraglit. But polish she did. She was surprised at how proud and pleased she felt to be wearing the uniform – she, who did not like to be bossed or ordered about, if she could possibly avoid it!

The training at Harrogate consisted of hours of square-bashing, which did nothing to improve the com-fort of her shoes, as well as freezing runs on the snowy Yorkshire Moors.

'It's so cold!' one of Audrey's room-mates groaned, when they came in after a bout of PT one morning, their cheeks pink and scalded by the wind and their fingers swollen like sausages. 'I suppose it could be worse, though. Heaven help us if it gets as cold as it was last winter.'

'We went skating on the river,' said another girl, who came from Maidenhead. 'It was frozen solid. I'd never seen anything like it before.'

They were both pleasant girls, and Audrey found that in the huts where they had been housed in Bridgnorth and in the digs here, she enjoyed the camaraderie. They sat in their rooms at night chatting and drinking cocoa, the wind whistling in through the draughty windows. It came as a surprise to her. She had always thought of Sylvia as the feminine, domestic one of the family. But here she was, enjoying sitting in her bed to keep warm, darning a sock with a needle from her 'hussif', as they called their sewing kit, and whiling away the evening with the girls. It gave her a warm, companionable feeling.

But she did miss home. Lying in bed at night, hearing the wind rattling the doors and window frames, she often longed to be back in her own bed. From a distance she saw her family differently, appreciating them now. There was Dad, exhausted from work, coming in faithfully every night; Mom always there, helping Marjorie with Paul, helping anyone who came along, Audrey realized. Mom's home was her safe kingdom, but she was always open to others who might be suffering. And Audrey missed Sylvia mooning over that old stick Ian, and Jack spouting Latin and thinking he was the cleverest person in the world. She often lay smiling, thinking of them with an ache of homesickness, and hoped they were all safe. And, though she would not have told anyone this, she thought a lot about Raymond Gould.

Raymond had been even more in love with Audrey than either she or he had admitted to anyone else, though Sylvia seemed to guess it. Audrey knew that one of the reasons Raymond joined the Navy when he did was that, try as she might – and, despite her dismissive words to Sylvia, she *had* tried – she could not love him back. Sylvia couldn't seem to understand this. If a man loved you, Sylvia seemed to think you were obliged to love him back. Audrey liked Raymond: why would anyone not like him? They had known each other for years, played together and been big chiefs to the younger ones. Raymond was a pleasant, polite, often sensitive boy and as they grew up she had watched him try to live up to all that his father expected of him. Stanley assumed without question that every generation must exceed the achievements of its parents. 'Progress!' he would cry. 'That's the aim of the human race.'

To which Ted Whitehouse would reply, 'Rags to riches to rags in two generations, Stan. It happens. No guarantees.' Which would enrage Stanley Gould, exactly as it was designed to.

Paul's birth had been like a massive, immovable tree falling across Stanley Gould's smooth highway. Paul had the moon face, slanting eyes and short limbs of a mongol child. He was sweet-natured. He could learn things, slowly, simply, if given time and patience. But he was handicapped. So far as Stanley was concerned, he was *wrong*. Paul would be lucky to fit into any school, never mind any of the King Edward grammar schools. His favourite pastime was waving madly at the trains through the garden fence. Paul was *not* progress.

Audrey grew up watching Marjorie Gould, as well as Raymond and Laurie, protecting Paul against the barely hidden revulsion of his father. But while Paul could not really understand the feelings that were directed at him, Raymond could. Raymond was sensitive. He also understood that he had not measured up, either. He was supposed to have been a first-class engineer, on the way to running his own firm, patenting his own designs. Instead, he had only just scraped through. He went into a profession that many parents would have seen as perfectly satisfactory. But to Stanley Gould, technical drawing was less than what he had in mind.

Late one evening, the summer before Raymond left, he and Audrey had sat talking at the bottom of the Goulds' garden. Everyone else had drifted away inside. They faced the railway, Raymond in his baggy shorts with his legs drawn up, arms linked loosely round them; Audrey in a skirt, her legs bent sideways under her. That was when Raymond told her he was planning to join the Navy.

'The thing is,' he said, 'maybe if I go and do that, and make a reasonable fist of it, the Old Man will look up to me a bit more. After all, he's never been in the services.'

Audrey was unsure what to say. She had sensed something like this coming. She sat quietly, listening and feeling sorry for Raymond. 'Maybe,' she said eventually.

Raymond sighed. 'He's always wanted such big things for us.'

'He's a bully.' The words slipped out and even Audrey was shocked at herself. 'I mean . . . Sorry, I didn't mean to . . .'

Raymond turned to look at her. She could feel him examining her very closely in the dusky light, as if he needed something from her.

'Is that what you think?'

'I think . . .' She hesitated, trying to be more careful. 'I think that's putting it a bit strongly. But surely it's wrong to expect other people to fall into line with the things you think they *should* be, if it's not what they want?'

There was a silence. Raymond turned to look ahead of him. 'Oh, Audrey,' he said quietly at last, 'you always are the one who can say what needs to be said. How do you manage to be so brave?'

'I'm blunt, the rest of the family would say,' Audrey laughed. 'They don't appreciate it much, I can tell you!'

'Laurie's more like you. I've never been able to stand up to the Old Man. I'm a coward, I suppose.'

'You're the eldest,' she stated.

'You're the eldest, too.'

'But I'm a girl.'

There was a silence that seemed full of feeling.

'Audrey,' Raymond turned to her and she had a sense of a great tension coming from him. 'Look, I know you don't feel the same.' He was struggling to speak. 'But –' His words came out in a rush – 'I can't seem to help it. I'm frightened to say this, because I know you don't want me, but God, I *do* love you, d'you know that?' He laughed as if at his own idiocy. 'I *really* love you, Audrey. There's just no one else like you – you're terrific!'

Audrey's heart beat faster and she blushed, though she knew, gratefully, that Raymond could not see. It was not from passion, though she was very fond of Raymond. She valued him as a good, kind person. But they had been over this before. Perhaps he was hoping she had changed her mind. Audrey was embarrassed by what she had caused, and by her lack of feeling for him. She should never have stayed out this evening, in this caressing summer air.

'I think I've been in love with you for years,' Raymond went on, his courage increasing. 'When we were young I looked up to you, and then it turned into – well, into something more than admiration.'

He took her silence to be not discouragement at least.

He moved close to her, about to put his arm round her shoulders.

'No!' Audrey leaned away from him. More gently she added, 'No, Raymond. Don't, please. Look. I've told you – you're my friend. You're like my brother! I've always liked you, but you know I don't . . . I've told you before.' She looked down, stroking the grass. 'I'm sorry.'

Raymond was already moving away again. 'No,' he said, trying to recover himself. 'I know. I *know*, really. I was just hoping . . . You're too good for me, Audrey. Too brave, too fierce. I'm not—'

'*Please*,' she said, so uncomfortable now that she wanted to get up and leave. 'Don't say that. I don't mean I'm better than you. You mustn't think like that.' She knew as she said it that, unfortunately, Raymond *did* think like that. He never thought he was good enough. 'I'm just not . . . Maybe I'm not ready for love, that's all.'

'It's okay,' Raymond said. He sounded wretched, but he was trying to pretend everything was all right.

It was close to dark and all she could see was his silhouette, his features so well known, so familiar. He was now a man, twenty-two and grown up. He was a man she could admire, but not one she was in love with.

'D'you remember,' he said suddenly, a smile in his voice, 'that time the bank caught fire, when we were all quite small? The fire brigade came and they all stayed for a cup of tea?'

Audrey laughed, relieved to be talking about something else. The sparks from the trains often set light to the dry vegetation on the banks in the heat of summer. They were used to it and kept buckets of water to hand. Mr Gould had a hosepipe. But that time the fire had got out of hand, burning right up into the garden, and the fire brigade had had to come and put it out, leaving tracts of black grass, which took weeks to recover.

'Laurie thought it was a party and they all made a big fuss of him. He kept going out with a box of matches for ages afterwards, thinking that was a good way to get another party. I had to watch him, because Mom was having Paul!'

They both laughed at the memory.

Lying in her chilly bed in Harrogate, Audrey sometimes found herself in tears thinking of those times, the carefree days of childhood games with Raymond and Laurie. It seemed so far away. And now it was overlaid by the much more recent memory of the memorial service for Raymond. She recalled their faces: Stanley Gould looking thin and uncertain; Marjorie bent and shrunken with grief; and Paul sobbing like a little child. Laurie, home on compassionate leave, looked gaunt and haunted, suddenly no longer boyish.

When she let herself think about Raymond she kept seeing the ship, the swelling grey sea, the terror and sadness of it – but she saw their faces as well, ravaged by the loss of him. Sometimes, once the others were asleep, she muffled her sobs in the bedclothes, weeping for the cutting short of Raymond's young life. She did love him in a way, for all the sweet childhood memories they shared. If only she could have felt the way he longed for her to do. At least then he could have died knowing that he loved, and was loved in return.

Now that she was at RAF Cardington, Audrey's WAAF life was to begin in earnest. With the icy February wind buffeting her face, she looked around at the base, at the huge hangars she could see in the distance. Across the building in front of them was a large sign: WELCOME TO THE ROYAL AIR FORCE. ALL NEW ARRIVALS REPORT HERE.

Already the language and ways of the services, and the Air Force in particular, were becoming familiar. Strange as the place was, there was a feeling of home. She looked forward to writing and telling the family all about it. Stepping past the cheerful WAAF driver with her bag, she returned her smile.

'Best of luck!' the driver called.

'Thanks,' Audrey said, and thought what a nice face the girl had.

Seven

''Ere, shift yerself, yer dozy mare – what're yer doing hanging about over there? This lot won't unload itself, yer know!'

The foreman's bawling cry reached Sylvia where she was standing at the end of one of the platforms, or 'decks', as she was learning to call them, in the top shed of Hockley Goods Yard, watching another train-load of wagons being shunted into place. They moved with crawling precision along the icy track or 'road' – another new term to her. A thin layer of snow whitened the rooftops round the railway yard and lay in smut-speckled patches on the ground.

When they told her she was going to be a porter, she had pictured herself working at Snow Hill, the main Great Western passenger station in Birmingham. She saw herself under the grand, over-arching span of the roof, pushing barrows loaded with passengers' suitcases. She would feel rather important and would overhear passengers exclaiming, 'Look at *her* – a lady porter! Well, that's a sign of the times.' When they told Sylvia she was being assigned to Hockley, the GWR Goods Yard for Birmingham, she was at first dismayed. She knew of Hockley passenger station, just across the tracks, but she had never been to a goods yard in her life.

The wagons ground to a halt with metallic shrieks. The loco stopped short of the shed and let out great whooshes of smoke and steam, which billowed into the freezing air. The guard climbed down to uncouple the engine, so that it could move on to its next shunting job. Engines did not go into the shed. The wagons would be eased back by means of a rope, around a capstan drum, to the stop-blocks. Further along the yard, an inspector was checking the labels on another set of wagons before they were shunted in. Shunters were moving among the numerous lines of wagons, calling to each other, sometimes in language fit to make her blush. Another engine was moving further back in the yard, and metallic clanging sounds rang out somewhere in the distance. The cold, smoke-filled air stung Sylvia's nostrils. She had her gloves off, tucked under her arm, and was blowing on her chapped hands, immersed in watching the scene, when the foreman started bawling at her.

'Damn you, you horrible little man,' she muttered, hurriedly pulling the gloves on again. 'You nearly made me jump out of my skin,' she added, though no one was listening.

She found she was fighting back tears. A childish urge came over her to stick her tongue out at her foreman, known as 'Froggy'. He was one of the rudest, most unpleasant individuals she had met in her relatively sheltered life and had already reduced Sylvia to tears more than once during this first week in the Goods Yard. Any mistake she made – and there had been quite a few – he was down on her like a ton of bricks. He was on at her for dropping things, trying to push the barrows instead of pulling them, leaving loads in the wrong place because she didn't yet know her way around properly, and generally being slow. Nothing was familiar to begin with, and Froggy was woefully bad at explaining things, so it was she who ended up looking foolish. It brought back all her old insecurities about being stupid and unable to do things properly, just the way it had been at school.

On top of that, all the muscles in her body were screaming from hours of heavy lifting and hauling of loaded barrows between the lines of wagons and the cartage area, where they were loaded onto the drays to go out for delivery in the city. Her back and shoulders felt as if she had been mown down several times by a tram, and her hands were so chapped and sore that she could hardly bear to touch anything.

Many times that week she had asked herself what on earth she was doing here, when she could be in a nice warm theatre. She thought wistfully of the stuffy darkness at the back of the stalls, of light pouring from the brightly lit stage and of the friends she had said goodbye to. But she knew that really she had done the right thing. Audrey's letters were full of the physical discomforts of the WAAF, although she was obviously enjoying it. And Sylvia knew she could put up with the physical pain, the cold and the arduous work, because in that week she had fallen head over heels in love with the railways. The place fascinated her. She just hated working with someone so discouraging and horrible.

Known as 'Froggy' on account of his odd, flat fingers (Sylvia wondered with a shudder about his toes, let alone other bits of him), the foreman's real name was Fred Bainton. When she had first started and was assigned to his team, he'd taken one look at her in her newly issued uniform – trousers, jacket, cap and heavy boots – and reeled backwards, rolling his eyes in contempt.

'Oh no, yer gotta be 'aving me on. Not another woman! What flaming use are you gunna be? I mean, don't take it personal, love, but this is man's work.' He shook his head in a manner that implied he was the one remaining sane person in a world of absurd folly. 'I don't need no one who can't pull their weight. The other 'un's bad enough, but at least that one's got some meat on 'er bones. But you: God almighty!' He'd stomped away, shaking his head with as much drama as Sylvia had seen on the stage of the Theatre Royal. 'Women,' he declaimed like something out of a Shakespearian tragedy. 'All they give me is cowing women . . .' She was, in fact, only the second woman so far to be taken on as a porter.

Froggy came hurrying along towards her now, a frantic, hunch-shouldered, weak-chested figure in his dark uniform jacket. He had a rodent-like face and bits of his thin hair squiggled out round the edges of his cap like little wet eels. Froggy's basic position was that he didn't like women and was absolutely certain they didn't belong anywhere near his kingdom of the railways. It seemed that no evidence you might give him would change his mind. He beckoned impatiently.

'What're you hanging about down 'ere for? It ain't no good standing there, dreaming about what yer boy-friend's gunna do for yer later – this lot's got to get over to Lawley Street.' He hurried past her, talking frantically. 'Not those two minks at the far end: they're for Winson Green. I don't know what those buggers've done bringing 'em in 'ere. The world's gone mad – and all I get's a load of cowing women . . .' This complaint echoed through almost any utterance that Froggy made.

Sylvia had been on the point of crying again at the scornful treatment she had from him earlier, but now she swallowed her tears down angrily. Right, she thought, a blush of anger and humiliation rising in her cheeks, I'll damn well show you, you little reptile.

She didn't want Madge, the other porter in her team, to see her crying, either. Madge was built like a prize-fighter, with legs like tree trunks. She was as tough as old boots and cut from a quite different cloth from Sylvia, who felt very feeble beside her.

'The first thing you need for this job is a pair of gloves,' Madge told her the first day in her foghorn of a voice, holding up her hands encased in tough leather gloves. 'And decent boots – you can get a good pair from 'ere, and they'll stop two and six a week off your wages till it's paid.' Sylvia had taken this advice, applied for the boots and bought the hard, brown gloves, which she was still wearing in. But her hands were only just recovering from their battering on the first couple of days. Everything they had to handle was rough and freezing cold to the touch.

The other two in her unloading crew came hurrying out from the mess rooms. Madge, whose surname also happened to be Porter – 'they couldn't 'ardly turn me down, with a name like that, could they?' – and the checker, Bill Jones, a quiet, decent man in his fifties. In the last few days Sylvia had been on the same shift as them, which started at six in the morning and ended at two o'clock. Bill, a short, sallow-skinned man with greasy brown hair and kindly eyes, was a live-and-let-live sort of character, who was kind about their heavy work and the efforts they were making.

He showed Sylvia around when she started the job.

'There's air-raid shelters up along there,' he said, pointing along the yard. 'We don't use 'em much – everyone tries to keep going. They're miserable holes to sit in, anyroad – but if it gets really bad . . .' He left her to finish the sentence.

He told her about the different sheds and about the Round Yard, which they could see over towards the passenger station. 'You won't need to work over there,'

Bill told her. 'That's a mileage yard – they charge them by the mile, like it says. Full loads only. But the customers have to organize the loading and collection, not us.' And there was Hockley Basin at the western end of the yard, where loads were moved on to joey boats to be carried further on the canal.

'Everything's had to be shifted around,' Bill told her as they stood looking across the yard. 'The offices, I mean – because of that lot.' He nodded at the shell of the main office block on Pitsford Street, one end of which was in the process of being rebuilt. 'I'll never forget that morning – after that flaming all-night raid in December, remember? I came into work and . . .' He shook his head. 'What a mess; you've never seen anything like it. The yard was full of rubble. All that bit of the block had come down along there. And that – that's the new Top Shed. That caught it a bit. But the main thing was the offices in there: all gone. They've had to shuffle them about to various places. Some of them are in the basement, others have moved over to Snow Hill. Terrible.' He looked very sorrowful. 'Still, they're doing a good job of putting it all back. But it's a mess. They're talking about giving you ladies some toilets of your own.' He smiled wryly at her. 'Early days.'

It was Bill who showed her the ropes, the basics about how the yard worked, and both he and Madge taught her the best way to lift things.

Madge, who looked about forty to Sylvia, was in fact twenty-eight. She'd spent all her working life in factories up until now and wanted a change. All Madge talked about was her 'feller', who was called 'Tone'. Tone was a boxer as well as working in a foundry. Madge talked a lot about his tattoos. Sylvia thought he sounded even more terrifying than Madge herself. But it was gratifying to see the short shrift that Madge gave to Froggy and his insulting whingeing.

'What's 'e got for us this time, then?' Madge demanded, striding towards her across the cartage area where Sylvia was now waiting. Every time Sylvia saw Madge, she was amazed by the sheer girth of the woman, her vast body wrapped in blue railway overalls. A variety of vehicles were lined up waiting: lorries, Scammell transporter trucks and carts with horses between the shafts. Some of the horses were snoozing. Others had their heads down, pushing deep into their nosebags. Sylvia loved the warm, comforting smell of the horses and always spent any spare minutes she had petting them. There were also cats in the yard for keeping the rats down, and that made her feel at home too.

Bill, the checker, had his lists under his arm. 'This is an LMS lot,' he said. 'A load of flour – to get across to Lawley Street.'

Madge made a face. 'That'll take some shifting. I 'ope you've 'ad yer oats, Sylvia.' She eyed the younger woman more carefully. 'What's up with you?'

'Nothing,' Sylvia wiped her eyes and attempted a cheerful grin. She didn't want Madge thinking she was a feeble milksop.

''As 'e been on at yer again? Look,' Madge said confidentially. She came up close, as Bill stood tactfully aside, and Sylvia caught her ripe smell of sweat and coal dust. Her cheeks had a pink, scrubbed look.

'Yer don't want to take any notice of 'im.' She jerked her head in Froggy's direction. 'I'd like to see that little runt doing our job. Tell yer what . . .' She leaned her florid face close to Sylvia's, sending a gust of breath laced with raw onion into Sylvia's nostrils. 'Any trouble from 'im and yer can tell 'im, I'll come and put 'is whatsit

68

through the mangle. That'll shut 'im up! Not that it gets an outing very often any'ow, I don't s'pose!' With a wink she moved away, her massive body shaking with laughter. 'Come on, you lucky lot – best get started.'

Sylvia followed, blushing to the roots of her hair as giggles rose inside her. She suddenly felt much better.

'Right.' Madge pushed her sleeves further up. Her pink, beefy arms were covered in dark-brown hairs. 'Let me at it.'

As Bill opened up the side of the wagon, or 'mink' (Sylvia was beginning to learn that the Great Western rolling stock was called by a whole menagerie of nick-names), she felt nervous again. Being so new, and with Froggy and a few of the other older men so hostile, all convinced that she wouldn't measure up, she always felt she had something to prove. The wagon was stacked full of enormous sacks of flour. Would she really be able to manage lifting them out? No one doubted it with Madge, who looked as if she could happily pick the men up with one hand and hang them on a hook to dry. But Sylvia was much slimmer and nothing like as strong.

The cartage deck was divided into twelve loading areas. Bill Jones was the checker for one of them. He called one of the drays over to line up ready. Sylvia, on her way to unload the flour, reached over and stroked the horse's warm nose. As she and Madge climbed into the wagon with the flour sacks she was seized by a fit of sneezing.

'Bless you!' Madge boomed.

'Ta.' Sylvia stood at the entrance to the full wagon, blowing her nose and wondering how on earth they were ever going to lift the sacks. 'I'm ready,' she said, trying to feel optimistic.

She seized the corners of the first big sack. It was a dead weight.

'You want to lever it round,' Madge instructed, heaving one of the sacks onto the barrow without much apparent effort. She had her knees bent, bracing herself. 'Come 'ere – I'll show yer.'

There was a piece of wood that they could use for pushing under the sacks and levering them up. Sylvia watched what Madge did and copied her. She found she soon got the hang of lifting and swinging the sacks across. They worked as fast as they could, barrowing the sacks across and loading the dray carefully, so that none of its load could topple off.

'I wonder where this lot's off to,' Sylvia said, arching her back to ease it for a moment, then sneezing again. Her face felt thick with dust. She pushed dark coils of her hair out of her eyes. 'I keep thinking about all the women who'll make bread somewhere with it.'

'Up north – Derby or somewhere; got to be, if it's LMS, ain't it?' Madge said, wiping floury sweat from her face. 'Poor cows,' she added, with unexpected tenderness.

Birmingham was served by both the Great Western and the London, Midland and Scottish lines. Some of the loads came into the city on the Great Western, but had to be transhipped to go forward on an LMS line. So the cargo had to be carted across town to another goods yard. During one tea break Bill had tried to explain to Sylvia the complications of checking off loads, and all the invoices required to make sure not only that every load got where it was supposed to, but also that the right people got paid for every stage of the journey. When he was halfway through Sylvia stopped him, laughing.

'I think my head's going to burst if you tell me any more. I never was very good with figures.'

Bill laughed too, kindly. 'Never mind. It is hellishly

involved, and it's not your job. Let the ones who do know get on with it! You're doing a good job where you are.'

This was a big boost of confidence for Sylvia, and she hoped Bill was not just being kind. And now, at night, when she heard the trains passing on the track beyond the garden and thought how she was part of it – 'a tiny link in the chain', as Audrey had written in her letter home – she thought of it all differently, with a new appreciation.

Eight

'So, Wizz, how's life on God's Wonderful Railway?'

'It *is* wonderful,' Sylvia said, snuggling drowsily against Ian's shoulder. She decided to ignore the edge of mockery in his teasing. 'Mostly, anyway. Even though I'm more tired than I've ever been in my life before.'

They were in the old armchair by the kitchen range, the cosiest place in the house now that the range was lit. Sylvia was on Ian's lap, his arms around her. Mom had gone next door to visit poor Mrs Gould. Dad and Jack were in the back room listening to the wireless, which stood on the sideboard by the table, with its accumulator. Every so often there was a burst of laughter from them, over the programme they were listening to. Cuddled up here with Ian, in the dim kitchen light, Sylvia felt so safe and warm – as if they could forget the war, the bombs and all the terrible things that were happening, just for a while. This was what it would be like when they were married, she thought.

'Really?' Ian wanted to know. 'Why's it so "wonderful?"'

She'd hardly had time to see Ian all week. There had been night after night of raids. Twice they had spent all night in the shelter.

'Anyway,' he went on. 'I thought you were going to be at Snow Hill – not stuck away in the goods yard. You can't *really* like it, surely?' His refusal to take her seriously was beginning to rile her again.

'You seem to think a girl can't be happy doing anything if she hasn't got a frock on!'

'Well . . . Yes, maybe I do!' he laughed, rumpling her hair, which she had let loose. All day she had to keep it tied up tight in a bun low in her neck, with her cap on top.

'And stop calling me Wizz!' she said, shaking her head away from his hand. Her dark hair lunged like a wild animal with a life of its own. 'Just because Mr Gould has called me that, ever since I can remember, doesn't mean I want you to. It makes me feel about six again. Now I'm doing a *proper* job, you can call me by a *proper* name, and so can everyone else.'

'That job doesn't sound very proper to me – not for a lady.'

'Oh, don't start off again!' She thumped him playfully in the chest. 'As if I haven't had that all flaming day from Froggy, the miserable so-and-so.'

'So tell me: you have a nasty foreman, your hands look as if you've worked for years as a washerwoman, you say your back hurts, your shoulders hurt, your head aches and you're so tired you can hardly stand up – so what's so very wonderful about it, hmm?' He jigged his knees so that she wobbled about.

'It's just . . .' How could she describe it? The smell of the smoke from the engines, the teeming railyard with the wagons shunting back and forth, the carriers' yard leading out onto Pitsford Street, full of horses and carts and trucks being filled up or waiting to go out over the weighbridge. There were all the loads, the metal stuff for munitions, the food and goods of all kinds coming in from, and going out to, firms all over the city. The offices

73

were busy with hundreds of people hunched over desks and comptometers, working out orders, writing letters and invoices. 'It's full of life and busy, and it's for the war effort. And even though it's ever such hard work, it's important and exciting! You never know what's coming next: flour one day, shovels the next – never a dull moment.' She found herself chattering about all the firms whose goods passed through the yard, reeling off names: GKN, Guest, Keen & Nettlefolds, Woolworths, the GPO. 'It's so *busy*. And Froggy gets all in a state about everything – he was actually jumping up and down on the spot the other day!' She laughed, thinking about it. She was learning to laugh and let Froggy's agitation wash over her.

Ian joined in her laughter, though a bit grudgingly, she thought. 'I'm beginning to feel jealous. It makes my work seem very dull.'

'No! It's just . . . the people are different from what you're used to.' Sylvia thought about Ian's quiet, formal family. Everything in the Westley household was in its place and just so. What on earth would they make of some of her workmates? She thought about Madge and the intimate punishments she threatened to inflict on Froggy Bainton and started to giggle again.

'What's up with you?' Ian asked, seeming a little irritated by her enjoyment and all the new things she was experiencing.

'I'd better not repeat it,' she said, suddenly solemn. 'You wouldn't approve.'

Ian gave an annoyed sigh and sat back, letting go of her.

'What's the matter?' Sylvia sobered herself, feeling she had been tactless.

'Oh, I don't know – this damn war.' He frowned. His

thin face had a creased, dusty look. 'I just wish it was over. It's changing everything. I just want to be back how we were – you and me. And for us to get married now and settle down.'

Sylvia was touched by this. 'Oh, I know – I want that too. But we're going to, aren't we – very soon?' They often discussed their wedding plans. 'And even if we just have to rent a room somewhere, it'll be ours until we can afford something better. Just you and me – and one day there'll be no bombs, no war . . .' She cuddled up to him again.

'Oh, we shan't need to rent,' Ian said, as if it was all decided. 'Ma and Pa will put us up for as long as we need. They've plenty of room over there.'

'Really? But I thought we—'

'Of course it makes perfect sense,' Ian said. 'It can't come too soon, as far as I'm concerned.' He sounded so gloomy that she did not like to argue, but her heart was sinking very low at the thought of living with Dr and Mrs Westley.

'I just loathe all this,' Ian was saying. 'All my pals going off, most of them anyway. Awful things happening.'

'Like Raymond.'

'Yes, exactly – like Raymond.' Ian had met Raymond Gould several times and had liked him. 'And it's turning you girls into . . . Well, you're not like you were before.'

'But I am,' she said, twisting round to kiss his cheek. Sometimes the age gap between them seemed even greater than it was. 'Don't be so grim. I'm exactly as I was before. Just in slacks sometimes.'

'That's just it.' Ian held her tight again, seeming vulnerable suddenly. 'At least you've got a skirt on now. Like the first time I saw you.'

She giggled. 'That was a dress.' She had worn a pretty summer frock that day at the fete when they met. Ian had called at the house soon afterwards. At first Sylvia was a bit awed by him, but she realized he was shy and awkward with women, and even his mother admitted that she had brought Ian out of his shell.

'All right, dress – it's all the same. That's my girl,' he whispered. His hand slid round and lay over her right breast. Sylvia squirmed with pleasure, turning her face up to his. Ian kissed her. His hand closed round her breast more tightly.

'God, Sylvia,' he broke off after a few moments. 'You're such a special girl. Don't change, will you, and become all mannish, like some of them? I couldn't stand that.'

'No, of course not,' she said, reaching up to stroke his smooth hair. 'Just because I have to wear trousers to work doesn't make me a man! Imagine trying to clamber in and out of those wagons in a skirt.'

Ian was looking intently at her. 'Oh God!' He took in a deep breath and let out a sigh of frustration. 'You know I believe in waiting – that it's the decent thing . . . But sometimes I wish – God, woman, sometimes I just want you so much.'

Her own body was full of longing. She could feel him underneath her as she sat on his lap and knew he was always trying to hold back, to do the right thing. She often imagined how it would be to be fully naked with Ian, to see his long, slender body and make love to him. And she also felt a bit sorry for him. Somehow she thought it was harder for a man to hold back and deny his urges. But it was unthinkable to go any further when they weren't husband and wife.

'Oh, Ian – I want you too.' She looked into his eyes.

'Look, we will be married. It's only a few months now.' With a pang she thought about the fact that she was going to have to give up work when she married him. And she had only just begun! Thank goodness it wasn't quite yet.

'Yes, and I suppose we'll have to have a wedding cake with cardboard on top, instead of icing, like everyone seems to be doing now?' he said scornfully. 'I don't want that for you, Wizz – I mean, Sylvia. I want us to have a better wedding, with everything how it should be.'

Wondering what had made him quite so grumpy tonight, she said gently, 'It docsn't matter about cakes and dresses, Ian, really it doesn't. It's *you* I want, for my husband.'

'Oh, Sylvia . . .' Ian was just reaching up to kiss her again when the kitchen door opened. A bar of light came in from the hall, and Jack appeared with exaggerated cautiousness.

'Hello, hello, hello . . . ? Is it safe to come in?'

'Oh, buzz off, Jack,' Sylvia said, leaning away from Ian and straightening her skirt, which had ridden well up her thighs. 'What are you after?'

'Hello, Jack,' Ian said, in a slightly forced way.

'Just come to make Pa and me a spot of cocoa,' Jack spoke in a mocking posh schoolboy tone, which he often put on. The hall light brought out the red sheen of his hair. 'Pater says it's time for beddy-byes.'

'Go on then – get on with it.' Sylvia scrambled off Ian's lap. 'Would you like a drop too, Ian? It'll be watery of course.'

'No, thanks. I'd best be off in a minute – while the coast's still clear out there. How're things with you, Jack?'

'All right,' he said. They started talking about football,

and then Ian asked if Jack was doing rugby this term. Sylvia looked gratefully at Ian. Now that the Gould boys were gone, Jack didn't get much attention. He had been overjoyed when Laurie came back on a couple of days' leave and had dragged him off to the park to play football.

As they were talking, the front door opened and Pauline came back in. Sylvia was struck by how pale and tired she looked, standing at the kitchen doorway. She greeted Ian.

'All right, Mom? Jack's about to go up.'

'I am indeed,' Jack said, holding up his cocoa as if it were a tankard of ale.

Pauline tutted, leaning on the doorframe. 'Bit late. Still, least it's quiet so far.'

'There's a drop of cocoa.'

'Wouldn't say no.'

'How's Mrs Gould?' Sylvia handed her the cup.

Her mother sighed and sank down at the table. 'Not good. Doing her best – you know Marjorie. Stanley's so—' She cut herself off, making a frustrated sound. 'Still, he's not going to change. It would just've been better if Laurie hadn't left as well. Marjorie barely knows what to do with herself, the poor woman.'

Sylvia could see that her mother was all in. Ian stood with his coat on, holding his hat.

'Sorry, love,' Pauline said. 'Mustn't dwell on misery.'

'Not at all,' Ian said, giving one of his stiff little bows. 'But I must be off.'

Sylvia went to the front with him to say goodbye. Ian held her close, his cheek against her forehead.

'Don't change, will you?' he said quietly, drawing back to look down at her.

'I'm not going to change, silly!' She laughed it off.

What was he so worried about? 'I love you, Ian,' she added seriously.

'Oh, I love you too.' He rallied and gave his sudden broad smile. 'See you as soon as we can.' He leaned down to kiss her again, seeming more light-hearted.

Nine

A few evenings later Sylvia answered a knock at the front door to find Laurie Gould on the step. He stood, with a sudden stiff shyness, in the dusk. Though it was March it was trying to snow, and a few flakes drifted down all around him, settling on his pale hair.

'I've got a couple of days' leave,' he said. 'We're being re-posted for flight training.'

'Gosh!' Sylvia said, then felt immediately foolish. 'Look, come in. It's so cold out there.' As he came through the door she added, 'So are you going to be a pilot?'

'Oh,' Laurie gave a little laugh, 'I don't know. They have to try us out and see whether we're fit for it.' He was putting on a brave face, but she could sense how much he had changed. He was thinner in the face, his boyish cheerfulness had become subdued and he seemed more serious.

They stopped in the hall for a moment. Sylvia felt her cheeks burn pink and was glad that it was rather gloomy. 'I just wanted to say,' she said, 'I'm so very sorry about Raymond. I never got the chance to talk to you properly, after the service and everything—'

'It's all right,' Laurie stopped her rather abruptly. Before he looked down at the tiles of the hall floor she saw the pain in his eyes. 'I mean, it's not all right, is it? But I don't know what there is to say.'

'Yes,' Sylvia said, seeing how difficult it must be, with everyone else's sorrow coming at him. 'Of course not.' As they stood there it felt so unfair that she was happy, having Ian and so many things to look forward to, while he was sad. And he was living so far from home now. Thank heaven Jack was not old enough to go, she found herself thinking. She realized she wasn't used to dealing with Laurie as an adult. She thought of him more as Jack's age, though of course he was quite a lot older.

'Look,' she said, 'Jack's out the back sorting out the rabbits, and Mom's here. Come on through.' She led him to the back of the house. Pauline was in the kitchen stirring a pot on the range with her sleeves rolled up. 'Mom, Laurie's come round to say goodbye. He's off in a couple of days.'

'We're going to Canada,' Laurie said.

'Canada!' Sylvia gasped. 'You never said . . . My goodness, *Canada*. Why?'

'They do most of the flight training over there.' Laurie shrugged as if it was all the same to him wherever he was.

Pauline looked stricken. 'Oh, so soon,' she said. Sylvia could see her biting back the words, *your poor mother*. 'But I suppose if you've got to go, then you've got to.'

'Yes,' Laurie said, in his quiet way. 'That seems to be how it is.'

'Come out and see Jack,' Sylvia said, as the atmosphere was growing more awkward all the time. She could see that Laurie, still grieving over his brother, was also in a state of nerves about all that lay before him.

They all ended up in the garden. Jack was chasing the rabbits back into their hutches in the gloom. Mr Piggles was already safely shut up for the night. One of the others had got out, and Jack was tearing down the garden after it.

'Oh dear!' Laurie said, attempting to sound jovial.

'Yes, it never ends,' Pauline said. 'We've had to put chicken wire all along the bottom down there, to stop them getting onto the railway.

Laurie went and joined in the chase, glad to have something to do. The snow was still whirling in the air. Sylvia ran in and fetched coats for herself and her mother and they stood huddled up, watching. Once they caught the rabbit, Laurie and Jack started trying to fool about together as they always did, but there was very little space left. It seemed sad, as if they had outgrown the garden. It was another sign that everything had changed.

Watching them, Sylvia found herself close to tears. She had never taken a lot of notice of Laurie, since those days when they were very little and had read books together. Laurie had soon left her behind and was forever reading or writing something. But he had often come round to their house, especially in the summer after Jack had gone to the grammar school and become keen on cricket. She thought of all those summer evenings, the sound of the ball on the bat, the clouds of gnats in the air, the boys' voices in the garden as the sun went down. Her heart ached at the thought of all those happy times when none of them had thought of dying young. She knew her mother was probably thinking much the same, but they stood in silence, their breath coming out in clouds on the air.

'Would you like a cup of tea, Laurie?' Pauline called eventually.

'Oh, no thanks,' he said, turning from laughing with Jack. Now, with his face lit up, he looked like the boy they knew, not solemn and tense. 'I'd better go. Mom wants me back.'

'Yes,' Pauline said sadly. 'I'm sure she does.'

Laurie and Jack gave each other friendly goodbye punches. 'See you,' Laurie said.

'Goodbye, love,' Pauline said gently. 'And tell your mother: she's knows I'm always here. Pop in before you leave, won't you?'

'I will. It's very kind of you, Mrs W.'

Sylvia could hardly speak when they got to the front door, there was such a lump in her throat. 'Good luck,' she said and almost added, 'Come back, won't you?' but bit the words back.

'Thanks.' Laurie turned towards home, then stopped and gave a little wave. 'See you!'

And as he turned at the gate Sylvia felt as if their childhoods were walking away from them with him.

.

As Laurie left the Whitehouses' door, knowing that Sylvia was standing on the step, he felt a powerful impulse to turn back, but did not do so. He was too aware of the distance between himself and Sylvia. The fact that he had joined up and was going off to another world made the gulf even greater.

Laurie could not tell whether Sylvia had any real idea of the huge change that was facing him now. How could she, or any of them? Like Dad, with all his brisk remarks about the technical side of it. But that was the easy part to imagine – the classes, learning how to operate the planes. The rest felt like looking over the edge of a cliff, into a void. He faced it with dread. He did not want to leave home and go halfway round the world, yet the thought of being here now, caught in the wash of his parents' grief, was too much to bear. He could no longer stand his father avoiding mentioning Raymond; or looking into his mother's face and seeing the raw pain etched on it. It made him feel utterly helpless. And he could never be any sort of compensation for their loss of Raymond. For his mother, her offspring were like a three-legged stool – her boys. Now, one of the legs of that stool had been sawn off, and the stool could not stand. Why even pretend that it could?

But Sylvia . . . He had always seen her as a kindly older sister. She was that pretty, sweet (especially compared with Audrey), rather timid girl who had been one of the constants of his childhood. He realized that he felt more pain at leaving her, and all the memories she evoked of summer gardens and games and carefree childhood, than at leaving his parents, who were now darkened by shadows of pain and regret.

He stood for a moment at his front door, knowing that Sylvia had not yet gone inside, but still shy of looking or saying anything more. Was she watching him? A second later he heard the click of the latch and knew she had gone. The street felt desolate, suddenly empty of her presence. In that moment a powerful sense of yearning twisted inside him. He longed for her to come out again. Was it just that he was going away that caused this heightened feeling towards Sylvia? All he wanted to do at this moment was go back to the Whitehouses' door, knock to be let in and settle down with Sylvia, see her smile and talk about old times. She felt like home, like everything he needed.

Trying to pull himself together, he went inside to where his mother was instructing Paul to lay the table for tea. Tea – such a childhood word, of crumpets and cake, and all of them together around the table in the cosy light. For a second his eyes filled, before he swallowed the tears away.

'All right?' His mother's voice was determinedly

cheerful. She looked up from the handful of knives (only four now, when it had always been five) that she had put down on the table. Laurie saw how thin her face had become, the skin closer to her bones. 'Did you see them?'

'Yes.' Looking down, he picked up the knives to lay them. Paul gave a yelp of protest.

'Let him do it,' his mother said.

Laurie handed Paul the knives. He looked up at his mother and, in spite of her fighting against it, her eyes were full of tears.

Ten

When she met Kitty Barratt that mucky winter morning, Sylvia had been at Hockley Goods Yard for about three weeks.

Hurrying to an early shift, she left Hockley passenger station and walked round to the Goods Yard entrance. A straggle of other people were going in the same direction. It was still dark and there was a sleety rain. Sylvia pulled her collar up and bent her head into the wet, trying not to let the miserable weather drag her spirits down. Everyone was hungry, almost all the time. The food available was never enough and she was often seized by a low, sinking feeling that could make her feel quite faint.

She had had a late night last night as well. There were fewer raids now and she and Ian had risked going out to a dance. It had been lovely to get dolled up in her pretty red and black frock with its swirling skirt, and see the pleased grin on Ian's face. He looked very dashing himself in his brown jacket and trousers, with a red scarf tucked in at the neck, his fine brown hair carefully combed back.

'Gosh!' He kissed her and looked her up and down approvingly. 'That's my girl. What a stunner!' From his jacket pocket he produced a red silk rose. 'For you, my dear.'

'Oh, Ian!' Sylvia cried. 'It's beautiful – and it matches my outfit. Where on earth did you get it?'

'Well, to be honest, it was my mother's. She said I could give it to you.'

'How nice,' Sylvia said, surprised. She didn't think Mrs Westley liked her very much, but she was touched. The rose looked lovely pinned at the neck of her frock.

Sylvia smiled to herself, thinking of the smoky dance hall, the band playing 'South of the Border' and the 'Java Jive' and so many of their favourite songs, and Ian holding her close to his strong, lean body. He was a rather awkward dancer, but she knew he was trying his best for her. She loved the feel of his muscular back under her hands as they danced, and they had some fun, though Ian did get a bit tetchy because she knew all the dances better than he did. It had almost been possible to forget the war for a bit, until they stepped out into the cold and the blackout again. She was feeling extra weary now, but it had definitely been worth it.

Turning into the yard, amid the gaggle of other trouser-clad workers, Sylvia caught sight of an unmistakably female pair of legs walking past her. For a moment she looked hungrily at the sleek shoes with their inch of heel and at the smooth, feminine stockings. How nice they looked, even if they were getting splashed up the back with spots of mud! Who was that girl? Sylvia wondered. She must have had a good supply of stockings before the war to be looking so good now. She caught a glimpse of the young woman's face under a dark felt hat with a narrow brim. Then she was gone, on her way into the offices. Sylvia felt a pang for a moment. There was something nice about being able to wear a skirt and dainty shoes to work, instead of the tough black boots she had to wear – not to mention working in an office instead of freezing out here.

Still, she thought resignedly, if I worked doing

anything in there, I'd only make a hash of it. I'm better off outside.

When she reached the Amenities block everyone was milling round, coming either on or off a shift. Sylvia didn't give the girl she'd seen another thought then. Men from last night's shift – women porters were not assigned to working nights – were all clocking out in the Time office, all tired and unusually quiet as they made their way home. Edie, the night cook who made sure the men all got a meal in the foremen's mess room, was on her way out too. When Sylvia came in, she saw Edie calling out to Madge, who was clocking in.

'Ta-ra!' she said. 'Behave yerself, bab.'

'Oh, I'll do that all right,' Madge said. 'Chance to do anything else'd be a fine thing. All right, Sylvia?'

'Hello, Madge,' Sylvia said as they went to put their things in the porters' mess room. Sylvia noticed that Madge looked weary and unusually dejected. 'Everything all right?' she asked, cautiously. She always felt rather young and foolish next to Madge.

'Oh, ar – I'm all right,' she said morosely. She looked as if she was not going to say any more, but then she added, 'Had a bit of a barney with my feller last night.'

'Oh.' Sylvia wasn't sure what to say, so she added, 'I hope you made it up all right.'

Madge heaved one of her ample legs up to tie her bootlaces and looked round. 'Oh, we made it up, but not before I'd given him a shiner. 'E always wants more than 'e's getting, that one. I said to 'im, "Yer can put *that* away right now. I ain't getting myself into anything I shouldn't." My sister's at home with Mom, with a babby, and 'er's only sixteen. I'm the sensible one, see.' Madge restored her foot to the floor with a thud and righted herself. 'It's all 'e ever thinks about – specially when 'e's 'ad a few. So I laid one on 'im – that'll teach 'im. Till the next time, any'ow. 'E's like a bull at a gate.'

Sylvia was blushing furiously at this surfeit of information. She had never before heard anyone talk like that in her life. It was certainly an eye-opener. Though she knew Ian was a decent man who wanted to do the right thing, she still felt pressure from him constantly to give him more, to go further, because his own desire was so strong. At least it's not just us, she thought. But she could hardly punch Ian, as Madge had apparently done, to keep him at bay!

Madge looked at her confused face and let out a loud laugh. 'Sorry, bab. 'Ave I spoke out of turn?'

'No,' Sylvia said, grinning suddenly. 'Not at all.'

The yard was busier than it had ever been: lines and lines of wagons full of ammunition and components, and every sort of equipment for the war effort pouring out of the factories to be sent south. Trains streamed in and out, and queues backed up, waiting to get into the shunting yard. The place was working at full capacity, and more. Sometimes staff from the offices were called out to work as porters as there was so much stuff to shift.

All that morning they were emptying wagons non-stop. By the early afternoon Sylvia and Madge were outside with Bill Jones, their checker, unloading a dray that had been filled from a joey boat in Hockley Basin. The boxes of nuts and bolts seemed endless as they worked in the unceasing drizzle, barrowing in loads from the yard to wagons in the shed and unloading them again there. It was very heavy work, not helped by the endless wet, the wheels of trucks and carts churning up the muddy ground.

By the time Sylvia was pushing one of the last barrow-fuls into the shed, she really felt she was running out of steam. Her face was soaked with rain, her clothes limp with sweat under her coat. She had walked miles, her shoulders were aching and her arms trembling with the effort of pushing the laden barrows.

'Right,' Bill said at last, signing off the list with a flourish. 'That's your lot, ladies! Time for a well-deserved tea break, I reckon.'

There was a burst of watery sunshine as they headed across for their break. The light reflected in the puddles across the yard, making them look like eyes, staring up at the sky. Sylvia caught sight of someone squatting down by the corner of the Amenities block, reaching out to stroke a cat. The young woman looked a little familiar, as did quite a number of the station staff by now. She had neatly bobbed, wavy fair hair. Sylvia moved closer, drawn both by the cat and by the person stroking him. The muscular tabby rat-catcher was known in the yard as Tiger.

'Hello, Tiger Tim,' said Sylvia, leaning over to stroke him. He arched his back and purred like an engine. 'Oh, you're in a good mood today.'

Just as the other girl looked up at her, smiling, Sylvia noticed her elegant black shoes and realized that she must be the same person she had passed that morning.

'He's a darling, isn't he?' the young woman said, looking up at her. Sylvia was immediately struck by her face. She had prominent cheekbones, large, soulful grey eyes and eyebrows plucked into a slender arch. Her voice was high and pleasant, although the next thing she said was drowned out by loud whoomp-whooping from one of the shunting engines behind, the shriek of a train whistle and the roar of a truck starting up, all at the same time.

Sylvia made a face, laughing and covering her ears. 'I didn't hear a word of what you said – sorry!' she said when things had quietened down a bit.

The girl stood up. Even in her heels she was almost a head shorter than Sylvia. She lit a cigarette and held out the packet. 'Want one?'

'Thanks,' Sylvia said. She didn't smoke often, but she liked the odd cigarette now and then. She leaned in to light it from the match the young woman offered, shielding it from the wind.

'All I said was: he thinks he's king of the walk.' She laughed as the cat rubbed against her legs. She was petite, with thin arms and neck, but a large bust for someone so small and an hourglass figure. Even in her sober office clothes there was something about her that made you take another look. Her hair curled attractively at her temples. She was not exactly pretty, Sylvia thought; there was something too unusual about her face, but with those huge eyes and her manner, she drew you in.

'So you're one of the porters?' she said, blowing out a mouthful of smoke, rather stylishly, Sylvia thought. 'I do admire you. Actually, I sometimes think you're lucky being outside, when we're stuck in that morgue there!'

'What d'you do?' Sylvia asked. She liked the warm, confiding way in which the girl talked to her. It was nice to meet someone close to her own age, who might be similar to her. With the Gould boys gone, and Audrey and Jane, her old school friend, away too, she did feel lonely, when she had time to think about it. She had grown to like Madge, but there was a gulf between them in age and experience.

'Oh, I'm a comptometer operator – very boring,' she

91

said, breathing smoke out through her nostrils. 'We used to be in there before . . .' She nodded her head at the wrecked office block. 'So they've moved us into a store-room, which is like the Black Hole of Calcutta.' She rolled her eyes.

'I wouldn't know where to begin with one of those compt . . . those machine things,' Sylvia admitted. 'I've no head for figures.'

'Oh, it's not difficult.' Leaning closer, in a way that made Sylvia feel strangely honoured, the girl went on, 'I'm Kitty by the way.'

'Sylvia.' She bent down to stroke the cat again.

'Nice having some animals around, isn't it?' Kitty said. 'I'd love to keep a cat, but . . .'

'They're no trouble,' Sylvia said. 'We've got two. And rabbits. We've got a big lop-eared chap called Mr Piggles. He's my little brother's really, but I end up looking after him a lot of the time. We keep hens as well.'

'Oh, you're lucky!' Kitty said. Sylvia decided that she did look pretty when she smiled. She had a wide mouth and a face full of vitality.

'It means we have eggs, at least.'

'That sounds ever so nice.' Kitty sounded wistful. 'My father doesn't like that sort of thing. There's just him and me. Mom died last year.'

'Oh,' Sylvia said, touched by this, 'I'm sorry – how sad. Where d'you come in from?'

'Handsworth Wood,' Kitty told her.

'That's a shame.'

'Why?'

'Only that we're over in Kings Heath. Otherwise you could have come round.'

'I could come,' Kitty laughed, with a merry, infectious sound. 'It's not the end of the earth, is it?'

'No, I s'pose not, if you could be bothered,' Sylvia said. 'We live near the station, but they're about to cut the passenger service. Savings for the war effort apparently – it's going to be goods only. You could get the bus, though.' She had a happy feeling that they were making friends.

As they stood talking, a couple of shunters sauntered across the yard. They stared brazenly at the two young women as they passed, one with a shunting pole in his hand. He leaned close to the other and said something and they both laughed. Sylvia saw Kitty follow them mischievously with her eyes. The yard was growing busier again, with trucks coming in, pausing at the weighbridge, then drawing up to be unloaded. Sylvia could see more teams of porters coming out with their checkers.

'I'd best go,' Sylvia said. 'No rest for the wicked. We'll be on again any minute. I must get some tea – I'm dropping.'

'I should think you are,' Kitty said. 'I don't know how you do it. But look, how about we get together sometime?' She threw her cigarette butt down and ground it under the heel of one of the neat black shoes. Wryly she added, 'Paint the town red?'

Sylvia felt her spirits lift and she smiled warmly. She had found a friend! 'That'd be nice,' she said as she backed away. 'I'd really like that. See you around.'

Eleven

Kitty Barratt stood in front of the mirror in her bedroom. It was still pitch-dark outside and she was getting ready for the early shift. As she leaned closer to the elegantly framed glass to apply her lipstick, the electric light above created interesting shadows under her cheekbones. However, it also made her look grey and washed-out. She rubbed on a touch of rouge, bared her small, even teeth to check they were not marked with lipstick, and dabbed at the corners of her mouth with a hanky.

Hands at her waist, she twisted back and forth to check her figure and her clothes. She had on a plain enough office outfit: a straight black skirt and a cream blouse covered by a sage-green cardigan. Her curvaceous, full-breasted figure would have looked impressive in anything. Her honey-blonde hair had a natural soft wave and was cut to jaw-length, curling neatly underneath and framing her forehead and large grey eyes. She patted the ends of her hair, wrinkled her nose, then gave a mischievous, self-satisfied smile.

'Go get 'em,' she purred. 'Kitty the cat!'

She stood listening for a moment. Was he up? Could she sneak out before the old sod was awake?

After hunting for her shoes, which she had kicked off last night, she held them in her right hand and opened the bedroom door with her left, wincing at its squeak. Her room was at the end of the landing. Tip-toeing along the red carpet, Kitty avoided looking at the next door, which she had to pass to go downstairs. For years it was a spare room in their generous-sized villa. But during those last months until she died last summer, Kitty's mother had moved in there. That room crouched in the house like a dark beast, full of agonized memories. Kitty still half-expected that if she went in there she would see her mother's grey face on the pillow, her eyes pleading away the pain. But, no, Mom was gone. Her mother had never been a strong woman, but she was the only heart the house had ever had. The maids had deserted them too, once Mom was gone. There was more work to be had now, and more cheerful places to spend your time. Only old Ethel stayed on, coming in for a couple of hours each morning.

Kitty ran swiftly down the carpeted stairs. At the bottom she slipped on her shoes before going out to the cold quarry tiles of the kitchen. She thought she was alone, that she had got away with it, but there he was in the chair, a dark-blue rug over his knees: Josiah Barratt of *J. Barratt & W. Stone – Non-Ferrous Die-Castings*, self-made industrialist, failed alderman and widower. He was a paunchy, balding man of fifty-five, stubble-cheeked this morning. He stared blearily as her as she came into the kitchen.

''Bout time,' he complained, pushing himself up in the chair. A belch rumbled up and escaped loudly. 'Get me some tea. What time is it?'

'Gone five,' she said. 'I'll put the kettle on, but I've got to go—'

'I said GET ME A CUP OF TEA, yer useless wench. You ain't going anywhere before I get my tea. I should've thought that was the least yer could do, for me keeping a roof over your pretty head. I'm starved, sitting here all night long.'

Well, why didn't you go to bed, you silly old sod? She kept this thought to herself, silently putting the kettle on. She winced at the way he spoke. Josiah Barratt was proud of the fact that he had come up the hard way: through the school of life and hard knocks, he had risen out of the Victorian slums. But he could turn it on, and talk posh in public when it suited him – when he wanted votes. Time and again he had stood for the Conservative Party in the council elections. He longed for his place of prominence, for civic recognition – even to wear the chains of mayoral honour. He'd lost again and again in elections, most recently to a smooth-cheeked public-school boy twenty years his junior, who had then proved his heroism by joining the RAF. Josiah was never going to satisfy his desire to call himself Alderman Barratt. The truth was that, even by Conservative standards, he was unpleasant. No one liked him.

At home he no longer put on airs. *If only Mom could see what he's turned into,* Kitty thought. Mom had been gentle and well-spoken, reared among the Plymouth Brethren. Josiah had dazzled her with his house, his successful business. He could turn it on all right.

Kitty always made sure she spoke well. She hated to sound common. Anything but be like him.

Her father groaned and stretched in the chair. A powerful stink of booze came from him and there was an empty Scotch bottle on the table.

'Pass me my boots,' he ordered. 'And yer can pass them an' all, while yer at it.' He nodded at his ciggies on the table in their plain, rationed packaging. Beside them was a little book called *Aircraft Recognition.* Her father was obsessed by the idea that they might still be invaded. 'They'll find a way, those scheming Krauts.'

Kitty passed him the boots. He pulled them on with a grunt, then lurched out to the back toilet to pass water. As the clank and whoosh of water assailed her ears, the kettle came to the boil, to her relief. She made tea as fast as she could.

'That's right, just bugger off and leave me,' he moaned as she went for her coat. 'I'm the one that puts the shirt on your back, yer know.'

No, you're not, she thought. I earn my own wages. She cast him an icy look. 'I've got to go.'

'What about my breakfast!' he roared. 'What does a man have to do to get summat to eat in this house?'

'Ethel'll be in later,' she said, going to the door. He didn't have to be at work for ages yet, and all he had to do was climb into his car. 'And I hope it chokes you, you old bastard,' she added under her breath.

And she was gone, seizing her coat and hat and hurrying out into the drizzle, out of the dark house where her mother had lived in fear. Never would Kitty let a man have power over her like that!

On the train she stood amid the packed crowd, hoping Ethel would remember to do the bits of shopping she had asked for. For a while she dwelt on practical details, and then she allowed herself to slip into a daydream about Joe Whelan. Would she see him today? And might Joe give her one of his special rides tonight?

Twelve

That afternoon Kitty stood on the platform at Hockley passenger station. She tugged her collar up against the raw wind, which carried sounds from the Goods Yard: the shunting of wagons and an intermittent clanging from the Round Yard, as if lengths of metal piping were being thrown to the ground.

'Come on,' she murmured, tapping her foot.

Would Joe Whelan be on today? She was almost sure he must be, and a thrum of excitement had begun within her. Her heart was thumping and her nerves were on edge. She felt that she couldn't bear it if he wasn't there today. The waiting was awful. She was hooked on his attraction to her. So what if he was old enough to be her father? The train guard was a big, good-looking man and she knew that the sight of her set him off-balance. She enjoyed knowing that he was full of desire for her.

Soon she and the other shuffling, muttering passengers heard the rhythmic puffing of the engine, and a plume of smoke appeared as it came on the mile-long journey from Snow Hill. When the train drew alongside the platform, Kitty positioned herself where she guessed the guard's van would stop. Before it had fully halted, its brakes squealing, she saw the door of the guard's van swing open and Joe standing ready to step out.

'Joe!' Kitty hurried over and greeted him with a dazzling smile.

Joe Whelan was a bear of a man in his late forties, who had come to Birmingham from Ireland in his twenties. He was stocky, black-haired, blue-eyed and very reassuring-looking, with a soft Wexford accent.

'Oh now, Kitty,' he said. He had his flags for signalling to the driver tucked under his arm, his whistle round his neck. 'Goodness now, what're you doing here?' His attention was mainly on the job, and the passengers boarding further along the platform. He looked agitated by her appearance.

'I wanted to see you,' she said, going up even closer to him and looking up into his eyes, making her own wide and appealing. 'Can I come with you, Joe?'

He looked around uncomfortably for a moment. Passengers were climbing into the carriages or, having disembarked, were walking swiftly away. No one was taking any notice of them. Joe hesitated. 'Get in then,' he half-whispered. 'I haven't seen you.'

Kitty nipped round behind him and stepped up into the guard's van. The stove was lit and it was very warm and fuggy. Two bicycles stood propped against the wall, alongside a wheelbarrow and various sacks and boxes. She heard the train get up steam again and Joe blowing his whistle. As they began to ease away, towards the next station at Soho, Joe stepped in and slammed the door shut.

She turned to him in the gloom. The expression in Joe's eyes was nakedly anxious, yet already full of the desire she knew he felt so strongly for her. She had met him on her journeys back and forth from Handsworth to Hockley and they had got talking. She had made up to him, there was no denying it. The man was like putty in her hands and she enjoyed the sensation of power it gave her.

'Hello, Joe.' She made her voice soft and seductive.

'Hello, Kitty,' he said, a little shamefaced.

She stepped closer. She knew she had the power to make him forget everything: his wife, his children, everything in his nature and his Catholic conditioning, which made his conscience scream that this was wrong.

'Where're we going today?' he asked. He picked up a cigarette that he had left burning on the stove and took a drag on it. The tip glowed orange for a second.

'I can't stay on today,' she said, moving close to him. Twice she had lingered with him beyond the two stops that took her home. She even bought a ticket once to take her all the way out to Wolverhampton Low Level, in order to ride with Joe before getting out and catching a train back. Joe had told her, wonderingly, that she was mad.

Each journey was spent in more of a fever of desire than the last – Joe's desire. Something about him tugged at Kitty's emotions. It was his lust for her that made her keep going back to him; her need for a sense of power, more than any fire that she felt in her own body.

'Kitty,' he said in a strained voice. 'You've got to stop doing this – coming to me. It's wrong. My wife Ann's not well . . .'

'D'you really want me to stop?' Kitty took her hat off so that he could see her face properly, and stepped up to him, putting her arms around him. Her full breasts pressed against his chest. She knew he would never be able to resist.

'God, girl,' Joe said helplessly. He threw the half-burned cigarette to the floor and ground it with his heel. 'God, now stop it, will you? What am I to do, with a girl like you coming on to me? I can't think straight.'

He looked down at her, then pressed her close to him, his burly body surrounding her, his mouth fixing on her upturned lips. He tasted of the roughest tobacco. They kissed for the rest of the short distance to Soho and, as soon as the train moved off again, Joe came to her and took her hungrily in his arms.

As they steamed into Handsworth station, Joe tore himself away from her. For a moment he looked dazed, still lost in his own arousal, like someone waking from a dream.

'God!' he said again. 'You make me want you, woman.'

Kitty was excited by his need. She had never had intimate relations with a man, not beyond these stolen kisses. But she had already had a taste of the way she could hook a man and make him hers. This was something she could do.

'Not now, Joe,' she said, tapping his nose with her finger. 'I've got to go.' She straightened her cardigan, deliberately pulling it tight across her breasts. She could see Joe gazing hungrily at them. She went to the door as the train halted, hissing steam. 'See you again soon.'

'When?' He reached for her shoulder. 'When will I see you?'

'I'm on the afternoon shift next week, I think,' she said.

Joe thought, put a hand to his head. 'I don't know when I'm . . . I can't think . . .'

'Never mind.' She reached up and pecked his cheek. 'See you as soon as I can.'

As she walked off along the platform she knew his eyes were following her. She could feel his gaze as if it was burning into her and she felt a purring sense of satisfaction. Heaven knew, these dark, horrible days of the war were bad enough. Something had to brighten them up a bit.

During a break the next day Kitty went out into the carriage yard at Hockley, hoping to find Sylvia, the porter she had spoken to. She seemed such a nice person, so sweet and pretty. Some of the girls in the office were nice enough, but Kitty, in her lonely life, was short of real friends.

For once it wasn't raining and a blustery wind was blowing that made it feel almost as if they were by the sea.

She found Sylvia standing by the head of the horse that was harnessed to the dray she had just finished loading, which was about to depart. The horse was a big chestnut creature with white fetlocks. Sylvia was looking up, one hand shielding her eyes, and talking to the driver. Kitty was surprised to see a girl perched up on the cart, an energetic, ginger-haired person with a very freckly face. Sylvia was laughing as they talked and was stroking the horse's muzzle fondly.

'Off you go then.' Sylvia gave the horse a quick peck on the nose. 'Ooh, you're lovely and velvety. Ta-ra!' she called up to the ginger girl, who slapped the reins and drove the horse forward. Sylvia stood watching, hands on hips, as it set off.

'Hello!' Kitty greeted her.

'Oh, hello,' Sylvia said. The yard was full of carts and trucks, bull-nosed Scammell transporters and porters, all hurrying to and fro. They both had to step back quickly to get out of the way of a Great Western truck that came roaring at them.

'Good heavens!' Kitty clutched Sylvia's arm for a second.

'That was close,' Sylvia said. Kitty saw that she looked very tired, though she seemed cheerful enough.

'Just thought I'd pop out and see if you were around,' Kitty said. She lit up a cigarette and smoked it stylishly, blowing smoke out at the side of her mouth. 'Fancy coming out sometime, for a drink or something?'

Sylvia looked uncertain. 'It'd be nice . . . The only thing is, what with my shifts and the raids, I have such a job seeing my fiancé. And I'm not very keen on pubs.'

So she's engaged, Kitty thought. A bitter feeling rose within her for a moment. 'I know,' she said lightly. 'It is *so* hard. I have a devil of a job seeing my feller as well. And I can't really invite you home – the old man's not keen on company.'

'I tell you what . . .' Sylvia looked across at the big clock in the yard just as Madge's voice came booming across to her.

'Sylv? Come on – shift yerself! We ain't finished yet!'

'Got to go,' Sylvia said. 'But how about you come round to ours? Everyone'd be really happy with some company. Only I know it's a bit of a way for you?'

Kitty was pleased. 'That's all right, I don't mind that. I'd like to come, if you think it's all right with your family.'

They fixed a time. Sylvia was off on Saturday, and Kitty realized she had the afternoon off as well.

'See you Saturday then,' Sylvia called, backing away towards the Main Shed. 'About four? Come and meet the menagerie!'

Thirteen

'Who is this person who's coming round then?' Ian asked, when he turned up on Saturday afternoon.

'Kitty?' Sylvia had been a bit nervous about telling Ian about Kitty. He expected her undivided attention. 'Oh, she works in the offices at the yard and she seems nice. I gather she's got a difficult home life and could do with some company. She likes animals as well, so I thought it'd be a change for her to come round.'

'Oh,' Ian said, rather peevishly. He went to hang his coat up in the hall. 'I rather hoped I'd have you all to myself and we could go for a nice walk.'

'We've got a couple of hours – she's not coming till four,' Sylvia said. She opened the front door again and peered out at the weather. It wasn't raining, though it was very chilly. Daffodils had pushed up in patches on the remaining strip of lawn at the back. 'It's not bad out here. How about we go to the park?'

'Okay, it'd be nice to get out,' Ian said, appeased, and reaching for his coat again. 'I've been rather cooped up all week.'

Sylvia was warmly dressed in a black skirt and cream jumper with woolly stockings and fleece-lined boots. Her coat was dark grey with white pinstripe squares faintly across it, and she had a jaunty grey hat with a little peacock feather tucked in the side. It felt very nice to wrap up in something other than railway clothing and set out on Ian's arm.

'You look lovely,' Ian said, smiling down at her. He had on a brown tweed coat and a brown and green scarf thrown sportily over his shoulder. Once they were a little way along the street he stopped her for a moment. 'Kiss?'

'People will see us!' she protested.

'What people?' He gestured along the deserted street.

'The curtain-twitchers.' But she reached up and kissed him, laughing.

They spent a lovely hour and a half walking arm-in-arm under the bare trees in Highbury Park and dreaming about the future. Daffodils were appearing across the park as well, yellow and hopeful above the dark ground.

'We'd better not be late back,' Sylvia said. 'I wouldn't like to be out when Kitty comes.'

When they got in, Sylvia saw that her mother was sitting in the back room in a blue haze of smoke and looking downcast.

'This has just come.' She held out an envelope and Sylvia recognized Audrey's handwriting. Sylvia took the letter, seeing that Mom was upset. Audrey wrote to them now and again and her letters were full of service life, her new friends and how busy and exciting it was. Sylvia read it out:

Dear Mom, Dad, Sylvia and Jack,
    I'll have to make this a quick one, but I'm afraid I'm writing to say that my leave, which we normally get after three months, has been cancelled for the moment. Very disappointing – I was so looking forward to coming home, and they can't tell me at the moment when I can get away. I hope as soon as possible, and I feel very browned off about it.

We're all working like mad and there's never a dull
moment (well, some of it's dull, but it's still busy!).
I'm now sharing a hut with a bunch of madcap girls
and we have a lot of laughs. We all went to the camp
picture house last night and they were showing *Tin Pan
Alley*, so we've all been singing the songs ever since!

Sylvia glanced at Ian, smiling, as they had seen the
picture together already. It was one of Sylvia's favourites,
though Ian thought it 'slushy'.

'She's starting to sound different,' she said. 'All that
funny language they have. And she went on reading:
"All is well here, suffice it to say." Ooh,' Sylvia laughed,
'"Suffice it!"'

I hope Dad's not overdoing it, nor you, Mom.
Glad to hear you've settled in at the Goods Yard, sis.
Well, that's a turn-up for the books – what does Ian
think? At least you've found a job that doesn't involve
any brain-work (wink)!

Sylvia was stung by this, and even more by the way
Ian joined in the laughter. She was just opening her
mouth to make an angry retort when they heard a knock
at the front door. Swallowing her rage – the sort of rage
that only an older sister can provoke – she said, 'That'll
be Kitty. I'll go.'

On opening the door, a cheering sight met her eyes.
Kitty, in a smart navy coat, shoes and hat, was peering
out from behind a large bunch of white narcissi with
orange centres.

'Hello!' Sylvia said happily, forgetting her wrath at
Audrey's comments. 'That was perfect timing – come in!'

'This is *ever* so nice of you,' Kitty said, stepping in.

'No, it's lovely that you could come. Everyone's at the back.' Sylvia took her coat. 'Well, except my dad and Jack, my brother. Come on through – this is my mom.'

Sylvia watched as her mother greeted Kitty in her kindly, comfortable way. Mom was always most at ease in her own home. 'Nice to see you, love. Come and join us. I'm sorry we're all in the back, but I haven't lit the fire in the parlour yet.'

'Oh no,' Kitty said, 'it's cosy in here. What a nice room.'

It was nice in a homely way, Sylvia thought, a cosy, well-used room with the table and chairs, fireplace and wireless on the sideboard in which they kept the crocks. On the mantel was a mix of jugs and candlesticks, a china horse, a silver cup that Jack had won at school for sprinting, and a jar full of dried lavender.

'I thought you might like these,' Kitty held out the flowers. 'Mrs . . . Oh, I'm sorry, I don't know your surname.'

'Whitehouse.' Pauline took the little bouquet, smiling with pleasure. 'Aren't they nice – but there's no need, you know, love. It's nice of you to come. Sylvia, find a vase; they'll look lovely on the table here. Come and have a seat in the warm, Kitty.'

'Take my chair,' Sylvia called over. 'I'll bring this stool.'

'Make us a fresh pot, Sylv?' her mother said. 'Reuse some of grouts. There is a bit of cake, although it's not up to much. It's got everything in except ingredients!'

Everyone laughed. 'It's surprising what you can do with no ingredients, Mrs W.,' Ian said. 'I bet it's delicious.'

Sylvia put the kettle on again as everyone greeted Kitty. She smiled, seeing her mother and, she thought, Ian too taking a liking to her new friend. And Kitty looked so nice and happy to be there. To make things even better, Brandy, the orange tabby, got up from her place in the corner and sauntered over to greet the new visitor.

'Hello!' Kitty said as the cat leapt up onto her lap, without any thought of asking permission. 'What a lovely warm thing you are!' The cat settled, purring.

'Don't let her claw you,' Sylvia warned. 'She's a devil for that.'

'I don't mind,' Kitty said. Brandy seemed to be in seventh heaven on her lap. 'I'd love a cat, but Dad's not keen on animals.'

'What about your mother, bab?' Pauline Whitehouse said. She sounded even more motherly than usual as she said it, as if she already had Kitty down as a sad little orphan.

'She died – last year,' Kitty explained. 'She'd been very ill, and . . .' She trailed off and they could all hear the break in her voice.

'Oh, you poor thing,' Pauline said. 'That's terrible. Have you got any brothers and sisters?' Sylvia stood, hoping Kitty didn't mind all these questions, but she seemed almost glad to be asked.

'No, just me,' she said. She eyed Pauline's cigarette. 'You don't mind if I smoke?'

'You go ahead, love,' Pauline said comfortably, lighting up herself.

They asked Kitty about her work at the yard.

'You're a comptometer operator?' Ian said. 'You must have a good head for figures.'

'Well, I suppose I have,' Kitty said. 'The machine does most of the work, really. But it does seems to come quite easily to me – arithmetic was my favourite subject at school, believe it or not.

'My sister's like that,' Sylvia said. 'Audrey. She's in the WAAF.'

'Oh, you've got a sister as well?' Kitty enthused. 'You are *lucky*, Sylvia.'

'Ha!' Ian teased. 'All that sisterly love.'

Kitty's brow wrinkled. 'Do you not get on?' she asked rather cautiously.

'Oh, she's all right,' Sylvia said, still stinging from Audrey's remarks in the letter. 'When she's asleep!'

As they were drinking their tea, Sherry, the brown tabby, came and rubbed herself against Kitty's legs and she laughed, seeming very pleased to be singled out.

'You're the favourite today,' Mom said. 'They're not always this friendly, you know.'

'Cats really do take to some people more than others,' Sylvia said. 'They obviously like you.'

'They can't stand me,' Ian said with a rueful expression.

'You don't smell right,' Sylvia teased.

Kitty was laughing, stroking both the tiger-striped cats. They went into ecstasies of pleasure.

'D'you want to come out and see the rabbits and the royal ladies?' Sylvia asked, once they'd downed their tea. 'We'll need our coats.'

'I'd love to,' Kitty said.

'I'll stay in the warm, I think,' Ian said. He looked sleepy. But Sylvia was pleased to see that he had taken to her friend. Ian was so clever that she was always a bit afraid he might look down on people.

Sylvia fetched their coats and led Kitty out the back. She looked round, seeming entranced with everything.

'You're so lucky,' she said again, taking Sylvia's arm as they went along the path in the chilly garden. Sylvia was surprised and warmed by this. 'Your family are so nice and – oh!' she exclaimed. 'All these animals!'

'Come and meet Mr Piggles,' Sylvia said.

When she lifted the big, floppy rabbit out to hand him over, Kitty laughed like an enchanted child.

'Look at him!' she said, full of delight. 'He's enormous – and all this fur! Is he going to be all right with me holding him?'

'Oh, he loves it, as long as you don't mind. He's a bit grubby.'

'I don't care about that,' Kitty said, holding her arms out.

Sylvia handed Mr Piggles to her, enjoying her pleasure. She couldn't help just looking at Kitty as she held the rabbit, at her strange mixture of delicate and ample features. With her slender limbs, there was something doll-like about her, yet she was curvy in all the right places to make her look very womanly. Kitty squatted, holding Mr Piggles and snuggling her face close to him.

'Oh, he's adorable! I've never had any pets.' She looked up from stroking the rabbit with a wide, delighted smile. 'Animals are so nice. Much nicer than people really, don't you think? But your family are lovely too, Sylvia. You don't know what I'd do for a family like yours – a brother and sister, and everything.'

'We're nothing special, you know,' Sylvia said, but she was pleased that someone liked something of hers. She showed Kitty round with pride, and they stood outside until they were too cold to stay any longer and had to go in and warm up.

Jack had just arrived home as they got in and, when she introduced Kitty to him, Sylvia saw him staring at her in fascination. She seemed to have that effect, Sylvia thought, proud that Kitty wanted to be her friend.

'Well, you're a handsome fellow,' Kitty said to him, and Jack blushed mightily and muttered something about needing to go upstairs. He was looking grubby and dishevelled.

Kitty and Sylvia laughed. 'Have I scared him away?' Kitty asked.

'Oh, he'll be back. He'll be too hungry not to come down – he's been playing football.'

Kitty immediately went over to the two cats, which were lying in a heap together by the fire, and stroked them again. Sylvia, feeling she was neglecting Ian, went over and sat with him. In a few minutes Jack came down again, having at least combed his hair, and tucked into slices of toast.

'Let's play something, can we?' he asked. 'Instead of just sitting around.' He loved games, and the family were more likely to agree to play if there was a visitor to entertain.

'Oh, can we!' Kitty said, full of excitement. She faltered, blushing. 'Sorry, I didn't mean to be so forward. It's just that I've never had anyone to play with!'

'Just for a while,' Mom said, smiling at Kitty's eagerness. She was knitting. 'You don't need me, do you?'

Jack brought in cards and Monopoly. 'What shall we do?' he said, excited that anyone was prepared to play with him.

'Monopoly, I think,' Ian said. Sylvia groaned inwardly. She found Monopoly hard going – all those cards to read, and it was so involved! But she didn't want to say so. She sat beside Ian, enjoying the fact that she was there with the man she loved and a new friend who seemed to be relishing everything about the afternoon. She caught Ian's eye and gave him a radiant smile. He laid his hand on her thigh and she shifted closer to him.

111

When Kitty left to catch her bus, she thanked the family with such feeling that Sylvia's mother said, 'Do come again, love, any time. We'll be pleased to have you.'

'That's ever so nice of you, Mrs Whitehouse,' she said. Sylvia was very touched to see tears well in her eyes as she spoke. 'I've had such a nice time, and it really means a lot to me to be in a proper family. Bye-bye, Sylvia – see you at work, I expect.'

'What a nice girl,' Pauline said, once the door was closed. 'And what a sad thing, her mother dying so young like that.'

'Come on.' Ian took Sylvia's arm. 'Let's go in the other room for a bit.' Sylvia knew he wanted her to himself for a while.

'Your father'll be home soon,' Pauline said. 'I must get cracking.'

'So did you like Kitty?' Sylvia asked Ian, scattering a few pieces of coal onto the fire in the front room.

'Yes, she was all right,' Ian said.

Sylvia turned to him. 'Just all right?' She felt childish asking, but it was important that he liked her friend. She felt entranced by Kitty, as if something new and important had happened, and she wanted Ian to feel it too.

'Well,' he shrugged, 'yes. You know – nice. What else d'you want me to say?'

Turning her back to Ian, Sylvia held a sheet of paper across the hearth to draw the fire, feeling suddenly enraged. Why was Ian so dismissive about things that were important to her? In the beginning she had told herself that it was because Ian was a man and he was much cleverer than she was. Why would he be interested in the little things she told him? She wanted to snap at him now, and tell him how fed-up with him she was. First over her job, and now this! But she knew she would feel even more foolish if she did, and he would tell her that she was being silly and would get the hump. In the end all she said was, 'I don't want you to say anything. Just don't say anything you don't mean, that's all.'

Fourteen

Kitty lay in bed that night in her blacked-out bedroom, wearing socks and a jumper over her nightclothes, trying to get warm. She knew her father was about downstairs, roaming the house, and it made her nervous. She had moved her heavy armchair across the door. Turning onto her side, she curled up tight, but sleep would not come.

She lay thinking about her visit to Sylvia Whitehouse's home. What a lovely, happy household! It filled her with longing. She had never known anything like that herself. Sylvia's mother was such a kindly, comforting sort, such a contrast to her own thin, frightened mother. For a moment the image of her mother's pain-racked face came to her and she forced it from her mind. Sylvia was so lucky, she thought bitterly.

On top of that, there was that fiancé of hers. He was obviously quite a bit older than Sylvia. He had a rather fusty look, Kitty thought, as if he ought to have been a vicar or one of those university men. But he seemed all right, and certainly had a good job. He obviously adored Sylvia – she was so natural and sweet-looking, with those lovely rosy cheeks and her striking dark hair. It was almost enraging how someone could be like that: so happy with herself and so innocent. It was enough to make you spit. Kitty felt very hard and old in comparison. When would Sylvia ever have thoughts like the ones she had about Joe Whelan? Kitty had had boys interested in her before, of course, but no one who had ever stuck around. The boys she met all seemed rather wet and timid compared with a big, grown-up man like Joe. Joe, over whom she had cast her spell . . .

She turned on her back and ran her hands over her body. Her breasts were such a good, ripe shape, it seemed only right that someone should see them and pay homage. She pictured Joe's face if they could only be alone together in the right place! He was already half-mad with desire for her, she knew, and she revelled in the sensation of seeing the blazing hunger in his eyes.

She had first met him the morning after a heavy air raid. On the train everyone looked exhausted, but they were more forthcoming than usual, all spilling out stories of the night before. Joe checked her ticket and exchanged a few words. He asked how things had been up her way. After that she'd seen him quite often. Kitty could not remember exactly when they had moved into the stage they were at now. He had begun to pause near her and chat. His eyes would linger on her longer than was quite usual; she would gaze back at him, wide-eyed.

One day, only a few weeks ago, she asked if she might see inside the guard's van. Already by then she could see the attraction written blatantly on his face. She asked before she had even boarded the train, making sure no one else heard. It was raining that day and everyone was hurrying to get on.

'Sure, it's a filthy day,' he said, trying to sound as if she had asked something reasonable. 'You'd better step up inside, quick.'

The van was dark inside. Joe had the little stove for brewing up at one end, so it was very warm and snug and there was a whiff of fried bacon. All sorts of bits of luggage were piled in there. Kitty even saw a parrot in a cage in one corner. The parrot was silent and looked pretty fed-up. Joe slammed the door shut and they stood looking at each other a moment.

'Well,' he said, as if wondering why he had allowed this, for he was now embarrassed.

'Your name's Joe?' she said, coming up seductively close to him, thinking what a fine, strong man he was, like a rock or a cliff. 'I'm Kitty. I've been waiting to be alone with you, Joe. I've been thinking about it.'

'Have you now?' he said helplessly.

'You know I have. And you have too, haven't you?' She laid her palms on his chest. 'Hello, Joe.'

Joe Whelan seemed paralysed. There was a terrible struggle going on inside him.

'Won't you put your arms round me, Joe?' she asked sweetly.

Awkwardly he did as she asked and she raised her face to him. Their eyes met in the gloomy van, and seconds later he pressed his lips hard to hers, clumsy with desire.

Now, whenever she saw him, it was the same. It had reached such a pitch that she knew that soon something had to change. She wasn't sure whether she desired Joe Whelan, or just needed to conquer him. Either way, she kept trying to think of ways they could be alone. She imagined unbuttoning her clothes, his face as he took in the sight of her . . .

Kitty jumped, her dreams interrupted by the sound of heavy footsteps outside her door. Her heart started pounding so hard that she could hardly breathe. The footsteps stopped. She was sure she could hear her father's heavy, inebriated breathing. The handle turned and he pushed the door, which gave an inch before it crashed up against the back of the heavy chair. There were several bangs, as if he could not take in that there was something blocking his way. Kitty could see light through the crack in the door, as if he was carrying a torch.

'Mary?' his voice said. 'What's going on? I can't get the door open.'

Kitty lay silent. He was very drunk. Whatever she said, he would not be able to take it in.

'Mary! Open this door, at once! I want yer. Let me in, wife. I need to have you.'

This had started in the past few months, since her mother died. Previously, he had drunk, but not like this. Somehow he was all right at the works, went in every day, the great Josiah Barratt, in his car with his bowler hat, a wide, lumbering figure in charge of his domain, doing very nicely out of the war, thank you. But once at home, he was like a different person. He had started drinking more and more heavily, showing his dependence on the woman for whom he had shown so little regard when she was alive, but whom he was now missing and was desperate for.

The first time he had come into Kitty's room she was already asleep. She heard nothing until she became aware of a light in the room and the fact that someone was trying to climb into bed with her. After a moment's fearful paralysis she leapt up with a shriek.

'Dad! What the hell are you doing?' She backed up against the wall. 'Dad, stop it. Wake up!'

He stank like a distillery and was almost past sense.

'Mary . . .' He reached out for her and pulled her roughly to him, fastening his stubble-edged lips to hers. The taste and sensation were horrible. Kitty pushed him away with all her strength and managed to scramble past him off the bed. She ran to the door and switched on the light.

'Dad! I'm not Mom!' Tears ran down her face. She would never forget the revulsion and sadness she felt at the sight of this pathetic man crouching on her sheets, staring at her with bleary, confused eyes. 'Get out of my bed,' she pleaded. 'I'll take you back to your bedroom.' She went over and pulled on his arm.

'Mary? I want Mary. You're not Mary!' He pushed her away.

'I'm Kitty, your daughter,' she sobbed. 'Mary's not here. She died. She's gone . . .'

Slowly it sank in and she persuaded him to get off the bed. It was as if he was waking out of a dream. He stood up, slow as an ox.

'I need to go. I'm going to wet myself.' And then he started crying. His shoulders started to shake and big, blubbering sobs came out of him.

'Come on, Dad – we'll go to the bathroom,' Kitty said, horrified by the idea that he might lose control of himself over her bedroom carpet. She led him along the landing, as if he were a big, frightened child, as both of them wept. She pointed him at the toilet bowl and waited to lead him to his bed. Once she was back in her own, she lay shaking and weeping with grief and revulsion.

Now he was out there again.

'Go to bed, Dad!' she shouted to him. 'I'm not Mom. I'm not letting you in.'

There were indistinct sounds of cursing and a few more bangs of the door against the chair and then she heard him shuffling off along the landing. She did not know if he went into his own room. She no longer cared, so long as he was not in hers.

Fifteen

Hockley Goods Yard now had to cope with the fact that there were more women working there than ever before. Even Froggy had begun to wear out his sarcasm and accept that the women were pulling their weight. By now some of the mess rooms and toilets had been allocated to women porters and other staff, and Sylvia sometimes ran into Kitty in the Ladies. Otherwise they occasionally snatched a cup of tea together during a break, but the place was so busy and the work so pressurized that it was hard. 'Us girls have to stick together,' Kitty said sometimes. Sylvia would laugh, but this felt an exciting and strong thing, as if they were pioneers in a world run by men.

'You'll just have to come round more on the weekend for a proper chat,' Sylvia told her the next week as they snatched a quick conversation. 'Although it seems such a bother for you.'

'No, it's not a bother – I'd love to,' Kitty said. 'I really enjoyed it last week. If your family don't mind . . . I could make a cake. We never really eat that sort of thing at home, so I could scrape enough together for one, I'm sure.'

'Well, we're never short of eggs, that's one good thing. But I'm sure whatever else you can lay hands on would be very welcome. Jack's like a goat – he'll eat anything!'

Sylvia always felt a pulse of excitement when she saw

Kitty's face across the yard or her waving to her along the passage inside. It was so good to feel she was making friends.

That week Sylvia was on the late shift, from two in the afternoon until ten at night. It meant doing quite a bit of work after dark, in the blacked-out yard. Shunting was especially hazardous at night, with the yard prevented from showing all but the minimum of light. Even the tender-engines had tarpaulins stretched across them, to hide the light from their fires, meaning that the trains were even more invisible. The lights in the Main Shed were shaded, the roof lights and windows all painted over or blacked out with roller blinds. But the work had to go on, day and night, to feed the war machine. Work went on even during air raids, and she lived in dread of there being one when she was on shift.

It was still bitterly cold. One evening Sylvia was pushing a barrow along the second deck of the shed in the dim light, heading for the wooden 'bridge' where she could cross over about halfway along the tracks, between two of the wagons. She passed a number of wagons covered by tarpaulins, which would hold food or all sorts of other merchandise. Behind them were open wagons of coal. Earlier the foreman she was on with that night – not Froggy, for a change, but a tall, thin, lugubrious man called Percy Price – had beckoned her solemnly towards him at the end of this second platform, or deck.

'I don't s'pose you've ever given a thought to how they heat the offices and why you can wash your dainty little hands with hot water, have you?' Percy asked, peering at her through his wire specs in the manner of one who has superior, if not sacred, knowledge. He was a new foreman to her – she hadn't worked with him before.

Sylvia pretended to consider. 'Er, no, I haven't,' she said sweetly. 'But I can see you're going to tell me.'

Percy stared at her for a moment, as if trying to identify the slightest trace of sarcasm in her voice, but failing to do so for sure.

'See them wagons of coal there, on the stop-blocks?'

'Yes?' She rested her empty barrow upright on its end. She really wanted to go across to the Amenities block to relieve herself, but she could see she was not going to get away easily.

'Well, hot water has to be heated by a boiler. And the boiler,' he pointed downwards, 'is under 'ere. Under this shed.'

'Ah,' Sylvia said. 'I see. Well, thanks, Mr Price.' She took hold of the barrow again and was just about to move off when Percy Price's eyes swivelled towards an untidy pile of boxes and crates on the other side of the deck.

'What're them lot doing there?' he said, his voice rising in annoyance.

'I don't know,' Sylvia said truthfully. 'It must've been the last shift . . .' Sometimes piles of stuff got left, if there was no loader available or the goods had been left next to the wrong wagons. Clearing them up was one of the yard's unpopular jobs, like cleaning out all the rubbish that got thrown down onto the tracks.

'Get it moved!' he commanded shrilly. 'Christ Almighty, you can't turn your back for one second around 'ere.' And he strode off along the platform on his pin-thin legs.

'All right, all right,' Sylvia muttered. Everyone was on

such a short fuse these days. The sheer pressure of work, on top of the nerves and food shortages of the war, made everyone tense and prone to fly off the handle.

She loaded her barrow with two of the abandoned boxes and wheeled them along to the carters' deck. She was about to go back for more, but her bladder was insistent.

'Blow it – I'll have to go!'

She hurried across and did her business. As she came out again, she could just see someone leaning against the wall a bit further along, and the glowing tip of a cigarette. Sylvia narrowed her eyes. Wasn't that Kitty? Moving a bit closer, she was sure it *was* Kitty and was just about to go and have a quick chat, when a large figure emerged out of the shadows and reached the woman first. The voice that spoke out of the gloom was definitely Kitty's.

'God, Joe, you made me jump!' Kitty stood up straighter, startled. 'What on earth are you doing here?'

Sylvia shrank back, curious to see what was going on.

The man leaned one hand against the wall, facing Kitty, as if wanting to trap her. He was a big, solid man and, even in the poor light, Sylvia could see there was something taut and intense about him. Was he threatening Kitty?

'What d'you think I'm doing here?' he said.

An engine came along the tracks then, whoomp-whoomping loudly behind them, and its whistle squealed. Sylvia couldn't hear a thing and, though curious, didn't feel she could hang about eavesdropping any longer. She wondered if Kitty was in any danger. The man looked so big and forceful. But Kitty hadn't mentioned any trouble, and Sylvia told herself it was really none of her business. She slipped back across to the shed to collect her barrow. But she kept wondering about it all evening.

Kitty did not notice Joe Whelan in the yard until he was almost beside her. The sudden sight of him set her blood thundering with panic. Joe was a big man and he seemed angry. It was alarming, him turning up suddenly like that, and the way he came right up close, staring into her eyes. But she tried to play it cool.

'I've got to see you,' he said, under cover of a train pounding along in the railyard.

'You've taken a chance coming here, haven't you?' Kitty said. She felt very vulnerable with him standing over her like that. She could feel the intensity of the man, the way he was holding himself, as if he was sufficiently pent up to explode.

'I knew I'd find you,' he said. There was whiskey on his breath, but he was in control of himself, just.

'How?' she giggled, uncomfortable with the way things were going. She had been caught on the back foot by him turning up suddenly. But she was excited by it too. He had come all the way here, for her!

'Look, Kitty.' He spoke fast, just above a whisper. 'I'm a married man. I've six children at home and a wife. I've been a good husband to Ann, a good Catholic husband.' He stepped back from the wall for a moment and wiped his hand across his forehead confusedly. Then he advanced on her again. 'I don't know what's happened to me. I've never . . . You see a pretty girl now and again – it gives a man thoughts. But you can overcome it, you *have* to.' He bunched his hand into a fist. 'But you—'

'Joe . . .' She tried to interrupt, though to say what, she wasn't sure.

'You come along and I'm – sure, I'm *mad* suddenly. Like a madman. I can't sleep, can't think of anything but you. I see your face every mortal place I look.' He moved up close again. 'Either meet me and satisfy me, or damn me: send me away without a hope. For God's sake stop taunting me, and say you'll do one or the other.'

She looked up at him, big-eyed. 'Joe,' she whispered. 'I'm eighteen. I'm a virgin.'

'Dear God,' he muttered, closing his eyes. 'I've one at home older than you.' Bitterly he added. 'You don't behave like an innocent.'

She reached for his arm and clung to it. 'I just wanted you to know, that's all. But how could we meet? Where?'

He looked up again. He seemed frantic. 'Would you? You'd meet me?'

Slowly she nodded. God help me, she thought.

'I know a place. Are you off at ten? Come to Tyseley.'

'*Tonight?*'

'Yes, tonight. Please, Kitty. Get on the train when you're finished here and wait for me on the platform at Tyseley. I'll be there.'

Once he had seen her nod, he left abruptly, disappearing along the yard into the darkness and the gathering night fog.

Sixteen

Back in the dimly lit office, Kitty calculated rapidly. It was a good night to be out. By the time she got in after a late shift, the old man was usually asleep or too far gone to notice whether she was home or not. She could always plead busyness at the yard, if by any chance he was still conscious when she got in. The war always gave that excuse. After that, for the remainder of the shift, she blocked out thoughts of what was going to happen. She sat over her comptometer, trying to warm her icy feet by rubbing them against her legs, and concentrated hard. She had always found that it was best to push from your mind things that are difficult to think about.

Only once the shift ended, and she was sitting in the dim blue light of the passenger train, did she face what she was doing. Her heart pounded faster. With trembling hands she lit a cigarette to try and calm herself. She avoided the eyes of other passengers close to her, some of whom she knew worked in the invoice offices at the yard.

Her mind drummed at her: *What are you doing? How could you have got yourself into this?* But she was helpless, compelled by something stronger than her own will.

When she got off at Tyseley passenger station it was very dark. Adjacent to the station was the railyard and the main GWR engine shed, where the engines were cleaned and maintained. A train was shunting slowly along the yard.

The other passengers who got off walked rapidly away, leaving her standing in the dark as the train's sound died away, towards Acocks Green. The air was thick with smoke and fog. She felt foolish, then scared. Sweat prickled under her arms and her hands were clammy, even in the cold night.

'Kitty?' It was a hoarse whisper to her right.

'I'm . . .' She had to clear her throat. 'Joe? I'm over here.'

'Come towards me,' his voice came to her. 'Here, walk close by the fence. Don't make a noise – there're people not far off.' The sheds at Tyseley worked all night, like everyone else now.

Kitty felt her way along with cautious steps, as Joe kept whispering to her. Suddenly she walked into his arm, which was held out in front of her, and she started.

'It's okay.' He pulled her to him, embracing her with the low fence still between them. 'It's okay, little girl. Oh, you came, sweetheart. You came to me.' His lips pressed against her cheeks. She felt the strength of him, the scratch of his stubble. 'Oh God, I was afraid you wouldn't . . . Come on down.' He leaned round and she found herself lifted in his bear-like arms, over the fence. When he set her down, the ground felt crunchy and uneven, as if she was walking on a pile of coal.

'Steady. Quiet now. I know where we can go.'

Joe led her by the hand, with Kitty following blindly in the dark, foggy yard. She had to put herself entirely in his hands. The air was dank and bitter with smoke and she could hear faint bangs and clangs from the sheds at the far end.

She realized they were walking alongside the tracks.

Kitty stumbled, though Joe seemed more able to see. Their footsteps on the cindery ground sounded terribly loud. She began to make out that there were dark, silent carriages beside them and, after a moment, Joe pressed her arm to stop her.

'We can go in here.' She heard him unfasten a carriage door. 'Up you go.' He half-lifted her onto the step, then followed her up and shut the door behind them. It was black as pitch and smelled musty.

'No one'll be bothering with this one till daylight,' he said. She heard rather than saw him go round the van, making sure the blinds were fastened down and, when he was satisfied, he switched on a torch, which made shadows heave up the walls. Kitty realized that they were in another guard's van, though there was nothing inside except an empty wooden crate and a pile of sacks in the corner. Joe put the torch down on the stove at the end, pointing it away towards the side wall.

'Joe,' Kitty found she was trembling. This was not how she had imagined things. She had dreamed of being in control, not of feeling tense and scared and in this cold place. 'Are you sure no one will come?'

'Well, if they do, they'll be up to the same thing,' he said, with a low chuckle.

'Could we light the stove? It's so cold.'

Joe considered. 'Better not. Someone might notice that.' But she could see he couldn't be bothered, did not want any delay. He came towards her. 'Oh now – you're here. I can't believe it, really I can't.'

Taking her in his arms, he immediately began to kiss her, immersing himself in his own desire. She let him for a moment, before pulling back. This was not her plan, to feel small and passive. She wanted to command him.

'Joe?' She looked into his eyes, asserting herself.

Trying to forget the cold, she began to unbutton her cardigan, then her blouse. He watched, entranced. She was wearing a pretty camisole and, as she pulled away the sides of her blouse, Joe sighed with pleasure.

'Oh, you little darling,' he said in a sentimental voice. 'I want to see you. I've dreamed of seeing you. It's all I can think about.'

'What about your wife?' Kitty said in an arch voice. 'Don't you see her?'

Joe looked down for a moment. 'We're not free with each other,' he said, with an air of shame. 'I've never seen her naked. She'll only undress in the dark. She's not like you, Kitty – it's the way we were brought up. And child-bearing – it takes it out of a woman. Ann's brought nine into the world and buried three. It's not been an easy life. But I've never played away. Not till now – till you. You've done something to me, Kitty. I can't even under-stand it. I can't seem to think straight about anything; all I can see is you.'

The sorrowful way he spoke brought out a tenderness in her. 'Joe, you know I'm not experienced. I wouldn't want you to think I'm—'

'Ah no, I don't mean you any harm, girl. Just let me see you, for God's sake. I'm that hungry for you.'

He began to caress her breasts through her clothes, but she drew back a little, pulling her camisole over her head and reaching round to unfasten her brassiere, peeling it away slowly. Despite her slim frame, her breasts were generous and heavy.

'Oh,' Joe said humbly. 'You're a taste of heaven, that's what you are.'

Kitty drew her shoulders back and he came to her, very excited, to lift and caress her, sucking and kissing, giving little grunts of pleasure. He pulled her close, pressing himself to her, his hands sliding down under her clothes to her buttocks.

'Take the rest of your clothes off,' he said. 'Just do it – for me.'

As she unfastened her skirt and took off her panties and stockings, so that she was standing barefoot on the gritty floor of the van, she could see Joe fumbling with his own clothes. Once she stood naked in front of him, he reached out for her, his eyes rolling in his head as he pressed himself against her body, thrusting with excitement.

'I'll not give you a child,' he said, with an effort. 'Just let me, woman . . . Let me come close to you.'

Kitty held him as he thrashed and pushed against her. She sensed that he was struggling.

'Get down,' he panted eventually. He led her to the pile of sacks, spreading them for her to lie on. They were coarse and smelled of dust. But she lay on the hard floor so that he could press himself against her belly, so close to coming that, after a few quick movements, it was over.

'Oh!' he cried, close to her ear. 'Oh God. God in heaven.' His voice held both ecstasy and despair. Then he was silent for a long time, so much so that she wondered if he had fallen asleep. She could feel her feet growing so cold that they were painful, and she shifted underneath him.

Joe moved and got up. He produced a rag from his pocket and wiped Kitty's stomach and then himself. They dressed again without speaking. She was shivering, her teeth chattering.

'I'll see you away,' he said. But he held her again, against his warm chest and belly, rocking her gently. 'God, girl,' he kept saying. 'God!' Kitty closed her eyes,

129

snuggling close to him, comforted by the big warmth of the man.

Eventually Joe said, 'How will you be getting home?'

She had scarcely thought. 'I don't know. I live in Handsworth Wood. I don't even know when the buses stop running.'

Joe sighed, obviously thinking. 'Best thing is if we stay here. We'll have to do the best we can with these sacks. You can have my coat. And we'll have to skedaddle early tomorrow, heaven help us.'

'What about your wife?'

'I'll tell her there was a job on,' Joe said, rather testily now. It was as if the reality of his wife and family was pressing back on him. He was laying out sacks on the floor. 'Come on, lie down next to me. I'll fold us one for a pillow – there's sacks and coats. I'll keep you warm, girl.'

Kitty looked round the bare, dusty van. What choice was there? And she was not afraid of him, at least. She lay down, shivering. Joe switched the torch off and lay behind her, covering them with his coat and some sacks. He put his arm protectively around her and some of his warmth seeped into her. In the musty darkness, Kitty thought about the other carriages stretching into the night. She prayed that her father had fallen asleep and had not missed her. But there was nothing she could do about it now.

'Goodnight, Kitty,' Joe said. After a second he added. 'Holy Mother – what a girl!'

And Kitty felt a moment of panic. What had she done? What did he want from her? She knew nothing, could decide nothing. Exhaustion overcame her. She fell asleep and slept surprisingly well.

Seventeen

Kitty began to come to Sylvia's for tea quite regularly. Sometimes their time off from the yard coincided on weekdays and Sylvia would ask Kitty over, knowing Ian would be at work and she was not missing time with him. Sometimes it was at weekends, when Ian was off and they were all together. Kitty seemed to crave company and said she didn't mind the inconvenience of the journey at all.

'It's just so lovely to come and be with a family,' she said. She seemed entranced with them all. And she never came without a gift: flowers from the garden or a cake she had baked.

'There's only the two of us at home,' she said one day, when she brought with her a fruit loaf with a thin scattering of raisins in it. 'And my father's not interested in this sort of thing.'

Sylvia was gratified to see that everyone had taken to Kitty. She had Jack's immediate attention whenever there was food about.

'Well, hell-o,' Jack enthused, peering greedily at the cake. He turned to Kitty, pretending he was smoking a pipe. He covered his shyness by joking about. 'I say, young woman, you can come round again. How about a chocolate one next time?'

'Jack!' His mother cuffed his head with a tea towel. 'Kitty may be a good cook, but she's not a magician.'

Kitty looked very pleased. 'I'll see what I can do,' she said to Jack, who looked adoringly at her. He did adore Kitty, but the cake was definitely a bonus. 'I might be able to dredge up a bit of cocoa from somewhere.'

They had some happy afternoons, whoever was in, round the fire, chatting and playing games. Sylvia's mother often looked after Paul Gould several times a week, to give Marjorie a break, and they played games with him and with Jack when he got home from school. Kitty was a lively presence. She was good with Paul and laughed her light, infectious laugh, which lifted everyone's spirits. The sound of her laughing would set Paul off on his own chortling. Sylvia saw that the whole family had taken a shine to her, even Dad.

'Nice girl, isn't she?' Mom said, after Kitty had left, the first day Ted met her.

'Seems all right,' Ted Whitehouse said, head down, hungrily eating his stew.

'Just all right?' Sylvia asked, though she knew this was high praise from Dad.

'She's heavenly,' Jack said dreamily, though as ever there was an edge of self-mockery.

'Oi, you,' his mother said. 'You're much too young to be having thoughts about a young lady like Kitty.'

'Oh, I shouldn't bet on it,' Ted said lugubriously through a mouthful of stringy beef.

'Ted!' His wife erupted. 'What a thing to say! He's only just thirteen.'

'Thirteen and a smouldering heap of masculinity.'

'Dad!' Jack was covered in blushes.

Sylvia laughed. 'Dad, you're embarrassing him.'

'Sylv, you're laughing like Kitty,' Jack said.

'Am I?' Sylvia said. She hadn't realized it, but she had been trying to sound like Kitty.

Ted was chewing thoughtfully. 'Pauline, what *exactly* is the matter with this stew?'

'It's got no onions in it, that's what,' his wife said. 'I couldn't find any, for love, money or anything else I might've tried.'

'Have we got none of our own left?'

'We finished them weeks ago. You know we did.'

'But you liked Kitty?' Sylvia kept on. She liked to hear nice things about her friend.

'Kitty,' Ted pronounced, 'is a fine specimen of English – I might even say British – womanhood.'

'Well,' his wife said, 'I s'pose you can't say fairer than that. There's a bit more spud, Ted, if you want some.'

One precious afternoon off, Sylvia and Kitty went out for a walk in Kings Heath Park. It was a bright spring day, but cold, so they wrapped up warm.

'I'm so tired,' Sylvia said. 'I need some fresh air to get me going.'

'I know,' Kitty agreed. 'If I stop for a minute, I fall asleep this week!'

Two nights ago there'd been another bad air raid and Sylvia and the family had been out in the shelter all night. It had been freezing cold, she'd had very little sleep and had to be at the yard by six the next morning.

They set off bundled up in coats, scarves and hats. Sylvia was very glad of her warm boots. The bright after-noon sun lit up the windows on one side of the street as they walked down to the park, and she felt suddenly uplifted and happy, despite her tiredness.

'It makes you appreciate every day, doesn't it?' she said to Kitty. 'All the awful things that have happened. Sometimes I lie awake and think about things. But the war's so terrible, my mind just sort of skips over it. I can't bear to think about it.'

Kitty shivered. 'It's true – it just drags you down.'

'Yes, come on, let's be cheerful,' Sylvia said as they reached the park gates. 'I don't s'pose that's what Hitler wants, so the more we do it, the better!'

Kitty laughed and suddenly slipped her arm through Sylvia's. Sylvia turned to Kitty, their eyes meeting happily. Kitty was so petite, and seemed so alone in the world, that she brought out a protective feeling in Sylvia. They set off into the green space, blowing clouds of white breath into the air. Although it was cold, Sylvia had a contented feeling of being close and cosy.

'It's been so much better at work since I got to know you,' she said. 'The first week I was at the yard I nearly gave up. What with flaming Froggy keeping on at me, jumping on anything I did wrong, and all those blokes who just think a woman can't do anything apart from cook and make up her face . . .'

Kitty giggled. 'You sound like one of those women – you know, suffragettes.'

'Not really,' Sylvia said. 'You should meet Audrey if you think I'm like that!'

'She sounds quite frightening,' Kitty said. 'She's a looker though, I bet.'

Kitty had been very taken with Pauline's family photographs in the front parlour. She had gazed for an especially long time at the one of Sylvia and Audrey together as little girls, shoulder-to-shoulder. 'How lovely!' she exclaimed. At the time Sylvia said, 'Well, it's lovely sometimes. But she's ever so bossy.' She had to admit that she missed Audrey though, now that she was away. She even missed arguing with her.

Now she said, 'Well, she can be a bit frightening. But

I'm beginning to see her point. Honestly, some of the men are so ridiculous. They seem to think girls are just made of cotton wool or something. How do they think babies get born? I'd like to see them do it!'

'Are you going to have lots of babies?' Kitty asked. 'With Ian?'

Sylvia was proud to talk about Ian. Bit by bit she and Mom were getting things ready for the wedding. Marjorie Gould had offered to make her dress, and it was soon going to be ready for a first fitting. Sylvia could sense Kitty's wistfulness.

'Babies? Oh, I expect so! It's funny – I haven't given it much thought. I suppose you just think that when you get married that's what you'll do. Maybe I'll have three, like Mom. But it seems such a way off at the moment that I can't take it in.'

'But July's not that far off!'

'It still feels years away to me – and we don't seem to have much time to think about it!' She glanced round at Kitty. 'What about you? Lots of babies, faces at the window?'

'Oh, yes!' Kitty said, her eyes lighting up. 'I don't want just one child, growing up like I did.' Her face fell and Sylvia was touched by her sorrowful expression. 'My own mother's life was so sad. She never had any real existence of her own. It was as if she was owned by other people all along, telling her what to do and who to be.'

'It sounds awful,' Sylvia said. Kitty had told the family that her mother had been one of the Exclusive Brethren, a branch of the Plymouth Brethren. Sylvia's dad grimaced when he learned this. 'Blimey. What a shower! I'm surprised she's as normal as she is. Mad as hatters, the lot of 'em.'

'They were so narrow and rigid,' Kitty said as they

stood staring at the murky pond in the park. A couple of mallards were floating about, without much apparent purpose. 'They wanted to keep very separate from the world and, when she left to marry my father, they wouldn't have anything to do with her.'

'At least she had you,' Sylvia said. 'That must have been nice for her.'

'But she was scared of my father. She was never allowed to step out of the house without his say-so.' Sylvia could hear the biting contempt in Kitty's voice. 'He's a cruel, arrogant man. He thinks everything is something you can buy for money. He'd say, "I bought you that new coat, or that carpet for the bedroom" or something like that. He thought that was what being a husband was. Just things. When she was ill, he hardly ever went in to see her. It was as if she was an old car that had broken down, and now she was no use to him. We had a nurse come in every day, but otherwise I looked after her. And all she did was worry about him. Was he getting his dinner? Had the maid starched his collars? She never thought about herself. And he's never thought about anything *except* himself. Look at your father, Sylvia. He's such a nice man. Can you imagine if your mother was ill? He'd care for her and go into her room and see her, wouldn't he?'

Kitty looked up at Sylvia, her big eyes full of tears.

'Yes,' Sylvia said. 'Our dad doesn't have a clue in some ways, but he'd look after Mom – course he would.'

'My father's a *monster*,' Kitty said, with such venom that Sylvia was startled and she broke down suddenly and began to cry. Sylvia put her arm round Kitty's jerking shoulders, moved by what she had heard.

'Oh dear, that does sound terrible,' she said. 'And you must miss your mom so much.'

'I do miss her,' Kitty said. 'But I don't want to be like her, or have a life like hers. She never *had* a life, that's the truth. Sometimes,' she looked up at Sylvia, eyes still brimming with tears, 'I wonder if there really are any nice men. I'm scared I'll never meet anyone or have a nice husband, and I'll just end up as a sad old lady on my own.'

'Oh, Kitty!' Sylvia laughed, while still embracing her. 'Don't be daft. You're only eighteen. There's plenty of time yet. Come on, let's walk on – it's getting cold.'

Kitty dried her face and tried to look more cheerful. Her nose had gone pink from crying. 'Thanks,' she said humbly. 'Sorry. I don't often let go like that. But the man I told you I was seeing has decided he wants to pack me in, so I'm feeling a bit down. And everyone at your place has been so kind. I've never met a family as nice as yours before.'

'They all really like you,' Sylvia told her. 'So look on it as a home from home.'

Later, snuggled up with Ian by the range again, when he came round in the evening, Sylvia told him about what Kitty had said.

'Poor thing,' he said. 'You wouldn't think her old man was such a sod, would you, sweet girl like that?'

'No – he sounds horrible.'

'There is something a bit little-girl-lost about her.'

'D'you think so? She always seems so lively.'

'Yes, but . . .' Ian shifted next to her. 'Ow, watch where you're putting that elbow! There's something mournful about her. The way she's tacked onto you, for a start. It's nice that you're so kind to her.'

'You don't mind? Her coming round if you're here, I mean?'

'Of course not. Well,' he gave her a squeeze, 'so long as we get *some* time to ourselves.'

'Of course we will,' Sylvia said, appeased by his encouragement. 'But I do think she needs some help – and I like her. Since my other friends have deserted me, it's nice to have a girlfriend to chat to.'

'Well, there you are. And she seems a very good sort. Very pretty too,' he added reflectively.

'Oi, you – watch it!'

As she was teasing Ian, a burst of laughter came from the back room over the sounds on the wireless. Sylvia and Ian chuckled at the sound of it.

'*ITMA*,' she said. 'Dad loves it.' She reached round and looked up at Ian and he snatched a kiss. 'And I love you.'

Eighteen

Audrey pulled the finished letter from her typewriter, adding it to the pile waiting to be signed and stifled another yawn. Tapping her feet with impatience, she gazed out of the window at the bright spring day. Voices called to each other outside, footsteps went past. Here she was, once again stuck in a stuffy office.

Her WAAF officer had left the room for a few moments. Audrey was left with the other secretary, a stylish, if scatty young woman called Miranda, who had worked in a London publishing house before she joined up. Miranda was an ACW1 (Aircraft Woman, First Class), a rank above Audrey, who was a humble ACW2. She was frowning at her shorthand pad, trying to decipher her latest scribblings, which, Audrey thought quietly, were really quite a mess.

'D'you mind if I open the window?' Audrey asked, half out of her chair.

Miranda looked up vaguely. 'Oh yes, do.' She retreated back into her notebook, a hand clamped over her forehead. 'Heavens, I can hardly make head or tail of this. Serves me right for last night, of course. My head's *thumping*.'

Audrey's head was *thumping* as well. 'Never again,' she said.

Miranda looked up with a wan smile. 'Did you make a night of it as well?'

'You could say that,' Audrey said.

Audrey was nursing not just her hangover, but also some sad feelings. At the dance last night she had met a boy who reminded her of Raymond Gould.

The camp gym doubled as a dance and concert hall and there were frequent 'dos' and 'hops'. The dances were packed with hordes of new male recruits on their basic training at RAF Cardington, all suddenly far from home and on the hunt for girls. Standing amid the energetic, jigging crowd last night, as boys in uniform swarmed around her and the other WAAFs, Audrey realized what it was she felt: under pressure to fall in love. The other girls in her hut – Cora, who was born in Jamaica, Pat from the Lakes, Joey (Josephine) from Liverpool, and Maggie and Victoria from the Home Counties – all of them were forever on about the 'boys'. Most of them, except Maggie, who was very shy and seemed to prefer food to anything in trousers, talked endlessly about their assignations, whom they had met and who had said what to whom. Audrey played along, and it was not hard to make dates with boys in the camp – there was an endless supply of them.

'Not like in the training camp I was in,' Joey said when they were chatting one night. 'We girls had to dance with each other – not a lad in sight.' Her dark eyes glinted with amusement. 'It was just like being back in the convent again. It's a lot more fun here!'

'I bet it is,' Cora laughed. She was big and blonde and always somehow seemed to have a supply of spirits (most often rum) hidden among her belongings.

Audrey found, secretly, that while a lot of the other girls leapt onto the dance floor with almost animal

140

enthusiasm, she felt lost and self-conscious, even though she tried not to show it. She knew the others would have been surprised at this. She seemed confident and there was nothing wrong with her looks. She could put up her hair very stylishly, and everyone said she was gorgeous with her oval, brown-eyed face. There was never any shortage of offers to dance. Yet somehow, though she had quite a good time, she had a sneaking feeling that the real fun started afterwards, once they got back to the hut, where the festivities often continued.

Cora often brought out one of her bottles and they talked and laughed late into the night, squatting on each other's beds in their nightwear – of which, as Victoria said, there was a 'glorious variety'. It felt so cosy and there was so much laughter that this, Audrey felt, was really the heart of life. She and Cora sparked each other off with their sense of humour, and it was all such fun. But she went along with the pretence that life only really began when the men appeared. And she was puzzled at herself. Hadn't she joined up for a bit more excitement than cocoa with a load of girls?

Last night she had stood at one end of the dance floor with Joey and Maggie while the band played and the room heaved with couples swinging to 'T'Ain't What You Do (It's the Way That You Do It)'. The air was fuggy and tinged with the smells of beer and sweat. Joey was soon snatched away into the dance by a young man. Maggie, who had only just stepped out of a girls' boarding school, took off into the corner with an equally shy-looking young man and they leaned against the wall talking, both looking terrified and blushing to their ears.

Audrey stood alone for a moment, but before she had time to feel awkward, someone jostled into her and almost knocked her empty glass out of her hand.

'Oh, I'm sorry!' A freckly face turned anxiously to her, topped by a head of red curls. 'Can I get you something else to drink?'

He had a strong accent, which Audrey thought was Scots, and was also quite tall. As she was five foot seven, that was always a bonus.

'Thanks,' she said, 'if there's any punch left. Otherwise, anything that's going would be nice.'

He elbowed his way back through the crush and she moved in the same direction and met him coming back.

'I hope you don't mind lemonade,' he said apologetically.

'Are you teetotal?' she laughed.

'No, I'm not. It was just the nearest one. I can go back for something else later.'

'It's all right. I could do with it. I'm thirsty.'

'Would you fancy a dance?' he asked. 'I'm Hamish, by the way.'

'I'm Audrey,' she said.

Once they'd had a drink they left their glasses and headed onto the dance floor. It was getting towards the rowdier time of the evening, when everyone would soon dance the Conga and end up snaking around the outside of the building. For the moment, though, the band was playing 'These Foolish Things', which, Audrey thought to herself, was a song that could even make *her* feel slushy and sentimental. She stepped into Hamish's arms and smiled up into his face. He returned the smile, but there was a seriousness about him that, she realized as the night passed, was what reminded her of Raymond. He didn't look at all like Raymond, but underlying his friendliness and his attempts at jokes was that similar sober steadiness.

'Have you been here long?' he asked, having to put his

lips quite close to her ear to be heard among the shuffle and chatter of the other couples.

'Since mid-February,' she said.

'Well, that makes you an old hand,' he said. 'I've been here two days!'

And you'll soon be gone again too, she thought with relief. The lads stayed for six weeks.

He told her he came from Aberdeen. 'And what about you?' he asked.

'Birmingham – can't you tell!' she said.

Hamish smiled. 'I'm not very well up on English accents; better at telling Edinburgh from Glasgow, that sort of thing.'

'Yes, I suppose you would be. Are you hoping to be a pilot?'

'If I make it. I'd like to be. Otherwise I'll have to settle for something else,' Hamish said. 'What do you do?'

Audrey grimaced. 'Secretarial. Very boring.'

His raised his eyebrows. '*Is* it boring?'

'Yes,' she said with feeling. 'It's about as interesting as staring at a blank wall all day. I'd rather be doing almost anything else.'

'Perhaps you could transfer?' he suggested. 'Is that allowed?'

'I don't know,' Audrey said, wondering. 'I've never really thought about it.'

'Balloons?'

She shook her head. 'Men only.'

RAF Cardington specialized in making and testing barrage balloons. Except in very bad weather there were usually a number of them floating like waterlogged fish above the camp.

'It's an interesting place this, isn't it?' Hamish said. His arm was resting comfortably across her waist at the back and she enjoyed the sensation. It made her feel feminine, which she didn't, very often. She felt too energetic and abrasive to be really womanly. 'I never knew a thing about it before we came here. I only put two and two together when I saw it was Shortstown – of course, the Short brothers! I remember reading about it. This is where the R101 airship was made, wasn't it? Those great big hangars, where they're making the balloons now. It's clever the way they've camouflaged them.'

The two of them chatted easily. Hamish told her he had three sisters, but was the only son. His father was a Church of Scotland minister. Audrey realized that he was well used to talking to people and she found him good-mannered, pleasant company. He asked about her family.

'So do you like the life?' he asked, as the dance finished and they stood clapping, waiting for another number to begin. 'I mean, apart from the job!'

'I do,' she said, realizing as she said it that she *loved* it and was having the time of her life. 'I like feeling more grown-up – getting away from home – don't you?'

Hamish grimaced. 'Oh yes! I'm the youngest, so you can imagine: I've got mother hens all about me. If I hadn't got away I don't think I'd ever have learned to fend for myself. Your sister hasn't joined up?'

'No, she's a real home bird, Sylvia is. Mind you, she surprised us all and has gone off to work for the railways. She goes about in overalls all the time – I'd never've expected it, but it seems to suit her.'

'Good for her!' Hamish said.

'In the Mood' was beginning. Every band seemed to play it sometime in the evening when there was a dance. Hamish held out his arms and looked at Audrey enquiringly. She nodded and they danced, laughing and pitching back and forth to the catchy tune.

She realized she liked Hamish. She wasn't sure how old he was – perhaps not even as old as her, like Raymond – but he had a grown-up, solid way about him. As they danced she tried to examine her feelings. Of course she hardly knew him, but she wanted to find herself attracted and sentimentally bound up with someone – even bowled over by love. It was what everyone else seemed to want.

It doesn't happen all in one night, she thought. And then she remembered Joey, from her hut, who had met a chap she liked within the first week. It had been hard to get any sense out of her ever since. Audrey wondered about herself, and whether anyone's heart really could be made of stone.

Could I fall in love with Hamish? she asked herself as he held her, strongly but gently. In fact he was everything good that a young man could be. He was handsome, polite, pleasant to talk to, and the way he held her felt right.

Stick around, young man, she thought. Could he be the one? When the dance ended, would he try and kiss her? Did she want him to? She wasn't sure. It seemed very soon. After they had congaed until they were all in a lather, and had more lemonade and danced a few quiet numbers, she could see that Hamish was keen to stay with her and was not trying to take off and dance with anyone else. Audrey felt the same. It was so much easier to stay with one nice partner if you could find one, than try your luck with anyone who came along.

As they left the gym and headed out into the scented night, Hamish stopped her and looked seriously at her.

'Thank you, Audrey. I've had a very good evening, and I hope you have.'

'Yes,' she said truthfully. He was a nice boy. Could she feel more for him than she had for Raymond?

'I hope I'll see you again? Tomorrow maybe?'

She agreed, and there was an awkward pause as both of them wondered how to part. But Hamish backed away. 'See you then,' he said gently.

'TTFN,' Audrey said, keeping her voice casual.

Sitting in her office now, she thought about Hamish. He had not been 'pushy' and kissed her, and she was glad of this. The extension of the party in their hut into the small hours with Cora's nip of rum had rather wiped Hamish from her thoughts for the time being, even though the girls had ribbed her about it.

'Who was that good-looking carrot-top you were dancing with all evening, Audrey?' Joey demanded, her dark eyes full of mischief. 'You looked as if you were well in there!'

Audrey had pretended to be enigmatic. Hamish – she didn't even know his surname, she realized. He was a nice boy. Raymond had been a nice boy too, of course, but she had not managed any sentimental feelings towards him. Did she feel obliged to love Hamish because she had not been able to love Raymond? And because she knew what they all knew, but tried not to dwell on: that in a few months' time, when his training was over, Hamish too could very easily be killed?

She rested her aching head in her hands for a moment, but, hearing the CO come back into the room, fed another sheet into the typewriter and began typing furiously.

Nineteen

April 1941

Just before Easter, Sylvia went into work to find two new female porters chatting in the mess room. They were both in their early twenties: one was a gawky, buck-toothed woman called Elsie; the other, small, dark-haired and plump, was Gina.

'The two of them together look like Stan and Ollie,' Sylvia laughed to Kitty. 'They just need a couple of bowler hats!'

Both of them were pleasant, and Sylvia especially warmed to Elsie. And it was nice to have more girls around. One day, when Sylvia and Madge came into the mess room for a break, Sylvia heard the two of them talking.

'I heard it's one of the passenger guards,' Elsie was saying. 'But I don't know who the girl is.'

'Well, someone told me it's one of the comptom . . . whatever they're called, the operators – from upstairs,' Gina said.

Sylvia listened, with her back to them, pouring tea for herself and Madge. My, those two hadn't wasted any time getting involved with the gossip! Sylvia hadn't really taken any notice of the bits of chat she'd heard on this subject, but now, as they mentioned the comptometer office, she wondered if Kitty would know anything about it.

'Have you heard anything about this, Sylvia?' Elsie asked. Her sticking-out teeth gave her a permanent look of rabbity cheerfulness, which made Sylvia think of Mr Piggles. It was what had made her like Elsie from the start.

'No more than you,' she said, coming to sit down. 'But there's always some bit of tattle going around. I shouldn't take any notice.'

'Who're you on about?' Madge asked, sitting down, legs apart, with her mug in one beefy hand. The bench shuddered under her weight.

'Some girl, works here,' Elsie said. 'Evidently this bloke – and he's a lot older, and a married man – is *besotted* with her.'

Madge shrugged. 'So what?' Madge liked to give off an air of being an expert on anything to do with men, which, Sylvia realized, she possibly was. Although her 'Tone' seemed to be enough of a handful by himself.

'I wish someone was besotted with *me*,' Gina said with a comical expression. 'There's hardly any flaming blokes left under fifty. And with us dressed up like this . . .'

'Yes – and this girl they're on about works in the offices,' Elsie said with comical dismay. 'Skirts and stockings: no wonder he's keen.' Elsie looked down at her skinny, trouser-clad legs. 'He's not going to look at us in this get-up, is he?'

'It could be worse,' Sylvia said, taking out a piece of bread and jam that she'd brought from home. 'You could be one of the grease monkeys at Tyseley. They've got a couple of girls in, cleaning the engines, now. They have to get right in underneath – can you imagine?' She

148

looked at the other two, who were hungrily following her food with their eyes, like a pair of dogs. She held it out to them. 'D'you want a bite?'

'What's this I hear about some girl in your office?' Sylvia said to Kitty as they walked across from Snow Hill to get the bus home. They couldn't get another train from New Street station now that the line to Kings Heath was cargo only. Going through town always made Sylvia feel sad. There was so much destruction and mess everywhere. She looked fondly at the Theatre Royal as they went past, but felt much happier in the job she was doing now. A pang went through her at the thought that she would have to leave, when she married Ian. She tried not to think about it. At least today she could have a nice cosy afternoon with Kitty while Ian was still at work.

'What girl?' Kitty said, frowning.

'Oh, it's just the gossip going around. She's supposed to be carrying on with one of the guards – a much older man; well, aren't they all!' She laughed. 'Honestly, it'd be like walking out with your dad. And apparently he's married.'

'I've not heard,' Kitty said, not seeming very interested. 'I suppose all sorts of things must go on. It doesn't really matter, does it?'

'Well, it does to the man's wife, I should've thought,' Sylvia said stiffly. She glanced at Kitty, who was staring stonily ahead of her, and thought she'd better change the subject.

'Will you see much of your father over Easter?' she asked.

Kitty turned and suddenly smiled. 'Oh, yes. I've said I'll cook a meal for him and his sister, my auntie. She lives out at Wylde Green, but they like to get together now and again.'

'Oh, that's nice,' Sylvia said, relieved to hear that at least Kitty had a little bit of family that she seemed pleased to see.

'Come on,' Kitty said, grabbing her hand. 'There's a bus there, look – race you!'

Never had Sylvia been so glad to be on an early shift, because she was back home when the air-raid siren went off, late one evening in April, just before Easter.

'Oh Lord – there goes Moaning Minnie,' her mother said, leaping instantly from her chair in the front, where they were listening to the wireless. Then she looked stricken. 'Oh! Your father!'

Sylvia felt a plunge of dread inside her. Her father was on fire watch at the Rover works. Jack looked up from his book, and for a second Sylvia saw fear in his eyes.

'Come on,' Mom said. 'Shift yourselves, quick! I hope that flaming shelter's dry.' Without Dad there, she sounded much more panicky and vulnerable.

They all rushed around as the horrible sound howled outside, jangling their nerves. It was getting on for half-past nine and dark.

'I'll go ahead,' Jack said, piling on his coat, hat and scarves. Man of the house for now, he took the torch and disappeared into the garden.

'Come on,' Sylvia said, hugging the flasks of tea. 'Let's get it over with.'

They put the lights out in the house and went outside. The air was thick with smoke and mist, and although the sky was quiet as yet, apart from the siren, there was an ominous, menacing feeling that made their hearts pound horribly as they felt their way along to the shelter.

'Go carefully, Mom,' Sylvia said. 'The path's slippery.'

'I hope Jack locked all the animals up properly,' Mom was murmuring. 'There's no telling when we'll get eggs again after this lot.' The chickens did not appreciate Hitler's intervention in their lives.

Jack's torchlit face appeared in the door of the Anderson. 'It's not too bad. No puddles.'

They all went into its dank atmosphere. It always seemed to feel colder in there than anywhere else. Within a few moments they heard the first of the planes. They filled Sylvia with a sick, familiar feeling of terror.

'Oh good Lord,' Mom said. 'I've got a bad feeling about this one.'

'Let's have some tea,' Sylvia replied, forcing herself to do something, to think of anything other than what was out there. As she bent down to pick up the flask, they heard the first crumpling sounds of explosions some-where quite close in the city.

It was another terrifying, seemingly endless night, with the banging of the ack-ack guns and the ominous wait for explosions. Sleep was impossible. The planes came and came, with their menacing drone, as if they would never stop.

'This is one of the worst,' Mom said at some point in the small hours. She smoked one cigarette after another. Sylvia knew she was fretting about Dad. What was happening where he was? Sylvia felt a band of tension tighten in her head.

Sometimes the planes roared right overhead and there were explosions very close by. They all doubled up, their arms clasped over their heads as the ground shook violently under them. Sylvia was overwhelmed by a feeling of powerlessness. She could hear her mother saying, 'Oh dear God, dear God!' in a muffled voice. As the shuddering and the sounds eventually died away, Pauline sat up again and reached for Sylvia's hand, clinging to it.

'Are you all right, love?' She sounded frantic.

'Yes – Jack, you okay?' Sylvia asked, leaning over to her brother.

'Yeah,' he said stoically, though she could hear a tremor in his voice. She reached for his hand with her other one and he did not shake her off. 'That was damned close again. It sounded as if it was in the next street.'

It was awful, waiting and waiting for this eternal night to end.

The All Clear finally sounded in the early hours. They all crawled out of the shelter, stiff, freezing cold, their stomachs acid with fear and lack of sleep. It was still dark, with a morning mist, and everything looked ghostly outside. The air was horrible, full of acrid burn-ing smells.

'It's not worth me going to bed,' Sylvia said groggily. 'I'll have to go in about half an hour.' When she went inside, she suddenly had to rush to the bathroom to be sick.

Later, stepping out into the street to go to work, it was with a sense of horror at what she might find on the way. Things in their street seemed normal, but there was a strong smell of smoke and the dank, musty stench of wet plaster from somewhere nearby. At the bus stop on the Alcester Road a middle-aged woman told her there had been a direct hit on Grange Road, two streets away, and that several people had probably been killed.

'It must've been terrible in town last night,' the woman said. 'It was non-stop.'

On the packed bus, Sylvia wondered all the way about her father. Had the works been hit? Was he all right? Once they were turfed off the bus – early, as it could not get to the stop – she made for Snow Hill. Walking across town, she gasped with shock at the destruction. She found herself in tears at what had been done to their city as she struggled to make her way along, with other people who looked equally stunned. The air was thick with dust. The buildings at the end of New Street where it met High Street had collapsed, leaving a huge, wrecked space. The mess, and the stench of smoke and gas and burnt tar, was appalling, mixed with the damp plaster smell of ruined buildings. Firemen were still hosing down the ruins and New Street was full of rubble and mess. The smoke and dust and mist of early morning were all clogged together, making her cough as she struggled along, trying to get a grip on herself and not sob out loud.

At Snow Hill her eyes widened even further. Parts of the precinct were in a terrible state and there was an atmosphere of barely controlled chaos. Inside, instructions were being shouted by railway officials and chalked onto blackboards, and people were scurrying about trying to make out how and whether they could get to work. She stopped one of the porters hurrying along the station passage, who looked her up and down, seeing her railway uniform.

'Can I get across to Hockley?' she said.

The man stopped his barrow for a minute. He looked haggard and was covered in pale dust. 'We've had direct

153

hits: platform one's out, the ladies' waiting room – it's all gone. Platform five's down – and eleven . . . There's a hell of a mess.' He seemed to need to tell her. 'Something'll be going through, but I couldn't tell you when.'

Sylvia went carefully down the rubble-littered steps to platform seven to have a look. Glass crunched underfoot. Squinting upwards, she saw that the glazed roof had been blown in and scattered all over the place. Platform five was a mess of rubble. Odd things were dangling from the girders above. Something that looked like a pair of trousers hung limply. Nothing felt quite real, as if she was dreaming.

I'll try and get a bus, she thought. There seemed slim hope of getting to work anything like on time this morning. She wondered, with foreboding, in what state she might find the Goods Yard, after last night. When she at last found a bus going in the right direction, she sat squeezed against the dusty window, unable to stop the tears of shock and exhaustion running down her cheeks.

Twenty

To Sylvia's relief, when she walked into the Hockley Goods Yard from Pitsford Street, things seemed, on the face of it, much as usual.

But the first person she met, as she clocked in, was Froggy. Sylvia waited for his curses to fall on her head for being late. Instead, Froggy was dancing about like a madman, his strange grin revealing gumfuls of dodgy yellow teeth.

'They missed us! Those buggers missed us . . .'

Sylvia started to apologize.

'I don't care where yer've been,' Froggy cut in. 'Yer 'ere now. Just get on with it. I want you in the shed, unloading with . . .' He named the checker and another male porter, and off he jigged.

'Well,' Sylvia said, hurrying to the mess room, 'wonders will never cease.' Nights of bombing took people in strange ways.

She felt better for being at work. Her sickness and aching head began to clear as she worked, full of the crazed energy that can come upon you after a night of no sleep. She was unloading a huge consignment of rivets and studs and other metalware to go across to the LMS line and, tired as she was, all the exercise let off some tension. It was good to see daylight, to get on with something with other people. She didn't envy her mother, worrying at home. But all the time anxiety niggled at her mind – was Ian all right? And Dad? Had anything happened to the works? She didn't hear any bad news, but every time she thought of the sights she had seen in the middle of Birmingham that morning, a plunging, sick feeling of worry went through her.

'God, what a night!' everyone was saying.

In their mess room at tea break there was more time for a chat. Sylvia already had the tea brewed when Gina appeared, dark rings of weariness under her eyes, but, like everyone, trying to put on a brave face. Gina was the oldest child in a large family and her father was a fireman. Sylvia knew she must be worried.

'Here.' Sylvia handed her a mug of steaming tea. 'Get this down you.'

'Hello, happy campers!' Elsie said, hurrying in. Sylvia and Gina laughed at the absurdity of this.

'Ooh, a cuppa tea!' She poured herself a mug.

'What the hell's up with you?' Gina asked. 'Were you the only person in town who got some sleep or summat?'

'Sleep?' Elsie beamed, looking rather manic and even more rabbity than usual. 'What's that? Remind me!'

In their pent-up state they all seemed to laugh at anything and everything. They sat in a little ring, in their trousers, jackets and heavy boots, caps on the benches beside them. A couple of other women came in and chatted by the stove, waiting for the water to boil again.

'Did you see that pair of cami-knickers hanging from the rafters in Snow Hill?' Madge chuckled after plonking herself beside them. 'There was all sorts up there this morning!'

Sylvia laughed. 'I didn't see them, but I saw a pair of trousers. The *mess*. It was awful.'

'I know – but I wonder whose knickers they were? They must be feeling a bit chilly this morning,' Gina said.

Madge snorted. 'Talk about washing your dirty linen in public.'

They all got the giggles, half-guiltily, but they couldn't seem to help it.

'Even Froggy was quite pleasant when I came in today,' Sylvia said. 'He was hopping about like a mad thing. I was more than half an hour late and he didn't even seem to notice.'

'Oh, you weren't the only one,' Gina said. 'The distance some people have to come. Did you hear, the police station was hit – Steelhouse Lane? I saw, on the way in.'

The others looked at her. It was hard to take it all in. As yet they had no clear picture of what had happened across Birmingham.

There came a tap at the door of the mess room and, looking round, Sylvia saw Kitty at the door.

'Hello,' she said. 'Come in.' Only then did she see the expression on Kitty's face and the unusually dishevelled state of her. Her clothes were crumpled, her stockings torn and her normally neat hair was unbrushed and full of dust. Sylvia jumped up. 'Kitty, whatever's happened?'

Kitty sank down on the bench beside her and burst into violent tears, in a way that tore at Sylvia's heart. All the women looked at each other in dismay. Sylvia put her arm round Kitty's heaving shoulders. 'Oh my goodness,' she said, distressed. 'What's the matter?'

Kitty was unable to speak for a moment and she was trembling all over. She gulped, tugging a handkerchief out from her sleeve to wipe her eyes.

'It's all gone – our house!' she cried. 'We had the most terrible night. I was under the stairs, in the cupboard, all on my own. My father wouldn't come, said he wasn't moving anywhere for anyone. He's *so* stubborn.' She banged her fist on her knee in frustration. 'When it got bad, I ran up and tried and *tried* to make him get out of bed, but he was . . . Well, he'd had a bit to drink and I couldn't wake him. I just had to go back down there by myself. And later – I don't know what time, I lost track – there was a huge bang! It was so loud and the noises just went on. It was pitch-dark. There was dust every-where – I was choking. I thought I was trapped under there. I thought . . . I was going to die.' She sobbed so much then that she couldn't go on.

'Oh, my,' Gina said. The other girls gave each other looks of horror and sympathy.

'It must have dropped in the garden – all the back of the house is gone,' Kitty went on. 'My father was in the bedroom at the back and . . .' She shook her head, tears pouring down her cheeks. 'When they came, he was . . . He never stood a chance . . . I had to show them where to look. I couldn't get out until the fire brigade came. I was just stuck. But the stairs didn't collapse. Otherwise I would have . . .'

'Oh, Kitty!' Sylvia said. 'How terrible.' Overflowing with feeling for her friend, she looked round at the others. 'Kitty doesn't have anyone else, you see – only her father.'

'They took him away,' Kitty said, wiping her blotchy face. 'I'll have to go and see my aunt, his sister, who lives in Wylde Green, and tell her what's happened so we can arrange the funeral. I wouldn't even know where to start on my own.'

'What about your things?' Sylvia tried to adjust her

mind. Have you got any clothes or anything? What about the house?'

'It's gone,' Kitty said bleakly. For a moment she stared ahead of her, as if this truth was only now sinking in, then she looked round at Sylvia, her eyes filling again. 'There's only the front wall still standing – like a shell. I've got no home, nowhere to go. I managed to get a few things out: a little bundle. But . . .' She put her hands over her face so wretchedly that Sylvia found she was crying as well. 'I couldn't think what to do, once they'd taken him. It was only a few hours ago. It feels as if it was days ago.' She brought her hands down into her lap and said, 'I couldn't think what to do, except to come here. I might be able to stay with Auntie – but she's quite frail and it's so far out. I haven't got anywhere else to go.'

Sylvia was wrung out with sorrow at the sight of her friend. It was bad enough having so little family, and now to lose even that seemed the most horrible thing possible. Once again, with a pang, she thought about her own father. *Please* let him be all right, she prayed.

'Look, Kitty, you must come back with me. I know that's what Mom would say. You can have Audrey's bed for now. We've got plenty of room.'

'Oh no, I . . .'

'You *must*,' Sylvia insisted. 'I'd feel bad if you didn't.'

Kitty looked round at her in wonder. 'Oh, Sylvia – could I really? I'd only need to stop with you for a few days, just until . . .' She stopped, as if suddenly faced by the bleak truth: *until what?* Her home was gone, and her father.

'Never mind that for now. You just come home with me.' Warmly she took Kitty's hand.

'Oh, Sylvia, that's so kind,' Kitty said, starting to cry all over again.

'It's the least we can do,' Sylvia told her, squeezing her hand. 'You can stay as long as you like.'

They travelled back to Kings Heath on the bus. It seemed to take an age. Some of the bus stops had had to be moved, as everyone tried, in all the wreckage and disruption, to keep the city moving and working.

As they got home Sylvia's heart was beating nervously fast. 'Mom?' she called as they walked in.

'I'm here, Sylvia.' Pauline came out of the front room. The look of her steadied Sylvia. She seemed calm and reassuring.

'Dad? Has he . . . ?'

'He's been home,' her mother said, and Sylvia could see her relief after hours of worry. She nodded a hello to Kitty. 'He had a dreadful night, but he's all right. He had a bit of a nap and went back to the works, but he should be home later. And Ian called in; he was in a rush, but he said to say he's all right.'

'Oh thank heavens!' Once again Sylvia was tearful. 'Look, Mom, I've brought Kitty home.'

As she explained what had happened, she saw her mother take in Kitty's filthy state, the little bundle of belongings in her arms that she had managed to salvage and her strained, tearful expression. Her face softened with compassion.

'Oh, you poor child,' she said. 'What a terrible thing. Of course you must stay here – give her Audrey's room, Sylv.'

'Oh, thank you, Mrs Whitehouse,' Kitty cried. 'I just didn't know where I was going to go. I'm ever so grateful. You're all *so* kind.'

160

'Don't you worry, bab,' Pauline said. 'You just come and make yourself at home. And in her comforting way, she took Kitty in her arms and embraced her as if she was one of her own.

Twenty-One

'Are you walking out with that red-headed chappie again?' Maggie asked Audrey, who was applying lipstick, peering into her tiny pocket mirror.

'Ummgh,' Audrey agreed, her mouth contorted.

'Aha,' Cora teased, and began singing the wedding march, 'Da da di-da, *da* da di-dah . . .'

'Oh, shut up,' Audrey snapped, putting the lipstick away. 'You lot are a right bunch of canting old biddies.'

'A bunch of *what*?' Maggie laughed. She loved to tease Audrey. ''Fraid I don't speak Brummy, dear.'

Audrey looked at her two friends, Cora was sprawled on the bed, looking very voluptuous. Maggie, plump and mousy-haired with a fresh complexion, was sitting on the side of hers, munching an apple and working on a piece of embroidery.

'Look, it's not like that,' she said. 'He's nice enough, but . . .'

'*Nice enough*,' Cora mimicked her. 'You really are the last of the romantics, aren't you?'

'Anyway, he'll be gone soon – goodness knows where. What's the point in getting too involved?'

'There is such a thing as a letter, you know,' Maggie said, looking up. 'You know, human communication.'

'Are you going to the flicks?' Cora asked. 'We're coming along later too – might see you there.'

'Oh, marvellous,' Audrey said sarcastically. 'Just what

I need: you two turning up.' She picked up her cap and gave the badge a rub along her sleeve. 'Right, I'm off. See yer later, old biddies.'

'Have fun!' Maggie said.

'Don't do anything we wouldn't do!' Cora called after her.

'I'm not likely to,' Audrey muttered, closing the door of the hut behind her.

It was a warm evening full of spring promise. She had said to Hamish that she'd meet him by the tobacco kiosk on the corner of one of the roads through the base. They were planning to go for a walk and then to a picture that was showing later in the evening. Audrey ambled along past the huts, each of which had a small garden of spring flowers and a lawn round it. She greeted people she knew on the way. Her shoulders were stiff, as ever, from sitting over a typewriter, and she circled them and breathed in deeply. It was lovely not to be cold. The winter seemed to have gone on forever.

When she got to the kiosk Hamish was not there yet, so she stood with her eyes closed for a few moments, enjoying the rays of the setting sun on her face. A smile turned up her lips.

I love it here, she thought. The life suited her. She loved the cosy hut with its neatly stacked kit, the attractive-looking base, the friendships and interest of it all. It was exciting, fun, full of purpose. Even if the job was a bore, it was still something more than typing in those gloomy offices in Birmingham. She had nothing to complain about, not when you thought about all these poor boys who were heading for terrible danger and often death. Boys like Hamish.

163

'Hello there – are you daydreaming?'

She opened her eyes, startled. Hamish's freckled face was smiling at her and she was reassured by how pleased she was to see him.

'I was just soaking in the sun,' she said. 'It feels as if it's a long time since we've seen it.'

'Shall we go for that walk?' he said. 'Make the most of it?'

When they were out of sight of the main buildings, Hamish took her arm. Things had moved on between them. Now, when they were together, they often kissed, and Hamish had told her he loved her. Audrey was thrown by this. Loved her? Did he really mean that? What was she supposed to feel? She liked Hamish. It would be hard not to like him – he was a kind, pleasant boy who had been very well brought up. But love? Soon afterwards she decided: what did it matter? He would be gone soon, off into Fighter Command. Anything could happen in the next few months. Why not tell him she loved him, as she had never managed to say to Raymond. What would be the harm?

So the next time when he held her in his arms and looked at her in that sweet, earnest way of his and said, 'You are so fine, Audrey. I love you. I'm bowled over by you', she looked back and mentally crossed her fingers. 'I love you too, Hamish,' she said, trying to sound as you would if you really meant it.

Hamish gave a little cry of joy and pulled her close. 'Oh my dear one!' he said, which Audrey thought was quaint, as Hamish often was. 'You make me so happy.'

They walked around the base arm-in-arm in the dusk, past the huge hangars and the shed where the balloons were fabricated. In the open area in front were two of the

164

special trucks equipped with winches for the balloon cables.

'You know,' Hamish said. 'If you get a storm, a lightning strike, you have to get those balloons down double-quick or they'll explode – all that hydrogen in there.'

'That'd be a sight,' Audrey said.

They chatted easily and, in a quiet corner behind one of the sheds, Hamish took Audrey in his arms again and kissed her hungrily. Kissing Hamish was pleasant enough, Audrey thought. He was a nice lad, funny and kind. Why would she not love him? Perhaps this feeling of vague pleasure was as good as it ever got? But if so, what was all that fuss about in books she had read and in the pictures? Her moderate feelings didn't seem to account for those passionately soaring violins and acres of love poetry. Was all that just a pretty lie?

Once again she felt guilty because she couldn't feel more, while Hamish seemed to feel so much.

As he drew back for a moment to gaze fondly down into her eyes, she said, 'Shouldn't we be getting back now? The picture'll be starting soon.'

Hamish looked faintly disappointed. 'Oh, d'you really want to see that? It's some Laurel and Hardy thing, I think.'

A Chump at Oxford was showing in the camp cinema that night. Audrey wasn't desperate to see it, but she didn't want to spend the whole evening with Hamish getting more and more amorous.

'I'd quite like to see it,' she said. 'Come on – let's. If we stay out here it'll just get cold.' She shivered. 'It's chilly enough now. We can always go and have a drink after, eh?' She squeezed his hand. 'How about that?'

Hamish looked appeased. 'With you, my dear,' he said, 'anything.'

A few days later Audrey was at her desk in the office. Though trying to look busy, she was fretting about Hamish. He would be gone in a few days to his next training camp and she had to decide whether she would keep in touch with him. Wouldn't it be false, leading him on?

She sighed and rested her head on her hand, looking out of the window. What the hell's the matter with me? she wondered gloomily.

'Are you with us?' A voice said, so close to her ear that Audrey almost left the seat. The officer for whom she worked, an energetic WAAF called Betty Masters, was leaning over her. Betty was a plain woman with brown hair scraped back and a long, upturned nose. She was the sort of person, Audrey thought, who, had she not been dressed in WAAF officer blues, would definitely be wearing tweed. She was also a person of abundant energy and intelligence.

'Did you hear what I said, Airwoman Whitehouse?' she enquired with a glint in her eyes.

'No, ma'am, I'm afraid not.'

'Right,' she said irritably. 'Then I suppose I shall have to repeat it. Because of the shortage of balloon operators, the powers that be in the service have decided to open the trade to women. There's going to be a lot of—'

'Oh!' Wide awake now, Audrey shot into a fully upright position. 'Can I do that – please!'

Betty Masters laughed, startled. 'What I was saying was: it's going to involve a lot of paperwork – which is your job, if I'm not mistaken.'

'Yes, ma'am, of course,' Audrey said, pulling herself together. But her heart was pounding with excitement. She had to persuade them to let her transfer, *had* to! 'But could I apply, d'you think?'

'You already have a skill,' Betty Masters said. 'Why on earth would you want to be out in all weathers, when you can work quite comfortably in here?'

'But there are loads of women who can do what I do,' Audrey argued, surprised by her own daring. She was so desperate to get out of that office and into something more active.

Betty Masters gazed, as if for inspiration, at the telephone. 'You're not irreplaceable, it's true. It's not up to me, though.' She turned. 'You'll have to apply, and then it's in the lap of the gods. But for now could we possibly embark on the paperwork – if it's not too much trouble?'

Twenty-Two

'Hey, guess what! Audrey rushed into the hut a fortnight later, bursting with excitement. To all the faces turned towards her she announced, 'I'm changing trades. They're letting me train as a balloon operator!'

Having made her announcement, she collapsed on the bed, sneezing. She had a heavy cold.

'What're you on about?' Joey asked. 'Women don't work the balloons.'

'They do now,' Audrey said through her hanky.

'You're transferring – *why* on earth?' Maggie asked as she lay draped across her bed. Maggie was also doing clerical work. 'Give me a nice cosy office any day.'

Cora, who had been looking for something under her bed, popped up beside it on her knees. 'By the looks of you,' she remarked, 'it'll be the death of you.'

'Thanks for the vote of confidence,' Audrey said nasally. 'It's always nice to know you've got such good friends.' She stood up to carry on telling them how pleased she was, and sat down again abruptly. 'Come to think of it, I really don't feel very well.'

Within hours Audrey's temperature had shot up, and Maggie and Cora reported her and had her moved over to the sick bay.

'Nice of you to get rid of me,' Audrey grumbled as

she was evicted from her bed in the hut. But she was not in any state to argue.

'Whatever it is you've got, we don't want it,' Cora told her.

'Heartless so-and-sos,' Audrey muttered.

'I'll bring your things – and a nip of something if I can smuggle it in. You're not just going to sleep that one off. It looks as if you've got the flu.'

As it turned out, she was not the only one. There were several WAAFs already laid up in the sick quarters and there had to be an area set aside for the women, in what had previously been an entirely male camp. Audrey was aware of others in the room, of people moving about and talking, but for a couple of days she lapsed into a feverish, almost unconscious state while the illness took over. She heard a female voice urging her to sip water, and felt its coolness sliding down her throat. Every so often she surfaced and was more aware of her surroundings: white walls, beds, light from a window. Most of the time, though, she was only half-conscious, with a hot, aching head, shivering body and very sore throat.

In her feverish state she had the most peculiar dreams, which involved Hamish, who kept asking her over and over again to marry him. Hamish had left the camp a few days earlier. In her confusion she was aware of both guilt and relief, though she had promised to write to him. Other dreams were about the balloon site. The barrage balloons reared towards her, bulky and suffocating, and she would surface, thinking she was screaming, but no sound came out of her mouth. Once she dreamed that Sylvia was sitting on her bed, holding Mr Piggles; but she then turned into Cora, who was urging Audrey to eat a poached egg, and when she woke and found there was no

169

one there, she felt bereft and homesick, wanting her mother. Hot tears of longing ran down her cheeks.

Gradually the symptoms eased and on the fourth day she woke, knowing that the worst of it had left her. Opening her eyes, she lay quietly, taking in both her own limp state and the surroundings. She could hear faint sounds from the base outside, but for the moment the room was quiet.

There were six beds in the room, but now they were all empty except for one opposite hers. Raising her head, she saw the shape of someone asleep under the bed-clothes and golden-brown, wavy hair on the pillow. She found herself wishing that Sylvia would pop up from under the bedclothes. Since her first few homesick days in the service, Audrey had not missed home with the ache she felt now. She imagined lying in bed, the sound of the wireless drifting up from downstairs, and she longed to see everyone again.

She must have drifted off to sleep again, because the next thing she was aware of was the arrival of a rattling trolley and a smell of toast.

'Ah, you're in the land of the living, are you?' The face of a blonde WAAF nurse appeared at her side. 'How about a spot of breakfast today? You haven't eaten a thing, and I'm sure it's time you did.'

Audrey nodded. 'Yes, please,' she whispered.

'Let's see if we can sit you up.'

The nurse was a tiny little thing, wiry and strong. She helped Audrey to lean against her pillows and brought her a boiled egg and some toast. Audrey felt the saliva rise in her mouth.

'Thank you,' she said, smiling.

When she was left with her breakfast, she realized that she was being watched from the opposite bed by a young woman with a round, friendly-looking face, who seemed familiar. Many faces on the base were familiar by now. The young woman, who was sitting up in bed writing something, raised her arm in a wave.

'Hello. Back with us, then?' She had a soft, girlish voice.

Audrey tried to laugh, but all she managed was a weak smile. 'Seems like it,' she said. 'Have I been away long?'

'You've been under a while, I'd say. But it was the same for everyone – nasty dose of the flu. I'm just a day or so further on than you.'

Once she had managed to get some breakfast inside her, Audrey started to feel a bit stronger. The other girl hopped out of bed and came over and sat on the side of Audrey's bed, plump in her nightdress, still holding a cup of tea.

'I'm glad you've come to,' she said. 'I've been getting a bit lonely.' Audrey was struck by the generous physicality of the young woman, her breasts large and heavy under the thin white cotton. I would've wanted to wrap up a bit more, Audrey thought. But the other girl seemed unselfconscious. She told Audrey her name was Dorrie Cooper and that she was a driver.

'Oh,' Audrey said. 'That's where I know you from! You brought us here the first day.'

Dorrie put her head on one side. She had pink, rather weather-beaten cheeks, a head of loosely curled honey-brown hair and big blue eyes. She had the look of a cherub, and Audrey imagined that Dorrie had probably looked much the same when she was only five years old.

'Yes, I remember,' Dorrie said.

'What, remember me? Why?'

'I don't know. I suppose some faces just stick in your mind. What's your name?'

'Audrey Whitehouse.'

'Where're you from – the Midlands?'

'Right first time,' Audrey said. 'Brum. Have I got that much of an accent?'

'Just a bit.' Dorrie grinned, showing a row of big, square teeth. Her smile was very infectious.

'What about you?'

'High Wycombe. Daddy owns a funeral parlour.'

'Does he?' Audrey said. They both laughed, not really knowing why it was funny. 'That's not a reserved occ, is it?'

'Oh, I don't know! Daddy's so ancient they'd never call him up anyway.'

She asked Audrey about her family and soon they were both chatting away about their homes and their lives before the WAAF, and since.

'The WAAF's the best thing that ever happened to me,' Dorrie said. She sat with one leg crossed over the other, twitching her bare leg up and down. 'I'd have loved to be something like a driver in Civvy Street. I wanted to drive big things like trucks or horseboxes – something with a lot of power. As well as writing, that is: that's what I really want to do, but you have to earn a crust somehow.' She laughed and Audrey enjoyed the infectious sound Dorrie made, as well as her energetic approach to life.

'Mummy thought I should do secretarial training, because that's what girls do.' Dorrie rolled her eyes. 'I think they assumed I'd work for Daddy.' Another roll of the eyes. 'Can you imagine? Like being buried alive – almost literally! I said I'd rather work on a farm, which Mummy was absolutely horrified about, of course. But I managed to persuade them that horses were a bit more respectable. So I was working on a stud farm. It was a nice job – a lot of mucking out, of course.'

'What about the writing?' Audrey said.

'Oh, I never really told them about that. Didn't want them prying. Anyway, when the war came and there was a chance to do something else, I jumped at it. In the meantime I'm always scribbling. I want to work for a newspaper.' She got up for a moment and went to her bed, holding up the book she had been writing in: blue with a marbled cover. 'My diary! Very hush-hush – evidently we WAAFs aren't supposed to keep them. Security and all that. But I've always kept one. You have to talk to someone!' She came and sat down again. 'But no point in saying anything about that to *them*. My parents don't understand literate people. Sorry, I'm babbling. How did you come to join up?'

'A bit like you really.' Audrey sat back, enjoying the conversation. 'Where I come from, for people like me, you can work in a factory, or a shop, or an office. So I did shorthand typing – well, shorthand at night school.' Audrey told her about her boring office job and then about Raymond. Dorrie listened intently.

'I suppose it was the shock, partly. We'd known each other as kids – all our lives really. And suddenly he was gone, just like that. He was on HMS *Esk*. It brought it all home: this is the only life we've got, and I wanted to do something apart from moulder away in an insurance office. I felt very bad about Raymond. He was . . . Well, he was very keen on me, and he told me so before he went. But I wasn't at all interested in him – not like that. Now I think I should have lied and said something nice to him. And then he was dead . . .' Her eyes filled with tears suddenly and she wiped them on the corner of the sheet. She was surprised at how easily she could talk to

Dorrie. 'Sorry. I feel very weepy at the moment. Must be the end of the flu.'

'It's all right, 'Dorrie said straightforwardly. 'I know. My brother was killed on the way into Dunkirk. It's bloody and awful, and what can you do except cry, and try and get back at them – the Hun, I mean?' She leaned over and patted Audrey's hand. She had strong, fulsome arms. 'Look, there's a wireless they'll let us listen to, if we want. I didn't like to ask for it while you were so poorly. But would you like it now? There might be some funnies on.'

Audrey nodded. 'Thanks.' Very happy suddenly, she put her plate aside and snuggled down under the bed-clothes. 'That'd be lovely.'

For the next couple of days there was no one in the women's sick quarters except for Audrey and Dorrie and, in that time, a close friendship was born. Both of them had visits from WAAF friends, and Cora and Maggie both met Dorrie. The nurse brought the wireless in on a trolley almost as often as they liked and they listened to everything: the news reports, big-band shows and Lord Haw-Haw's sinister voice. And above all they laughed: at the radio and at each other. On a couple of occasions they were laughing so much that the nurse came in and told them off.

'You're supposed to be ill!' she said, though her own lips were twitching.

Dorrie, who was by now feeling more energetic than Audrey, spent her time knitting a voluminous red jumper and writing her diary. Any time a nurse or anyone else came in, she hid it under the bedclothes.

'I've always had a diary, more or less ever since I could

write,' she said. 'Life wouldn't be the same without writing everything down.' She hugged the book to her chest. 'I get a new one about twice a year – I've got heaps of them locked away at home.'

'What on earth d'you write about?' Audrey asked. She was still content to lie about, feeling limp, and not do anything much. Even the thought of writing exhausted her. She felt a pang of guilt: she had not sent a letter home for some time. Sylvia had written saying there had been a terrible raid and a friend of hers was living with them because she had been bombed out.

'Just everything. What's going on, what I feel about it, who says what.' Dorrie held up the book. 'All my life goes in here. Even you'll probably go in here – in fact, I'm certain you will!'

Audrey squinted at the label on the front. 'That doesn't say Dorrie. What's your name?'

Dorrie blushed and rolled her eyes again. 'I'm afraid it's Dorothea.'

'Blimey,' Audrey said. 'I thought Dorrie was short for Doreen – it is, where I come from!'

'I wouldn't mind being called Doreen,' Dorrie said seriously. 'You can call me that, if you want.'

'I'll stick to Dorrie,' Audrey said.

They spent a lot of the day talking, in between meals and the naps that Audrey, especially, needed. And they talked well into the night, lying in the dark with no one else to disturb, sharing many details about their lives. Dorrie seemed fascinated by Birmingham and Audrey's life there. Her own upbringing in High Wycombe she described as narrow and cheerless.

'I was always the naughty one,' Dorrie said, chuckling. 'I had a little schoolmate called Jimmy, and one summer holiday we got up very early, sneaked right out to the edge of town and rode the farm horses. We got one of them to stand up close to the fence – it was quite a tame old thing and we both managed to get on the same horse together. We plodded around on it for a bit. It was misty and the grass was soaking wet, so when we slid off him we got wet bottoms. And then we sneaked home again before anyone noticed. It was the best!' She laughed, remembering.

Audrey felt quite envious. It was hard to imagine living so near to the countryside. She told Dorrie the story of little Laurie Gould setting fire to the cutting bank, to get the fire brigade back.

'You live by the railway – you lucky thing! I love trains. If I'd been a boy, I'd've gone to be an engine driver.'

'Just like every other boy in the country,' Audrey said.

'Yes, but I would've done it. They just *talk* about it.'

Dorrie said that her father had been appalled at the thought of her joining up. 'Daddy's view of women is that you go to school for a little while, so that you can help handle your husband's correspondence and add up a bit and not look too much of a dumb cluck socially. He thinks women should all be like Dora Spenlow in *David Copperfield* – have you ever read it? You know, she just wants to hang around him and hold his pencils while he's writing. She's absolutely sickening. Daddy hates it when a woman thinks for herself and, if you disagree with him, dear God! You'd think the sky had fallen in. Mummy goes along with it and then secretly does what she thinks is right, which I think is ridiculous and just pandering to him. Anyway, I just can't fit in with what they think I should be: a little married lady in another little married house. Oh no – thank God for the WAAF! What's your mother like, Audrey?'

'Mom? Oh, she's all right,' Audrey said. Thinking about it, she realized that her parents, while exasperated with her sometimes, had never tried to crush her. 'Mom's quite frightened of life, I think. I don't think things were easy when she was young, and she's very protective of us. My sister Sylvia's much more timid and homely, but I've always been the tomboy one! But they're all right. I miss them.'

'No leave lately?'

'None ever yet.'

'What?' Dorrie's voice came through the darkness indignantly. 'Not since you joined up? Well, you must be eligible for some soon. Don't you want to go home?'

'Yes,' Audrey said. 'I do.' Thinking about it as she lay for hours in bed, she realized just how much she wanted to see everyone.

Twenty-Three

'Oh!' Jack enthused when he came home from school to discover that Kitty was to stay with them. 'Does this mean she's going to make cake?'

Kitty, who was at the table peeling potatoes, laughed merrily. 'Of course I'll make cake, if you like.'

Everyone had gravitated towards the kitchen that afternoon. Even Jack was hanging about, sitting sideways in the armchair, his legs flung over one of the arms. Sylvia was amused to see that Jack could hardly take his eyes off Kitty. Now Kitty had had a wash and was dressed in her spare clothes, she was looking very neat and attractive. They all urged her to rest, but she was adamant that she was not sleepy and wanted to be as helpful as possible.

'I managed to salvage my ration book, Mrs Whitehouse,' she told Pauline. 'And I'd be happy to shop for you whenever I can, if it helps.'

'That's nice of you,' Pauline said. She was at the table chopping onions, tears pouring from her eyes. 'That'd be a big help. Oh, these onions! It's a miracle to have them, I know – I queued for three-quarters of an hour to get them, but they don't half make me stream.'

'Let me do it,' Kitty offered. 'I don't mind.' Sylvia smiled at her friend's eagerness to please.

'So, will you make chocolate cake?' Jack persisted. 'You did say you would.'

'Oh, shut up, Jacko!' Sylvia said, pretending to lob a potato as him. 'Poor Kitty has just lost her home and her father, and all you can think about is chocolate cake.'

'I'll have to go and buy a few clothes,' Kitty said. 'I did manage to find the little money that was in the house – Dad kept a bit of spare in the bureau at the front. Better I have it than someone comes in and sees what they can get.'

'Well, it's yours – your father's anyway,' Sylvia said.

'I know,' Kitty said, 'but I still felt peculiar taking it.' Her eyes filled with tears. 'He was such a hard man. I wish . . .' She shook her head, unable to get to the end of the sentence.

'I'm sure we can find you a few things of Sylvia's and Audrey's,' Mrs Whitehouse said. 'To tide you over anyway.'

'You're so kind.' Kitty looked round at them all with tearful eyes. 'You already feel like a family to me. I never knew people could be so nice.'

'Don't you worry,' Pauline said. 'Everyone's got to stick together, that we have.'

As she spoke they heard the front door open.

'Dad!' Jack cried.

Usually Ted came in calling, 'Pauline?' But today he came into the kitchen and just stood quietly at the doorway.

'Hello, love,' Pauline said. She wasn't the sort to rush into her husband's arms, but Sylvia could see the relief written all over her face.

'You all right, Dad?' For a moment Sylvia felt like crying as well. The night had been so awful and they were all exhausted.

'I'm all right,' he said quietly. His dark eyes took in

the homely activity in the kitchen and he gave a tired smile.

'I'm just boiling the kettle, love,' Pauline said. 'Ted, Kitty was bombed out last night. She's going to be stopping with us for a bit.'

'Bombed out?' he said, standing straighter. 'What happened?'

'Well, it was a bomb,' Jack said.

'Don't be smart with me, lad,' his father said.

Kitty explained what had happened, and Sylvia could see that her father was affected by hearing her story.

'It was a terrible night,' he said, shaking his head. He looked at Pauline. 'You heard about the tunnel at Fawley Grove?' Sylvia's mother looked at him, shaking her head. 'Those poor souls, about a dozen of them. They took shelter in that tunnel under the railway – there was a direct hit.'

'Oh, my word,' Pauline said. They all stood, appalled.

'You stay as long as you need to,' Ted said to Kitty.

'Go and sit down, love,' his wife instructed. 'You look all in. I'll bring you your tea.'

When Ian came round later, they all sat in the front room. Nearly all the talk was again of the previous night, of what had happened in different parts of the city. Ian was very sympathetic towards Kitty.

'You poor girl,' he said. 'And I'm so sorry to hear you've lost your father.'

Kitty became tearful again. 'I still can't quite take it in,' she said. 'I know I didn't always see eye-to-eye with the old man. But no one should have to die like that.'

Sylvia and Ian did manage a few minutes on their own

that evening. Kitty took herself off to bed, saying she was all in, and they decamped to the kitchen again.

'Well, here we are again,' Sylvia joked. 'When I think of courting, I'll always think of the smells of onions and disinfectant.'

Ian laughed. 'I don't care what it smells of – at least we have a chance to see each other,' he said, pulling Sylvia close and kissing her hungrily. For a time they were wrapped up in each other, kissing and cuddling.

'How long's she staying for?' Ian asked.

'Kitty? I don't know. She doesn't seem to have any family apart from this old aunt.'

'Well, I suppose she'll have to go there in the end, won't she? She can't just stay with you forever.'

'Why not?' Sylvia said. 'Anyway, I couldn't really not invite her back here, could I? Not when she had nowhere else to go. Don't you like her?'

'Oh yes, she's perfectly all right. I was just thinking of your family. She's in Audrey's room – I don't know what she'll have to say, if she comes back.'

'Well, she hasn't as yet,' Sylvia said, irritated that Audrey should be such a major consideration when she wasn't even here.

Sylvia felt very grateful to her mother and father for their kindness to Kitty. And Kitty was full of enthusiasm for the family and tried to be as helpful as she could at every turn. As the days passed, the girls travelled to Hockley together when they had the same shift pattern. Sylvia found she loved having Kitty living with them.

'To tell you the truth, Audrey and I have never been close at all,' she told Kitty one night, when they were both sitting in Audrey's room. 'I suppose we're too

181

different. I've always felt as if I'm in her shadow and,' she made a comical grimace, 'she's ever so bossy!'

Kitty was propped against the pillows, her knees under the eiderdown. Brandy the cat, which had taken a shine to Kitty, was on the bed, purring loudly as Kitty stroked her. Sylvia sank down onto the bed and started rubbing her hair with a towel.

'I'd love to have had a sister,' Kitty said wistfully.

Sylvia straightened up and looked at her. She leaned over and touched Kitty's hand. 'Well, you've got one now – if you'll have me.'

Kitty looked moved. 'Oh, Sylv, do you really mean it? That's such a nice thing to say!'

'Course I mean it,' Sylvia said. Kitty's new sorrows had made Sylvia feel even more tender towards her.

'I feel so alone.' Tears ran down Kitty's face suddenly, though she quickly wiped them away. 'But it's so nice to be living here and being allowed to be part of your family for a little bit. Your Ian's such a nice man as well.'

'Yes,' Sylvia said. 'I'm ever so lucky, but . . .' Her own colour rose as she found the confession slipping out. 'Well, I love him, of course I do. And I'm so glad we'll soon be married, even though I'm not sure about living with his family. But . . .' Blushing heavily now, she said, 'Ian is very – I mean, he wants to get married so that we can, you know, take things all the way. I don't want . . . Well, it's not that I don't want it, but I think you should be married, and it's too much of a risk. He gets very . . . Well, I suppose it's frustrating for him.'

Kitty was staring at her with wide, sympathetic eyes. 'Oh, that must be so difficult. But I do think you're right. It's better to wait. It would make getting married more of a special thing, wouldn't it?'

'Have you found this – with boys you've been out

with?' Sylvia asked. 'I feel so silly asking, but I haven't had a lot of boyfriends. One or two when we were quite young. And then Ian came along, and bingo! That was it. But he does get quite grumpy, and I feel as if I'm doing the wrong thing, denying him.'

'Oh, I'm sure you're not,' Kitty said. 'I'm not the most experienced person with boys. I always find I'm too shy with them. Maybe that's one of the things about not having any brothers. You don't know how to talk to them. But Ian will respect you for being like that, won't he? And then you can have a lovely white wedding. I'm sure that's how it should be, Sylvia. And your dress is nearly ready too; you must show me – it'll be lovely!'

Twenty-Four

May 1941

The late spring brought warmer weather and fewer raids. Sylvia found her work easier without the harsh ache of cold in her fingers and toes, and with a proper night's sleep. But the news of the war grew more and more desperate. The family gathered round the wireless to hear one piece of bad news after another: the encirclement of Tobruk by the German tank commander, Rommel; the German invasion of Greece and the capitulation of the Greek government. It was hard to say anything after such news. Everyone looked at each other and then waited for something funny to come on to take their minds off the dark despair of it.

Amidst it all, though, in some ways Sylvia was happier than she had ever been. Their modest wedding plans were going ahead. Sylvia's dress, a slender pearly silk shell, which had been fashioned out of another dress, fitted her perfectly and was almost ready now. Marjorie Gould had done a lovely job on it. When Ian's mother, Mrs Westley, heard that their neighbour was making Sylvia's dress, she said snootily, 'Oh, aren't you going to have a professional tailor?' But Sylvia knew that making it was something to distract Marjorie from her sorrow, and in any case, by then she had already started. To her enormous relief, Ian had told her that soon after the wedding they might be able to rent a couple of rooms from a friend of his father's in Moseley. So she might not have to live under Mrs Westley's chilly eye after all!

With the wedding only two months away, it started to feel real at last. Sylvia would have to give up work. She would be moving out of her family home and would lose her cosy times with Kitty. Mom was happy for Kitty to stay on as a lodger, and Sylvia knew she would see a lot of her, but she was starting to feel very nervous. All these changes felt strange, and the joy of getting married was tinged with sadness at the other things she would lose.

Life in the Goods Yard was as busy as ever. Sylvia's job seemed even more precious now, as she knew that she would soon have to leave it.

One morning she was in the middle of unloading a flat cart stacked with heavy boxes into one of the wagons. Wheeling her empty barrow back out to the delivery yard, smiling at a joke one of the carters had just told her, her face sobered at the sight of a burly figure hurrying into the yard. Something about this large man caught her attention. He had his head down and seemed intensely preoccupied. She realized she had seen him before.

A voice called to him from along the yard, 'Oi, Joe! You after Pat's cheese ration again?'

The man did not react, did not even seem to hear the joke directed at him. The shunters, like Pat Sheehan, had extra cheese rations because they did such heavy work. Sylvia remembered that this big man had been into the yard a number of times, looking for Pat. The men were cousins, she had been told. And he was the man she had once seen talking to Kitty. She turned, slowing her own

185

progress to watch him for a moment, as he disappeared across the yard.

'It was you told her, wasn't it, you stupid bastard?'

Joe Whelan caught his cousin, Pat Sheehan, by the throat and pinned him up against one of the stationary minks. They were in the shunting yard, hidden in a spot between the tracks occupied by two long lines of wagons. Pat, a strong, wiry man seven years Joe's junior, was taken by surprise and found himself sandwiched between Joe and the faded W of the GWR letters painted on the wagon.

'Joe! What the . . . ?' Pat protested. But Joe had him in a terrible grip and he could feel the force of the man's anger. Though Pat struggled hard, he could not shift him. Joe was as strong as steel and explosive with rage. 'For God's sake man, what's got into you? Get off me!'

'It was you – it had to be. You said something to Ann . . .'

'No, Joe! What did I say to Ann: about what? I haven't even laid eyes on her . . .'

But there was something too shrill in his denial. It didn't ring true. Joe felt the muscles in his arms bunch tighter as he squeezed Pat's throat. 'Liar!'

'For pity's sake . . .' Pat was starting to choke. He seized Joe's arm and wrenched it away from his own throat with all the force he had in him. Joe's arm gave, and Pat doubled up, coughing and cursing. 'What the hell's got into you, Joe Whelan? You're a madman!'

Joe was panting as well, his colour up. They faced each other in the shadow of the wagons.

'Well, Pat, if it wasn't you, who was it, then?'

Pat Sheehan looked along the track, towards the goods sheds. An engine was getting up steam on the other side of the wagons.

'It wasn't me, Joe!' Pat almost had to shout over the whoomping of the train. 'It could have been anyone. Anyone who knows her, I mean.'

'What the hell's that supposed to mean?'

Joe advanced on Pat, looking as if he was about to grab his throat again.

'Joe, back off.' Pat held his hands up to defend himself. 'I can't be talking if you're going to keep throttling me . . . Look, everyone knows you've been carrying on with that girl. You've been spotted with her, more than once.' Seeing Joe's darkening expression, he hurried on. 'There's no need to be looking like that. Is it my fault if you've been caught out fornicating? How could you, Joe – and be so careless about it? The walls aren't blind, and people will talk. If someone's told Ann, then I'm sorry, though I'm not surprised. But it wasn't me.'

The energy seemed to drain out of Joe and he sagged miserably. 'God knows, Pat, what am I going to do? As if Ann wasn't in enough of a state already.'

'Why d'you do it then, you fool?' Pat demanded. Things seemed simple to Pat Sheehan. Right was right, wrong was wrong. And he was married happily enough.

'I couldn't help myself.' Joe spoke to the cindery ground. 'God knows, I tried.'

'Not hard enough, by the look of things,' Pat said scornfully. 'Ann's a good woman. Shame on ye.'

Joe was turning away as if he had something else on his mind now. He walked off, along the narrow path between the tracks.

'Good luck to you, mate,' Pat Sheehan muttered, rubbing his neck where Joe had squeezed him like a madman. 'Looks as if you're going to need it, you silly old fool.'

Joe staggered back to the goods yard. His blood was up and he was full of explosive rage and frustration. He felt drunk, even though he was dead-sober. His control over his life had been snatched from him. The one thing in the way – the block over which he stumbled again and again – was Kitty Barratt, from whose eyes and scent and body he could not free himself.

He knew she worked somewhere in the big building at the side of the yard and he steered himself there. What was it she did again? Some sort of number-cruncher . . . He lurched into the building, past caring what anyone else thought. His wife was sitting at home, pale as a stunned fish. He had done that: him, no one else. His was the heavy conscience. But there had to be some result from causing such distress. Kitty had to come to him, to be his. The thought of it made tears press at the back of his throat.

People appeared out of rooms. Joe asked, asked again, until he was down in the murky depths of the building. A door was ajar before him. Women young and old hurried in and out.

'Yes?' A matronly figure with spectacles stopped him. 'Who are you looking for?'

'Kitty Barratt. I have a message.'

'She works in there.' The woman inclined her head. 'But . . .'

He was looking into a room full of desks and female heads bowed over calculating machines, fingers punching them very fast, as if they were a kind of musical instrument. For a few seconds everyone looked the same, cogs in a machine, hair colours all blending in. And then he saw her: her hair, her astonishing curving figure, so neat and beautiful at the desk.

'Kitty!' He thought he had just breathed the word like a sigh of appreciation, but heads shot up all around the room, including hers. Those large grey eyes took him in. He saw her face register who he was, and the dismay and disgust that widened her eyes and chased away her initial look of surprise. She sat quite still, her mouth slightly open, seeming to have no idea what to do.

'Kitty, could you come out and speak to me . . .' he began saying, knowing already that he sounded pathetic, instead of commanding, and not like someone with a real message to impart other than: *God, Kitty, I can't live without you. I'm enslaved by you, body and soul; don't make me suffer like this* . . . And she was already shaking her head, her face appalled, looking around for someone to help rid her of this embarrassing spectre.

An older woman with her hair tied back austerely in a bun stepped up to him.

'What is it you want?' she asked sharply.

'I need . . .' He was crumbling, but forced himself to keep going, to stand upright and try to sound like a man who had something sensible to say. 'It's important that I speak to Miss Kitty Barratt.'

The woman glanced at Kitty, who had half-stood up and was shaking her head, mouthing *No*, and Joe was mortified by the look of desperation on her face. All the other eyes in the office were fixed on him. He could feel their curiosity, their amusement. He knew he was setting himself up as food for gossip, but it was too late. He couldn't stop himself.

'*Kitty!*' he begged.

'Do you know this man?' the harridan with the bun asked, and Kitty started to shake her head.

'No – sort of. I mean, he won't leave me alone.' She hung her head.

'Ah now, Kitty, come on!' Joe burst out. 'Don't be like that. Just come out here and talk to me a minute, for God's sake.'

'If you don't leave, now,' the harridan said, 'I shall have to call for assistance. If I were you, I should go without making any more fuss.'

He was trembling. 'Just let me speak to her,' he said in a low voice, appealing to the woman. He looked across at Kitty, his eyes pleading, but she looked away and sat back down on her chair.

'Just go, please – now,' the woman, who seemed to Joe like Kitty's gaoler, commanded him.

He knew he was beaten. But, as he turned, he couldn't help himself. He shouted out, 'Meet me later, Kitty. I'll be waiting for you. I'll wait!'

And then he was outside, scarcely knowing what he was doing.

'What on earth happened today?' Sylvia asked, as soon as she and Kitty were on their way home. News of the incident with Joe Whelan, the guard from Tyseley, had travelled fast. The man had come in, shooting his mouth off, demanding to speak to Kitty Barratt.

'The bloke made a right exhibition of himself, I heard,' Elsie had told Sylvia as they were working together, shifting more sacks of flour. Tiger, the cat, was prowling round inside the wagon, making sure he was not disgraced by overlooking any rats.

'Was he a big bloke, quite old?' Sylvia squatted down

to stroke the cat, which grudgingly accepted this attention.

'I don't know,' Elsie said. 'I never saw him. But he's got it bad, by all accounts, whoever he is.'

As she stood next to Kitty now on the crowded train from Hockley, Sylvia could see that her friend looked upset.

'It's just . . . Oh, Sylvia.' Kitty looked up with big eyes from under the brim of her hat. 'I've never said anything about him, because I thought it was all over . . . He's an older man who just got a thing about me. He wouldn't leave me alone. But it all started around the time my father was . . . you know, the bombing, and I had so many other worries.' Sylvia saw Kitty's eyes fill and she looked away for a moment, trying to gather herself. 'It's quite sad really,' she went on, still tearful. 'He's nearly as old as my father and he thinks he's in love with me.' She looked round anxiously for a moment. 'Oh Lord, I hope he's not the guard on duty today. I thought he'd seen sense; that it was all over. He's not a bad man, but he's just kidding himself. I just haven't known what to do.'

'Oh, poor you!' Sylvia said, squeezing her arm. 'It must have been a shock.'

'It was. He came into the office, demanding to see me, even after Miss James had asked him to leave. I felt such a fool. Everyone was staring. I just didn't know where to put myself.'

Sylvia tried to tease Kitty out of it. 'I suppose you can't help being so pretty that men keep falling in love with you!'

Kitty pulled a face, wiping her eyes. 'But they don't, do they? Not the right ones – men of my own age. Not that there are many of them left around here at

191

the moment. They're either so young they're in short trousers or over the hill.'

'I know,' Sylvia said, 'let's do something nice tonight, cheer ourselves up. Play some games or something.'

'Will Ian be coming round?' Kitty asked.

'I think so, yes. Why?'

'Well, I don't want to be a gooseberry, you know, get in your way. You must both get sick of me being around.'

'Don't be silly!' Sylvia said, affectionately. 'Ian and I will be married and in our own place soon. We'll have all the time in the world. And he's been saying what fun it is to have you around. If we set up some games, Jack'll want to join in – even Dad maybe. Let's make a night of it, shall we? You can put all that trouble out of your mind.'

Kitty looked a lot more cheerful. 'That sounds lovely. All of us playing together!'

Twenty-Five

'Audrey's coming home – she's got leave at last, in a couple of days!' Pauline announced as soon as Sylvia walked in from work, after an early shift. Sylvia could hear the happiness in her mother's voice. 'She says she's got something to tell us.'

'Well, I hope it's good news,' Sylvia said, sitting on the bottom step of the stairs, wearily pulling off her work boots. 'How long's she coming for? She'll want her room.'

'A few days, she says. She's been poorly, apparently.'

'Kitty can come and sleep in mine,' Sylvia said. 'I'll make her up a bed on the floor.'

As she went upstairs, Sylvia felt a tingle of excitement. It would be good to see Audrey. And she knew Audrey would like Kitty!

By the time tea was ready that evening, Kitty was still not home.

'I expect she'll be here soon,' Sylvia said. 'They do keep them very late sometimes.'

'We'd better get on and have it,' her mother said. 'Your father needs his meal. I'll keep some for her.'

They sat round the table in the back room. The evenings were lighter now and the curtains were still open.

Ted looked round the table. 'That girl not here, then?'

'*That girl* has a name, Ted, as you well know.' His wife was spooning something pale onto his plate. 'And the poor wench's not long buried her father, so be kind to her.'

'That's rotten,' Jack said, for once not making fun.

'Pauline,' Ted said, eyeing his plate. '*What* is that?'

Jack snorted with laughter and Sylvia saw her mother stiffen. She rested the spoon for a moment and fixed her husband with a forbidding eye. '*That*, Ted, is potato pie with turnip and a bit of swede . . .'

Sylvia couldn't help smiling with Jack at the gimlet-like stare their mother was directing across the table.

Ted turned his dark eyes innocently upon his wife. 'Any onion, by any chance?'

'One,' she said, digging the spoon determinedly into the pale concoction again. 'Cut up very small. It was the only one we had. And there's a bit of cheese on top.'

'Sounds nice, Mom,' Sylvia said carefully.

'So where's that wench, then?' Ted asked, surrendering to the food. Though he seemed fond of Kitty, he always talked about her in a joking way and Sylvia realized that it was because he was shy of a young woman who was not his daughter.

'Working late, I think,' Sylvia said.

Her father was tucking into his turnip-flavoured meal. 'This is all right, Pauline . . .'

'Thanks very much,' she said tartly. 'We do our best.'

By the time Kitty came in it was nearly half-past nine and dark. They had started to worry. Ian had come round, and Sylvia was with him in the kitchen.

'I'm so sorry, Mrs Whitehouse,' Sylvia heard Kitty

saying. 'There was ever such a lot to do today – it all just got piled up on us and we had to stay till it was finished.'

'It's all right, love,' Pauline was saying. 'It can't be helped, if there's a job to do, can it? I've kept you a bit of tea . . .'

Sylvia and Ian jumped apart as her mother and Kitty came in.

'*Sorry!*' Kitty said to them. 'Oh dear, there's no peace with me around, is there? I'll take it in the back and leave you to it.'

'It's all right,' Ian said politely. 'It sounds as if you've had a long day?'

'Oh,' Kitty wilted, 'it's endless. Piles and piles of it. Thank you, Mrs Whitehouse, that looks lovely.'

'Well, you're the first person who thinks so,' Pauline said.

'We'll come and keep you company, won't we, Ian?' Sylvia said, pulling him by the hand.

'If you say so, my dear.'

Kitty laughed. She looked rather flushed, Sylvia thought, as if she had run from the bus stop.

Sylvia was still feeling guilty that she had not been able to go to the funeral with Kitty. It had been held in Wylde Green, right in the middle of one of Sylvia's morning shifts. Kitty had asked timidly, as if she didn't want to bother her, when her shifts were that week, and then said, 'Oh dear, that's a pity. The funeral's on Tuesday morning.' Sylvia had not liked to ask for a change at such short notice, when it was not for a close relative.

'I'm sure Mom would go with you, if you like?' Sylvia had offered. And Pauline had said the same, but Kitty had refused even to contemplate it.

'You've done far too much for me already,' she had

said. 'And it's such a long way to go. I've got Auntie there, and her son. She's quite a kind old soul really. But thank you for offering – it's ever so good of you.'

Sylvia noticed now, as Kitty ate, that there was something very tense about her mood. She looked flushed and on edge. Poor thing, Sylvia thought, it must be terrible, being so alone; she's ever so brave. And Kitty kept up a cheerful conversation, asking Ian about his day. She seemed fascinated by his job and often asked him about it.

'I wish I'd been able to do something like that,' she said as they had a cup of tea after her meal.

'It takes quite a bit of training,' Ian said, rather stiffly. Sylvia realized that Kitty enquiring about his work was one thing, but her imagining that she might actually be able to do it herself was quite another, in Ian's book! Sylvia chuckled inwardly. Ian was not convinced that any woman could manage a job like his.

'Kitty's very brainy, you know,' she told him. 'Not like me.'

'I've always been quite good with numbers,' Kitty said. 'But I'm sure there's a lot more to it than that.'

'Yes, a good deal,' Ian said rather dismissively.

'You must be ever so clever,' Kitty said. Her eyes were shining and Sylvia thought how pretty she was.

'Oh well, I don't know about that,' Ian said, crossing one leg over another. He was enjoying the attention.

'Yes, you do,' Sylvia gave his elbow a playful shove. 'You know you're a clever clogs all right.'

Ian laughed. 'Well . . .'

'I like clever men,' Kitty said, getting up to take the cups and saucers into the kitchen. 'I always think they should be cleverer than me – and you certainly are, Ian!'

'Kitty,' Sylvia said, seeing a long, dark smudge down

her back, 'you've got a nasty mark on your blouse. How on earth did you do that?'

Kitty looked startled for a moment. 'Oh no!' She twisted round to try and see it. 'I'll go and wash it. I must've rubbed up against something at the yard – you know what it's like. I'll just finish the washing-up, and then I'm off to bed. Night, all!'

As soon as she was safely in Audrey's room with the door shut, Kitty stood by the cheval mirror and twisted round to look at the back of her blouse. Tutting with annoyance, she slumped down onto the floral eiderdown on the bed. All her smiling cheerfulness vanished. She lay back, exhausted and dispirited.

Never, ever was she going to let Joe Whelan any-where near her again. He had lost any sign of caution or common sense, barging into the offices like that, making a complete mockery of her and of himself. She had wanted to die with shame. And to cap it all, he was waiting for her when she came out of work, lurking around like an old dog, even though she had made it clear she never wanted to see him again. Her cheeks burned with humiliation, thinking about what had happened.

'For goodness' sake, Joe!' she erupted as soon as they were far enough away along the street. 'Haven't you made enough of an exhibition of us both today?'

And now he looked so slumped and defeated. The man she had initially got to know at least had more dignity about him. She marched on, trying to get as far as possible away from the yard and anyone they might know. Fortunately there was a distraction on Pitsford Street. A horse had fallen, pulling a cart up the slimy cobbles at the steep end of the road. There was a commotion and a crowd trying to help.

'Ah, don't be like that, Kitty,' Joe said, trying to keep up with her. 'You don't know how I feel. I can't live without seeing you. Why're you being like this?' He tugged at her sleeve to stop her and she shook him off.

'Because . . .' She turned on him, fiercely. She wanted to shout at him: *Because you're an old man – it's an embarrassment having you following me around, and I don't want to see you any more!* But his face was so wretched, and she knew he wasn't really a nasty man. She couldn't say it like that.

'I can't stop thinking of you, girl.' They stopped at the corner of a road, by a wall. 'I can't think of anything else. You're sending me mad, so you are.'

'Joe,' she said desperately, but more gently. She *had* to be rid of him. The whole thing had become tiresome to her: he was pathetic and a burden. And gossip was flying around the yard. 'We can't keep on like this, can we? I'm young, and you're married. It's just not on, is it?'

Joe put his head down, as if in acknowledgement of the truth of her words. He was leaning against the wall with one hand; with the other he lifted his cap off and wiped his arm across his forehead. 'God!' he said miserably. 'God in heaven. She knows – my wife.'

'Oh, Joe – no!' Kitty was horrified. This was all becoming too real, too messy and nasty. She longed for him to turn and walk away, to vanish.

'Come with me.' He took her arm and tugged on it. 'I know it's got to stop, Kitty. It will stop – from today. But have pity on a man. I need you: one last time, I promise. Just do it for me, just once more. I worship you, Kitty. Just set me right and I'll leave you alone.'

'What?' she said, horrified. But she could see that he

was in such a state that he could not think straight or master himself. 'What d'you mean? Where?'

'Anywhere,' he said. They walked a short distance, then he pulled her in through the gates of the cemetery and along to a deserted corner.

Now, lying on Audrey's bed, her eyes tight shut, Kitty could not stop remembering Joe's frantic panting and thrusting against her. She had just let him, to get it over with, so that she could say goodbye and that would be that. He had pulled off her cardigan and undone her blouse, which rubbed against the wall and must've got soiled in the process. Her underwear still felt damp and sticky from the results of his exertions.

Kitty turned on her side and curled up, miserably. She'd have to go and wash out her things when no one else was likely to notice. But at least that was over. She was shot of him.

'Don't come near me again, Joe,' she'd told him afterwards. Now that he had had what he wanted, he was full of agreement.

'I know it's wrong,' he said humbly. 'But you're a very special girl, Kitty.' In parting, he kissed her cheek so sweetly that she almost liked him again.

She lay now, feeling dirty and wrung out with exhaustion, and thought about the meal she had just eaten, sitting there with Sylvia and Ian. Sylvia with her man, who thought he was so clever and superior. Little goody-two-shoes Sylvia had everything. Kitty's hand grasped at the eiderdown and she held a handful of it tightly. She was filled with a savage, bitter feeling and her mouth twisted.

When she first met Ian she had thought him a rather boring old stick. She could see that he thought himself a cut above Sylvia and her family, however polite he was.

He was quite an attractive man, though: nice and tall, with good strong shoulders and, especially when he smiled, a pleasant-looking face. How would it feel to be taken in the arms of Ian, a tall, lithe man like that, instead of an old one like Joe? *Hello, Ian*, she imagined herself saying and moving closer to him, closing her eyes as she lifted her face to him. And she could win him: he would be captivated, full of desire, unable to help himself . . .

Kitty forced herself to her feet to get undressed. Sylvia was such a dreaming, trusting sort, she thought. She never suspected the worst of anyone. It had been so easy to convince Sylvia last week that she was spending the day at Wylde Green, at her father's funeral. She had set off, making them think she was off across town, when in fact she had spent the day at work as usual. It would never occur to them that she was not telling the truth – and she certainly didn't want them thinking otherwise.

Twenty-Six

'Look who's here!' Pauline called as Sylvia walked in, and a moment later Audrey appeared out of the back room.

'Oh, you made it,' Sylvia cried, and went to hug her. 'Look at you!' She stood back and admired the smart WAAF uniform. Audrey had taken her cap off, but she had kept her hair up, fashionably rolled back from her forehead and neatly rolled at the back. She obviously wanted the family to see her at her smartest. 'Ooh, you feel thin, Audrey. Are they looking after you properly?'

'I'm perfectly fine,' Audrey said, and Sylvia could see that she did look fine, and happy and excited. 'I've just had a dose of the flu, that's all. Before that, I was putting on weight on stodgy WAAF food. Anyway, look at you, as well.' Sylvia was still dressed in her work overalls.

For the moment they felt almost like strangers and greeted each other with new respect. They all sat round drinking tea and catching up with each other.

'I'm beginning to feel left out,' Jack complained. 'It's a bit much that I'm not old enough to join up.'

His mother turned on him. 'You want to stay out of uniform, my lad,' she said. 'It's different for the girls. Audrey's not going to be flying any planes, are you?'

'Not very likely,' she said. 'But that's what I was going to tell you. I'm retraining – as a balloon operator!'

They all looked suitably stunned.

'What's a . . . ?' her mother said. 'What, you mean the barrage balloons? They don't have women doing that – it's a nasty heavy job.'

'They do now,' Audrey said. 'And they train at Cardington, so I don't even have to leave. I talked my CO into letting me transfer, because they're recruiting. Anyone can take over the clerical stuff.'

Sylvia chose not to rise to this remark. Although she knew she couldn't possibly do the clerical stuff, Audrey had not deliberately set out to be mean to her. In fact, Audrey seemed more relaxed and easy-going than Sylvia had ever seen her before.

'Well, I never,' their mother said. Sitting there in her apron, she suddenly seemed rather small compared with her two budding daughters. 'Oh, Audrey love, do be careful. I hope you're going to be all right.'

'Well, yes,' Audrey laughed. 'I hope so too. But I'm sick to the back teeth of mouldering away in that office, I can tell you.'

'So who's this Kitty person?' Audrey asked later. 'Mom says she was bombed out?'

Sylvia explained a little. 'Don't worry – she'll be moving out of your room.'

Kitty came back shortly and they were introduced. Sylvia was rather annoyed with Audrey. Despite Kitty's sweet insistence that she must have her room back, Audrey was a bit offhand with her, Sylvia thought. She wondered if Audrey felt that she had been replaced in some way, which was of course ridiculous.

Audrey settled in, rested, popped out to see a few friends who were still about, for a while that first evening, and enjoyed making a fuss of all the animals.

'No eggs taste as good as ours!' she said, looking fondly at the hens.

The second evening, once everyone was home, they all sat round after tea, with the teapot on the table in its knitted cosy, listening to Audrey's stories. Sylvia could feel her excitement about all her new independence and new friends. She talked about her pals she shared her sleeping quarters with, and about a new friend she had made called Dorrie.

'She's a scream,' Audrey said. 'We were in the sick quarters, had the place to ourselves, and it was the best rest cure I've ever had.'

'It sounds as if you have more fun than work, down there,' Mom observed from over her knitting.

'Yes – d'you ever actually *do* any work?' Jack asked. Dad chuckled.

They chatted and teased the evening away. Before it was too late, Audrey got up.

'I'm going to hit the sack,' she said.

She looked across at Sylvia. 'Come and chat to me for a minute, sis.' She rolled her eyes upwards to indicate that she meant in her room.

'All right,' Sylvia said. Surprised and pleased, she looked at Kitty, hoping she didn't mind. 'But I'll need my bed soon too. I'm all in. I'll be up soon, Kitty.'

'You two go and catch up!' Kitty said, smiling.

Sylvia sat on the bed in Audrey's room and watched as her sister rearranged a few things pointedly, as if to say: *This is* my *room*. She asked Sylvia about work and talked about how excited she was to be changing trades again, chatting as she leaned towards the mirror to wipe off her mascara. Sylvia watched her sister: her tall, lean body, so intimately familiar, yet now also, in some ways, a stranger to her. Audrey looked slender and strong and even more magnificent, she thought.

'So,' Audrey said. 'All set for the wedding?'

'I think so. Marjorie's doing a lovely job on the dress. Kitty's helping her too – sewing on some pretty little pearl beads. She's being such a help. You are going to be here, aren't you? Or is being a bridesmaid not a priority in the WAAF?'

'It should be all right,' Audrey said. 'I've already put in a request. Come hell or high water, I'll be here, kid.'

Sylvia laughed. 'You'd better! Your dress would be far too long for Kitty, if I had to get her to stand in for you.'

After a pause Audrey spoke in a different tone, her face still close to the mirror. 'You know, you want to watch that one.'

'Which one?' Sylvia said, but she already knew Audrey must mean Kitty. Her heart pumped faster with the resentful irritation that only her sister could arouse in her. There she was, thinking they were going to have a nice cosy chat. 'What d'you mean?'

Audrey stood upright suddenly and their eyes met each other's in the glass. 'You want to watch her with Ian.'

'*Ian?*' Sylvia burst out laughing. 'Who – Kitty? Audrey, what the hell are you on about?'

'Ian: remember him? The rather pompous – there, I've said it, sorry, but he *is* – man who is supposed to be your fiancé.' She explained that she had been out that afternoon to see the mother of a school friend who had also joined up. 'When I came back in, I knew Mom was out because she'd gone shopping, but I could hear voices. There they were, the two of them, in the back room, at the table, thick as thieves, playing checkers or chess or something.'

Sylvia felt a cold, instinctive plunge of fear inside her. Her instincts raced before her mind, which quickly caught up and told her not to be so ridiculous.

'Ian was here? This afternoon?' she asked carefully. 'No one said.'

Audrey turned round then. Sylvia tried to find some joking or malice in her face, to say that her sister was trying to stir up trouble. But instead she saw genuine concern, almost an apology for saying anything. 'He was here all right.'

Sylvia struggled to make sense of this. 'I suppose he thought I was on an early shift as well and came to see me . . .' She rallied herself. 'Look, Aud, I don't know what you have against Kitty. She's a friend; she's so nice and she does ever such a lot to help round here. It's not what you think – that's ridiculous!'

'Sylvia.' Audrey came and sat next to her, talking very seriously. 'I'm not trying to make trouble for you, honest to God. I'm not jealous that you're getting married or anything like that, as you might be thinking. You know me,' she gave a little laugh that made Sylvia feel suddenly fond of her. 'Not one to get myself tied down, if I can help it. But that girl, Kitty, is a piece of work. Take my word for it. I've seen the type. There are a few of them around me at Cardington. Nice as pie to your face, but . . . There's just something about her that's not—' She stopped as if she didn't want to say too much. 'You need to watch her, that's all I'm saying.'

'Oh, for goodness' sake,' Sylvia said, getting up to go. 'I've heard enough of this rubbish. Why d'you have to come home and be so poisonous about my best friend?'

She went, feeling furious and churned up, to her own room, where she found Kitty climbing into her temporary bed on the floor. Kitty looked so sweet and pretty, and she glanced up and smiled as Sylvia came in. Almost all Sylvia's doubts melted away. What on earth was Audrey going on about? She was imagining things; she'd just breezed in and was reading the worst into everything. But Sylvia just wanted to make sure.

'I was just chatting to Audrey,' Sylvia said, pulling back her bedcovers and adding casually. 'She said Ian was here earlier?'

'Oh, yes – didn't I say?' Kitty said through a yawn. 'He was looking for you. I think he thought you were on an early . . .'

'I did tell him,' Sylvia said, lying down.

'He must have forgotten. 'Anyway, he didn't stay long – just for a little chat. He's so *polite*, isn't he? A real charmer. I think he felt it would be rude not to stay and talk to me, even though of course it was you he really wanted to see. Then Audrey arrived, so he thought it was safe to leave, I think. He seemed a bit scared of her! He's a nice chap – you're very lucky, Sylvia.'

Although Sylvia was worn out from her day's work, she lay awake for a long time. She tried to recapture her fury with Audrey. How dare she come back here, bossing people about and making accusations, saying such horrible things about her friend when she barely even knew her? But she had to admit to herself that Audrey, though bossy and opinionated, was not small-minded or spiteful. It was not in her nature.

She looked up into the darkness and thought about all the times Ian had been here lately. Was Kitty flirting with him? She was certainly her charming self with him, giggling at his jokes, full of life when he was about and smiling at him. But that was just Kitty being Kitty, wasn't it? Audrey must just have got it wrong.

But it was a long time before she slept, and even then she had shapeless, uneasy dreams.

'Post – for you, Audrey!' Jack called the next morning. Sylvia heard the conversation, though she was still in bed. Kitty had gone off to work, but she had the luxury of a lie-in.

'For me?' She heard Audrey run down the stairs, but Jack must have met her halfway up.

'A postcard.' Jack spoke teasingly. 'From someone called Dorrie.'

'Oh!' Audrey sounded pleased. 'She's my friend – at the base.'

'Goodness,' Mom's voice floated up from the hall. 'You've only been away a couple of days.'

'Not the same around here without you,' Jack read, before Audrey snatched it from his hand.

'Get off, Afterthought! It's none of your business.' She came upstairs again and shut herself in her room.

Audrey was obviously very caught up in her WAAF life, Sylvia thought. She felt a little wistful, wondering if she should have joined up. But to do what? She was better off where she was, she knew that really.

The rest of Audrey's leave passed without any upsets. Sylvia did not want to fall out with her, so she said nothing more about Kitty. Audrey went back to the WAAF, promising to get home again for the wedding. Life hurried on, busy at the Goods Yard and at home, full of talk and laughter with Kitty and the family, and snatched times with Ian.

When she next saw Ian, at the weekend, she found

herself wanting him jealously all to herself. She insisted that they went out, leaving Kitty in the house. Sylvia wanted it to be a happy afternoon, like so many they had had before, but both of them were tired and out of sorts.

'Let's just walk,' Ian said, once they'd left the house. 'It's a nice enough day.'

Sylvia couldn't think of a better suggestion. She felt tired and strangely lifeless. However much she told herself what Audrey had said about Kitty was utter nonsense, the creeping doubt had been eating away at her all week. But she was angry with herself for allowing Audrey to put bad thoughts about Kitty into her head, when Kitty had been nothing but a staunch friend.

This was the time of year when the trees were in leaf and all the flowers were coming out and she was supposed to be full of plans. She and Ian were getting married in just a few weeks! But she felt as if she was shrivelling inside, and however much she told herself not to be so stupid, the feeling would not go away.

Taking Ian's arm, Sylvia walked along, trying to be bright and cheerful. Ian had his long coat on and his trilby and looked very distinguished. As ever she felt a surge of pride in being seen with him. She asked him bright little questions about his work – she had long since realized that he did not really want to hear about hers. Ian answered wearily. Things felt out of sorts. They walked the streets, hardly noticing where they were going.

'Are there any other things we need to do for the wedding?' Sylvia asked after a silence.

'Oh, I don't know,' Ian said. 'All the important things seem to be under control. All that remains is the stuff you girls like to see about: dresses and suchlike.'

'Yes, I suppose . . .' Sylvia said. Ian seemed so absent-minded about it all. Was it just that? Sylvia asked herself. Or was she reading the worst into his every mood now? 'Ian?' She stopped him and made him turn to her. 'Is everything all right?'

He hesitated for a second, then put his hands on her shoulders. 'Of course, Wizzy. Why not?' But Sylvia felt there was a stiffness to his response.

She looked up into his face, finding herself suddenly on the brink of tears. 'You would tell me if there was anything wrong, wouldn't you? I'd hate to think . . .' She couldn't go on, her throat ached so much. 'It's just, you seem so far away.'

He looked down at her and gave a tired smile. He squeezed her shoulders, then reached down and pecked her on the lips. 'Not at all! I'm just a bit tired, that's all. Blame work. Blame Hitler. One way or another, he's wearing all of us out.'

Twenty-Seven

'What's the matter with you, Sylv?' Pauline asked, seeing her daughter staring into space as if she was in a trance. 'You're not having second thoughts – about Ian, I mean?'

'Oh – no!' Sylvia said. 'I do feel a bit funny, though,' she admitted. She could not explain it. It was as if there was something happening just out of her reach, like the whistle that a sheepdog can hear, too high for the human ear, but which alters the direction of the flock. 'I don't really know why. Wedding nerves, I suppose. Or just tiredness. Now the raids have stopped, maybe it's a reaction.'

The Germans had turned their attention to invading Russia. 'Huh,' Ted had said when they heard the news. 'Those flaming Reds can have a turn for a bit.'

'Hmm,' Pauline spoke in a muffled voice, searching for something in one of the low kitchen cupboards. 'The girls have been a bit peculiar as well. Isabella's laying like mad and Victoria hasn't produced for days.'

Sylvia smiled at the way her mother measured everyone by the chickens. 'Well, I don't think I'm going to lay an egg, anyway,' she said.

Mom straightened up and gave her a look. 'I should hope not,' she said.

*

A few days later she and Kitty travelled into work, chatting easily together. Over the weeks that had passed Sylvia had put her mind at rest over her silly suspicions and what Audrey had said. Trust Audrey to make a drama! She had just jumped to the worst possible conclusion. During those weeks Ian had been round and they had spent plenty of time together alone, and things had felt much as they always had. And now Kitty was talking excitedly about a soldier called Bill, home on leave, whom she had met last night when she and some of her fellow office workers went out for a drink in town.

'*Ever* so dishy,' Kitty enthused as she and Sylvia were getting ready for bed. She was pink-cheeked and lit up with excitement. 'He's blond and very tall. And he asked me for my address, so I'm hoping for some letters.'

'Oh, that's lovely, Kitty,' Sylvia said, truly pleased for her. It was surprising that someone as lovely-looking as Kitty would not have a young man – except that there was a young-man shortage.

Now, as they stood packed into the bus, Kitty was still talking about Bill. 'I suppose I'm going to have to be writing letters – one of those long-distance relationships. All rather romantic, though!'

'That's one way of getting to know one another, isn't it?' Sylvia said. 'And the boys in the forces love getting letters. Mom keeps going on at me to write to Laurie Gould.' She rolled her eyes.

Kitty frowned. 'What – Mrs Gould's son next door? I thought you liked him?'

'Well, of course I do. Laurie's all right. But I can't imagine that he'd really want to hear from me.'

When they got to the Goods Yard they parted and Kitty went to her office and Sylvia to the Amenities block to leave her things in the mess room.

Elsie was in there and she greeted Sylvia. Sylvia felt a pang of guilt when she saw her. She would have liked to spend more time with Elsie, but she was so caught up with Kitty. Elsie had a look on her face of someone who knows something grim and wants to tell you about it.

'Have you heard?' she said, after a few moments. She leaned round from tightening her boot laces.

'I don't think so,' Sylvia joked. 'Or, if I have, it went straight past me.'

Elsie stood up. 'You know that bloke, the big Irish one who came and barged into the offices that day?'

'Irish bloke? He's not been round again, has he?' Kitty certainly hadn't mentioned there being any trouble.

'No,' Elsie said. 'I don't think so. He had a thing about one of the girls down there. Thing is, Sylv, some-one said that the name he was asking for was that girl who's living with you: Kitty Barratt.'

Though this was no surprise, a fat worm of unease turned in Sylvia's stomach. Kitty had made light of what had happened, saying that he was just someone who had a bit of a thing for her. So far as she knew, everything had settled down long ago.

'Well, he did cause a bit of a nuisance to her,' Sylvia said. 'What about him?'

Elsie sat down on the bench. 'It's been going round that he was involved with some girl here: if not Kitty, then someone else. His wife's not been well and . . . Well, apparently he got up the other morning and found she'd – you know . . . done herself in.'

'No!' Sylvia cried, appalled. 'Oh no!' She sank down on the bench beside Elsie, who was not a gossip-monger and looked genuinely upset.

'I thought he looked quite a nice sort of a man,' Elsie said.

'How did she – the wife, I mean . . . ?'

Elsie made a gesture towards the ceiling. 'They say he had to cut her down quick, so his kids didn't see anything. There's six of them apparently. I mean, those poor kids . . .'

Sylvia heard that Elsie was tearful, and the thought of all those bereft little ones made her feel like crying herself.

All that day while she was working she kept thinking about the man, Joe Whelan, and his family, and the sadness of it weighed upon her. It was the shunters who had heard the news, because of Pat Sheehan being Joe's cousin. Even amidst all the busy day's work, the news dragged everyone down. With the war causing so many deaths, this one seemed especially cruel and unnecessary. Sylvia didn't see Kitty until the end of the shift, but all the time uncomfortable thoughts were niggling at her. What the hell had happened, and what did Kitty have to do with it?

'So,' Sylvia said, stacking up the plates near the sink, where Kitty was getting ready to wash up. 'You'll have heard?'

She deliberately started this conversation about Joe Whelan in front of her mother. She was starting to realize that when she was alone with Kitty she was so drawn in by her friend that Kitty could have told her anything and she would have believed it. She still reproached herself for feeling any suspicions about Kitty. But this was over something truly serious.

'Heard what?' Kitty said, casually swishing soap in the water.

'About that guard, Joe Whelan.'

She saw Kitty's shoulders stiffen. Then she turned, her face full of a sad concern, which Sylvia found reassuring.

'I didn't know you'd heard. It's absolutely *awful*, isn't it?'

'What's that?' Pauline asked. 'Not more bad news!'

Kitty turned and leaned her back against the sink, drying her hands on a cloth. 'It's so sad. There's a guard, from Tyseley, who often used to be on the passenger train from Hockley. I haven't seen him lately. He's . . . well, quite a bit older than me. And I'm afraid he got rather keen on me, even though I kept telling him . . .' Her eyes widened. 'It was so difficult. There was a time, a few months ago, when he started following me about – turned up at the yard a couple of times. I don't know if you ever saw him, Sylvia. I had to be quite hard on him and tell him to leave me alone.' She looked down sadly for a moment.

Pauline perched on one of the chairs at the table and Sylvia could see her mother listening attentively. It felt like a sweet moment, with them all talking and confiding together. Sylvia felt the tension begin to ease inside her. There was an explanation after all – Kitty was not responsible.

'Anyway, he came back to the yard a little while ago. I'd almost forgotten about it all by then, so I got a terrible shock when he came bursting into our office, demanding to talk to me! Miss James, who's in charge of our office, made him leave. I don't know why he was behaving like that, but Miss James saved me from a very awkward situation.'

'Oh dear,' Pauline said with a sigh. 'Older men do make terrible fools of themselves sometimes. And you're such a lovely little thing. Is it any wonder?'

'Well, I don't know about that,' Kitty said. 'But I do

know that I never gave him any encouragement. But now . . .' She put her hands over her face. 'Oh, it's so dreadful I can hardly bear to think about it!'

Sylvia and her mother exchanged glances.

'His wife's taken her own life,' Sylvia explained gently. She saw her mother's face stretch in shock.

Kitty burst into tears on hearing this and they moved close to comfort her, standing each side of her. Kitty sobbed for a few moments, then tried to speak, wiping the tears from her cheeks.

'I've been asking myself over and over again: was it my fault? I never asked for anything from that man – I just wanted him to leave me alone.'

'Why didn't you say?' Sylvia asked, with her arm round Kitty's shoulders. 'You never told us you were having all this trouble.'

'Well, it was embarrassing; and I didn't want to bother you when you've been so kind.'

There was a click and slam of the front door.

'That'll be Ted coming in,' Pauline said.

'Pauline?'

'I'm in the back, love,' she called.

Ted appeared at the kitchen door, took one look at Kitty's tearful face and the huddle of women and retreated, saying, 'Oh good Lord!'

They all rolled their eyes at each other.

'Do you think it's my fault, Mrs W.?' Kitty said pleadingly.

'Not by the sound of things,' Pauline said on her way out to see her husband. 'But it's a terrible sad thing, that it is.'

Twenty-Eight

June 1941

Kitty sat in her room, waiting for the rest of the household to settle down for the night. Since saying a yawning goodnight and going upstairs, she had changed from her usual skirt and blouse into a little black dress, which she had bought and kept hidden in the back of the wardrobe. She had redone her make-up and pinned her hair back. It looked both neat and stylish. She knew her new man: he liked women to be women. Not like poor old Sylvia these days. Those awful trousers that the lady porters had to wear made them look anything but ladylike.

She got up and twisted this way and that in front of the cheval mirror. Oh yes, she thought, smiling at herself in the sleek black dress; yes, *sir*. She patted her hair, dabbed eau de cologne behind her ears and sat on the bed again, drumming her fingers on her thighs. Audrey's alarm clock on the dressing table said a quarter-past ten. She had told him she would be able to get out by half-past at the latest. Time crawled. The clock's tick seemed deafening and its sound increased her inner tension. She wished she could think of something to do – anything – to pass the time until she could risk creeping downstairs. Sylvia would soon be asleep, because work always tired her out. But tonight it seemed to take forever for Mr and Mrs Whitehouse to get themselves up to bed. Feet thumped up and down the stairs and Pauline's voice came through her door, 'Well, Ted, where on earth have you put it? It must be somewhere . . .' and muffled replies from him.

'Go to sleep all of you,' Kitty hissed. At *last* the door of their bedroom closed.

She drew in a deep, ragged breath. *This is living!* she thought, with a little smile. This excitement, of a man wanting you. It lit up everything: the gloom of war and the tedium of her office job. It made her feel she was doing what she was put on this earth for. Kitty Barratt – *femme fatale.* She giggled to herself.

Finally, at almost half-past ten, she got up and checked her face and hair once more in the mirror, picked up her raincoat and shoes and clicked off the light. The door opened with a squeak, which make her wince. God help her, if Mrs W. or Sylvia came out! She'd find some excuse, though: she was good at that. Taking some of her weight off the stairs by leaning on the banisters, she slipped downstairs and out of the front door, quietly leaving it on the latch. It was a mild June night – damp, but not raining.

As arranged, she walked a little way along the street, towards Kings Heath Park, before she heard his voice, low and very cautious. 'Kitty?'

'Yes, coming!' she replied, also very softly. There was a half-moon in the sky. In its light she could see a shadowy figure moving towards her, tall and handsome, just the sort of man she had always wanted. Ian Westley had come out to meet her, and her alone.

As soon as he came close, he took her in his arms. 'Kitty, darling! There's a girl. You got out all right?'

'Yes – I had a bit of a wait, but I think they're all asleep.'

He was looking down at her and in the dim, silvery light she could see his entranced expression.

'God, you're lovely,' he said. 'I'd have waited up all night to see you – don't you worry.' His lips sought out hers and Kitty kissed him back, enthusiastically. Ian held her close for a moment and then said, 'It's a bit awkward meeting like this.'

'I know,' Kitty said in a shamed voice. 'But it's so hard to know what else to do, in the circumstances. There's nowhere to go really, is there?'

'Come and walk in the park – it's quite dry,' Ian said, taking her arm. He glanced at the sky. 'Not quite a bomber's moon, but it's clear enough. At least they don't seem to be coming over nowadays.'

'Or nowanights,' Kitty added, and Ian laughed, squeezing her arm.

'You're a sparky little thing, aren't you?'

They walked to the end of the road and slipped into the park where the darkness was almost total, but where it felt safe and private. Kitty was electrified with excitement. She knew what Ian wanted of her. Sylvia had told her enough about his frustration with her; that he was an energetic man who needed a woman. And Kitty planned to give it to him, but not yet. It was much too soon. She didn't want Ian to think she was fast. She would have to play her timing very carefully, because she had real designs on him. He was a catch – and she hadn't got long. Ian was getting married. She must play things to the letter.

'Ian, dear,' she said, as he stopped in a dark spot along the path to kiss her again. She stopped him for a moment.

'I – oh dear! This is awful. But I can't seem to help what I feel for you . . .'

'God, Kitty, I can't get you out of my mind,' Ian said fervently. 'You're just such a girl, a *woman*, I mean. Just the touch of you!' He ran his hands down her sides, over the generous curve of her hips.

'I know,' Kitty made an anguished sound. 'But I feel so badly about Sylvia. We can't go on like this, deceiving her and carrying on behind her back. You're getting married – it's only a matter of weeks now! Her dress . . . all the arrangements.'

Ian groaned and leaned his forehead against Kitty's. 'I know. I feel a complete heel. It's caddish behaviour towards Sylvia, and I know it. But I've never met a girl like you before, Kitty, one who's made me feel so completely . . . Oh!' He flung his head back, ecstatically. 'So free, and full of . . .' He seized her hand and tugged it. 'Full of joy and silliness. Come on – let's dance!' He seemed about to start twirling her round.

'Ian!' Kitty stopped him. What the hell was he playing at? She was full of the need to pin him down, to know that she would *have* him – if not now, then sometime soon. 'Don't, please. We must talk. This is terrible. We are both deceiving Sylvia, and she's such a good person,' she appealed to him, wondering if he could see her wide eyes in the darkness. She needed Ian to see her as a helpless innocent. 'She's been such a good friend to me.' She put on her most imploring tone. 'Taking me in after all my troubles. I wouldn't want to hurt her for the world. Whatever we do, we can't go on deceiving her. We'll have to tell her the truth.'

'I know,' Ian said, immediately sobering down. They walked along together. 'Sylvia will come round. She's a good sort. I'd only make her unhappy in the long run, if we were to marry and find we weren't suited. You have to go where your heart leads, don't you? And my heart . . .' He swept her into his arms again and kissed the end of her nose. 'My heart leads very much to you, Kitty Barratt. You are the woman for me.'

'Oh, Ian,' Kitty said, her heart leaping with triumph and relief. Ian was the sort of man who would look after her: a professional man with a good job. He would devote himself to her. 'You are so wonderful. And I know you're definitely the man for me. The moment I saw you, I had that feeling – did you know, the way I did?'

'No, my darling, I didn't, but I do now. I certainly do.'

Later in the night something woke Sylvia. She opened her eyes, suddenly wide awake, though she didn't know why. All seemed quiet, but then . . . Was that a faint movement she could hear? Maybe it was Mom, or someone else, going to use the bathroom.

She decided to go herself, to settle herself down. She got up, not bothering with slippers. On the landing she almost bashed straight into someone in the dark. Both of them exclaimed, with loud gasps.

'Is that you, Kitty?' Sylvia hissed. Whoever it was had grasped hold of her arm and smelled strongly of eau de cologne.

'Yes,' Kitty whispered.

'God you made me jump!' She could feel that Kitty was fully dressed. 'What the hell're you doing?'

'I've just – look, come into my room a minute.'

They crept into Audrey's room and Kitty switched on the light. For a few moments they squinted at each other. Kitty was holding her shoes in her right hand, with her left clutching the two sides of her cardigan together as if to keep warm. She was all dolled up in something Sylvia had never seen before.

'Oh dear, caught in the act!' Kitty said. Sylvia could see that she was pink-cheeked and bright-eyed. 'Naughty, naughty me, sneaking out . . .' She put her shoes down quietly and turned to Sylvia with a coy expression. 'Only Bill had another one-day leave and used it specially to come and see me – can you believe it! He's being posted tomorrow and he doesn't know where, the poor thing. Oh, Sylvia – it's so awful, all this uncertainty. You're so lucky that your feller is reserved.'

She sank down on the side of the bed and tears welled in her eyes as she looked up at Sylvia, whose emotions were immediately ones of sympathy and sorrow. Poor Kitty – so many sad and difficult things seemed to happen to her. Sylvia sat on the bed beside her, her eyes full of concern. She didn't even think to ask how Kitty had known that Bill had turned up so suddenly.

'Oh, don't worry,' Kitty said. 'You mustn't stay up losing sleep over me. I'll be all right in the morning. Only,' she sounded tearful again, 'I think I love Bill, and I'm going to miss him *so* much.'

Twenty-Nine

July 1941

There would never be a day in the following months when Sylvia would not ask herself how she had missed the betrayal going on right under her nose.

One ordinary July day Sylvia was on an early shift, barrowing loads as usual. A week of good weather had broken up into storms, and the Goods Yard was soaking wet and filthy with churned-up mud. Steam from the locomotives met the clouds as if they were long-lost relatives, and the smell of smuts and mud seemed more intense on the air.

She worked away, enjoying the sense of power that she had now in her body. Her limbs had grown thicker and stronger and she felt at home in the place. Even Froggy Bainton had had to accept that the women could do their jobs and were not to be mocked.

Kitty was on a late that day and their paths did not cross. Madge, whom Sylvia was working with, arrived at work with a shiner on her left eye and the ridge of her cheek badly swollen. Apart from muttering darkly about a disagreement with Tone, she scarcely said a word all day, which Sylvia found unnerving, but she was too scared to ask anything. It made for a long, silent shift, though.

Teatime at home came and went without Kitty. They ate without her, as shifts and transport were all unpredictable.

'They *are* working late tonight,' Pauline remarked as eight o'clock came and went. They read and listened to the wireless. Ted rustled the paper and Pauline was unravelling an old grey jumper to knit up into something else. 'I think I'll do socks,' she said to no one in particular.

It wasn't until much later that they really started to wonder.

'Mom, she didn't come in earlier and just fall asleep, did she?' Sylvia said, as the clock hands were inching towards ten-thirty.

'I never heard her come in,' her mother said. 'But I s'pose she might've done. It's a bit late now – don't wake her, if she's fast asleep.'

'I'll just check,' Sylvia said, getting up with a yawn. She was already undressed for bed and padded upstairs in her slippers.

She slid open the door of Kitty's room and listened, not liking to switch on the light. Was that breathing she could hear? The clock was ticking loudly on the chest of drawers. Moving to the bed, she gently ran a hand along it. The mattress was cold and unoccupied.

Once she had turned on the light, it took her moments to make sense of what she saw. The bed was empty, as she had half-expected. But so was the chair and the chest of drawers, other than the few things Audrey had left. Kitty's usual chaotic mess of stockings and shoes was not there. The floor was eerily clear. Frowning, Sylvia went to the cupboard and looked inside. There was nothing there except Audrey's few things.

Her heart started pounding. This made no sense. Had

Kitty been kidnapped, spirited away in some fashion under their noses? Or was it something to do with Joe Whelan and all that trouble?

'Mom!' She ran downstairs, not caring whether she woke Jack, and burst into the front room. 'She's not there. Kitty, she's gone, and so have all her things.'

It was not until the next day that they understood the true situation. That night they agonized about telling the police about Kitty's disappearance, but decided against it.

'The wench has packed her bags and gone,' Ted pointed out. 'What're they supposed to say about that?'

Pauline's face was pinched tight with worry. 'It seems so unlike her,' she said, pulling her dressing gown tightly around her. 'Why would she leave like that, all of a sudden, without saying goodbye? So peculiar – and she's usually a good-mannered sort of person. I hope she's not in trouble.'

Sylvia remembered the night she had met Kitty creeping in up the stairs. 'I wonder if it's to do with that soldier she met – Bill. She seems very keen on him, and she's been writing to him. Maybe he came back suddenly . . .'

'All the same,' Pauline said, sounding annoyed now. 'After staying here so long, rent-free and the lot, you'd think she might've thought to say goodbye before she went off. I'd've thought the girl had better manners.'

It did seem very strange for Kitty to leave without a word of thanks or explanation, and none of them could make the least sense of it. Sylvia barely slept. She lay tensed, listening for the sound of Kitty creeping back in.

She racked her brains for an explanation and realized, as she did so, that there were a lot of things she didn't know about Kitty. Far too many things, in fact.

When Sylvia got home after her shift the next afternoon she had barely got into the house when her mother came out of the back room. Sylvia could see at once that there was something badly wrong. Pauline, who almost never cried, had been crying.

'Mom, what's the matter?' Sylvia threw her jacket onto a hook and went to her mother immediately. 'Is there news? Is it Dad, or Kitty? What's happened?'

Jack was at home after school and even he looked very solemn.

'Go and feed the animals, love,' their mother said to him. 'While I speak to Sylvia.'

They went into the back room and Pauline said gently, almost as if she was talking to a vase that might crack in two, 'Sit down, bab. I've got some news to tell you, and . . . Well, to tell you the truth, I can hardly bring myself to say it.'

Sylvia sat numbly, staring at her. She laid her suddenly clammy hands on the dusty black knees of her work trousers. Her mother sat on the chair beside her.

'God, Mom, what's happened?'

'Mrs Westley came round here this morning,' Pauline began. Her eyes searched her daughter's for any clue that Sylvia might guess what she was about to hear, but she looked utterly bewildered. 'I'll just have to come out with it.' Her mother spoke in a rush now, as if to get it over. 'When they got up this morning, Ian wasn't at home. They found a note from him saying that he had gone away and that, by the time he came back, he would be married to someone they had never even heard of . . .' Pauline hesitated, 'called Kitty Barratt.'

Sylvia heard a cry forced out from between her lips, a yelp of pain, though her mind had barely even registered what her mother was telling her. Her chest felt as if there were tight ropes round it.

'Married?' Her voice sounded high and squeezed. 'Kitty?'

Her mother nodded slowly. 'I've been trying to take it in ever since. So has Ian's mother, for that matter. She seemed furious with me, as if I'd set all this up. "Who is this person he's run off with?" she said. And I had to tell her who Kitty is – not that I know really. But *Ian*, I mean . . .' She stopped, out of words. 'How did this happen? How *could* he – a stick-in-the-mud sort like him? I just can't believe it.'

Sylvia swallowed. She felt as if her head was full of loudly rushing water that was drowning out her thoughts. All the things she thought she knew and hoped for were jumbled up together, overturning, as if her life was washing over an enormous waterfall. She and Ian were to be married, in just a few days' time . . .

'Is this true? How can it be true?' She got up and hurried across the room as if there was something she could do to make it not be true, and reaching the door, realized there wasn't. She rushed back to her mother and knelt down in front of her, her eyes full of anguish.

'What are you telling me? *I'm* marrying Ian! We're getting married . . . He's my . . . We –' She broke into distraught weeping and her mother reached forward and wrapped her arms round her daughter's shoulders.

'My poor babby. Look, come and sit up here . . .' With tears running down her own cheeks, Pauline took Sylvia's hand and pulled her sobbing daughter onto her lap as if she was a little child again. 'My poor, poor girl,' she said. 'I can't take it in, either, but that's what Mrs Westley said. Of course she's terribly upset as well, that Ian—'

'But Ian wouldn't do that!' Sylvia insisted, sitting upright again. 'He wouldn't. He's a proper person, a decent man. He's *mine*. He just wouldn't.' She looked at her mother. 'The note. Did she . . . ?'

'She didn't show me, no,' Pauline said. 'She said that he was full of apologies to everyone that we were all making arrangements, and that we'd feel put out and disappointed, but that he'd decided he'd got to do this and "follow his heart".' She quoted these words bitterly. 'He said he was very sorry to hurt you, and that he feels a coward for not telling you face-to face . . .'

'He *is*! He's a coward. A horrible, low-down—' Sylvia cried. 'And *her*, what about her? She's run off with him – has she really?' Even now, with the memory of Kitty's sweet, winning face before her, she could not believe it. How had this happened? Then she thought of Kitty creeping up the stairs that night. She had said she went to meet that man Bill. But had that all been lies? Surely Kitty had not been with Ian that night? She put her head down, sobbing. It was all too much to take in.

'I can't imagine what he's thinking of – or her. It's beyond me, really it is,' Pauline said. She looked completely drained.

'Audrey.' Sylvia spoke through her tears. 'She said not to trust Kitty, and I thought she was just being silly. That she was jealous or something. How could Audrey see it, and not me? Why am I so blind?' She got up, stunned, to move from her mother's lap to another chair where she sank down. She put her head in her hands. 'I thought they were my two best friends,' she said.

Pauline got up, her movements slow, as if she was in pain. 'I'll make us some tea,' she said, with a despairing shake of her head. 'I'm sorry, bab. I'm sorry to have to tell you, and I'm even more than sorry it's happened.'

'My best friend,' Sylvia said slowly, 'and my fiancé.' She still sat, grounded by shock, as her mother went out to the kitchen. 'Kitty and Ian. Ian and Kitty.' She sat whispering it again and again as the bitter truth of it began to sink in.

Thirty

Audrey came striding across the camp at RAF Cardington, chatting with a group of other young women who were training on the balloons with her. All dressed in heavy blue overalls, they had spent most of the day in the old R101 hangar, learning preliminary skills before being let loose on sending up the barrage balloons outside. Today they had spent learning how to splice ropes and disentangle and organize the ropes and wires from which the balloons were suspended and guided into position. Audrey's hands were covered in cuts from the wires, her shoulders ached from turning the winch and her back from bending and straightening and pulling on ropes, but she would not have exchanged her new job for anything.

'Last one to the NAAFI's a cissy!' one of the other girls cried.

They all started to run, shrieking and clomping along in their heavy boots, in search of tea and bread and butter. Audrey joined in, already fond of this solid, energetic group of women. At least two of them had grown up on farms. It was all so much better than being in the office. Audrey loved being out in the open air and wearing clothes that made moving about easy and made her feel strong and competent. It was summer time, the sun was shining and life felt very good.

As they neared the NAAFI she heard a low, familiar

whistle and looked round. Dorrie, just coming off shift herself, was waiting, her eyes alight with amusement. Audrey left the other WAAFs, who were gambolling towards their well-deserved tea, and went over to her.

'What the hell's so funny?' she asked. But she was happy to see Dorrie. The sight of her always did Audrey good.

'I just can't get used to you in that get-up,' Dorrie said. 'You do look fully operational.'

Audrey wagged a finger at her and put on an earnest voice. '"I'll have you know, each one of those balloons is three times the size of a cricket pitch." According to our new instructor, Sergeant Reynolds, who takes it all *very* seriously.'

Dorrie spluttered with laughter again. 'Lucky old you. Here, look.' She drew some envelopes out from under her arm. 'I collected the post. There are two for you.'

'Two? Oh, ta!' Audrey took them, staring curiously at the envelopes. She sighed at the sight of the small, precise handwriting on one. 'Oh dear, Hamish again. And whose is this writing – oh, it's Mom's. That's a turn-up for the books! She must be missing me.'

She saved Hamish's envelope for later and ambled towards the NAAFI in the sunshine, opening her mother's letter.

'I'll get the tea,' Dorrie said.

Audrey found a space to sit among the chattering WAAFs, all downing tea and slices of bread and margarine. But she was soon oblivious of them, lost in the world of her mother's letter. 'I'm afraid I've got bad news to tell you,' it said, in Pauline's looped hand:

It's about Sylvia. She's in a very bad state. That Kitty Barratt and Ian have done the dirty on her and run off together. They're supposedly getting married! We still can't really take it in. I don't know what to say to comfort her. The wedding's off, of course, but I hope you'll still come home, Aud. It would do her good to see you.

Mom wasn't much of a letter-writer because in normal times she seldom needed to write to anyone. She mentioned that Dad and Jack were going along all right and that Marjorie Gould was bearing up. 'She misses Laurie, of course. But she thinks he's safe, being in Canada. I hope she's right.' She ended, 'Take good care of yourself. Come home, won't you? Love, Mom.'

Audrey folded the letter and sat staring ahead of her. Dorrie soon appeared with two cups of tea.

'What's up?' she asked, cautiously. 'Not bad news?'

'I knew it!' Audrey looked round at her friend, a savage rage rising inside her. 'I don't know how I knew, but I could just see she was a little *bitch*.'

'Blimey, Aud, what's happened?' Dorrie said, startled. 'D'you mean that girl at home – the one you didn't like?'

'*Yes*.' Audrey banged her fist on the table so that the cups jumped, and some of the others looked round. 'God, if I could get my hands on that sneaky, grovelling little piece of work. You should have seen her: "Yes, Mrs Whitehouse; no, Mrs Whitehouse; let me do the washing-up, Mrs Whitehouse; oh, poor little me, everyone's so kind to me . . . "' Audrey spoke in a mocking, saccharine tone. 'I just couldn't understand it. Sylvia was so taken up with her – but then that's Sylv for you. If the Devil popped in one afternoon, she'd sit him down and make him a cup of tea. But our Mom's usually a lot quicker on the uptake than that. She took all of them in, that Kitty – but not me. There was just something about her.'

'You said. Insincere.'

'Yes, *false*. It stood out a mile to me. And as for Ian.' Once more Audrey ground her fist on the tea-stained table top. 'God, if I could get hold of him, I'd have a few things to say to him. He's only gone and run off with Kitty.'

'No!' Dorrie digested this for a few seconds, looking appalled. 'God, how awful! Mind you, sounds as if she's better off without him, if he's just going to run off at the drop of a . . . whatever it is you drop in these situations.'

'Well, I never thought much of him. He was all right. But he was quite a bit older than her, and he always liked to feel one up on Sylv, because she's sweet and doesn't think she's very clever. She's a lot cleverer than him in some ways. I thought she was always trying to turn a blind eye to his faults, personally. But all she wants is to get married and have a nice home, and – you know, all the usual.'

'Poor girl. That's rotten.'

'I must write to her tonight. I'll go home on leave anyway – Mom wants some moral support.' She groaned. 'God, my poor little sis. We're like chalk and cheese, us two, but she's a good sort, Sylv is. This is the last thing that should've happened to her.'

Audrey sipped her tea, seething with fury. She was so angry she felt her fists clenching, thinking of all the things she'd like to say and do to Ian Westley and Kitty Barratt. Her rage even stopped her noticing the pain from her cut hands.

'What did you say?' She realized Dorrie was talking to her.

'I said: what about you? Is that what you want, too? Marriage, I mean.'

'Me?' Audrey shrugged. 'Oh, I've never been one for wanting to get married. It just feels wrong, having some man ruling your life all the time, deciding everything. No – I *don't* want it.' She looked round at Dorrie, realizing in that moment how strongly she felt. Even Hamish, gentlemanly though he was, always assumed that she would just fall in with his plans. 'I want to decide things for myself – and get out and see a few things.'

Dorrie smiled, and for a second Audrey saw in her face a look of happy relief.

'Me, too. It's nice to find someone else who's not just dreaming of a white wedding.'

'Oh, not me,' Audrey laughed, clinking her teacup against Dorrie's, like a toast. 'Not even a black one!'

Audrey opened the letter from Hamish later, when things were quiet in their hut. The only other person in there was Maggie, who was lying on her side, facing the other way and reading a book. There was a box of chocolates open on the bed and every so often her hand reached out and ferreted about in it. Her mother sent her boxes as a treat.

Audrey sat back on her bed, boots off, but still in her overalls, her long legs stretched out, the muscles aching and feeling pleasantly tired from her day's work. Nowadays she never noticed the lumpy, uncomfortable bed. She slept like a log.

Hamish had left some weeks ago to do further training in Fighter Command. Since then he had written faithfully to her, and each of his letters made Audrey feel worse than the last. Hamish always told her that he was well and that training was progressing. He always added, in his restrained way, that he was missing her and very much wanted to see her. This letter ended with the words, 'Thinking of you always, as ever, Hamish.'

Thinking of you always, Audrey thought, gloomily. It was hardly the heights of passion, was it? The truth was that unless Hamish wrote to her, she almost never gave him a thought and she was glad he had gone. Although he was a nice lad, she had found him dull company. His gentlemanly but persistent petting oppressed her. When she was kissing him she was thinking of other things, like whether she had finished all the typing that the CO had given her, and what there might be for tea. This did not seem a very good sign. Should she not feel aroused and want to respond?

What was all the fuss about with men and women? She felt it was her fault, some deep lack in her. She had had a handsome man kissing her – in fact, there had been several handsome men over the past weeks. There was never a shortage, and Audrey, with her dark-eyed looks and outgoing personality, was always in demand. Every time a new one came along she lived in hope. Perhaps this would be the one who would steal her heart, would make her feel something. It was nice knowing that someone was attracted to her, it was true. But usually she ended up in the same state of boredom tinged with melancholy at the lack that she felt in herself. It all seemed wrong when there was old Sylv, desperate to get married. But Audrey's emotions were just not involved, and she couldn't seem to get her body involved, either. The men didn't seem to care about this, she noticed. A few touches and they were off.

She sat back with the letter folded on her stomach.

Oh, Hamish, she thought desperately, why don't you

just give up?

She had only written back to him once, before deciding it was a waste of time. Yet still Hamish kept writing, imploring her to reply.

She slipped the letter in among her things and tried to forget about it. She thought she would probably never see Hamish again. He'd been posted miles away, up the east coast. At first he had been talking about visiting her on his leave, but since she had not answered any more of his letters there had been no further mention of it.

Maggie turned over onto her other side and looked up at Audrey. She licked her chocolatey fingers with narrowed eyes.

'What's up with you?' Despite her soft, kittenish looks, Maggie could be quite sharp.

'Oh . . .' Audrey lay back with a groan. 'Just life.'

'Men trouble?'

'In a way.' Audrey sat up, genuinely wanting Maggie's advice. 'It's just – one of the lads I went about with a few weeks ago . . .'

'That red-headed one? He was very sweet on you.' Maggie held out the chocolate box. 'Here, have one. Mainly nuts left, I'm afraid.'

'Thanks.' Audrey took something with half a hazelnut on top. 'I know, that's just it. He keeps on writing, and I don't want . . . I mean, there's nothing in it for me. I wish he'd just stop, but it seems so unkind to tell him.'

'Audrey,' Maggie sat up, looking very earnest. 'Just *write* to him, for heaven's sake! It doesn't matter if he's not the love of your life, or even close. Those boys could all be dead soon. Where's he gone, d'you know?'

'Fighter Command. Norfolk.'

Maggie looked sad. 'Two of my brother's school pals

died in Fighter Command – Battle of Britain. Only twenty-one, both of them.' She leaned forwards. 'You don't have to marry him, Audrey. Just give him something to look forward to while he's still here.'

Audrey stared back at Maggie, ashamed. The dark waters of Raymond Gould's death washed through her head again. 'Yes. You're right. I've been stupid about it. I will write to him.' As soon as I've written to Mom and Sylvia, she thought. They were the ones who really must come first. She could imagine only too clearly what a state her sister must be in.

Thirty-One

She managed a brief visit home for the two days she had been allocated for the wedding. In fact she did not see as much of Sylvia as she expected, for she insisted on working her shifts throughout the time.

'There's no point in me mooning around here, is there?' she said. 'Sorry, Aud – but you can keep Mom company anyway.'

Against the dark serge of her uniform Sylvia's face looked very pale and sickly, and Audrey could see she was bottling up all her hurt and sadness. Instead of her usual sweet self, she was silent and snapped at everyone when they asked her anything.

'I don't know what to do for her,' Pauline said to Audrey. The strain was telling on her as well. She had dark rings under her eyes. 'I've told Marjorie to hang on to the dress – not let Sylvia see it. I don't know what to do for the best. If I could get my hands on that Kitty . . .'

'And flaming Ian,' Audrey said. 'Let's hope they go to hell in a handcart.'

She did her best to offer comfort and a listening ear, but Sylvia was not ready to open up. Audrey was relieved to get back to RAF Cardington. That was where her real life was now, she felt.

*

The realization hit her like a blow.

'Of course, you daft thing,' Dorrie said, when she saw Audrey's downcast face. 'What did you imagine – that you'd just stay here?'

'I just thought . . .' She trailed off. 'Yes, I s'pose I did.'

Audrey had only just realized that once she finished her ten weeks of training, she would be posted to a balloon site elsewhere. She had visualized staying on at RAF Cardington for the remainder of the war with her friends, and the usual routine; and, above all, with Dorrie. She was horrified by the thought of leaving.

Dorrie shook her head. 'Doesn't work like that, dearie. You're a pawn on the big service chessboard for the duration. So we all have to be brave!'

Audrey started calculating how long she might have left. A few weeks anyway. 'Well, we must make the most of it!' she said.

It was a very happy time. She and the balloon team were now learning their skills outside. They were driven on trucks out to the green open space of the base. Here they spent the day putting into practice all they had learned about rope knots and letting out the wires from the winch. They knew how to inflate the balloons from hydrogen cylinders. As the balloons filled, they paid out the ropes as the bloated, fishy shapes rose into the sky above them, tugging for their freedom. They had to learn how to put the balloons 'to bed': deflating them, getting them captive on the ground and rolling them up. It was heavy work, but the girls all worked well together and Audrey enjoyed it all, the challenge of it, even on not-so-fine days when the rain beat into their faces.

She enjoyed all the camaraderie and jokes, and the huge appetite they all worked up. Their instructor, Sergeant Nick Reynolds, a fair-haired, athletic man, had obviously taken a liking to her as well and there was an atmosphere of friendship and fun. She felt she was having the time of her life, feeling active, powerful and useful all at once. At least, she thought, if they re-post us, some of us might be sent somewhere together.

What filled her with a sense of desolation, every time she thought about it, was the prospect of leaving Dorrie. As the weeks went by, the two of them grew so close that they spent every possible moment together. They went to the pictures on the camp or sat in one of their huts chatting. On free days, for a change of scene, they might go into Bedford to the Corn Exchange, where you could get tea and a scone with bramble jelly. In the long summer evenings they would find a place to sprawl on the grass outside and talk and laugh, until long after dark had fallen and the midges were biting.

Audrey turned down quite a few possible dates with RAF lads. The prospect of a long evening drinking and listening to the thoughts of a boy she didn't care about, ending probably with him wanting to take her to a dark spot and go as far as she would let him, left her cold. How much more fun it was to sit with Dorrie, to talk with absolute freedom. Dorrie was interested in everything – especially people and politics. And they laughed! Audrey thought she had never laughed as much in her life as she had since knowing Dorrie. Seen through her friend's eyes, everything became humorous, even when they were talking seriously. As the weeks went by, they talked more about their families, their feelings and their experiences. About everything – or almost everything.

Audrey kept pushing her own confusion from her mind. These feelings of excitement when she saw Dorrie – the fact that this girl was the one who filled her with joy, longing and tenderness – wasn't this what falling in love was supposed to be like? She pushed this thought away. How silly! That couldn't be. She'd soon be gone from here anyway, so why not just enjoy the fun?

The two of them took a leave day together and got passes to go to London.

'I've never been before!' Audrey said, full of excitement.

'Well, it's looking pretty battered,' Dorrie told her. She had been a number of times with her parents, to go to plays and see the sights. 'The poor old girl isn't looking her best. But you must see her anyhow. Everyone should see London.'

They travelled up to London crushed into a railway carriage, some fellow passengers in service uniforms, others not. Both of them were wearing WAAF uniforms – skirts this time, with short-sleeved shirts. Audrey had a letter from Sylvia, which she had saved to read on the train. Once they had set off, she opened it and read it with growing astonishment, her anger boiling up again.

'My God!' she erupted. Ears were flapping all around as she spoke, but she was too furious to care. She passed the letter to Dorrie. 'You'll never believe what's happened now.'

Her eyes followed Dorrie's, reading the lines of Sylvia's painstaking, childlike writing:

> There's been another horrible shock. Dad called us over yesterday to look at the paper. There was a bit announcing the death of one Josiah Barratt of Barratt & Stone Castings . . .

Dorrie looked round at her, frowning. 'But . . . ? Is that . . . ?'

'Yup,' Audrey said. 'The father. Of Kitty Barratt. The one who was killed when they were bombed out – or not, as it turns out.'

Dorrie gasped, staring back at the letter. Sylvia went on to say that Josiah Barratt had been found dead in his office over the works one morning, his heart having apparently given out the night before. The piece went on to say that he died intestate. Though he had one surviving daughter, she had been absent from home for some months and so far could not be traced.

Dorrie was looking truly baffled by now. Audrey explained heatedly, not caring who heard.

'According to Kitty, they'd been bombed out and the old man was killed. That's how she turned up living with us – and Sylv, of course, took pity. But that was all a lie as well.' She raised her voice slightly. 'Old man Barratt was alive and kicking, and getting on with making a tidy sum out of the war effort, thank you very much – when Kitty told us he was pushing up the daisies. Now he's actually dead, and he must either not have made a will or destroyed the one he had made.'

Audrey was dimly aware that all ears in the carriage were now tuned in, riveted, to what she was saying, despite the fact that they were all pretending to read their newspapers and fiddle with cigarettes.

Dorrie turned to her, her grey eyes wide with in-credulity. 'She couldn't have lied about something like that, surely? Saying he was dead when he wasn't!'

'Oh yes – and she did. My God, she's a piece of work. You wouldn't believe it, would you?'

'But didn't he report her missing? You'd think the

police would have come and checked out where Kitty worked.'

'P'rhaps he didn't care. Or thought she'd run off with a man – and good riddance. Not much love lost there, I don't think.' Audrey gave a sharp sigh. 'My poor little sis.'

Sylvia's letter was not very long, but through it Audrey could feel all her hurt and misery.

Dorrie shook her head. 'Some people!' she said. Both of them became uncomfortably aware of the attentive atmosphere in the carriage. Audrey looked round and the middle-aged man opposite held his copy of *The Times* up even higher in front of his face.

'Mind you,' Dorrie lowered her voice to a whisper, moving closer to Audrey, 'my grandmother was a bit like that. My father's mother. She's dead now, but she used to come out with some corkers. They lived a few miles from us. She spent the last couple of years of my granddad's life telling everyone he was already dead, even when he was quite obviously there, walking about around the village.'

Audrey frowned. 'Why?'

'I don't know,' Dorrie said. 'Not that I remember this – it was when I was a baby. I don't think she liked him very much.'

'Well, yes, it does look like it,' Audrey said. Their eyes met and they both creased up, having to stifle their giggles in the strangely silent carriage, so as not to make fools of themselves.

It was a muggy, overcast day. The train pulled into King's Cross and they walked through the shade of the enormous station and out into the crowds. Dorrie caught hold of Audrey's elbow so as not to lose her. The battered, sooty splendour of London burst in on them. Audrey looked round her, awed.

'It's lovely,' she said to Dorrie. 'It feels so big! Oh, look – balloons!'

They could see a barrage balloon in the distance, tugging gently on its ropes. The girls looked at each other and laughed with happiness.

'So,' Dorrie said. 'Where d'you fancy going?'

They walked and walked, taking in the sights and following the river. They ate the packed lunch they had been provided with, looking out over the sheen on the sludgy water and watching the boats. By mid-afternoon they found themselves at Lyons Corner House in Oxford Street.

'Come on,' Dorrie said. 'Let's go and have a sit-down. I'm gasping.'

Audrey was amazed by the size of the place as Dorrie led her inside. She followed her friend's energetic, curvaceous shape through the food hall and up to the tearoom, feeling a sudden explosion of happiness inside her. This was so exciting, so exactly what she wanted of life! Here, with Dorrie, she felt she had all she needed. When they reached a table in the enormous tearoom, with the orchestra playing softly in the background, she was smiling broadly.

Dorrie looked at her as they sat down and a smile lit up her own face.

'Happy?' she asked.

'Yes,' Audrey said, 'I've just *loved* today. Seeing everything. All those grand places. I know everything's covered in sandbags and there's so much wreckage, but it's still a grand place. You feel you could really *do* something here, don't you?'

'Yes,' Dorrie said. 'That's just it. Not like the sleepy

hole I come from. I'm going to come here and beg a newspaper to let me write for them! When it's all over, I mean.'

'I want to live here after the war too,' Audrey said, full of excitement. Suddenly she wanted to plan everything, for them to pledge to do it all together. But just as she was about to speak, the nippy came, in her black uniform and little cap, to take their order.

Dorrie asked about cakes, winking at Audrey. 'I'll treat you, kid. They must have something, even these days.'

When the waitress had gone, Dorrie looked around. 'I've been here a few times with Ma and Pa – before the war, obviously. We came up to see a show now and then. Ma used to insist that we did something not related to death, just occasionally!'

'Lucky you,' Audrey laughed. She sat drinking it all in: the huge, pale room with its ornate columns supporting the ceiling, and tables stretching off in rows almost as far as she could see, now occupied by families and couples all enjoying a treat. There was a festive atmosphere, with the sweet smells and clinking of spoons on china and the chatter all around them. A little girl at a table across the aisle stared intently at them. Dorrie winked at her and she looked away.

Dorrie looked around her dreamily. 'One day,' she said, then stopped.

'One day what?'

Dorrie looked as if she was going to say something important, but then she sat back in the chair and just said. 'Yes – when it's all over. Things have got to be different then, haven't they?'

'How d'you mean?'

Dorrie shrugged expansively. 'I don't know. Not so

244

hemmed in and constrained. Something's got to come out of this war – less of a class divide, more fairness, letting people just live their lives how they want to,' she finished, sounding almost angry.

'I suppose,' Audrey said. She wasn't used to such talk. She could hardly imagine how things might be different.

The nippy arrived again and laid out their tea and scones.

'Ooh,' Dorrie said with relish. 'Look – strawberry jam. What a treat!'

Once they were alone again she said. 'D'you know, we'll be able to get away for a weekend soon. Neither of us have had much leave at all since we've been at Cardington. How d'you fancy coming and staying at home with me for the weekend? I'd love to show you around all my haunts.'

Audrey looked into her friend's eager face. For a moment she had a sensation of falling into something, and wanting with all her being to be swept along. It was a feeling she could barely understand.

'Wouldn't they mind?'

'No, of course not.' Dorrie seemed to be choosing her words carefully. 'We wouldn't be any trouble – we'd be out most of the time anyway. It's just never easy with them; and since Piers was killed, it's . . .' She shook her head. 'But what they want is for me to be normal, and this sort of counts as normal, I suppose.'

Audrey was completely bewildered now. 'You're normal enough, aren't you? What're you talking about?'

'Oh, I don't know,' Dorrie said wearily. 'Whatever I do, they don't think it's the right thing. Pa is so pretentious – hence our names, for a start – and both of them want me to be the sort of girl who would become secretary to a *top man*.' She made a face. 'What they would really have liked is for me to go to finishing school in Switzerland and learn how to pick up a hanky from the floor without showing my knickers, and talk as if I've got a mouthful of mothballs.'

Audrey was laughing at her friend's indignation. 'They got the wrong daughter then, didn't they?'

'They absolutely did! They've always wanted to be "in" with the right people, but where does a funeral director fit in socially? So far as the toffs are concerned, they're trade, and therefore beyond the pale. Whereas they see themselves as many cuts above the butcher and fishmonger, who are also trade – except the right people don't see it that way. It's all very, very stilted and ghastly. I was a tomboy and, even when I grew out of that, I've never been able to fit the mould. That's what I mean about the war – it must break these moulds. Look at us: the RAF wouldn't have touched us before the war, and now they've found out that it doesn't take five women to do one man's job, there's no going back, is there? God knows, I hope not anyway. You see, Audie,' Dorrie leaned passionately across the table, 'these are all the sort of things I want to *write* about.'

Audrey watched her friend, her face full of intelligence and animation. She was saying things that filled Audrey with a new sense of excitement. It was so different from Mom, who never wanted to rock the boat in any way; or from Sylvia, bless her, with her romantic, timid approach to the world.

'What're you thinking?' Dorrie said, peering at her.

'I'm wondering why you'd want to be friends with me,' Audrey said. 'I come from somewhere very different—'

'You're from somewhere *real*,' Dorrie interrupted. She seemed to be almost quivering with emotion. 'Which isn't full of small-minded, feudally inclined snobs. Believe me, Audrey.'

'But that doesn't mean people aren't stuck, in their own way. In thinking things can't change.'

Dorrie gazed at her, looking into Audrey's eyes as if she was trying to decide something vital and was looking for a sign. She reached over and touched Audrey's hand for a moment.

'Come, anyway, and stay. Just for a weekend, or whatever we can get off. I've got lots to show you. How about it?'

Thirty-Two

August 1941

The Coopers' house was in a side street close to the Corn Market at the centre of High Wycombe. It was a smart brick terraced house three floors high, with the family business on the ground floor.

By the time the girls arrived, having walked from the station, Audrey was feeling sticky and dishevelled. The weather was very close and sultry. She was also rather nervous. Apart from her time in the WAAF, she had never been away from home and had certainly never stayed in a little place like this that felt so quiet and respectable. She looked at the smartly painted black front door and the green-and-gold sign above the front window, which read: 'REG. COOPER & SON – FUNERAL DIRECTORS'.

Audrey turned to Dorrie. '"And Son"? So your brother . . . ?'

'Yup,' Dorrie said briskly. 'Piers had gone in with Pa. It wasn't what he wanted. He was more of an outdoors type, but as the parents said: you can't earn a living playing cricket. Piers jumped at the chance of joining up, because it got him out of here. I suppose they can't face taking the sign down.'

'It must all be a bit grim – as a job, I mean,' Audrey said.

'You get used to it.' Dorrie seemed distracted, and Audrey realized that she too was nervous about seeing her parents. 'Come on, let's go round the back.'

A narrow alley led them to a walled-off back yard. Audrey could hear hammering from the outhouse along one side of the yard, and she caught a pleasant whiff of sawn wood.

'Do they make the coffins here?' she whispered. She felt giggly suddenly with nerves.

'Yes, we had to find someone to replace the lad who worked here. It's not a reserved occ – you'd think it might be.' Dorrie went to a green back door and rapped on it. Rolling her eyes she said, 'Let's get it over.'

The door was opened by a young woman with a pale, pointy face and scraped-back black hair. She looked hostile for a second, until her face softened into a smile.

''Ello, Miss Dorrie. Your mother said you was coming back for a visit!'

'Hello, Susan,' Dorrie said as the skinny young woman stood back to let them in. 'How're you keeping?'

'I'm all right. Yes, I'm all right.' She seemed very flustered. 'But . . .'

'What's the matter?' Dorrie asked. She and Audrey stood in the dark back kitchen with the young woman, who looked as if she was about to dissolve into tears.

'Oh, it's nothing. It's just that my mother's none too well again, and I can't help but worry . . .' Tears began to run down her cheeks.

'Oh dear, I am sorry, Susan,' Dorrie said in a kind voice. 'But I'm sure you're doing your best, and the neighbours are very good with your mother, aren't they?'

Susan wiped her face and tried to rally herself. 'Oh, they are – yes. Just sometimes it all gets on top of me.'

Audrey had the impression this was a problem that had gone on for a long time.

Dorrie reached out and gave the young woman's arm a squeeze. 'You're very good to your mother. She's a lucky woman.'

Susan was trying to find a brave smile, when they heard footsteps.

'Dorothea?' A face appeared at the door. 'I thought I heard voices.'

'Hello, Ma.' Dorrie went and kissed her mother, rather stiffly, and Audrey immediately had the impression that Dorrie was humouring her, that she had to put on a show for her. 'This is my WAAF pal, Audrey Whitehouse.'

As they made polite greetings, Audrey took in the sight of Mrs Cooper. She was a lean, rather stringy woman with hair darker than Dorrie's and more tightly curled. A twirling lock of it hung over her forehead. Her complexion was sallow, and she had bruise-like rings under her eyes. Audrey could see in her a resemblance to Dorrie, in the large eyes and shape of the face, but it was as if Mrs Cooper had been sucked dry. Whereas Dorrie was rounded like a golden, fleshy plum, her mother seemed a shrunken-up version, like a dried prune. She thought about Marjorie Gould for a moment. It was terrible, what loss and grief did.

'Susan, do make the girls a cup of tea,' Mrs Cooper said. 'Come through, and we'll show you where're you're sleeping. I'm afraid you may have to be in the attic,' she told Audrey.

'Oh, that's all right,' Audrey said.

Behind her mother's back Dorrie turned and winked at her. Audrey was startled by this.

'Where're you from, Audrey?' Mrs Cooper asked, stopping at the foot of the stairs.

'Birmingham,' Audrey said. She felt shy and subdued suddenly.

'I see,' Mrs Cooper said. She sounded weary.

Climbing up behind her, Audrey wondered what 'I see' meant.

'This is my room,' Dorrie said, going into the one that looked out over the back and putting her bag down. Audrey had a glimpse of a pale-green counterpane. The main bedroom was at the front and there was another door that she knew, without asking, must have been Piers's room. They took her up to the attic, which Audrey liked as it gave a good view. The floor was covered with brown linoleum and there was a bed with another pale-green counterpane, a chair and a small chest of drawers.

'I'm afraid it's rather spartan up here,' Mrs Cooper said.

'No – it's nice,' Audrey said. 'Thank you, Mrs Cooper.'

Dorrie's mother gave a stiff smile. Seeming preoccupied by other things, she went to the door.

'There'll be tea in a moment – do come down, Dorothea.'

'We'll be down,' Dorrie said.

Dorrie seemed amused by something and Audrey could not work out what, but she was too busy looking around. She found Mrs Cooper strange, but told herself: what did it matter what the woman thought of her? She was only here for two days after all.

'What a poor summer this is,' Dorrie said, looking

out. 'At least it's dry, though. Let's get out of here this afternoon, shall we?' She seemed restless and ill at ease. 'There are two bikes – are you okay on one?'

'Oh yes, I'll manage. Dorrie?'

'Umm?' Dorrie turned from the window and came and sat beside Audrey on the bed. 'You're here. I can hardly believe it.'

'Your mom – has she changed a lot since, you know, Piers . . . ?'

Dorrie's eyes clouded. 'No. Not changed really. I'd say she was just more so.'

The Coopers' business took up the front room and yard of the spacious terraced house. There were two more rooms at the back, apart from the kitchen and scullery, which served as a parlour and a dining room. Audrey found the house forbidding. The dining room was small and crammed with dark furniture. The back parlour contained the expected ration of chairs, the upholstery all dark green, a table and fireplace, the fire tools neatly lined up, their brass handles polished. There were side-tables with the requisite newspapers and half-finished knitting and letters. And in the window stood a vase of faded yellow yarrow, giving off a musty scent. There was nothing wrong with the place, nothing jarred. But it was lacking in the sort of homeliness that Audrey was used to.

She wondered what Mr Cooper was like. When he appeared for the midday dinner that Susan had fretfully produced, Audrey saw a compact, grey-haired man, who hurried up to her and shook her hand forcefully. She could see where Dorrie got her energy from.

'How d'you do,' he said with a brisk nod, before

sitting at the table and dealing with his food in an equally fast and curt manner. He had greeted Dorrie with a peck on the cheek. 'Back home then?' And little else.

Audrey was puzzled by the whole set-up. At home, when she went on leave, everyone was full of questions, pleased to see her, and there was the usual chatter and teasing and Jack fooling about. There was a warmth to it, she thought, that she had taken for granted. She realized with a pang of fondness that she had a nice family, and she felt a rush of love for them, missing them as she sat in this odd, chilly room.

Mrs Cooper did ask them both questions about WAAF life, and Audrey a few about home. Dorrie talked more than Audrey, telling them about the balloon training, about how strong Audrey was and a little about her own driving. But as she talked Audrey felt that Dorrie's parents didn't approve or want to know.

'What did you do before the war?' Mrs Cooper asked after a time.

'I worked in an insurance office – as a shorthand typist,' Audrey said.

'Ah, now that seems . . .'

'I didn't enjoy it much,' she said firmly.

By the time the stilted meal had finished with a dismal lump of chocolate shape and some tinned pears, Audrey was starting to wonder whether Dorrie could really be the daughter of these people at all. Talk about cuckoo in the nest! She wondered what Piers had been like, but no one ever mentioned him. Dorrie dealt with her parents with a cool, detached and almost amused manner, as if they were strangers she had just met and whom she had to put up with for the moment.

Audrey had never been so glad to get to the end of a meal.

Thirty-Three

'They're not really what I was expecting,' Audrey said.

The two of them were cycling along a country lane, the verges lined with hawthorn and cow parsley. Audrey, who was the taller of the two, had said she would ride Piers's bike, although it had a crossbar. Dorrie was riding her own. She had shown Audrey the Abbey and the Rye, the green parkland in High Wycombe, but seemed very keen to get out of the town and it was soon left behind by the two fit, fast-pedalling young women.

Dorrie laughed. 'The parents, you mean? So what were you expecting?' She seemed light-hearted now that she was away from there. Both of them had changed into civilian clothes, and Dorrie had on a peach-coloured skirt and a white sleeveless blouse. Audrey had brought a cotton frock with her, covered with navy-and-white flowers. The day was overcast, but warm and muggy.

'I don't know. They just seem very . . .' She didn't want to be rude, so discarded the words *cold, dull, odd.* 'Very – just not like you, that's all.'

'No, they're not like me. Or, at least, I try not to be like them. Well spotted!' Dorrie turned and grinned. Audrey thought how lovely she looked, with her brown forearms and round, pink face. She felt a pang of tenderness for her, seeing this strange family and sensing there were all sorts of difficulties that Dorrie was always brave about.

'D'you think I could meet your family sometime?' Dorrie asked, seeming suddenly bashful.

'Yes, course you can. I'd like you to,' Audrey said, panting a little as they were cycling uphill along a dry, white track.

'They sound nice,' Dorrie said wistfully.

'Yes. I s'pose they are.'

'Mine aren't *not* nice. They just don't . . .' Dorrie paused. Audrey was not sure if she was catching her breath or if she didn't know how to go on. 'I suppose I'm just not the daughter they hoped for.' Before Audrey could reply, Dorrie went on, 'Come on – we can really get up speed down here!'

They crested the hill and started to go down, Dorrie swooping ahead, her hair flapping. Audrey followed, hardly using the brakes and letting the bicycle rush downhill, with the wind against her face.

'Whoooooo!' she heard from Dorrie, whose legs were flying out, off the pedals.

Audrey heard her own laughter. It bubbled up, free and happy, and poured out of her all the way down the hill. The warm, billowing air caressed her skin. Pure joy filled her at the speed, at the excitement of it and at this carefree being here with Dorrie, whom she would rather be with than anyone in the world. She let her own legs fly free. Then the track levelled off and soon they were going uphill to the top of another rise.

At the top Dorrie braked in a gateway.

'That was bostin!' Audrey said, going to join her. 'As they say, where I come from.'

Dorrie's brow crinkled. 'You what?'

'Black Country for "wonderful"!'

Dorrie smiled. 'I love it up here. Let's stop for a bit, shall we?'

The gate looked over a field of barley, which stretched gently downhill to dark trees at the field boundary. It seemed very quiet suddenly, with only the breeze sending whispering waves through the ripening crop.

'It's so lovely,' Audrey said, breathing in the warm, barley-scented air. 'And you can see for miles.'

'Let's go in.' Dorrie got off the bike. 'We can just leave these by the gate.'

There was a grassy verge along the edge of the field. Sitting down on it, they could just see over the barley and down the slope of the field. A small plane laboured across the hazy sky and, afterwards, the place seemed even quieter. Audrey could hear birds in the hedge, a bee droning past. Then a burst of birdsong came from somewhere high, an insistent little cry. She looked up, but could not see anything.

'What on earth's that?' she said.

'It's a lark. They hover right up high. Haven't you heard one before?'

'I don't think we have many larks in Birmingham.'

Dorrie gave a vague smile. She was sitting with her arms wrapped round her knees. She seemed suddenly far away. Audrey felt shut out from her thoughts and wanted to bring her back.

'Have you always biked out here?' she asked.

Dorrie raised her head. 'Yes, lots. It's freedom. Home's always felt hemmed in. They're all right really – my people, I mean. But since Piers died . . .' She shook her head and trailed off into silence. For a few moments she gazed across the field and her eyes narrowed. Then she said, 'Sometimes I think I'd like to go and live in America. They don't have all this class nonsense. Not like here, anyway.'

'I thought you wanted to live in London.'

Dorrie looked round at her, serious suddenly. 'I *do*. Yes.' She inched closer. 'Oh, Aud – when the war's over, let's do it. Let's set up in London and be different from all this! Shall we? Are you game for that, too?'

Audrey felt excitement flare in her. London, a new, different life – and with Dorrie! It was all she wanted, she realized. The two of them, like adventurers together, exploring the world, doing new things, different from everything they had ever known. For a second she thought of Sylvia. It was terrible, what had happened, but thank *goodness* she wasn't going to marry stodgy old Ian. Other things might be possible for her as well.

'Yes! Shall we?' She looked hungrily at Dorrie. '*Can* we? God, d'you think it'll ever be over?'

'Of course it will.' Dorrie was looking deep into her eyes, and Audrey was taken aback by her intensity. She felt herself washed along in Dorrie's passion for everything. She had never met anyone like this woman before. All she wanted was to be with her, to make a life – nothing else seemed to matter. Inside she felt emotions swelling, her heart beating hard. Nothing seemed quite real. She was acutely conscious of Dorrie's physical closeness, of the swell of her breasts under the white cotton, her eyes, her lips, the by-now-familiar, salty, wonderful smell of her.

For a moment they sat with their eyes locked together. Without looking away, Dorrie slowly, as if fearfully, put her arm round Audrey's back and lay it across her shoulders, its weight at first light and tentative and then, as Audrey did not react, she rested it more definitely. Neither of them spoke. Audrey could feel herself breathing very lightly, as if not to disturb something shy and delicate in the air around them. Her heart thudded. As Dorrie moved closer, still not taking her gaze away, she knew they were going to kiss and that it was what she wanted. She could not think about the name that anyone else might give to what was happening. She knew that she felt desire; that Dorrie was the only person she had ever felt this for; that she was going to kiss her back.

Dorrie's full lips met hers, and a moment later they were lying back in the grass in each other's arms. Audrey could hear little urgent sounds of desire as they kissed, and wasn't sure which of them was making these noises as their hands moved over each other's bodies. She only knew that she had never felt or been touched like this before, and that this, and Dorrie, were all she desired. As they held each other, she felt Dorrie's body begin to shake, and realized she was sobbing so hard that there was scarcely any sound.

'Dorrie?' Audrey moved onto one elbow to look down into her face, full of concern and tenderness. Dorrie's face was pink and contorted, as if with pain. Audrey gently wiped her wet cheeks with her fingers. 'Don't cry,' she whispered. 'Why are you crying?'

'Because I'm not alone any more,' Dorrie murmured. 'I'm so happy – I can't believe it. With you.' She buried her head in Audrey's shoulder, and Audrey held her, very gently, as she wept again.

Mrs Cooper had managed to get hold of a chicken and, with Susan's help, made a nice meal to celebrate Dorrie's visit home. The four of them sat round the table that evening, and Audrey warmed a bit more to Dorrie's mother. She was more relaxed and talkative by the evening. Mr Cooper was friendly in a clipped, distant way. Audrey felt that she could not imagine ever having a real conversation with him. He fired little questions at her – What did her father do? Had it bad up in Birmingham, had they? – without paying much attention to the answers.

One of the questions was, however, 'Got a man-friend then, have you?'

'Well,' Audrey said. 'No. Well, I did have. But he was at Cardington with us and he's been posted quite far away for further training. So we write, but I hardly ever see him at the moment.'

Mrs Cooper looked at her with sympathy and approval. 'This terrible war,' she said. 'But you'll be together one day, I'm sure. Would you like a few more peas?'

Dorrie was looking at Audrey across the table in a wide-eyed, innocent way.

'Audrey's a great one for the boys,' she said. Audrey felt the toe of Dorrie's shoe press against her shin as she spoke and avoided looking at her.

'Quite right,' Mr Cooper said, as if for something to say.

The feeling that none of this was quite real came over Audrey again. She was just floating her way through it, like a dream. But it was a dream that included Dorrie, and that was what mattered.

The weather changed that night, the stifling mugginess building all evening until the storm broke after they had all gone to bed. When they went up, Dorrie whispered, 'See you later' to Audrey. Audrey lay waiting in a suspense of excitement and strangeness. Under cover of the growling thunder, Dorrie crept up to the attic room and into Audrey's bed. They did not speak about what was happening. It was as if to name anything would have been to break the spell of their stay. With little whispers and stifled laughter, they kissed and explored each other's bodies, just a little. They were hesitant and careful with each other. Mostly they lay pressed together in each other's warmth, whispering and laughing. Audrey felt soaked in wonder and pleasure, a sense of being utterly in the right place.

The next day was the first really fine one in a long time and they spent as much time outside as they could. Dorrie gave some time to her mother in the morning. Mrs Cooper stopped home from church to be with her, and Audrey stayed in the attic and left them to talk in peace. But after lunch the two girls set off on the bikes and explored again, taking to the wild, more isolated tracks out in the country.

'I always think of all this as mine,' Dorrie said, as they paused again at a high vantage point. 'I've explored it so much. And not many people come up here.' She stood looking across the undulating land, her hair blown back from her face. Audrey watched, enchanted, full of a mixture of passion and tenderness that made her legs feel weak. My Dorrie, she thought. Lovely Dorrie Cooper. And she had a moment's daydream of the two of them sharing a flat in London, both going out doing jobs. What jobs? She had no idea. But it would be daring and new and good.

'To think of those vile Germans marching across all this,' Dorrie said fiercely. 'With their tanks and their boots, and all that revolting shouting they do. Never. They must never be allowed anywhere near.'

Audrey laid her bike on the ground and went up behind Dorrie, putting her hands round her waist. She nuzzled against Dorrie's moist neck, her cheek against Dorrie's hair. She knew that what she felt for Dorrie was desire, but it was not something she felt able to give a name to. It was as if it was something separate entirely from what she might have done with a man. She just followed her strong, overwhelming instincts, without naming or questioning them.

Dorrie made a small sound and twisted round in Audrey's arms.

'Come into the field,' she said.

They lay side-by-side, arms entwined, looking at the puffy clouds moving across the blue. Dorrie said, 'I love you, Audrey. God, I do!'

Audrey kissed Dorrie's peachy cheek. 'Love you too, Dor. You're the best thing that's ever happened to me.'

Dorrie turned her head. 'D'you mean that?'

'Course. You're my mate. What else?'

Dorrie seemed reassured. She squeezed Audrey tightly. 'I've found you, my girl. Found you at last. It means everything to me.' She looked round at Audrey with wide eyes. 'It takes someone brave,' she said. 'Not everyone's as brave as you.'

On the way back to the camp, on the train, they sat with Dorrie's WAAF jacket folded casually on her lap, to hide the fact that for almost all the journey they were holding each other's hands.

Thirty-Four

Sylvia slipped out of the house that afternoon, shutting the front door quietly behind her. She patted the pocket of her raincoat to make sure she had the letter with her. The summer had mostly been a washout, and though it was dry at the moment, she took the coat in case of another storm.

It was her day off and she waited until Mom was outside hanging the washing before she slipped away. She could not face any more of Mom's concerned questions about where she was going or how she was. Being in the house made her feel so sad and oppressed that she just had to walk and walk and tire herself. Scarcely thinking about where she was going, she turned in the direction of Moseley village.

It was a month since Ian and Kitty had taken off and much of that time she had spent in a numb state, going through the motions of life. There was nothing much that her family or friends could say to comfort her. Even Froggy noticed and kept making remarks like, 'Eh, you're wasting away. You need some meat on yer bones if you're gunna do this job!' and 'Eh, give us a smile, wench!' Elsie, Gina and the others were kind, realizing Sylvia would just need time to get over it.

At first she had been unable to believe or accept what had happened. For days she thought it must be a mistake and that Kitty would come back, smiling in her lovely way and saying there had been another explanation altogether for their disappearance. Sylvia knew really that this was a hollow hope. What other reason could there possibly be? But at first she just could not believe it of Kitty or Ian. How could she have been so blind, when they were deceiving her, right in front of her eyes?

It was about a fortnight later when Dad came in from work, his expression grim, and opened up the day's *Evening Mail* on the table.

'Pauline, come and look at this. Sylv,' he added in a careful, apologetic tone, 'you'd better look too.'

They all leaned over the column about Josiah Barratt.

'Are you sure that's the same man, Ted?' Pauline asked.

'That's what the wench said – Barratt & Stone. I'm certain. How did she think she was going to get away with that: pretending her old man was dead?'

'Well, she did get away with it, didn't she?' Sylvia said. An acid taste rose in her mouth as she read the piece about Josiah Barratt's death. Kitty's actions had shaken her to the core. Never, in her sheltered life, had she imagined anyone could be so deceitful. 'We all believed her.'

'What sort of a person would make up a thing like that?' Pauline said, staring at the paper, still half-disbelieving. 'I even offered to go with her to his funeral – no wonder she didn't want me to!'

Her father closed the paper. 'The wench must be warped in the head,' he said. 'That's all I can think. 'You know: bats in the belfry. But if I could get my hands on her, after what she did to you, Sylv . . .' He threw the paper onto the sideboard. 'The deceiving little bint.'

Jack was utterly outraged on Sylvia's behalf and kept pronouncing phrases such as 'Perfidious woman!' and

'Treachery!' but Sylvia could see that under his clever-clever pose, he was very angry and shaken at the way Kitty had taken them all in. He even came up to her, once or twice, and silently wrapped his arms around her.

But there was nothing anyone could do to ease her misery and the double sense of betrayal. She had been so badly hurt and, on top of that, there was all the embarrassment of having to cancel the wedding. Mrs Westley was mortified and, strangely, Sylvia liked her better now than at any other time. It was too late now, though, for that to make any difference.

The worst part was feeling so alone, as if part of her had been cut away. She missed being engaged, being part of a couple and all that meant. It meant feeling wanted and attractive, instead of rejected and worthless. Her future and all her hopeful plans of a home of her own, of grown-up life and babies, had been taken away. She found herself often in bitter tears. But despite all her family's care for her, the feeling that everyone had their eye on her to see if she was beginning to 'get over it' got on her nerves. It was such a relief to be alone.

When she had been walking for a time she found herself at the entrance to a churchyard in Moseley. On impulse she pushed open the wooden gate. It was very quiet inside, with no one about. The grass needed cutting; it was long and lush after all the rain. Sylvia walked past the church, along a path between the graves and yew trees, until she saw a secluded spot under a tree at the far end, beside an ivy-covered wall. She took her coat off and laid it on the ground to sit on. Looking up into the branches, she saw to her surprise that it was hanging with small, ripening apples. It seemed strange, but nice to have a tree blooming with fruit near the graves.

She sat for a moment, hugging her knees and taking in the calming peace of the place. She could hear small birds and the rattling call of a rook. Clouds passed swiftly across the sun. A breeze stirred the leaves. Sylvia reached into her pocket and lit up a cigarette. She never used to smoke, but everyone smoked these days. The cigarette was soothing, and the old building and the graves around her made her concerns seem less terrible, more just a part of the long sweep of time. She wondered about the people buried close by. What joys and calamities had made them either laugh or weep?

As that terrible month had passed, she began to single out particular feelings from among the swamping misery. One feeling surprised her now – an emotion that she could barely admit to. Sitting here, staring at the lichen-covered grave of a young woman called Mary Jane Friar, who had died in 1897, she knew that the feeling was relief. She did not have to marry Ian. She did not have to spend her life trying to keep up with him, to prove herself in some way. It was very hard to admit, but she had never felt Ian's equal. He was older, cleverer – he assumed, at least. Sylvia's lack of confidence allowed him to think of himself as superior. She had always felt as if she was about to let him down, and all the while let him think himself above her. It was all rather tiring.

Now that she hadn't seen him for several weeks, and had become more used to the loss of his physical close-ness, she could feel other emotions that she had always pushed into the background. There had been a pressure from him: *Be what I need you to be. Be the woman I need – pretty, ornamental and a bit dim – to make me look impressive as a man.*

Sylvia stared across the lush graveyard. She could see now that the trouble had started when she went to work for the railway and had become – in Ian's eyes – less of a woman. It was not just that she wore trousers and boots. She had gained other things: confidence, strength and a real feeling of being part of it all. Ian had not liked the fact that she was developing a mind of her own.

Sylvia stubbed out the cigarette and picked a buttercup that was growing in the grass. She stared into its golden-yellow depths.

'You wanted someone like Kitty, who'd simper all over you,' she whispered. 'Who would build you up. But sooner or later you're going to find out what she's really like, heaven help you!'

She placed the flower down and reached into her coat pocket, finding a treasured object there. She was filled with a sudden, reassuring feeling of warmth and excitement.

Soon after Ian left, Sylvia had bowed to pressure from her mother and written a brief letter to Laurie Gould. What was the harm? she thought. It took her mind off things for a short while, especially as writing was still quite an effort for her. But at least Laurie was one person who understood this. She did not tell him what had happened, not then. She just wrote a bit about her job and said that everyone was all right. She tried to reassure him about his mother. 'Your Mom's getting out more now,' she had told him:

My Mom and yours, and another few ladies, have set up a knitting circle. Some of them are in the WVS and they sell things in the shop. But it's mainly so they've all got a chance to meet and have a natter. They take it in turns to go to each other's houses, and when they came here it all sounded very cheerful. Paul goes along too and gets lots of fuss made of him. Mrs Simmonds is teaching him to knit – so far he's got a yellow scarf about an inch long and he keeps going round showing it to everyone!

It was not much of a letter, she thought, but she had done all she could.

Laurie must have replied almost the same day he received it. He told her he had been selected to be a navigator and was training at the Air Observer's School near Toronto. He chatted about his pals and some of the new things he'd learned and about the warm welcome some of the Canadians had given them. He had been to local homes for meals and been treated royally. Everyone was so kind and friendly. He said he liked Canada and would even think of living there, after the war was over. 'Sometimes I just think all of it's quite mad,' he wrote:

We're all so young, and a lot of the blokes training as pilots have never even driven a car – then we're all being put in charge of these huge planes. If you stop to think about it, it's madness. But then I suppose there are a lot of things it's better not to stop and think about in this war. Some aspects of life here I could do without – some things about living cheek by jowl with a whole load of other lads can be . . . Well, I won't go into detail. But most of them are terrific. And it can be enormous fun.

At the end, he wrote:

I'm really sorry, Sylvia. Mother told me what happened – with Ian. She says you're not yourself and

267

everyone's worried about you. Sounds really rotten.
I wish with all my heart that I could find a way to
cheer you up. I suppose I'm a bit in awe of you, as
you've been like 'a big sis' to me – you and Audrey
too, though Audrey's far more frightening! Anyway,
this is just to say that I do hope you'll be feeling better
soon, Sylv. If Ian could treat you like that, well . . . I
don't want to say anything bad about him, as I know
how keen you were on him, but what a fool he was to
let you go, that's all I can say.

She was touched by the letter. It felt strange, the idea
of writing letters to Laurie. Little Laurie Gould! But
he was not so little now. She was having to adjust to the
fact. And she had known him all her life. He felt safe and
kind. She wrote back quickly, suddenly feeling that he
was someone she could turn to, telling him more about
what had happened, about Kitty. Again Laurie must
have written back the day he received it and, when she
received that letter, she did the same.

It was Laurie's third letter that she took out to read
again now. It truly warmed her heart, and she had carried
it with her ever since it arrived:

Dear Sylvia,
    I may not be able to write much today, but I want
to get another letter off to you. Thanks for yours – it
means such a lot to hear from you, and I liked your
descriptions of the Goods Yard. Your 'Froggy' foreman
sounds a bit of a character! I've discovered from being
away that I like writing letters. It's like talking to you,
but different somehow. You can think more about what
you say.
    I hope all is going well at home. It does seem very

quiet over here, and safe. But they're keeping us busy. I'm in class most of the day, learning all the stuff a navigator needs, and sometimes I feel as if my head's going to explode with things like dead-reckoning (which means working out where you are – if only it was as simple as it sounds!). Anyway, time is too short to bore you with the details. Otherwise, we have also been exploring the town. I'm coming to the conclusion that now the novelty of Canada has worn off, I really prefer good old England after all. Everything here is too spread out and a bit too new. It just doesn't feel right – although I suppose one could get used to it. I'd love you to see it and tell me what you think.

I feel very shy saying this, Sylv, but I don't half miss you. I've realized, being away from home, just how much you mean to me. Well, maybe I had already begun to realize, but now I know for sure. You're a great girl, and I find myself thinking about you so often and wishing we could sit and chat, with all the time in the world. I don't want to say too much because I know you're grieving for Ian. And us being childhood pals – well, maybe it would be a challenge to change into a new gear, if you like. All I will say is that there's a heart that beats faster, over here in Canada, every time I think of you, and I want you to know that. I hope you won't think the worse of me for saying so. Whatever you feel about me, just know that you have a very big admirer, who thinks of you with great fondness and appreciation.

The letter finished with a few more remarks about daily life, but it was this last paragraph that Sylvia read again and again. She was struck by how good Laurie was at saying on paper what he felt. And his words struck a chord deep within her – the feelings of this boy who was suddenly a man.

She read the letter several times and for a moment held it close to her heart, picturing his kindly face and remembering his voice. His words had stirred feelings in her that made her happy in a calm, warm way.

'Laurie Gould,' she said, out loud, 'you're a nice, nice man. Come home soon.'

They day was darkening. Looking up, she saw the clouds gathering overhead. Folding the letter safely into her pocket, she got up to hurry home.

Thirty-Five

'Are you with us today?' Sergeant Nick Reynolds walked up behind Audrey.

She jumped, startled back to the present moment. 'What? Oh, yes, sir, I am.'

She and three other WAAFs were standing in line holding one of the balloon ropes on the airfield, in front of the huge hangars. It was another warm day and she was enjoying the feel of the sun on her upturned face. The balloon was tugging against their restraining hold, so there was a pleasing pull on her muscles. She was the last in line today, at the back.

Nick Reynolds kept moving, as if he had come all this way just to inspect their work. But as he walked past Audrey he breathed, very low, 'Fancy a drink tonight? Eightish?'

Audrey nodded, almost without thinking. It would have been hard to refuse. As Nick walked away towards another group of WAAFs, the girl in front of Audrey turned and made a face at her. 'You're in there, by the looks of it!'

Audrey gave what she hoped was a mysterious smile. Narrowing her eyes, she watched Reynolds's departing form. He had a straight back and carried himself well, his short fair hair neat against his head. She liked the way he walked. *A man*, her mind offered the words. *Go for a drink with him. He's a man – a nice one. Normal. That's what you are. A normal woman going out for a drink with a good-looking man.*

As soon as she and Dorrie had arrived back late on Sunday night they had released each other's hands and launched themselves among all the other girls in their huts. They had been so busy that Audrey had scarcely seen Dorrie since. In fact she had been throwing herself into activities and socializing. Caught between aching to see Dorrie, who above all people she longed to see, and fearing and dreading it, she kept herself in constant motion. Even when they were not working, she was cleaning her bed space in the hut and chatting feverishly to Maggie, Cora and the others – all the while trying not to think about what had happened in High Wycombe.

Now that they were back here, the whole thing felt like a dream. She only let herself remember when lying in bed, when doing so was so full of memories of Dorrie's fulsome body lying beside her. What had really happened? They had not done anything much at all, she told herself. There had been those snatched kisses, caresses under the bedclothes. But the thought of Dorrie – her full breasts, her lips – immediately filled her with an ache of desire. She almost tried to persuade herself that Dorrie was just being friendly. They were just pals – girls together. They had not talked about it. It all felt like a beautiful, loving dream. But now, back here, whatever could it mean? She felt ashamed, and terrified of anyone finding out. She tried to imagine taking Dorrie home, her Mom and Dad knowing what had gone on, and she was full of horror. Whatever happened, whatever you might call it – it had to stop.

At the end of their afternoon shift, once they had the balloon securely bedded down and put away, the transport came out to the airfield to pick them up. Audrey saw a familiar shape at the driving wheel. With a melting sensation inside, she saw Dorrie's bouncy hair under her cap, the shape of her face and the quizzical angle of her slender eyebrows. Audrey's body gave a throb of recognition. She took a deep breath and prepared to act normally.

Dorrie turned the truck with its winch, braking near the balloon squad. Her eyes sought out Audrey.

'What're you doing here?' Audrey called to Dorrie, trying to sound as if she might be talking to someone with whom she wasn't besottedly in love, whose very outline didn't make her feel like taking her in her arms.

'We had to do a swap,' Dorrie called, with no further explanation. But Audrey knew what the explanation was: Dorrie had managed to exchange jobs with someone else, in order to be close to her. Sitting perched on the back of the open truck, Audrey knew that her feelings were at war with each other. As soon as they stopped, she knew Dorrie would find a way of speaking to her. While this was exactly what Audrey longed for, she also knew she would try to fight it and avoid Dorrie. What else was there to do? They could hardly carry on the way they were at the Coopers' house, could they?

She jumped down as soon as the truck braked and started walking briskly away towards the NAAFI, laughing and chatting with some of her squad.

'Audrey!' She heard Dorrie's voice ring out behind her and she felt like a betrayer, turning casually to her as if to say, 'Oh – who are you again?'

'Hang on,' Dorrie said, running to catch up.

'You go on,' Audrey said to the others.

'There's a picture on tonight, if you fancy it,' Dorrie said. Now that they were alone she seemed edgy, as if she was afraid of Audrey and what she might say.

'Oh,' Audrey said. 'The trouble is, I've just said I'll go for a drink – with Nick Reynolds. Sorry, Dorrie.' She saw her friend trying not to show that she was hurt. 'He just asked me, when we were out on the field. It was difficult to say no.'

'Okay, never mind,' Dorrie said lightly. Audrey was about to turn away when Dorrie said in a low voice, 'Aud – I'm missing you terribly.'

Audrey stared at the ground. She felt the blood rise in her face, in a whole confusion of desire at the very sound of Dorrie's voice, yet embarrassment at her words. What if anyone heard? They were two women! This was unnatural – it could not be happening.

'Well,' she said, all awkwardness now, and unable to meet Dorrie's eyes. 'I miss you too. But we're back here now, aren't we?' She turned and walked away.

She met Nick Reynolds at eight and he invited her to come to the sergeants' mess. He was waiting near the entrance when she arrived and gave his easy smile at the sight of her. He was a good-looking, relaxed-seeming man, whom Audrey had realized was quite some years older than her – over thirty, she thought, looking at him as he greeted her.

'Good timing!' he said. 'Come on – let's get a drink.'

As they turned into the entrance to the mess, she felt his hand on her back, gentle, but as if steering her.

Audrey felt a combination of reassurance and irritation at this.

The mess was rowdy, with jazzy music blaring out and lots of male chat and laughter and smoke. There were other WAAFs sprinkled about, and Audrey caught sight for a moment of Cora's pale hair across the room. Cora waved and mouthed something at her, but she didn't catch it.

Nick brought the half of bitter that she had requested and sat next to her with his pint. 'Cheers!' He grinned, holding up the glass. 'At last you've agreed to come and have a drink with me. That feels like something to celebrate.'

It was an effort to say much in the mess as it was so noisy, so she gave him a smile, wondering why a nice man of his age was not married. Then she wondered if he was, in fact. She had never asked. She was not sure she wanted to know.

'How long've you been here?' she asked, having almost to shout.

'Only about twenty minutes,' he quipped.

Audrey put her head on one side. 'You know what I mean.'

'Oh – months. Forever.' Nick had to lean close for them to hear each other. His powerful body pressed against her shoulder. Audrey shifted on the bench. She had her uniform skirt on and eased it a little further down. 'They brought a few extras in, when the women were taken onto the job, but I was here before, training the blokes. You must've seen me around.' He took a drink and then said, 'Well, you've not got much longer here, have you? You'll be trained up by the end of the month. How're you finding it?'

'It's hard work,' Audrey admitted. 'I've found

muscles I never knew I had. But it's much better than sitting in the office.'

One of Nick's friends came up then, with a WAAF whom Audrey didn't know, and the four of them chatted for a time. The WAAF was rather a posh girl from Kent, who kept talking about her horses, and Audrey found her rather snooty. She was glad when they moved away and Nick suggested they go out and get some air. 'This is one of the few really fine days,' he said. 'Make the most of it, shall we?'

The sun was just setting as they went out into what could almost be called a balmy evening. Nick took Audrey's arm and she linked hers through his, feeling his hard, manly warmth beside her. Unlike Dorrie, he was much taller than her.

This is the proper thing, she thought, and her thoughts were like a harsh running commentary. I'm walking arm-in-arm with a man. She was glad there were a lot of personnel around to see them. Audrey White-house with Nick Reynolds. Man and woman. All as it should be.

As soon as they found a quiet spot, beyond the huts, Nick began to kiss her. Audrey responded enthusiastic-ally. She was a woman and she was attractive to men. This is what she should be doing, what was expected. But all the time, as Nick's kisses became more forceful and passionate, it was as if Audrey was viewing the whole thing from the outside. And she was glad when she heard people passing them, hoping she would be seen in Nick's embrace.

Nick pulled back for a moment, an aroused, almost drugged look on his face. 'God, you're a cracking woman, you are, Audrey. I thought that the moment I saw you.' His hand pressed into the small of her back, bringing her closer. 'Christ, I want you.'

She was desirable then. She was a real woman. But she felt trapped by his need. How could she get out of this?

'It's early days,' she said, drawing back. But she did not want to close the door on his attraction to her. Nick was nice enough, when he was not in this state. And she needed to continue seeing him. 'No need to rush, is there?' she added lightly.

When she got back to the hut and climbed into bed, she found a note tucked under the bedclothes. The lights were still on and she looked around to see if anyone was watching her. None of the others were taking any notice. She wondered when on earth Dorrie had put it there, and if anyone had seen, because she knew immediately who it was from. Keeping it well down in her lap, she opened it: *Let's meet tomorrow. I'll be driving you again. D x*

Thirty-Six

Audrey slept very badly that night. Her dreams were full of looming faces: Dorrie's and Nick's, both huge and distorted, both trying to make love to her. In the dream she kept pushing them away and running across the airfield, which was endlessly enormous. She had an idea that she might catch hold of the ropes of one of the balloons and be pulled up into safety. As she was swept off her feet she woke with a gasp of panic, the blood thudding in her ears.

After a few minutes, tears came. She felt so confused, afraid of what she felt – barely knowing what she *did* feel any more. Being with Dorrie that weekend was one of the best times of her life. She loved the talking and joking, the way their eyes met with such understanding and mischief. But the other things – the desire, the way they had slid into each other's arms. Surely that was wrong and unnatural? She dug around for the word in her mind. *Homosexual.* Was it? Surely that was just men? She'd seen one or two WAAF girls in pairs, which the other girls nudged each other about. 'Those two are, you know . . .' this usually with a wink, ' . . . *close.*' But that was not her, was it? She turned over in bed in an agony of feeling, remembering the hurt she had seen in Dorrie's eyes when she said she was going out with Nick last night. It was as if she had to make a choice between the two of them. If only Dorrie was a man, she found herself thinking. But then she wouldn't be Dorrie, would she? She almost groaned out loud with the ache of it all.

Dorrie was not driving them the next morning, to Audrey's disappointment and relief. They spent another warm day out on the airfield with the balloons and then did a couple of hours' rope-splicing. Now they were more familiar with how to do things, it was easier to chat and she managed to forget her troubles for a time.

She only saw Dorrie at the end of the shift, drinking tea in the NAAFI. As Audrey walked in, she spotted Dorrie immediately, at a table laughing with another driver. She was taken aback by the moment of jealousy that she experienced, seeing Dorrie smiling into the other girl's face. Then Dorrie caught sight of her and waved, smiling.

'Hello, Aud – come and join us!'

Audrey fetched her mug of tea, feeling a wave of light-heartedness come over her. Perhaps she was just being silly. Dorrie was her friend, that was all. Maybe she was just a bit more physical than some girls, but did that matter? After all Dorrie had been away to board-ing school, and those girls were always a bit odd, she'd heard.

'Look at the state of you,' Audrey said as she sat down. Dorrie's face was blackened with smears of oil and her nails were filthy.

Dorrie made a face. 'Is it that bad? I'll go and ablute when I've had this. Joan and I,' she nodded at the other girl, a rather horse-faced woman who smiled toothily at Audrey, 'have been driving some top brass about. Fairly top brass, anyway. Unfortunately, in my case, the car broke down – himself was none too pleased!'

Audrey laughed. 'Oh dear. Bet you weren't popular.'

'No. A visiting wing commander – he was trying to catch a train as well. I got him to the next one, and he was pretty civil about it. In fact I thought he was going to pat me on the head.'

'I'm glad it wasn't me,' Joan said. 'I'd have gone all to bits.'

'No, you wouldn't,' Dorrie said, preparing to bite into a dry-looking currant bun. 'You'd have got your head under the bonnet like anyone else. So,' she looked at Audrey, 'you been out on the field all day?'

When they had finished tea and chatted for a while they all got up to leave.

'Fancy coming along with me for a bit?' Dorrie said, casually, to Audrey.

Audrey, longing to put things right, agreed to go to Dorrie's hut. The place was almost identical to the one Audrey slept in, though it was fractionally less tidy. Dorrie's bed was at the far end. On a bed close to the door a gaggle of WAAFs were gathered around chatting, having just come off duty. Audrey realized it must be someone's birthday, as there seemed to be cake involved. Another girl, further down, was lying staring at the ceiling. As they passed her, Dorrie made a face.

'Man trouble, I think,' she whispered. 'She's unlucky in love, that one.' Louder she added. 'Look, just wait here a sec. I must go and sort my face out.' She draped her towel over her shoulder and rummaged among her things for a bar of soap. 'Back in a tick.'

Audrey sat on Dorrie's bed as she disappeared off to the ablutions hut. Bursts of laughter came from the girls at the other end and then a ragged rendering of 'Happy Birthday'. The unhappy-looking girl didn't stir. Audrey wondered about asking her if she was all right, but thought the better of it. She looked around. A dark corner of something caught her eyes, sticking out from under Dorrie's pillow. It took her a moment to realize that it was her diary. Usually Dorrie kept it hidden away in a little white drawstring bag, but she must have pushed it under there in a hurry.

She looked away, but a strong impulse of curiosity overcame her. What did Dorrie feel about her – about what had happened? Would she have written anything? I can't look, she told herself. That's sneaky and deceitful. Her heart pounded faster. She looked around the room again. No one was taking the slightest notice of what she was doing. Leaning over slightly, she pulled the blue book from under the pillow, glancing nervously at the door.

Opening it to recent pages, she saw Dorrie's looped, clear handwriting. Dorrie always wrote with a fountain pen, in blue-black ink. Quickly she turned to the latest entry, dated 2 September, written last night. It said simply:

I feel so lousy and miserable. Audrey's avoiding me like the plague now. The inevitable, I suppose. Maybe I was wrong. Alone again.

The words pierced Audrey painfully. From Dorrie's manner, it was impossible to see that she was feeling so bad. Flipping back, a word jumped out at her from an entry written a few days earlier: *lesbian*.

I love Audrey so much. The words won't come out of my mouth because I'm so frightened to burst this magnificent bubble of happiness that we have. She's the *one*, I think – the one I've been looking for all this time. Never have I known such a sense of peace in myself. I know I'm a lesbian – I suppose I have always known it, since I was old enough to think about it. But Audrey – oh God, I don't know if she has any idea what I feel, or what she is, and I'm so terrified of losing this. I fear she'll run away from me and I could not bear that. Oh, for a world where we can all just be the people we were meant to be, instead of all this hiding and pretence and having to fit the mould.

I know some girls just pair up here, but I'm a more private sort – I can't stand the thought of them gossiping and pointing the finger, the way they do. I suppose this makes me a coward. I want to speak to Audrey, to hear her say loud and clear that she's mine, that she'd stand by me through anything – her and me together, whatever. Maybe it's too soon. Perhaps it will always been too soon. *I can't say it.*

Audrey's eyes dashed along the lines, eating up the words, torn between joy and exultation at how much Dorrie felt for her, and the appalling shock of *that word*. Cuddles and kisses were one thing; unspoken feelings, looks, even holding hands. But seeing that word, *lesbian*, she was filled with panic. Didn't it mean sordid things, secrets and being outcast? *Queer.* Shoving the diary back under Dorrie's pillow, she hurried out of the hut, glancing left and right to see if Dorrie was coming, but there was no sign of her.

She tore along to her own hut and threw herself, panting, on the bed.

Maggie watched, bemused. 'Where's the fire?' she said.

*

It wasn't hard to find Nick Reynolds that night, or any other night, because most days she saw him during training, and Nick was very keen to meet her later again, for a drink. She smartened herself up, dabbed a bit of lipstick on, lent to her by Cora, and put her hair up.

'You going with that bloke I saw you with the other night?' Cora asked, also titivating before a date.

'Yup, that's the one,' Audrey said breezily.

'Might see you later then – mine's a corporal.'

Audrey looked round and smiled. This was more like it. Meeting men: the whole game of men and women, the courting procedure. She slotted herself back into it with determination. No one was going to call her queer. For a moment she imagined Sylvia's baffled face, if Audrey was to announce that she had taken up with a woman.

'But, Audrey, *why* on earth?' she would say, with her innocent look. 'Imagine what Mom and Dad will say. People will talk . . .' Good old Sylv – straight as a die.

It was just unthinkable. She might have been a bit of a tomboy, but that didn't make her one of *those*. Dorrie would just have to get over things. Then, maybe, they could be friends.

She put her jacket on and patted her hair. 'Coming then?' she asked Cora. 'We might as well go together.'

They set out across the base, laughing and joking. It was a relief to be with someone uncomplicated and fun.

'Hello, Beautiful,' Nick said, when she met him outside the sergeants' mess.

Audrey smiled. She knew she looked good, and she was feeling very healthy and fit from all the balloon work. She felt strong and powerful – and feminine, she thought, enjoying the desire she could see in Nick's eyes.

They spent a couple of hours talking and drinking. Nick was keen on sport and could talk endlessly about cricket and football. Audrey listened politely, though she had never played either and therefore did not find them especially thrilling as a topic of conversation. But Nick did take an interest in her and asked about her family, her home life. She asked about his, but all Nick said was, 'Oh, nothing much to say. Mother, father, one sister. No excitements!'

For her last two weeks at Cardington the warm evenings ended up in much the same way, in a dark spot somewhere on the base with Nick, in each other's arms, kissing for a long time. Nick kept pushing things further and further. It was very clear what he wanted, and Audrey was having to work hard to fend him off.

Audrey got back to her hut one night, during the first week when she was seeing Nick. She came in screwing up her eyes against the light, her lips feeling bruised and her cheeks tingling from the rasp of Nick's stubble.

Cora had got in just before her and everyone was getting ready for bed. Just as Audrey sat down to unlace her shoes, Cora came over and sat beside her with a solemn face. As ever, she looked immaculate. Audrey could visualize her in her department-store job, recommending nail varnish and face powder.

'Nick Reynolds,' Cora said, as if checking she had the right name.

'Yes,' Audrey said. 'What about him?'

Cora hesitated. 'You do know he's married?'

Audrey wasn't sure if she actually gasped out loud. She felt a plunging sensation of shock. Emotions followed: dismay, but then also a floating sense of relief.

Nick could not expect any commitment from her. He was not free. No wonder he was not keen to talk about his personal life.

'I thought he might be,' Audrey said. She felt a blush rise in her cheeks.

'The chap I was with tonight knows him – and the wife as well. There's a child, too. Just thought I'd better say, so that you're not the only one in the dark.' Cora got up to head back to her bed. 'All up to you entirely, of course. None of my business. I just didn't want to see you heart-sore, darling.'

Thirty-Seven

It was not too difficult to avoid Dorrie on such a big, busy RAF base. Audrey and the other balloon trainees were out almost all day, and Dorrie was not their driver. Nor did she seek Audrey out. They both did their jobs, and mostly their paths never crossed. Once or twice in the next week Audrey spotted Dorrie in the distance, both times walking alone, with her head down.

The second time she saw Dorrie coming along one of the camp roads heading towards the huts. Audrey dodged back down a side-road, praying that Dorrie wouldn't come along there. Dorrie kept walking without even raising her head. As she passed the end of the road and Audrey saw her familiar form moving past, she was filled with agony. To anyone else, Dorrie might seem lost in thought. But to Audrey she appeared utterly dejected. All she longed to do was to run and put her arms round her.

But she shook that impulse away with a sense of horror. No, her head told her coldly. Dorrie was a queer, and she wasn't. Simple as that. Surely Dorrie must have got the message by now? What had she made of Audrey disappearing from the hut the other day? Had she worked out that Audrey must have looked in her diary and seen her terrible, dirty thoughts?

But the moment Dorrie disappeared ahead of her, Audrey felt absolutely miserable. It was like a light being turned off, leaving her in foggy gloom. The extent of this feeling frightened her as well.

'Damn it!' she cursed, marching along towards her hut, angry now, though she could not have said why. She had a date with Nick tonight and she had to prettify herself. God knew, she was a woman, wasn't she? That's what women were supposed to do, not moon about drooling over other girls – that was *queer*.

'I've got other fish to fry,' she told herself determinedly. What did it matter if Nick was married? They were only having a bit of a drink together. It wasn't as if she wanted to marry him herself, was it?

As she readied herself for the evening she hardly dared ask herself what it was that she did want. *A man*, was all she could think. *I need to know that I'm attractive to a man.*

They went out to a pub that evening, a few miles out of Bedford. There was a small group of them, and one of the men had the use of a car. Audrey found herself among a collection of people she did not know at all, apart from Nick. It was best that way. Even though Cora had spoken to her only in friendship to warn her about Nick, she didn't want Cora watching her every move.

The driver and his girlfriend, Violet, sat in the front. Audrey and Nick were squeezed in the back with two others, a man and another WAAF called Elizabeth. She was rather buxom and space was tight, so Audrey spent the journey on Nick's lap, her head bent so as not to bang her head on the roof of the old Morris. Nick had his arms round her waist. While he chatted to the others, Audrey tried to sit in as unprovocative a position as possible, although she could sense Nick's excitement. All the while his left hand, closest to the door, was gently stroking her back. She felt a combination of excitement and embarrassment and throughout the journey did not turn to look at him once.

They all piled out and went into the busy little pub: Audrey and Nick; Elizabeth, the WAAF orderly (though not one Audrey remembered seeing when she was in the sick quarters), and her RAF boyfriend, Richard; and Joe the driver and Violet, a slender, ginger-haired girl. It was a warm evening, the sky was clear and tinged with mauve at the horizon. They joined others who had spilled out onto the grass at the back, which sloped gently down to a stream. They were a nice enough crowd. Audrey took a liking to Violet, who was not a WAAF, but said that she worked, for the duration, as a telephone operator at Bedford railway station.

'My sister works for the railway as well,' Audrey told her.

Violet's face lit up. 'Does she? Where?'

'Birmingham. She's a porter.'

'Crikey!' Nick laughed. 'I bet she's built like a prize fighter.'

'No, she's not at all,' Audrey retorted. 'She's lovely and slim – and very pretty. She's just doing a good job for the war effort.'

'Like you girls on the balloons,' Nick said. Joe and Richard laughed, though Audrey couldn't see what there was to laugh about. She knew they *were* doing a perfectly good job. Nick took a drag of his cigarette. They all had cigarettes, the smoke wafting away on the light breeze. 'Hey,' he put his arm round Audrey. 'Don't take on. I'm sure your sister's a little cracker.'

'She *is*,' Audrey said.

'Pretty as you?' Nick looked deep into her eyes.

'Prettier.'

'Bring her along next time!' Joe joked.

Audrey was about to reply that Sylvia was engaged to be married, when she realized that this was long out of date. She wondered how Sylvia was feeling now. She must write to her! The days were so full, and passed so quickly, that she hardly ever got round to it.

The boys were laughing at something. Audrey dragged her mind back to the present. Elizabeth was too far away from her to get talking, so she struck up a conversation with Violet, who turned out to come from a large family, having six brothers and two sisters. They spent most of the evening chatting about home and their jobs.

'I was glad to get out, to tell you the truth,' Violet said. She wrinkled her nose, which was scattered with freckles. 'I was stuck in a wet-fish shop before, so when the chance came to go into the railways, I jumped at it.'

Audrey laughed. 'You must've stunk!'

'I did!'

'I was doing clerical work. It made me want to bang my head on the desk with boredom. You can see why people get married, just to get out of it.'

She expected Violet to look shocked, but she nodded. 'You can, but that's no answer, is it? My mum and dad shouldn't've gone near each other with a ten-foot barge pole, but they're stuck with each other now.'

Audrey wasn't sure what to say. She realized that her own mother and father were quite happy, compared to a lot of people. 'Oh dear,' she said. 'Like that, is it?'

Violet nodded. 'It's like that all right. But what can they do? They've got nine children.' She looked away, to the sky in the far distance. 'I'm not letting that happen to me.' She smiled. 'Look, the moon's coming up – it's nearly full. Isn't that lovely?'

A big, golden disc was rising slowly above the fields, fresh and beautiful, as though to greet a world filled with peace. A pair of ducks flew over, yakking urgently in the gentle evening air. For a moment they all looked, in silence.

On the drive back, once again Audrey had to sit on Nick's lap. As the journey progressed, and now that they had been drinking, she could feel him becoming amorous, his hand finding its way up to stroke her breasts in the darkened vehicle. She kept trying to fend him off, but it was hard work. Nick was not going to let her go easily when they got back to the base.

'Come with me afterwards,' he kept whispering. 'I need you, Audrey. I need you badly.' She could smell the drink on his breath. And the beer she had drunk gave her a devil-may-care attitude. It was fate. Whatever would happen would happen. And it was a heady feeling to be needed so much.

As they drove back to the edge of the town, Nick called to Joe, who was driving, 'Stop, will you, pal? Audrey and I've got someone we've got to go and see. We can walk back to Shortstown from here.'

By the time she had begun to gather her thoughts, it was too late to protest. She and Nick were climbing out of the car at the very edge of town, where the houses petered out onto the country road. The others called out ribald goodbyes and there was nothing she could do about it. She was already half-walking, half-running as Nick tugged on her hand, back away from the town.

'Come on,' he urged her. 'I know where we can go!' He slowed, realizing, even in his half-drunk state, that this was no way to woo a woman. He turned and wrapped his arms round her. 'God, Audrey, you're a cracker, you are. I don't know what you do to me. I can't stop thinking about you every minute of the day.'

He pressed his lips to hers, clumsily, forcing his tongue between her teeth. She tasted tobacco and cheap Scotch. He released her and began to pull her along the road again. Audrey, with a cold feeling of helplessness, abandoned herself to fate. She had only the most basic knowledge of what men did, even now, after all these evenings of Nick fumbling at her in dark corners, his hands finding their way into the most intimate places he could manage, panting with frustration that he could not go any further.

'Here's a place.' They were among the fields again now, in the moonlight – a bomber's moon, she thought. Nick ran to a five-bar gate and vaulted over it, turning to help her climb over, which was made more difficult by the fact that she was wearing her WAAF skirt.

Once inside the field it was hard to see, despite the moon.

'Are those cows over there?' she asked fearfully.

'They won't take any notice,' Nick said. 'Here – come along here.'

There was a soft squelching feeling as she moved her right foot forward. 'Oh no – ugh! I've trodden in it!'

'Just wipe your foot off on the grass,' he ordered impatiently. She obeyed, taking her time.

Nick reached for her and pulled her into his arms again. 'Now's our chance.' His voice was low and urgent. 'I need to have you, Audrey – none of this playing around. There's only so much I can stand. I need to have you properly.' He pulled her hips in towards his own, to make her feel how stiff he was, then stepped back to unbutton.

'Take your things off,' he ordered her.

This was being a woman, she thought. What she had to do . . . As she drew down her underwear, he reached for her hand.

'Feel – this is how much I need you.' He pulled her to his upright cock and made her close her hand it round it. All she could do was obey now. It seemed too late for anything else. She was surprised at how hot it felt, how smooth. He moved against her hand.

'Lie down,' he said. 'Now, for Christ's sake.'

She lay beneath his weight, her eyes tightly closed, and knew she was doing the right thing; that this was a fast-moving stream that she had to allow to carry her away.

Thirty-Eight

October 1941

Sylvia carried the pail of chicken feed out into the dying light of the afternoon.

'Here you are, girls!' She scattered the feed into the run and the hens lunged at it. There had been some replacements of the five original 'royal ladies'. Victoria had escaped one night and was never seen again – 'A fox, I expect,' Mom said – and Eleanor and Isabella had both taken sick and died. So Elizabeth and Lady Jane had been joined by the 'Andrews Sisters', LaVerne, Maxene and Patty, and by a new, noisy cockerel called The Duke.

Sylvia stood watching them with her arms folded. After a moment she realized she was humming – 'He's the boogie woogie bugle boy of company B' – and was so surprised that she stopped. I don't feel so bad any more, she thought, with a faint smile. Although all her miserable, betrayed feelings could still surface very easily, there were cracks of light in the darkness.

These past months had been the worst time of her life. Thoughts about what Ian and Kitty had done were so bitter and hard to cope with that at times she felt she might go mad dwelling on it. Worst of all was going out: to town, or the journey to work. She lived in dread of meeting either of them, yet at the same time she was

293

always looking for them, as if she still needed to see them to believe that what had happened was actually true. Once she did think she saw Kitty, in the distance in New Street, and hurried to catch up, not knowing what she was going to do when she did. But the young woman with Kitty's colouring must have turned in somewhere and Sylvia lost her. She had no idea where Kitty was working now – she could have found a job in any of the offices in the city. She had seen no sign of Ian. Between them, the two of them had punctured the simple, innocent way in which she had seen life before. They had given her a harder, more sceptical view of things, and especially of men.

Sylvia went and picked up the pail. Jack can do the rabbits, she thought. A goods train was rumbling past, but as the sound died, she heard something else, the sound of off-key singing coming from the Goulds' garden. She realized Paul must be out there, and she squeezed round the end of the chicken run and looked over the wall. Paul was playing with a box with wheels fixed on either side, pushing it back and forth, in his own world. From the back, with his thick, blond hair, he looked quite like Laurie.

'Pauly?' She had to call him a few times before he noticed her. He hurried over to the wall, beaming with delight at seeing her.

'Is that your go-kart, Pauly?'

He laughed and pointed. 'It's a car!'

'It's very nice. I bet it goes fast. Aren't you chilly though, love?' He only had a short-sleeved shirt on over his trousers. 'It's getting cold out here.'

Paul looked down at himself for a moment, then up at Sylvia again, grinning all over his round face.

'Laurie's coming!' he announced.

Sylvia felt a shock of excitement go through her. Laurie had told her it would be soon, but had not been able to say exactly when. 'Laurie – is he? When, Pauly?'

Paul waved his arms. He didn't know. 'Laurie!' he repeated happily.

'Paul!' Stanley Gould came outside and stood with his hands on his hips. 'What're you doing out here, lad? Come on, your mother wants you. Oh, hello, Sylvia – I didn't see you there.'

'I was admiring Paul's go-kart,' she said.

'Oh, yes,' Mr Gould said dismissively. 'Come on, Paul – you get yourself inside.'

Paul blundered away across the garden, making his little noises and holding his arms out. He liked pretending to be a Spitfire. He disappeared into the house.

Mr Gould, who was a tight, tetchy man these days, was about to turn away. He obviously had things on his mind. Sylvia spoke up quickly. 'Paul said Laurie's on his way home, Mr Gould?'

'Is that Sylvia?' she heard Marjorie's voice, and then saw her come hurrying out in her apron, holding half a cabbage. 'Hello, love – yes, we had a wire from Laurie, just this afternoon. He'll be home today or tomorrow!'

'He's been posted to Lincolnshire,' Stanley said. He seemed to soften a fraction. Everyone loved Laurie – how could you not? 'But they've given him a bit of leave.'

'That's nice for you,' Sylvia said, her heart beating harder.

'Ooh, yes – we can't wait,' Marjorie said. She came over to Sylvia. 'And I know you've been writing to each other, love.' Her voice was warm with approval. 'He's looking forward to seeing you.'

Sylvia felt herself blush and was glad it was so dark.

'Thanks, Mrs Gould,' she said, touched.

'Must get the tea,' Marjorie said. 'I'm sure Laurie'll be round, soon as he can!'

Stanley Gould stood for a moment as if lost in thought.

'That's nice news,' Sylvia said.

'Oh, ar,' he said. 'It is. Marjorie's very pleased, that she is. Must get on,' he added, turning purposefully towards the house.

Sylvia watched him walk away. Marjorie's pleased, Marjorie's upset. These were the only ways Mr Gould ever let you in on what he was feeling.

She hugged herself with excitement. Laurie was back in England!

Up in her room Sylvia took out her bundle of Laurie's letters from her chest of drawers. She smiled at the sight of his messy, left-handed boy's handwriting. She remembered him hunched over the table for the ordeal of forming his letters, his brow pulled into a frown and the tip of his tongue curled out to touch his nose. Sylvia still imagined him writing like that now, the letters looked so tortured.

Laurie had written to her regularly from Canada and she had found his letters the brightest light by far in a dark time. As the weeks went by he seemed to become more, rather than less, homesick. And he confided in her his worries about his parents. Having lost Raymond and with him away, he knew things must be difficult. When Sylvia wrote back she tried to paint things as optimistically as she could.

Sitting on the bed, she pulled out one of the letters and leaned back against the wall to read it:

It's good to hear from home, Sylv – and I like hearing about the yard! Your muscles must be hard as iron by now. It makes me think of the trains going by at home. It's things like that you really miss: noises and smells. I find myself getting all sentimental about odd things that over there you barely notice. I miss listening to the wireless and the smell of everything – the grass and winter mornings – and even the smoky, foggy stink of dear old Brum!

I found myself thinking about Snow Hill the other day. It was about the most exciting place in the world when we were nippers, because if we went to Snow Hill station it meant we were going away on holiday. We never went there at any other time. Dad used to take us to Devon, some years – d'you remember us going off? We all wished you could all have come as well. But the best bit was going to Snow Hill, everyone crowding onto the platform and cheering when the train pulled in. Dad lifted me up, so I could see the loco with the smoke pouring out. And he'd say: *Look, that's a King, or a Castle, or whatever it was* (I never remembered details the way Raymond did). And there was that enormous clock on platform seven, and the one in the ticket office where everyone used to meet. Right now, I can't think of anything better than pulling into Snow Hill and knowing that someone would be waiting there for me under the clock – and especially if I knew that someone would be you, Sylvia.

Smiling, she pressed the letter against her body and lay back for a moment. So Laurie was almost home. A

297

strange, apprehensive tingle went through her. Laurie had been writing to her all this time because he was homesick, and she was part of home. And she had gladly written back. His kind, affectionate letters had been the thing that had brought her through these awful, painful months. But how would it be when he came home and they were really together, face-to-face?

When he came at last, two days later, she was upstairs changing out of her work clothes after an early shift. There was a tap at the front door, followed by a burst of male voices and laughter. Jack had just got home and he and Laurie were in the hall, clowning about and play-fighting. She rolled her eyes fondly. Thumping each other seemed to be the boys' best way of showing how pleased they were to see each other.

'Hello, love,' her mother's voice floated up from the hall. 'Jack, pack that in – poor Laurie's hardly over the step. Ooh, lad, haven't you *grown*? I can't get over it! Sylvia's here – I'll call her . . .'

Sylvia went down the stairs, her heart thumping like a little piston and feeling self-conscious as the eyes of not just Laurie, but her mother and Jack, followed her every move. She saw Laurie's eager face turned up to hers and immediately she knew her feelings had not been a mistake. She was filled with excitement and a shy tenderness. Laurie had changed out of his uniform by now, into his old brown trousers and a navy sweater, so that he looked like the old Laurie, only more grown-up, his blond wavy hair shorn close to his head.

'Hello, Laurie,' she said.

He smiled broadly. 'Hello, Sylv.'

'Come on – kettle's on. I might even be able to rustle

up a few biscuits, if you speak to me nicely,' Mom said.

Pauline and Jack went into the kitchen. For a few seconds Sylvia found herself alone with Laurie. After all these years when she had noticed him hardly more than the chairs and tables, now she was acutely conscious of him. He had filled out and grown into a strong, impressive-looking man, despite his still-youthful face.

Laurie was smiling at her, his eyes full of delight. For just a second before they followed the others, he took her hand and squeezed it, looking questioningly at her. She smiled, feeling a blush spread up her cheeks, and squeezed his hand back like a promise.

A few minutes later Marjorie and Paul also came round, Marjorie bringing half a cake, which they added to the tea and biscuits, all sitting around in the back room. It felt like a celebration and Sylvia could see Marjorie's relief and happiness. Her eyes were brighter than they had been in weeks and she laughed and smiled. Everyone hung on Laurie's words.

'Your father'll want to hear all this again when he gets home,' Marjorie said. 'But you tell us anyhow.'

Laurie talked about Canada and the training and his pal, Victor, who had also gone out to train there, determined that the only thing in life worth doing was being a pilot.

'Trouble was, he just couldn't do it,' Laurie said. 'He had an almighty job getting the thing off the ground, and an even worse time landing. He couldn't seem to judge heights or distances – he crashed two kites, trying to land!'

'Kites?' Jack asked, drinking all this in.

'That's what we call the planes.' Laurie was awash with RAF terms.

'Oh, my word!' his mother said. 'He can't have been very popular.'

'He wasn't. They knew it wasn't really his fault, but obviously you can't have that. So they sent him over to train with us as a navigator. He thought the world had ended to begin with, because he'd failed as a pilot, but he got stuck in, in the end.'

'It must be the most important job, what you're doing,' Sylvia said. 'I mean, if you got lost . . .'

'We're a team,' Laurie said. 'No one's more important than anyone else. From bomb-aimer to—'

'Oh!' Pauline gasped, a hand going to her chest. 'Bomb-aimer!'

'We're going into Bomber Command,' Laurie said. He looked down at the table for a moment. Pauline and Marjorie exchanged looks.

'I know, love,' Pauline said quietly.

Sylvia felt a chill come over her. She didn't really know what being in Bomber Command involved, but they had been on the receiving end of bombing here all right. But no one wanted to spoil the party. They got Laurie to tell them about the pranks and other fun he'd got up to in Canada. Sylvia watched him, impressed by how much he had changed. Laurie had been a shy boy who had difficulty making conversation or looking you in the eye. But now he had grown used to talking with strangers and had developed a direct, lively gaze. As she watched him, feelings grew in her – warm, loving feelings. She just enjoyed being in the same room, watching his quick smile, hearing his familiar voice. His presence was so much lighter and younger than Ian's. It felt like coming home. There was such a feeling of rightness that she had to stop herself sitting there wearing a permanent soppy grin. In fact she saw Jack looking at her in an amused sort of way once or twice.

Once tea was over, Jack insisted that Laurie come and help him feed the rabbits and hens. As he got up to go out with Jack, Laurie leaned over to Sylvia. 'Can I see you a bit later?'

She looked up and smiled yes.

'It's always difficult to find anywhere to be on your own in this house,' Sylvia said when he came back in. Ted had come home by now and greeted Laurie warmly. But even Jack got the hint and the rest of the family melted away and left them alone in the back room.

'Let's sit at the table, shall we?' Laurie said. He looked around fondly. 'I've got so many good memories of sitting here – and this afternoon's been another one. It's the cosiest place I know.'

They sat down by the table and chatted for a bit. Laurie asked after Audrey.

'Oh, she's all right,' Sylvia said. 'Seems to love the WAAF. Duck to water.'

Laurie smiled. 'I can imagine.'

'In fact she loves it so much we hardly hear from her. She doesn't love us any more!' She said it as a joke, but all the family were a bit hurt that Audrey seemed to have forgotten their existence.

'Oh, I expect she's just got caught up in it all,' Laurie said. 'The life's very busy.'

'Huh!' Sylvia said. 'I dare say she could find time, if she put her mind to it.'

After a bit more chat they were suddenly at a loss. Despite their letters and fond words and Laurie having grown up so much, it was hard to move from being friends as children to something more adult. Laurie sat with his arms folded on the table and looked down at the blue cloth, as if searching the table top for inspiration. But once he met her eyes again he was surprisingly direct.

'I've loved getting your letters,' he said. 'It's kept me going – it really has.'

'It wasn't so bad over there, was it?'

'No, I didn't mean that. But it throws you back on yourself, not having any family or anyone familiar around. You start to think about what really matters to you. And where we're going, Bomber Command . . .' He trailed off and just gazed at her. She was moved by the intensely loving look in his eyes. He reached out and took her hand, asking permission with his eyes, and she opened her palm, her pulse racing.

'I thought I might find you looking very pale and sad,' he said. 'If I'm honest, I've wanted to go and punch Ian's lights out, for what he did to you.' There was a flicker of a smile. 'Not that it would have helped.' He squeezed her hand. 'But you look . . . lovely.'

Sylvia blushed at the warmth of the compliment. 'It was all a bit of a shock,' she said. 'But I've got over it now, though.'

'Have you?' His eyes searched her face.

She nodded. 'I can still get really angry sometimes. But maybe I had a lucky escape. I don't think Ian was quite what I thought. Because he was older I just thought he was wiser than he was, I suppose. But if he could be taken in by Kitty like that, I'm well rid of him.'

To her annoyance, tears filled her eyes. She wiped them away. 'Sorry. Brings it back.'

'Hey,' Laurie shifted closer and held one of her hands

between his in a way she found deeply touching. 'It's okay. I've realized, being away and everything . . . It's not a lot of fun being in the services sometimes, but they do keep you busy and make you feel that everything you do is *for* something. Being at home's much harder. Like my mother – and yours – just having to keep everything going, when it's all much worse than it was before.'

'The railway's a bit like the services in some ways,' she said. 'They make you feel it's all *for* something, too – and it is. But the best thing, over these months, has been hearing from you. It's made all the difference.'

'I thought of you every day – all day. Well, maybe not quite,' he laughed. As he spoke he gently caressed her hand. 'I had to do a spot of navigating now and then, but it was as if . . .' He stopped to think. 'Being over there, I saw everything differently. I saw *you* differently. I know you've always looked on me as a kid brother, and I didn't think you could ever feel what I feel for you now. But age doesn't matter that much, does it?'

'It doesn't matter,' she said. 'And you don't seem younger – not now.'

Suddenly there were even more silences in the conversation as they couldn't stop staring into each other's eyes.

'You're so lovely,' Laurie said in wonder. His face moved closer to hers and she saw the pale down of hair on his upper lip, his scattering of freckles. 'Sylvia, Sylvia. I've been dreaming of seeing you.'

'It's so strange,' she said. 'All this time you've been here, right in front of me . . .' And as they both leaned forward to kiss each other, they both knew what she meant.

1942

Thirty-Nine

January 1942

'I still can't even *feel* my hands and feet,' Elsie groaned, clapping her gloved hands as she and Sylvia pushed their empty barrows across the cartage area of the shed. The Goods Yard outside was white with snow and a flurry of flakes was coming down again. Elsie's nose was red with cold and her eyes were running. It was close to the end of the shift and she was still cold, even after toiling back and forth all day.

'Never mind, we're nearly done,' Sylvia said. She and Elsie often worked together now. 'You're too skinny, that's your trouble. You want some more flesh on your bones.'

'Thanks,' Elsie said, with the irritation of someone who has spent much of her life failing to gain weight. 'Ey-up,' she added, as a young lad dashed past them as if looking for someone. 'He's a new one in the offices. Poor little bugger – I s'pect they've sent him out to fetch the Fog Book.'

Sylvia laughed. This was one of the favoured initiation rites for young clerks at the Goods Yard. Some fool's errand would be found to get them running anxiously around, only to end up with a very red face.

'They sent one out to fetch a bag of sparks for the

fireworks a few months back!' she laughed. She called to him. 'Eh!' The boy jumped. 'Yes, you! What've they sent you out for?'

The lad, pale, weedy and nervous-looking, swerved in her direction. 'I've been told to fetch a porter called Sylvia White . . . White-something. D'you know which one she is?'

'I do,' Sylvia said solemnly. Elsie was grinning beside her. The lad was so earnest. 'That'd be me.'

'There's a bloke at the gate asking after you,' he gabbled, as if delivering the message would be a weight off his mind. 'Says you're expecting him.'

'Oh!' Sylvia gasped, her heart hammering with sudden excitement. 'Oh, ta very much.' Without stopping to explain to Elsie, she upended her empty trolley and tore across the yard. The air was full of whirling snowflakes. Could it be – could it really? He'd said he'd be coming soon. Like Audrey, apparently, he couldn't be here for Christmas . . . But now, could it really be . . . ?

Through the whiteness she saw Laurie standing just inside the gate, keeping out of the way of the weigh-bridge. He had his hands in his pockets, a black scarf wrapped over his chin, but no hat and his hair was coated in snowflakes. He looked cold and a bit uncertain. When he caught sight of her hurrying across the busy yard, he leapt into life. Looking round to check that no vehicles were heading for him, he ran to meet her. Without thinking, they flung their arms round each other, at which a ragged round of cheers and applause rose from the carters and porters around the yard.

'I can't believe you're here!' she cried, kissing his cold cheek. Everything was suddenly lit up with joy. He was here – really here! 'Oh, look at your hair!' She started gently knocking the snow off him.

Laurie grinned. 'I only got in a couple of hours ago, but I had to come and find you – and see this place.

He was about to kiss her when both of them became aware of the commotion they were causing. Sylvia stepped back, blushing, as one of the men trying to drive a truck past shouted, 'Don't mind us, bab – we've got all day. There ain't no war going on or anything.'

'Sorry!' she called, blushing again, but saw that he was grinning.

'My goodness, this is a place, isn't it?' Laurie said, looking round. He seemed fascinated. 'I've never been in one of these yards before. Mighty busy, isn't it?'

'I'm nearly finished,' she said, feeling very proud and active in her work clothes. 'I've got one more load, then I can stow my trolley and get my things. Come over here and I'll show you round.'

Once they'd finished, she showed him the yard and round the shed. It was full of trains loading and un-loading, porters hurrying back and forth, tarpaulins being fixed on, loads being checked. They walked along to look out over the shunting yard and the roundhouse.

'The cut's just behind there,' she said. 'And there's the coal store – and look, they're just bringing this one in.'

A line of wagons was clanking to a halt in the shed, the engine letting out a long swoosh of steam outside. Sylvia could see that Laurie was loving seeing it all.

'I wonder what's in there?' he said.

'Could be all sorts of things,' Sylvia laughed. 'We get just about everything through here. Even a goat or two!'

'This looks really hard work. You're amazing, Sylv!' He looked at her with happy admiration and put his arm round her back for a moment.

'Well, I'm glad you think so,' she joked. But she was

delighted. Laurie was genuinely appreciative of her, and it was such a change after Ian.

Laurie came and met her off her shift the next day too. Gina and Elsie soon caught on to the fact that an admirer was coming to meet her. She received plenty of teasing.

'It's certainly better seeing you looking a bit more cheerful,' Gina told her, as they chatted during one of their breaks. 'Instead of like someone who's just been to a funeral.'

'Thanks, Gina,' Sylvia said. 'I'll try to look overjoyed at all times.'

'By the look of that feller of yours, you won't have to try too hard. He's mad about you – it's written all over him.'

'You want to hold on to that one,' Elsie said.

'He's a good 'un all right,' Sylvia said, grinning.

During the few snatched hours she and Laurie managed to spend together on his leave, it didn't take Sylvia long to realize that she was more in love than she had ever been in her life before. As well as Laurie's kindness and respect towards her, there was a comfort in being with him that went very deep. They knew each other's lives and families so well that there was no having to prove anything, or struggle to measure up, as she had felt she had to do with Ian. Being with Laurie was so much better – so right! They could reminisce together and share old jokes as well as new ones.

Laurie only had two days of leave. Without saying anything to each other, they both decided they would not talk or think about the war. Now that the Americans were in the war after the Japanese bombing of Pearl Harbor, there was more of a sense of energy and optimism. But it did not take away the fact that Laurie was now in Bomber Command. None of it was over, but for the moment they wanted to be a young couple who could think about the future and dream dreams, as if there was no war to ruin them.

They went on snowy walks on both days, in the remaining afternoon light after Sylvia finished work. Arm-in-arm they wandered into the wonderland of the parks. The branches were two-tone, with their top layer of snow and the grass a white swathe several inches deep, crossed here and there with lines of footprints. The second day they took Paul as well and he ran up and down shrieking like a small child and demanded a snowball fight, which they gave him, keeping it gentle and good-natured. Paul got bored with that and whirled off, skipping across the snow so that they had to run to keep up. When they all arrived back at the Goulds', pink-faced, laughing and half-saturated, Marjorie sat them down and fed them tea and bread and jam and looked happier than Sylvia could remember in months. Mr Gould seemed chirpier too. Both the Goulds were delighted that Laurie and Sylvia were in love.

'Thanks for taking Paul with you,' Marjorie said, watching the boy gobble down his tea. 'I just can't keep up with him these days. I hope he was good?'

'Course he was,' Sylvia said. 'You were ever such a good boy, weren't you, Pauly? And he had a lovely run around.'

Everyone wanted to see Laurie, so the times he and Sylvia had alone were very precious. That first night they stayed up late in his house, sitting on the rug by the dwindling fire. They did not switch on the wireless. Their hours together were already slipping away far too fast.

'Come here,' Laurie said, holding out his arms. Sylvia went to him and sat between his outstretched legs. 'That's better,' he said. 'I don't want to let go of you, ever.'

She laughed, loving the feel of his arms round her and him nuzzling the side of her face with his cheek. They were already so at ease together, in just a few days, knowing they loved each other, and it was as if neither of them could contemplate anything other than spending all their lives together. It felt like a strange, wonderful miracle.

'What shall we do after the war's over?' she said.

Laurie was silent for a moment. 'I don't want to go back where I was before. Not to that office. I want to be somewhere there's no one ordering you about all the time. In the country – maybe I'll be a farmer.'

'A farmer! You don't know the first thing about farming.'

'I could learn,' he said. 'I've learned to navigate a plane – you can learn pretty much anything, if you put your mind to it.'

Sylvia was impressed by this new confidence in him.

'Wouldn't you like to live in the country?' he asked. 'Somewhere pretty, with flowers and fields . . .'

'Yes,' she said dreamily. Then she turned to look at him. 'I don't mind where I live really, so long as it's with you. You're what I want – that's all.'

He looked seriously into her eyes and for a second she saw a flicker of fear, as if a thought had come to him, but he banished it.

'Of course I'll be there with you. There's nowhere else I want to be, Sylv. So long as . . .' He stopped. 'Best not think too far ahead, eh? Not now. But God, I love you,

Sylvia, like nothing and no one else. You're my mainstay.' He hugged her even closer to him. 'Just stay here and carry on being just as you are, and I'll always be thinking of you.' He kissed her passionately and she lay in his arms, warm and happy. His voice suddenly very serious, he said, 'I don't want you to think . . . When we're together, like this, I'd like things to go further – God, I would! If things were normal – I mean, I wouldn't think of us going further until we were married. But now, when you never know . . .' He sounded embarrassed, but he needed to say it. 'I just don't want to cause any trouble for you – push things too fast. After all, we've only just found each other.'

Sylvia twisted round and placed a finger across his lips. She was moved by his trying to talk about it. Much as she desired him, she was not ready yet, not quite. 'Sssh. I know. It's all right. Everything's perfect, like this, my love.'

His body shook gently with laughter and he kissed the top of her head. 'You're wonderful.' After a few moments he said, 'Has Audrey found anyone? What's she up to – apart from balloons and all that?'

'She did mention someone called Nick,' Sylvia said. 'But that was when she was still training, so I don't know if they see all that much of each other, now she's down south – somewhere on the edge of London. She doesn't get round to getting in touch much, and we haven't seen her in ages. But no doubt she's going along just fine and dandy, bossing everyone else about!'

Laurie laughed. 'No doubt. She'll find some big strong RAF officer, I expect, and have a whole clutch of kids.'

'Audrey?' Sylvia said astonished. 'Oh, I don't think

313

so! She's always been very determined that's not what she wants. Doesn't want to be tied down and all that.'

'Oh,' Laurie said. 'Well, we'll see. Most people don't know what they want until it arrives.'

She looked up at him. 'No. But now you've arrived. Aren't I a lucky girl?'

She was not able to see Laurie off when he left, because it was during her working hours. They had to say goodbye very early in the morning, Laurie getting up to see her before she went to work. They stood in the Goulds' hall, locked in each other's arms. Sylvia couldn't help crying at having to part from him.

'It seems such an age until you can come again,' she said, clinging to him. 'Promise me you won't do anything dangerous.' She knew this was absurd even as she said it, but she did not want to think about the danger he might be in.

'At least it's not Canada now,' he said.

'Lincolnshire feels like the ends of the earth to me,' she said despondently.

'It'll soon go by,' he said. 'And write to me, won't you? Your letters are the best.'

'My letters are terrible,' she sniffed, looking up at him with a half-smile now.

'They're not – you're much better at it than you think.' But he held her close and she could hear that he was upset too. They just needed to be together, that was what they had discovered. They were part of each other: it was as simple as that.

As she walked away from the house in the snowy darkness to catch the bus, she took his warm embrace with her and their loving words. 'Always remember, I love you and love you,' Laurie had told her. 'That's all that matters, ever.'

It was desolate coming home that day, and the days afterwards, knowing it would be weeks before she saw him again. Getting back to Kings Heath, and knowing that their houses were empty of Laurie, felt so sad. She knew Mrs Gould must also be feeling it terribly. Even Ted commented on it.

'Seems very quiet, now the lad's gone,' he said, settling down with the paper that evening.

'He'll be back,' Pauline said, trying to jolly everyone along, as she had doubtless had to do with Marjorie Gould as well. It struck Sylvia then just how strong her mother was. She held fast, always quietly trying to support other people.

Sylvia told herself she had to settle back into a routine. If she kept busy, the days would pass and, however much she missed him, she had the pleasure of Laurie's letters to look forward to.

It didn't stay quiet for long, though. The second night after Laurie left, there was a tap at the front door, just as they were about to get the tea ready.

'Who on earth can that be?' her mother said uneasily.

'I'll go,' Sylvia said.

She went along the dark hall, not bothering to put the light on, and pulled the door open. It took a few seconds to make sense of the shape on the step, standing half-turned away as if looking out along the street.

'Audrey?'

Sylvia saw her sister turn and stare at her stonily for a second. Then her pale face contorted and she burst into tears, her shoulders heaving as if her distress had been long held back. Sylvia noticed the suitcase then, lodged beside her on the step.

'They've thrown me out!' she sobbed. 'The WAAF – I've been dismissed. I had to come home – I've nowhere else to go.'

Forty

They stood round, shocked and bewildered. Audrey sat at the kitchen table, with Sylvia and Pauline standing on either side of her and Jack lingering in the doorway. It was so rare ever to see Audrey cry that this in itself was extraordinary. Her hair was loose and she was wearing her own clothes – no more WAAF uniform now. She suddenly seemed smaller.

Steam poured from the kettle on the stove. All thoughts of getting a meal ready were forgotten.

Sylvia was about to comfort her sister, but Pauline moved first, leaning on the table with both hands. 'You'd better tell us what's happened, Aud.' Her tone was controlled, but Sylvia could hear the anxiety in it.

Audrey hung her head. 'I've been kicked out.'

Pauline's face was very grave. 'What've you done? You must've done summat bad to've been . . .' Her voice hardened and her body seemed to become tougher and more forbidding, as if she was reverting back to ways of behaving and speaking from an earlier time in her life, which normally she tried to forget. 'Out with it, wench – what've you done?'

Audrey flinched as if Mom had hit her. She raised her head and said, 'Tell Jack to go out.'

Mom gave Jack a look and he didn't argue. They heard the door click shut and his tread on the stairs.

'Well?' Mom demanded. Sylvia felt as upset by the

317

change coming over their mother as by Audrey's distress. Her stomach tightened with dread. What on earth could Audrey have done to merit such harsh punishment?

'I'm four months gone.'

Gone, Sylvia thought. She can't have left the WAAF four months ago – where has she been all this time? But the sharp inward suck of her mother's breath and the cuff she administered across the side of Audrey's head tilted her mind into what was happening. *Gone.* Four months *gone*.

'You stupid, dirty . . .' Mom couldn't seem to think of the right words to convey her fury. 'You . . . Oh!'

She sank down on a chair by the table, staring ahead of her. She swallowed, then banged her fist on the table. Sylvia expected Audrey to fight back, as she always would have done, but not this time. She sat hanging her head.

'You silly, *stupid* girl!' was all Mom could think of to say, but she said it with intense feeling. There was a long, awful silence. Audrey stayed hidden under her hair. 'Sylv,' Pauline said eventually, in a low, controlled voice. 'Make that tea.'

The kettle was still boiling away, unheeded.

As she obeyed, her hands trembling, Sylvia heard Mom say menacingly, 'Are you quite sure?'

'I've felt it moving.'

'Dear God, what in heaven's name is your father going to—? How *could* you? Have you got any idea—?' Chopped sentences dropped from Mom's lips. She was red in the face now and working herself up. 'I've got to get out of here, or I'll do something I regret,' she said, pushing her chair back. She stopped at the door. 'You *stupid little bitch*!' she hissed. 'Of all things, I never thought *you* . . .' She hurried out of the kitchen

318

and they heard her feet banging on the stairs. A door slammed.

Sylvia was left alone with her weeping stranger of a sister and a full pot of tea. She did the only thing she could think of: poured out two cups, put in far more sugar than the ration allowed and sat down beside Audrey. She was reeling with shock and confusion. A baby? Was that what Audrey was saying? How could she have let this happen? She had never seen her mother so hard and cruel. But she had never seen her sister so low and upset, either. At last she dared to put her arm round Audrey's shoulders and felt her begin to tremble.

'I knew you'd be kind,' Audrey said, her voice cracking. 'You're always the one who's kind.' She rested her forehead on the table and broke down again, into distraught weeping. 'Oh God, sis – it's been so awful, I can't tell you . . .'

'Oh, Aud,' Sylvia said, feeling her own tears welling up. 'What on earth are we going to do?'

'I tell you what I'm going to do,' Audrey said, sitting bolt upright. 'I'm going to get this thing inside me taken away and adopted, and then I'm going back to the WAAF. That's what *I'm* going to do!'

Ted Whitehouse walked into all this a short time later. Pauline had come down, her lips seeming glued together, and was going through the motions of making everyone's tea, slamming saucepans down as if she was trying to kill ants in the process. She hardly seemed to know what she was doing, and no one dared say a word to her. Sylvia hung around the kitchen, staying close to Audrey, as she couldn't think what else to do.

Their dad walked in the back door, his coat speckled

with snowflakes, holding a bicycle pump. He took in the overwrought household, his wife's angry thumping about and Audrey's tear-stained face. Sylvia gazed beseechingly at him.

'What the hell's going on?' he asked with caution, clinging to the bicycle pump. He nodded at Audrey. 'What's she doing here?'

Audrey looked up at him desperately, said, 'Oh, Dad, I'm so sorry!' and burst into tears all over again. Mom cut into a potato as if it were someone's neck. She laid the knife down suddenly, put her hands over her face and, in a distraught voice, cried, 'Oh, I don't know what's happening to this family!'

Sylvia realized that Dad was looking to her, as the only other almost dry-eyed person in the room, for an explanation

'Audrey's in a bit of bother, Dad,' Sylvia said, just in case this was not obvious.

'Right,' he said. He laid the bicycle pump on the table. 'Let's get to the bottom of all this. Come in the front, with me and your mother.'

'I want Sylv there as well,' Audrey insisted. Sylvia was touched by the way Audrey had latched onto her. She couldn't seem to face their parents on her own.

It seemed the right thing to go to the front room; it added a solemn note. Dad hadn't even taken off his coat. The snow was melting into dark spots. Their mother stood with her arms folded, as if holding herself together. Sylvia could feel waves of strong, fearsome emotion coming from her, and that was the worst thing of all. It made her quake inside. What on earth had happened to Mom? She was rough and ready in some ways, but she was usually kind. They all stood in the front room until Ted said, 'Well, sit down, for goodness' sake.'

As they moved to their chairs, Sylvia glanced at her sister and saw for the first time the slight bulge of her belly and a thrill of horrified wonder went through her.

'Well, what's going on?' Dad demanded.

'Are you going to tell him, Audrey – or shall I?' Mom said, her voice coming out in hammer-blows. 'Half the street'll know soon, so you'd better let your father in on it.'

Audrey looked down into her lap. Sylvia's heart was pounding. From the side-table the photograph of herself and Audrey as dark-eyed little girls looked across at them, both grinning. She felt a sudden acute pang of grief.

Audrey stood up suddenly, pulled out the edges of her cardigan and stood sideways on to her father. 'There you are, Dad.'

Ted looked at her as if she'd gone mad. 'What're you doing?' Though her belly was a bit enlarged, it was not big enough for it to be immediately obvious what she meant.

'The wench is in whelp, Ted.' Pauline's voice lashed the room.

'Can't you see?' Audrey's voice was harsh as well. 'I thought it was going to be obvious to the whole street, like Mom says. I'm having a baby, Dad. I'm just about four months gone. I'm not married, and I've been kicked out by the Air Force. I'm soiled goods – see?' She tried to stick her front out even more.

'Sit down and stop that,' Mom said furiously. 'Anyone'd think you were proud of the fact, you little hussy.'

'Oh, hussy, is it?' Audrey fizzed into fury. 'Call me a hussy, when you've not asked me what happened . . .'

'What happened?' Mom was losing her temper. If her daughters had known it, she was now sounding exactly as she'd vowed she never wanted to – just like her own mother. Sylvia cringed, listening to her. 'What d'yer mean, what happened? Unless you're different from any other woman since Adam and Eve, it's pretty obvious what's happened! You dirty girl: you're a disgrace, that's what you are – you with all yer lip. Now see where it's got us all; another mouth to feed and a bastard child on the way.'

Sylvia began to cry then. It was horrible hearing Mom talking like that, so rough and cruel.

'Pauline, knock it off!' Dad commanded. Sylvia realized to her astonishment that her father was close to tears. This was almost more upsetting than anything. 'For God's sake, woman, how's that going to help?'

'Well, is he going to marry you?' Mom started off again.

There was a silence. Even the clock seemed to tick louder in agitation.

'No,' Audrey said. 'He can't.'

'Why, love?' Dad asked, holding out a warning arm in Mom's direction to stem her outraged flow.

Audrey looked round at them, sullen and bitter. 'Because he's already married to someone else.'

'Oh, for heaven's sake!' Mom erupted. 'You mean you didn't even trouble yerself to find out beforehand?'

Ted shook his head, wringing his hands. He unbuttoned his coat suddenly and threw it off, onto a spare chair.

'So that's it,' he said, somehow seeming reassured. 'You were taken in by some Joe sweet-talking you . . .'

'Well, how does that make it any better?' Mom was

launching into a speech when Audrey almost shouted over her.

'No. It wasn't like you think!' Sylvia saw her sister's stubborn, perverse pride reassert itself. Audrey was perched angrily on the edge of her chair. 'I knew he was married. I just liked him, that's all.' She stared defiantly back into their confused and appalled faces.

'Jack?' Sylvia tapped on his bedroom door. Her brother was, as usual, at the little table in his room, wrapped in a rug and doing his homework, his hair rumpled from running his hands through it. He looked up at her with troubled eyes. 'Tea's ready.'

'What's going on, Sylv?' He closed his book. 'I heard Mom shouting. What's up with Audrey – what's she done?'

Sylvia sat down on the bed. She breathed in deep. 'Audrey's . . .' She found herself blushing in front of her almost, but not quite (at fourteen), man of a brother. 'She's going to have a baby, Jack.'

Jack's face moved in various directions, from being close to laughter, to incredulity, and finally to something like horror. He pushed his chair out and leaned over, staring at the floor. Eventually he said, 'Is she getting married then?'

'No.'

He looked up, frowning. 'Why not? That's what women have to do, isn't it, if they get into trouble?'

Sylvia felt anger flicker into life within her. She felt passionately protective of Audrey. Her reaction surprised her. She might have expected to be glad to see Audrey taken down a peg. But this was too serious for that. She knew her sister – she may have been difficult and hard to live with sometimes, but she was no fool. It wasn't only Audrey who was to blame. And just when she needed Mom to be kind, she had turned into someone they hardly recognized. It was all frightening and horrible.

'The man who is the father is already married,' she said bitterly. 'So obviously *he's* not in trouble.'

'You know what I mean.'

'Yes, I do. You automatically think it's all Audrey's fault.'

'No . . .' he said wavering. 'But it is, in a way, isn't it? You can't just go having a baby without being married. I mean, what are we going to tell everyone? I can't tell my friends, or have them round here, if she's – well, like *that.*'

Sylvia got up, so enraged that she wanted to hit Jack, even though she saw that he was right in a way. It was a disgrace. Everyone would be gossiping and pointing the finger at Audrey as a loose, fallen women. She could just imagine some of Jack's snooty grammar-school friends making jokes about Audrey in their donkeylike, just-broken voices. It would all be seen as Audrey's fault. It was grossly unfair.

'Well, Jack.' She stood over him, gripping her hands together. She was trembling with emotion. 'You can decide where you stand, can't you? Are you going to put your friends – and what they might say – first, or are you going to look out for your sister?'

Jack flushed red. 'Women aren't supposed to behave like that,' he said mutinously.

Sylvia clenched her hands even more tightly to stop herself giving him a good slapping as her temper boiled over.

'What the hell would you know about it?' she yelled. 'Now, come and have your sodding tea and treat Audrey properly – right?'

Forty-One

'Sylv, come up with me?' Audrey whispered in the hall after they had eaten a silent, excruciating meal, with no one able to look each other in the face. Sylvia felt sick and had to force her food down.

'I'll be up,' Sylvia said. She gripped Audrey's fingers for a moment. 'I'd better help Mom with the washing-up, or she'll create.'

But when she went into the kitchen she was greeted by the words, 'Just get out of my sight – all of you,' uttered from her mother's hunched figure by the sink. Pauline didn't even turn round to see whom she was speaking to.

Sylvia didn't know what was more upsetting: the way Mom was acting, or Audrey vowing she was going to give away the baby. She crept upstairs. Show-tunes were jazzing out of the wireless in the back room. Dad must be trying to drown it all out.

She tapped on Audrey's door and found her lying on the bed. She wasn't crying, just lying there staring towards the window.

'This room reminds me of Kitty,' Sylvia said, closing the door and going to sit on the edge of the bed.

Audrey grimaced. 'I was right about her, wasn't I?'

'You were. More than right.'

'I don't know why. It wasn't something I could have described, exactly. Just something about her – as if she

326

had bad bits in her, like a potato. You couldn't seem to see it.'

'But, Audrey,' Sylvia said, tearful again suddenly, 'if you could see that, why couldn't you see it with this man? The . . .' She nodded towards Audrey's stomach. 'The father – what was his name?'

'Oh, him,' Audrey said lightly. She put on an arch, dismissive tone. 'It doesn't matter about him, or what his name is. I shan't be seeing him again.'

'Did he lie to you?'

Audrey considered. 'Not exactly. Someone else told me he was married. He just never said.'

'That's lying.' Sylvia took her shoes off and curled up on the bed. Audrey drew her legs up for a moment to let her sit back against the wall. Sylvia felt so sorry for Audrey, but she was also somehow happy that her sister wanted her company, in a way that she never had before. She liked the feeling of being close and confiding.

'I s'pose it is,' Audrey agreed. She obviously didn't want to talk about him much.

'Were you in love with him?' Sylvia asked sympathetically.

'I liked him a bit, that's all,' Audrey said. She spoke lightly, almost mockingly. 'Look, I don't really want to talk about him. It's over.'

Sylvia stared at her. 'I don't understand you,' she said carefully. 'If you weren't in love with him – *really* in love – why did you go with him? Like that, I mean?'

Audrey sighed and shifted onto her left side. Sylvia looked at her sister's long, pale face and the curve of her dark brows, and thought how lovely she was – and now how vulnerable. She felt another surge of tender protectiveness towards her. 'Well, I suppose I just wanted to get it over with. Find out what it was all about. You know: have an adventure.'

'But a baby! Audrey, you're having a baby!' Her exasperation shifted to wonder. She didn't want to talk about what Audrey was planning to do afterwards. 'God, I can't imagine it. How does it feel?'

'It's been awful.' Audrey's face crumpled again.

'Oh, sis . . .' Sylvia reached out and they held hands across the counterpane.

'I couldn't tell anyone,' Audrey said through her tears. 'At first I thought I'd just caught some lurgy. I kept feeling sick – and I was sick a few times. The work on the site is so hard; some days I got up and thought: I can't, I just can't go out there and do it, feeling like this. But I couldn't keep reporting sick. I felt as if I was living in a nightmare and one day I'd wake up. I was so ashamed, and I knew someone would guess sooner or later, but at the same time I couldn't let myself believe what had happened. Even if he hadn't been married, I was posted miles away from him by then. He doesn't even know. What would be the point? He's got a child already. So I just kept telling myself to keep going. I fainted a couple of times. The sick bit stopped after a few weeks, so that was better. It was so strange, though, because I kept frantically thinking of ways I could get rid of it. Some of the girls talked about remedies, you know – I wasn't the first WAAF to catch for a baby, by a long way. One girl had left Cardington just before I did, so there was talk . . . And I kept thinking of jumping off things, and what I could do to get rid of it. But then every time anything came near me, I was placing my arm across my belly and thinking: Don't hurt me. Don't hurt the baby! And at the same time as all that, I couldn't really believe there was a baby at all.'

Sylvia listened, full of sympathy. 'I don't know how you managed.'

'I've never felt more exhausted in my life. And the worst of it was not being able to tell anyone.'

'But what happened? Did you tell them in the end?'

'Someone guessed. One of the other girls. She didn't report me, she just said, "Audrey, sooner or later you're going to have to tell someone." She was quite kind really.'

'So you did?'

'I did.' There was a bitter pause. 'And that was the end of the WAAF for me.' She started crying then, in a sad, bereft way, which wrung Sylvia's heart. 'I can't get over how stupid I've been,' she said as the tears ran down her cheeks. 'I loved the WAAF – it's the best thing I've ever done – and now it's all over; at least, if I'm stuck with this thing. I know it's a baby really. But I don't want it – I don't! I just want to go back and get on with my life.'

'Would they have you back – after, I mean?' Sylvia said.

Audrey avoided her eyes. 'If I get rid of it. Probably.'

This seemed too terrible to think about. 'But what if . . . I mean, if someone looked after it?'

Audrey gave a harsh laugh. 'What, like Mom, you mean?'

For a moment this had entered Sylvia's head. She felt like offering to do it herself, but it looked impossible and overwhelming. 'Oh, Audrey.'

'What a mug, eh?' She shifted again, as if uncomfortable, and they loosed hands. 'We're quite a pair, you and me. I'm just going to have to take what comes for now – all the tittle-tattle. I can hardly pretend I'm a war widow round here, can I? I'll just have to brave it out. And then when it's over . . .' Sylvia saw her trying to harden her feelings, but instead her eyes filled with tears. 'Well, I'll be rid of it, won't I?'

Sylvia stared at her, thinking how brave Audrey was, but at the same time she was horrified by her. How could she think of giving her baby away? Would Mom make her do it? It seemed so cruel and unnatural.

'What about you?' Audrey said, wiping her eyes. 'Are you feeling any better – about Ian?'

It was Sylvia's turn to sigh. 'Yes, well . . . If I think about it all, I can still get worked up. It's not even Ian I'm bothered about now, not really. I miss him in a way, but what really upsets me is being deceived. I think Kitty hurt me even more than he did.'

'Silly bitch!'

Sylvia could not deny this.

'But something else has happened.' She looked down shyly.

Audrey lifted her head, looking momentarily mischievous. 'Are those red cheeks I see? Come on, Sylv: who is he? Do I know him?'

'You do.' She looked up, a smile breaking over her face. 'It's . . . well, it's Laurie.'

Audrey looked blank. 'Laurie? What, Laurie Gould? *No!*' She lay back, letting out the first laugh Sylvia had heard from her since she had arrived home. 'You can't mean Laurie, Sylv – I mean he's sweet, always was, but he's only about twelve!'

Sylvia laughed as well, understanding why Audrey found it funny: little Laurie from next door.

'I know, but you haven't seen him in ages, Aud. He's grown up. He's much bigger than me now, and he's been in the RAF – in Canada and everything. And he's just so *nice*, so kind and easy to talk to. You'd hardly know him in some ways, he's changed that much. After Ian, Laurie

just seems so much better a person. You'd like him –
really you would.'

Audrey lay back, her face serious now, as she saw that
Sylvia meant it. 'Little Laurie. Well . . . You're not having
me on?'

'*No.* Cross my heart.'

They looked at each other and Sylvia blushed again.

'You really are in love, aren't you?'

Sylvia did not miss the wistful tone in Audrey's voice.
She smiled. 'I do believe I am.'

'Well,' Audrey said. 'At least something good's happened.'

'Aud.' Sylvia laid her hand on her sister's thigh. 'I'm
. . . I was going to say I'm sorry, but it seems an awful
thing to say about a baby. But Mom'll come round, I'm
sure she will.' Even as she said it, she was not sure it was
true. After a silence she added, 'I can't stand seeing her
like that.'

'I suppose, when it's one of your own,' Audrey said.

'Yes, but – it just doesn't seem like her.' She sighed.
'Look, we'll stand by you. I will, you can be sure of that.
And help any way I can. We'll all be all right, if we stick
together. Sticks and stones. Who cares what people say,
eh?'

'Thanks, sis,' Audrey said. She sat up, tearful again,
and held out her arms. Sylvia shifted closer and the two
of them put their arms round each other and sat rocking
gently, in a warm, comforting embrace.

Forty-Two

Audrey woke from a vivid dream. She was leaving RAF Cardington, walking to the gates, bag in hand. The transport was waiting to take her to the railway station and away from there forever. She wept in the truck and, as she woke, she was sobbing. When she opened her eyes in the blacked-out room she could only sense, rather than see, where she was. Home. It wasn't all a bad dream that she could chase away with the daylight and find herself back on the balloon site, happy and active. In fact it was not RAF Cardington that she had been sent home from, but a smaller balloon site on the north-eastern edge of London. But in the dream everything most precious to her had been brought together, only for her to have to leave it all over again.

Muffling herself in the bedclothes, she lay crying, quietly. In those moments she even missed Nick. They had both known that her time at Cardington was coming to an end. Nick made the most of her being there, and Audrey let him – it was as simple as that. The worst thing was knowing she only had herself to blame. She had allowed Nick to make love to her four times, and on one of those times she had caught for the baby. She cried a little, thinking of his good-looking face, his kisses. But she knew it was hopeless. She did not want Nick. She had wanted to prove she was a proper woman – she had used him just as he had used her. She knew that Nick was not the real source of her heartbreak.

The WAAF was a large part of it. The life she had loved, which had been snatched from her. But thinking back to her last days at RAF Cardington, her most painful memory was the hurt and bewilderment she saw on Dorrie Cooper's face.

All that last month she had avoided Dorrie. It was for the best, she told herself. If Dorrie was one of *those*, then both of them had to face up to the fact that there was no future for them together. She certainly didn't want anyone else getting the idea that she was one of *those* herself. The thought of being labelled as queer brought out in her a primitive dread.

But she felt so sad and ashamed about the way she had treated Dorrie. If she saw her on the base, she would turn and walk away. If Dorrie was in the NAAFI canteen or any other social meeting place, Audrey made sure she did not go in. She was on constant alert. She kept this up for most of the last month, going out with Nick on many nights, or teaming up to go out with other girls like Cora. Dorrie kept out of her way – she was not a fool. She had got the message quickly. Audrey was grateful for her tact.

But one night, during her last week of training, she did see Dorrie. Audrey came back to the hut one night, after going out with Cora and a couple of other WAAF girls. As they reached the door in the warm night, Dorrie suddenly stepped out of the shadows.

'Oh, Audrey,' she said, in a relaxed, friendly tone that did not attract the others' attention. 'I just need a quick word with you . . .'

Audrey stopped. It would have seemed odd not to. The others went on into the hut. Dorrie stopped in front of her in the darkness, and Audrey could feel the intensity of her gaze.

'Just come for a stroll, will you?' Her voice was dignified, but Audrey could sense a well of emotion behind it as she added, 'Please.'

They turned to walk along the row of huts, past the bathhouse and down the road. Gaggles of service people passed them, talking and laughing loudly. Neither of them spoke until they were further on, in a quiet part. They walked out onto the open base, past the looming, shadowy hangars. Eventually, when they were in a space that seemed deserted, Dorrie stopped and turned to her.

'You read my diary, didn't you?'

Audrey felt ashamed, as if she had acted in a petty way. There was no point in denying it. 'Didn't you want me to?'

Dorrie looked away for a moment. 'I didn't leave it there specially, if that's what you mean, no. But sooner or later we would have had to say something. I thought . . .' To Audrey's horror, her voice began to crack. She was not used to seeing strong, carefree Dorrie crying. It buckled her heart. 'I thought,' Dorrie went on, through tears that she could not seem to prevent, even though she was struggling against them, 'that we had said something already. Not in so many words, but . . . I thought you understood, that you were . . . I love you, Audrey. You're – I thought—' She stopped, unable to go on, and put her hands over her face, weeping brokenly.

'Oh, Dor.' Audrey's throat was aching with tears as well. She felt terribly guilty and regretful for the way she had treated Dorrie. 'I didn't realize . . . I mean, I was scared. And I didn't know what you felt, not really. I just saw that word and I panicked. I've never thought of myself like that. I don't know that I am one of *those*.

334

I just . . .' She thought of Nick. Nick was nothing, compared with this. But Nick had been impossible anyway. She had chosen Nick *because* he was impossible. Maybe she just needed the right man. How was she supposed to know? She stood watching her friend in helpless confusion. 'Come here,' she said eventually and they walked into each other's embrace. Dorrie was trembling with long-pent-up emotion, and she sobbed and sobbed in Audrey's arms.

'I'm sorry, Dor,' Audrey kept saying, feeling Dorrie's hair against her cheek and all the emotion pouring out of her. 'I just don't know. I do love you – course I do. But I don't know if it's like *that*, or what. I'm so mixed up, I don't know what I am.'

Dorrie calmed down after her first rush of emotion and wiped her eyes. 'Oh God,' she said, taking a deep breath. She put a hand on her chest. 'I've been full of this *ache* ever since that day. Just here. I haven't been able to get rid of it, as if I'd swallowed a stone.' She looked at Audrey and gave a brave smile. 'I'm sorry too – I rushed you. It's just, I've known for so long . . . about me, I mean. I don't really know how, but I just knew. I've just never found boys – or men – of any relevance. Some are nice, of course. I like some men a lot. It's just that all my emotions seem to turn to women. Maybe some of us are just born like that, I don't know.'

Audrey realized that she, growing up, had never once thought about it. The question had never crossed her horizon.

'You're going soon,' Dorrie stated bleakly.

'Yes – next week.'

'I'd . . .' Dorrie hesitated. 'I'd hate to lose you completely. Write to me, will you?'

'Course I will,' Audrey said, relieved. She would have

hated to lose Dorrie too. Now she'd be at a distance, and it all felt safer.

They hugged, friends again in a fragile way. As they parted, Dorrie reached up and kissed her cheek. 'Thanks for all the good times,' she said warmly, but with a hint of self-mockery.

Audrey lay thinking of this encounter now, her tears still flowing. She had left the camp without any more goodbyes to Dorrie. It was when she was working at the other camp outside London, with some of her fellow trainees and some new girls, that she started to feel queasy. The full horror of the fact that she was expecting a baby came upon her among strangers. Now that she was out of the WAAF, everything that had happened seemed to remove her even further from Dorrie. Here she was at home, disgraced, after an affair with a married man she never loved, and carrying his child. How was anyone supposed to understand that? How could she possibly write to Dorrie now?

What had kept her going so far was the thought that she would go back. She would rid herself of this baby, go back to the WAAF and pretend it had never happened. But what she had to face was that she could never go back to what she really longed for. Even if she gave this baby up to be adopted and went back to the WAAF, she would be sent to some balloon site somewhere among strangers. What she longed for so desperately was the WAAF at Cardington, with Dorrie. And, whatever else happened, that was gone forever.

Audrey felt a terrible sense of despair during those first days at home. Sylvia was working late that week, so she sometimes saw a little of her in the morning, but then she was out until late and returned home exhausted. At first Sylvia felt like her only ally. The men of the family just didn't know what to say to her. Dad had not been unkind, but he instinctively wanted to leave all this sort of business to the womenfolk. Jack was so appalled he could hardly look at her. And Mom was no better.

Audrey moved round the house like a shadow, keeping out of everyone's way. She knew her mother enough to realize that she had to let it all sink in. Things improved a bit the second day when Marjorie Gould called round. Unlike most visitors, she didn't knock at the front, but appeared suddenly from round the back.

'Pauline, you there?' Her head appeared round the back door. 'Ooh, hello, Audrey, I didn't know you were home! All right, love – got a bit of leave, have you?'

Audrey smiled and her mother said quickly, 'Come in, Marjorie. How's Laurie getting on?'

Marjorie was wearing a dark-pink jumper and clutching her arms across her ample chest to keep warm. She perched on a kitchen chair, looking troubled. 'Oh, I think he's going on all right. I expect your Sylvia knows more than I do.' She sighed and then looked round, smiling bravely. 'I'll just have to hope he's all right. I don't like to think about it.'

There was a silence, then Pauline said brusquely, 'Well, Marjorie, you'll have to know sooner or later . . . But don't go canting in the street, will you? Everyone'll find out soon enough, as it is.'

'Goodness, Pauline, what's happened?' Startled, Marjorie loosed her arms and sat up straighter, as if preparing herself.

'Shall I tell her, Audrey?'

Audrey looked down into her lap, nodding. She could

feel the unpleasant burn of a blush spreading up her neck.

'Audrey's been let go by the Air Force,' her mother said. 'She's in the family way.'

There was such a long silence that Audrey looked up and saw Marjorie Gould trying to work out what to do with her face. Whatever shock or horror may have registered at first, Audrey had missed it. By the time Audrey looked up, Marjorie was looking at her with tender confusion.

'I take it he's not going to marry you then, bab?'

Audrey shook her head. 'Already spoken for, as it turns out,' she said.

'Oh, my . . .' Marjorie said. 'Oh dear. Well,' she paused and her eyes filled. Smiling through tears she said, 'You know, I'd never've said this before the war and all that's happened . . . I know it's wrong, not to be married and everything. I know Stan'll carry on about it, and there'll be others airing their opinions too, but . . .' The tears escaped her eyes. 'I'd give anything to have a little baby in the house these days. Now Raymond's gone and Laurie's away, and there's just . . .' She stopped to wipe her eyes. 'Per'aps it's wicked of me, but a new life to hold – ooh, Pauline, I almost envy you, I really do.'

To Audrey's astonishment, she saw her mother's eyes fill with tears as well. She put her hands over her face and her shoulders shook with grief.

'Pauline?' Marjorie leaned in to her, shocked. 'Oh, bab – don't take on so bad. We'll all pull together, won't we? Never mind everyone else and their tittle-tattle; it's family that counts.'

Audrey watched her mother try and regain control of

herself. What she later realized were long-buried sobs came forcing themselves out of her. Marjorie looked across at Audrey with wide eyes, grasping that there was something else afoot, because this was so unusual for Pauline. She stood up and put her arm round her friend's shoulders. Pauline rested her elbows on the table, hands still over her face. Audrey felt tears pricking at her own eyes.

'What is it, Pauline?' Marjorie said gently.

Eventually Pauline wiped her eyes roughly. Still shielding her face with her hands, she said in a tight voice, 'I'll say this, just once. I don't want you to go on about it – any of you.' Very quickly she said, 'My mother was a harsh woman. I've always tried not to be like her. I had a little sister. She was called Lena . . .'

Audrey stifled a gasp. Mom had always led them to believe she had two brothers and one sister, Jean. Who was Lena?

'She caught for a babby with a man when she was sixteen. Our mother told her to pack her bags. She wasn't going to face the shame of a bastard baby in the house. Lena begged her, but it was no good; Mother turned her face against her. She left, our Lena, with a bundle of clothes and ten shillings. I've never seen her from that day to this.'

'Oh dear God.' Marjorie sank back down onto the chair. Audrey sat in shock, unable to stem her own tears.

Her mother still didn't look at her, not then, but she turned to Mrs Gould. 'Oh, Marjorie,' she said, reaching for her hand. 'I'm finding this very hard to come to terms with. But you've just said the best thing a friend could ever say.'

At last she turned to Audrey. 'I've never wanted to be like my mother,' she said. 'She was heartless and cruel and . . .' She shook her head, fighting back more tears. 'Somehow we'll just have to try and make the best of it. And, Audrey, you'll give that child away over my dead body.'

Forty-Three

Sylvia sat on her bed with the door closed, glad to have some time alone. It was her afternoon off and she knew that Audrey was asleep, or pretending to be, in the next room. There had been so much emotion in the house over the past few days that they were all exhausted. The girls were still reeling from the shock of what their mother had told Audrey and Marjorie, though she flatly refused to say any more about her lost sister or anything that had happened.

'I'm not going over any of it, digging all that up,' she said. 'There's no more to say – the past's dead and buried, as far as I'm concerned.'

The sisters had gone over and over it, when they were alone together upstairs, wondering, guessing. But it was so upsetting to dwell on it. And Mom was adamant: they were to say no more about it. All Sylvia wanted to think about now was Laurie. She loved him so much, she longed to lie and daydream about him! How quickly things had fallen into place with him, so that he had become utterly important to her. All that bitter betrayal by Ian and Kitty had led her to this – that was how she had come to see it. It was her blessing.

She had a pad of paper in her lap, but sat for a long time staring out at the colourless sky. If only Laurie could walk through the door now. The thought of seeing his young, kindly face and feeling his arms round her made her ache with longing. She loved receiving his letters, which he usually kept as light as possible, relating stories of what he and he pals had been up to, pranks and jokes. He always ended by telling her how much he loved and missed her, and that he was counting the days until he could come back on leave again.

Sylvia sighed and began to write: 'Dearest Laurie . . .' Immediately she ground to a halt. If only she could talk to him face-to-face! She never found writing easy, at the best of times. 'Since I last wrote, we've all had a bit of a shock,' she wrote. 'I want to tell you, and not keep anything from you.' Briefly and straight-forwardly she told him about Audrey's arrival home and about the baby. Somehow it didn't feel right to tell him about her lost auntie. That could wait until they were together.

I feel so sorry for Audrey. She's had a terribly rough time, staying in the WAAF, trying to keep working. I really don't know how she managed, because she just seems exhausted now. One of the good things is that she and I are getting on much better. Everyone's having to try and get over the shock in their own way. Dad's been okay really. Mom was more furious than I've ever seen her, quite nasty really and so harsh, though she's calmed down now. And Jack can hardly look at Audrey. I do wish you were here to talk to him, because I know you could make a difference. It's awful and shameful for Audrey, but it's not as if the father is going to have to take the brunt of any of it – he doesn't even know.

Maybe your mom's already told you all this? She was so nice and kind when she heard what had happened, and it's kindness that counts, isn't it? How is punishing Audrey or being nasty to her going to help anything now?

She paused again, then wrote:

It feels so peculiar, the thought of a baby. And the thought of people gossiping about us. But, as your lovely mother said to us, if your friends turn against you, then they weren't really your friends in the first place, were they?'

I miss you so much, my darling Laurie. I hate this horrible war for taking you away, just when we have found each other, and for making you do such difficult and dangerous things – that's how I imagine them anyway. I think of you so much: you're with me in everything I do. Write to me soon, when you get time, dearest. I'll be waiting.

With all my love, Sylvia

Once the first shock of the news was over, Marjorie said to Audrey, 'What're you going to do for the time being? You don't just want to hide in the house for the rest of it, surely?'

Again Audrey was very grateful to Marjorie. She had already begun to think the same thing.

'No, I don't. I was thinking I might get a job.'

'A job?' her mother snapped. 'What, with you sticking out the front, for all to see?'

'But married women are working all over the place now,' Marjorie corrected her gently.

*

Audrey took the first job she was offered, as a typist at an engineering works in Rea Street. It was an easy bus ride away. Before she set out to look for work, Audrey told Sylvia afterwards, Mom stopped her in the hall, when she was already in her hat and coat.

'She looked me up and down and said, "Hang on a minute. I've got something you'll need." She went upstairs and came down with a brass ring. She said it had belonged to her own mom, that she'd never been able to afford anything better, and even that had been in and out of the pawn shop.' Audrey's eyes filled as she reported this. 'I don't know what's got into me these days,' she added, halfway between laughter and tears. 'I can't seem to stop crying!'

'I'm nearly as bad,' Sylvia said, wiping her own eyes.

'She told me I should wear the ring and I should call myself Mrs something – I stuck to Whitehouse, so I didn't get in a muddle. And then she said, you know, arms folded the way she does, "I don't like what's happened Audrey. I don't like it one bit, being shamed in front of my neighbours. But you're my – flesh and blood, and I'll not turn against you – I've seen too much of that already. And *that*, that child in there, is the last one who's to blame, the poor little thing." I was just beginning to get emotional, thinking: Oh, Mom's coming round to being all right with me. Then she gave me one of her looks and said, "You *stupid* girl" and waltzed off into the kitchen!'

Both of them were laughing through their tears.

'Well, that sounds like Mom,' Sylvia said. 'But she is coming round. Thanks to Marjorie.'

'Yes,' Audrey said, then with an impish look, 'Marjorie, as in *Laurie's mom*, eh?'

Sylvia blushed, but she was pleased. 'She was nice to

you, wasn't she? I mean, she's known you since you were knee-high – we must feel almost like her own.'

'She'll make you a nice mother-in-law, won't she?'

'Don't say that,' Sylvia said with a shudder. 'Don't tempt fate. I daren't think about that, with Laurie going up in those planes – about any of it.'

The sisters were silent for a moment. Audrey reached over and squeezed her arm.

The winter crawled passed. The news was dark and terrible, with Japanese troops reaching further and further across the East. When, in February, the news was announced that Singapore had fallen, the family all sat around the wireless in the back room, listening intently. Pauline stopped knitting. The Japanese had moved with terrifying speed through the Malay peninsula.

'Oh, my word,' Pauline said eventually.

Ted got up and clicked off the wireless. 'We made the roads too good over there,' he commented. 'They've swarmed across it like bloody little yellow ants.'

There was no good news from anywhere. It was still freezing cold. Sylvia's toes were burning with chilblains. She confided in Elsie what had happened to Audrey. After the initial shock, Elsie was sympathetic and it was good to have someone to talk to who was outside the family. Jack kept his friends away from home, but he gradually began to get used to his sister's condition, even though he was very embarrassed by it and didn't want to talk about it. Laurie had slipped a note to him in with a letter to Sylvia, advising him to try and put his sister before anything else, and Sylvia was sure that had helped.

Audrey grew bigger and the baby started to show more and more. She had to put up with nasty comments from a few people in the street, but Audrey was quite good at holding her head high and brazenly ignoring them – especially as it was no one she had much respect for anyway. The people who mattered, ultimately, were on her side. She only shared her hurt and her worries with Sylvia.

'I don't mind what they say about me,' she said one day. 'Nosy busybodies. But when he's born – or she – I don't want them making him feel . . . You know what people can be like.'

Sylvia nodded, worried as well. People could be so cruel. 'We'll just have to cross that bridge when we come to it,' she said. Audrey had stopped talking about giving the baby away. Sylvia didn't ask; she didn't want to revive the subject.

Despite all the worry and trouble, it was nice having Audrey home, to have another girl to talk to apart from Elsie. She was fond of Elsie, but after Kitty, she was now less trusting with anyone who was not family. Laurie wrote regularly and she always carried his latest letter with her. The feel of the folded paper tucked into her pocket made her feel happy and gave her strength.

In March she received a letter that specially affected her. Laurie had found a place to be alone, and it was an unusually emotional letter:

We came back from a training flight early this morning. I can't say too much, of course. While we're up, I try not to think of the whys and wherefores of what we are preparing for. Besides, on the job we are all kept very busy, so there's no time for navel-gazing. But sometimes, when you get back, well, you can't help thinking your own thoughts. We don't like to talk about it between us – not too good for morale, I

346

suppose. Mostly we try and joke and keep each other's spirits up. No one wants to drag the rest down.

Tonight I miss you more than ever, my dearest one. I'm writing by torchlight and it seems very dark outside this little ring of light. I only wish you were here in it with me, and we could talk and talk. I know that would make things feel right. I know things between us have gone faster than they might have done without the war. We might have sat looking at each other for years without seeing how we are best for each other – that's what I feel anyway. All I needed was there, all the time, just over the garden wall! If I'm truthful, what I should like to do tonight is fly to you – somehow! – and take you in my arms, and make you promise to marry me, and for us to have a home and stay together forever. D'you think you'd agree? I hope so with all my heart.

Sylvia was deeply touched by this letter. She didn't take it as a proposal of marriage exactly, as Laurie was obviously feeling low, and somehow it didn't feel quite like that. But she knew they were both thinking of it, hardly daring to hope that, once the war was over, it was a dream that might come true.

Forty-Four

April 1942

Audrey sat at her desk in the poky office above the works in Rea Street. Each day, all day, she typed invoices. Finishing the one she was working on, for some machine component or other, she pulled it out of the typewriter, yawning until her jaw almost cracked. The loudly ticking clock on the wall told her that it was still only three o'clock. Her head was muzzy and all she wanted was to put her head on the desk and sink into sleep. She looked longingly out of the window at the sunny April afternoon and dreamed of getting up from her desk, surrounded by the other yawning typists, walking out into the sunshine and never coming back.

Not long now, she told herself. If she worked fast, she might be out before five. She was almost seven months pregnant. The one good thing about having this baby was that soon, she need never come back here again. All the same she was grateful to be earning money. And thank goodness it was a job sitting down.

Determinedly, she rolled another sheet of paper into the typewriter, pulled her chair closer into the desk and started typing.

*

348

Once work was over it still felt warm outside, even though the sun was beginning to sink. There was a hopeful breath of spring in the air. Instead of going straight to catch the bus, Audrey cut along Moseley Street and went into the park. Walking made her more breathless now. She was still quite tidy at the front, but the weight of the baby was starting to tell and she ambled along. Afternoon sunlight slanted low across the park. She found a bench looking out across the grass and the flowerbeds full of primroses. There was still half a cold-meat sandwich left in her bag and she ate it, ravenously.

The walk seemed to have stirred the child inside her and she could feel forceful little lunges of life.

'Oh, keep still, you little bugger,' she murmured, resting her hand on the swelling life of her belly. A sense of utter despair washed through her, as it did whenever she allowed herself to stop and think. Here she was, carrying Nick Reynolds's child, a fact of which he was completely ignorant and which, knowing him, he would not have cared about, either. His life would go on as before, while hers was ruined. Here she was, stuck at home, having lost the life she really loved. Once the baby arrived . . . And here her mind slid away from the reality facing her. No one had ever told her much about how a birth actually happened. And afterwards? She still dreamed about giving the child way, of escaping home again. Except that her mother was adamant that no flesh and blood of hers was being given away ever again. And, in the deepest part of her heart, Audrey felt that the decision had been taken from her and she was grateful.

She knew Mom was appalled at her for bringing a bastard baby into the family. What mother wouldn't be? But now she seemed prepared to fight almost to the death to defend it, no matter what. At least Audrey now understood why. Dad had been all right, in his way. Sometimes, when she walked past him in the house, he would reach out and squeeze her shoulder, or just say, 'All right, wench?' He could think of nothing more to say, but wanted to tell her that he felt for her. Those moments, when anyone was kind, were the ones that reduced her to tears. Thank heavens for Sylv, she thought. They'd always been like chalk and cheese, but now she felt closer to her little sister than ever in her life before. She thought of Sylvia and of the glow that had come over her because of Laurie. Lucky Sylvia! Audrey envied her, in a way, but knew she could never be like her.

The baby throbbed in her again. 'Ssssh,' she said, stroking a hand over her swollen belly. 'Settle down, will you?' She longed to feel more fondness for the little thing in there. Even though it was not the baby's fault, it still felt like a burden that had wrecked her life.

She sat looking out at the grass in a storm of shame, regret and frustration. All these weeks at home had meant a battle with these feelings. Sometimes she wanted to rage and cry out at what she had allowed to happen to her. She had deliberately courted danger. For what? Just to prove that she was a woman, like other women, and not a . . . freak. Even as the word came to her, she felt wrong and cruel to use it of Dorrie. If that's how Dorrie was, then good luck to her. But Audrey didn't want to be dragged into that, no matter how fond she was of her. She could barely admit to herself how much she missed Dorrie, just as she had missed her every time she was with Nick. Nick was like an unlit candle by comparison. What I need, she kept thinking, is a man who's like Dorrie.

Dorrie had written to Audrey once while she was in

London. By that time Audrey was feeling so sick and desperate that she had never replied. If Dorrie had written again, she didn't know whether the letter would ever reach her. Perhaps the WAAF would send it on. But maybe Dorrie had got the hint. What was the use in keeping that up now? Dorrie would surely hear what had happened sooner or later. It was awful to think of Dorrie finding out the stupid mess she'd got herself into.

She knew she had to cut herself off from the WAAF and forget about it. Come what may, she had to face the future – a future she had made for herself. But sitting there that afternoon, looking over the sunlit grass, this knowledge felt almost more bitter than she could bear.

Forty-Five

May 1942

Sylvia woke suddenly, her blood racing. Opening her eyes in the darkness, she knew something had startled her out of sleep. A few seconds later she heard a noise from next door. Audrey – it must be.

She slipped out of bed and stood listening at Audrey's door. She could hear her moving about, and a muffled sound came from inside. Full of dread, she pushed open the door.

'Aud? Oh Lord, are you okay?'

She saw her sister's slender figure kneeling on the floor next to the bed, her pillow in front of her to stifle her cries. Her hair was a dark skein down her back. She was too intent on what her body was doing to turn and look at Sylvia.

'It's started,' she gasped. 'Ages ago . . .'

'Oh, sis – already? Why didn't you wake me?' Sylvia went to her and put her arm round Audrey's shoulders. In the seconds before Audrey shook her off, she felt that her sister was drenched in sweat.

'I wet the bed,' Audrey said, hanging her head, panting between each attempt to speak. 'And then it started, hard . . . It's gone on and on— Oh!' Another wave of agony swept her words away and she groaned into the pillow.

'I'll get Mom.' Sylvia felt weak and shaky. It was terrible to watch such pain and feel so helpless.

'No!' Audrey tried to say, but so feebly that Sylvia could tell she didn't mean it.

'Don't be silly,' Sylvia said. 'You can't carry on like this on your own. We need to get the midwife!'

She ran to her parents' room. It was Dad who woke most easily, and within minutes he was dressed and wheeling his bike out.

Mom hurried in to see Audrey, her hair in a plait and pulling her old blue dressing gown round her. Sylvia could see that she was in a state as well, though trying not to show it.

'Oh, bab – look at you! Why didn't you wake us sooner?'

Audrey moaned in reply. She had gone deep into herself and did not want to talk. She was concentrating hard on what she had to do.

Sylvia saw her mother beckon her to the door. 'I'm going down to put some water on. Stay with her. She looks quite far on to me . . . Your father'll be back with the midwife soon.' With an anxious backward glance, Pauline went to the stairs.

Sylvia was about to return to Audrey's side when she heard a whisper across the landing. 'Sylv!' Jack had come out of his room. 'What's going on? Is it Audrey?' He looked young and anxious standing in his pyjamas.

'Yes, the baby's coming.'

'Is there anything I can do? Is she all right?'

'You could go and ask Mom – she might want some fetching and carrying. And, Jack,' she said as he was about to dash off, 'after this is over, you could try being a bit nicer to her. It wasn't just her fault you know. It takes two.'

Jack hesitated, looking down. 'All right,' he said, before disappearing downstairs.

Audrey's pains seemed to be getting worse. She groaned and writhed, and after one especially bad contraction she cried out, 'Oh, when will it be over? I can't do it any more, Sylv. I'm so tired.'

'Oh, Aud,' Sylvia said, almost in tears. 'It'll soon be over. It will. You're doing ever so well. Just hang on.'

She could smell her sister's sweat and the room seemed stuffy. She pushed the window open a crack and fetched a cloth to wipe Audrey's head with, praying all the while that Dad would soon be back with someone who had some idea what they were doing. Mom ran up to check on things as the water was boiling, and sat agitatedly on the bed beside Audrey's prone figure as she gasped and groaned.

'Oh dear,' Pauline kept saying. 'Oh dear, oh dear. That's it, love – it'll soon be over.'

Sylvia saw that her mother's face was full of anguish. She knew Mom was thinking that Audrey was having to go through all this with no husband to support her, and bring forth a child that would have no father. It was a very bad start in the world.

After what seemed an age they heard the back door open, and voices – a woman's voice. Sylvia sighed with relief.

'Oh, thank God!' Pauline said.

The midwife was a red-headed, frail-looking young woman. As Dad said, after it was over, 'That wench didn't look strong enough to post a letter, never mind deliver a baby. But she can ride a bike like the clappers – I had a job keeping up.'

She had intelligent blue eyes and a quick, competent manner.

'Audrey?' she introduced herself. 'I'm Nurse Bailey, and we're going to deliver your baby. Now in a moment, when you're ready, I'd like you to get up onto the bed so that I can see how far you're getting along.'

Audrey groaned. The thought of moving seemed too much for her. 'It's wet,' she murmured.

'I'll get a clean sheet,' Mom said, hurrying off. 'I'm sorry – I hadn't realized . . .'

The young woman examined Audrey, and Sylvia felt terribly awkward and embarrassed. The idea of someone poking about in your private parts with other people watching seemed terrible to her. But Audrey barely seemed to notice. She kept her eyes closed and moaned from time to time.

'We can see how far on the labour is by how widely dilated the cervix is,' the midwife said, as if this was quite a normal conversation. Sylvia had barely any idea what she was talking about. But she did understand when the young woman's brows contracted into a puzzled, then worried, frown. She withdrew her hand, cleaned herself up and spoke gently to Audrey.

'How long have you been like this?'

'I don't know,' Audrey gasped. 'Hours and hours. Soon after we came to bed, I . . . The wet . . .'

'That'd be about eleven o'clock, I should think,' Pauline said. It was now nearly four in the morning. 'Is everything all right, Nurse?'

The young midwife took a deep breath and said, 'Well, this is a first labour. But there's very little progress at all with the dilation of the cervix. As her waters have broken . . .' She hesitated, thinking for a moment. 'I think we should call the doctor.'

Pauline Whitehouse ran from the room and they heard her shouting, 'Ted! Get your bike out again and get the doctor!'

Even before the doctor came, Sylvia felt a cold grip of fear take hold of her. Audrey looked so young and slight lying there, eyes closed as if she had gone very far away from them all. She was gripped by frequent, agonizing bouts of pain, rolling and writhing on the bed. As the pain seeped away she lay very quietly, as if she had slipped away from them all.

'Mom,' Sylvia whispered urgently, 'what's going on? Is it supposed to be like this?'

'I don't know,' her mother said. She was twisting the soft belt of her dressing gown round and round in her worry. 'It wasn't like that for me. The doctor'll be here any minute – then we'll see.'

The waiting was unbearable. Sylvia watched Audrey, full of a cold, sick feeling, not helped by the bodily smells in the room. As soon as they heard the doctor arrive they all rushed to the top of the stairs, as if that could hurry him into making things all right.

Dr Gibbons, a rotund, balding man who stank of pipe-smoke, seemed incapable of speed. Even Audrey's cries of pain, which Sylvia felt would have made her spring to the ends of the earth, did not manage to galvanize him into getting up the stairs any faster. Sylvia clasped her hands to her lips, biting on her fingers as he examined Audrey. Please, please let him make it all right, her mind said, over and over again.

But Dr Gibbons stood up abruptly, snapped his bag shut and commanded, 'Call an ambulance.'

There was a glimmer of dawn as the man and woman in charge of the ambulance loaded Audrey into it. They carried her out on a stretcher, looking frighteningly pale. Everyone wanted to help, but there was not much to be done except comfort each other.

Sylvia noticed the kindly voice of the ambulance man. He had a soft Welsh accent. 'Nearly there,' he said to Audrey as she moaned in pain. 'We'll be in the ambulance in a minute. Soon have you safe.' Just as they reached the doors a fit of pain overcame her. She convulsed on the stretcher, trying not to make a noise, but her moans seemed to echo between the houses. A couple of people who were setting off to work on bicycles passed, staring. Sylvia realized with a shock that going to work was what she should have been doing too. Everything, apart from what was happening to Audrey, felt like another existence.

As they at last got Audrey settled in the ambulance, the man, about forty and with a round, gentle face, turned to them.

'Any of you going with her? You can, you know.' He was going to travel with Audrey. The woman was the one driving.

They heard Audrey's voice from the back of the ambulance. 'Sylv! Come with me. I want my sister!'

Sylvia and her mother looked at each other. 'I'm supposed to be at work,' Sylvia said. She both wanted to go with Audrey and dreaded the thought of it. Then she looked down at herself. 'I can't go like this: I'm in my nightdress!'

'She wants you. Run and dress – quick. I'll go to the Goods Yard and tell them,' Pauline said.

Sylvia tore upstairs and flung on some clothes in seconds. As she ran out to the ambulance her mother pressed a half-crown into her hand. 'Take this – you don't know how long you'll be there.'

So Sylvia found herself climbing up into the back of the ambulance and driving away through the quiet morning, reaching for her sister's hand.

Forty-Six

If it had not been for the ambulance man, Sylvia thought she might have passed out with worry. Audrey looked so bad. Sylvia had never seen anyone giving birth before and she didn't know how it was supposed to be. What was wrong? Audrey seemed so remote, and at the end of her strength. But the man talked quietly to her. When she screamed in pain – a worse pain, it seemed, than any that had gone before – he held her hand and, as she lay back, tenderly wiped her hair away from her face. He also talked quietly to Sylvia, and the journey to Selly Oak passed more quickly than it might have done.

'She your big sister?' he asked.

Sylvia nodded, mute with anxiety.

'You're quite alike,' he said. 'Both very pretty.' His tone was one of genuine observation, not as if he was trying to butter her up.

'Quite alike,' Sylvia said. 'Except for the hair.' She pulled at a strand of her unbrushed, chaotic mop. 'And if you knew us.' She searched his face, the gentle grey eyes. 'Is she going to be all right?'

'Oh, I expect so,' he said gravely. Did she imagine that he looked worried too?

'She's very brave, my sister,' she found herself saying. 'Very brave and strong.' Tears came suddenly and she put her head in her hands.

'It's all right,' the man said. He touched her shoulder, just for a second. 'Don't worry.'

When she looked up again he was gazing intently into Audrey's face as if willing her to be all right.

When they rushed Audrey away, Sylvia sat in the side-room where she was told to wait, feeling desolate. The ambulance man had told her his name was Colin Evans. He had wished them both the very best. Then he was gone. Sylvia realized then that she had been up most of the night and was feeling very low. She went to see if she could at least find a cup of tea. In the corridor she met a woman pushing a trolley.

'Is there anywhere I can buy a cup of tea?' she asked.

'It's a bit early for that.' The motherly woman poured her a cup. 'Here, this is for one of the wards, but we can spare you a cup, bab – you look all in.'

Sylvia began to cry again. 'It's my sister. I don't know where they've taken her. She's having a baby. Some-thing's wrong . . .'

'Oh dear,' the woman said kindly. 'Well, you'll hear sooner or later. Go on, drink up – it'll do yer good.'

Sylvia thanked her and went back to the room and its uncomfortable chairs. She started to shake, as if she was going to pieces. She was filled with fear and dread, certain that she was never going to see Audrey again. Sitting back, she allowed herself to have a quick, sharp weep. Then, overcome by sheer weariness, and despite the hardness of the chair, she fell asleep.

'Miss? Hello, Miss?'

Someone was touching her shoulder. Nothing made sense for a moment when she opened her eyes to see a small, white room and a young woman with brown eyes and a white nurse's cap looking down at her. Then it all came back.

'Oh!' She was about to leap up. 'What's happened? Audrey – where is she?'

'Are you Miss Whitehouse?'

Sylvia stared stupidly at her. 'Yes. Has my . . . ?'

'Your sister is still under. I mean she hasn't come round from the anaesthetic. She won't be able to see you until later. They delivered the baby by Caesarean section.' She smiled then. 'A little boy.'

'Oh!' Sylvia's heart was suddenly beating so fast it made her feel quite peculiar. 'A boy! Oh, are they – is she . . . ?'

'She's recovering well,' she nurse said. 'But it was an emergency. They needed to get him out quickly.'

Sylvia burst into tears. 'Thank heavens!' she sobbed. 'I thought she was going to die.'

'Oh no, she's going to be all right,' the nurse said. 'But why don't you go home and rest for a while? She can't see you yet. If you come back later, during visiting hours, I'm sure she and the little one will be much more ready by then.'

Sylvia walked out, dazed, into the now sunlit May morning. As she stood waiting for the Outer Circle bus, it hit her in a blaze of amazement. Everything was all right! Audrey had had her baby and she was going to live! She realized how terrified she had been the night before. Now she felt like turning cartwheels along the street. All she wanted was to get home and tell Mom and Dad and Jack, who would all be fretting themselves silly.

*

361

Most extraordinary of all, Mom had let Jack stay home from school. Never had such a thing happened before, even at the height of the bombing when they were all exhausted. Only Dad felt he had to get to the works. Marjorie was waiting with them, with Paul, and as soon as Sylvia opened the front door they all rushed towards her.

'She's all right. And she's had a little boy! Everything's all right.'

Her mother put her hands over her face in tears of relief and gratitude. 'Oh, thank heavens – oh, my little girl! I thought I was going to lose her.' Marjorie comforted her, tears running down her cheeks as well.

'A boy!' Jack said. 'How long before he can play football?' But then his face crumpled and he rushed upstairs, embarrassed to let his emotion show.

'Well,' Pauline said, wiping her eyes. 'A baby boy. Now the fun and games'll really begin. Look what Marjorie's brought us.'

In the back room was a big pram.

'I hadn't the heart to part with it,' Marjorie said. 'I've kept all sorts of bits and pieces in it – nothing dirty, though. And I've given it a good clean-up for her.'

'Oh, I remember that!' Sylvia said. She had seen Marjorie pushing Paul around in it. 'It's lovely.' In tears herself, quite wrung out with emotion, she said, 'So, we are keeping him, Mom?'

Pauline's face took on a hard, determined air. 'We're keeping him. Whatever anyone thinks, he's family.'

As they were making a much-needed cup of tea, Jack came downstairs again, looking watery but under control. 'Look,' he offered, 'I'll bike over and tell Dad, shall I?'

*

Sylvia and her mother caught the bus back to the hospital that afternoon. Pauline admitted that she had forgotten all about heading over to the Goods Yard to explain what was going on, so on the way Sylvia called them from a phone box. The woman's voice on the other end was disapproving. 'We'll have to dock your pay.' Sylvia couldn't have cared less.

Audrey was lying quietly when they went in, but as she saw them come to the bed, she gave an exhausted smile.

'Hello, Mom, Sylv.'

'How are you, bab?' Pauline asked softly, sitting beside Audrey. She wiped her eyes, determined not to get too emotional again.

'Very sore. But I'm okay. I feel so weak . . . He's doing well, they say. They'll bring him in a minute.'

Audrey couldn't remember much about what had happened. 'It was a shock when I woke up here. And then, just a few minutes ago, a bloke came and asked how I was and said he'd brought me in the ambulance. I couldn't even remember him!'

'I'm not surprised, the state you were in,' Sylvia said. 'That was kind of him. His name's Colin. He's ever such a nice man.'

'Yes,' Audrey said. 'He seemed it.'

A nurse came up and said to her, 'Well, it's nearly his feeding time. Shall I bring the little fellow through?'

From the nursery there came the distant sound of babies crying. Women lay recovering on the surrounding beds. A few minutes later the nurse came back carrying a little bundle wrapped in a white blanket. As she handed him to Audrey, they saw a rosy face, his head topped by a slick of dark hair.

Sylvia knew her mother had deep reservations about

363

this baby, but she could see her being drawn in by his sheer loveliness. She wondered what Audrey felt. She was showing every sign of loving him as any mother would.

'Oh,' Pauline said, and a soft expression that Sylvia had never seen before came over her face. 'He's beautiful. He looks just like you did.'

Audrey flashed a sudden watery smile. 'Does he?' She gazed at him as he lay in her arms. 'I still can't take it in. One moment I'm asleep – then they show me . . .' Tears suddenly ran down her face. 'It doesn't seem right somehow.'

'You laboured hard for him, love,' Pauline said with surprising fierceness. 'You just had a little help with the last bit. What weight was he?'

'Seven pounds nine,' Audrey said. 'He feels even heavier, now he's come out. Here,' she offered. 'D'you want to hold him?'

Sylvia and their mother both had a hold. Sylvia felt the warm weight of the little boy, and his mysterious baby-smell. In amazement she took in his twitching face, his tiny lips and nose.

Audrey watched them getting acquainted with her son. 'Mom,' she said softly, 'they say I have to stay here for a few days.' Then, with more vulnerability than Sylvia had ever seen in her, she went on, 'I couldn't part with him – not for anything.' She swallowed and added. 'Mom, I'm sorry.'

Pauline looked up from gazing at her grandson and said, without rancour, 'Too late to be sorry. Now we're just going to have to get on with it – and think of this one's future.'

Forty-Seven

30 May 1942

Laurie Gould sat crammed into the hut, shoulder-to-shoulder with all the other men awaiting their final briefing. The air was full of smoke. Everyone needed something to calm their nerves before take-off.

'Tonight's the night,' the Lincolnshire station commander told the assembled air crews. 'The plan is on. Some of you will be familiar with the destination.'

They had spent that morning carrying out aircraft checks, flying out over the North Sea to make sure everything was operational. All day the airfield was alive with activity: refuelling, maintenance checks and 'bombing up', for what was clearly going to be a massive raid. Trailer after trailer of bombs had moved across the base, some packed with incendiaries, others with high explosives, all to be stowed in the waiting planes. They had been in no doubt that this was to be a Big One. Now, at last, they knew the intended target: Cologne.

Sitting beside Laurie was Sam Masters, their crew's flight engineer. Nudging Laurie, he held out a packet of Lucky Strike. Laurie took one. 'Thanks, chum.' He lit up and drew on the cigarette, trying to ignore the cramping in his guts. It always took him like this. Nerves got everyone, one way or another. Some chaps couldn't stop talking. Others went back and forth to the latrines. Almost all of them smoked. It was important never to think about what you were doing or allow the imagination to take over. That was the way to a complete funk. You had to joke with all the lads, and block out thoughts of anything other than the job ahead.

The weather was fine, the commander's brisk voice was saying. The moon was due to be full tonight and the skies clear, though there might be moderate cloud cover over Germany, which might make their life slightly easier. He outlined the route on the map. Laurie listened with exceptional care. It was his job to get them there, guiding the Avro Manchester with his plotting and calculations. His stomach churned again and he drew in some deep breaths to try and calm himself.

The build-up was always bad, but this was by far the biggest mission that he personally had been on yet. The Luftwaffe had wreaked massive damage on Warsaw, Rotterdam and Belgrade. The RAF had replied by bombing Rostock and Lübeck, Essen and, already, Cologne. Now they were going on the biggest raid ever – with more than a thousand bomber aircraft. The centre of Cologne was to be obliterated. The word 'Coventrate' had become a new one in their language, since the devastating raids on Coventry.

'That's all,' the commander concluded. 'Best of luck to you all.'

They ate a meal, got kitted up and waited. By eight o'clock they were climbing into the trucks that would take them out to the airfield. Laurie was once more crammed in with his crew, Sam Masters on one side of him and Ron Williamson, the wireless operator, on the other. There was the odd remark passed, a snigger of laughter, but mostly they were quiet now, reflective, keyed up for what lay ahead.

Every few minutes Laurie reached inside his flying jacket for the reassuring feel of the folded sheets of paper. Pressed close to his heart were Sylvia's two most recent letters. Thinking about his lovely Sylvia was his refuge, his dream. A pang of longing tightened his chest. Here was the world with this beautiful woman in it, his old friend, now his love. Everything was lit up in a blaze of loveliness, now that their feelings for each other had grown into the sweet, loving thing they were. And here he was, caught up in this wretched war, wasting every day of his life away from her, in this terrible, destructive job of work.

Frustrated anger coursed through him. What was life for? For this? Being carried out to a dark airfield, from where he would fly to the country of other men, to wreak on it massive destruction? And all this when he could be at home with his girl, getting married, loving her and doing good, wholesome things that offered him a future. Would he ever see another dawn after this one? *Six weeks' life expectancy in Bomber air crews*, they were told, when they arrived. *Make your will, lads.* That was something he had never told Sylvia. There were already too many men who had not come back – two of them the best friends he had made, the ones he would joke with in the crew room. For a few seconds he was filled with utter desperation. He pulled himself back from this, taking deep breaths again. He forced himself to think of Sylvia and nothing else.

Earlier in the day he had found time to write to her. The letter would surely already be on its way, ready to greet her in the morning. He had memorized many of the words from her letters to him. He knew they were an effort for her, and he carried them close to his heart as his own personal mascot.

Audrey had had the baby, Sylvia had told him, in the first letter. She described what had happened, the long night and Audrey's distress, her own fear and then, at the end of it all, this beautiful little boy! 'He really is such a sweetheart,' Sylvia told him:

I'm afraid Aud has been rather weepy for the past few days, though Mom says that's often how it is after a birth. But it's so sad that things aren't better for A. I feel desperate for her sometimes. She's very attached to the little boy and making a fine job, which is lovely to see, though she still hasn't given him a name. I know Mom thinks he should be christened, but she doesn't want to go to the vicar with A. not being married. There's no sign of the father, of course. A.'s adamant that there's no point even in telling him about the child, though I would have thought he could at least give some money to provide for him, married or not. I do have to try not to say the wrong thing.

Mom and Dad are doing their best, and the person who has been the most help is your mother, bless her! She's round all the time – can't seem to keep her eyes off the little man. She just wants to coo and hold him, and never mind where he came from. Thank goodness for her – there are enough busybodies out there who like to condemn people, and I'm sure A. will have to cope with enough of them. So having someone like your mother around is a tonic for all of us. And it's so nice to be able to write, my love, and tell you about how it really is.

Laurie had smiled reading this, but there was a deep sadness to the smile. He knew his mother loved babies, but he knew too that she had had hopes for Audrey and Raymond. Perhaps this baby was like a replacement for the child that Raymond never had with Audrey – or with anyone. Laurie knew, with a sour feeling, that his father would never allow himself such an indulgence. Dad, ever tight and relentless, always expecting more from everyone than they could give. But Laurie was glad for his mother, that she could take so much pleasure in this little child.

I so wish you were here. We are busy as ever, but I still find plenty of times to miss and miss you. Sometimes I dream that I'll look up when I'm at work and you'll come walking across the yard, like you did that day, and you'll tell me the war's over and you're never going away again. Well, a girl can dream, can't she? And one day maybe that'll happen.

I'll make a date with you, my love. When you're coming home, send me a wire with a time on it. All you have to say is 'Meet me under the clock' and I'll be there – whatever time of the day or night!

He closed his eyes as the truck jolted them towards the waiting lines of aircraft. Now it was all before him, the long, dark hell of never knowing when you might be blown out of the sky. He had to take a piece of heaven with him, and she was that heaven. *I love you, Sylvia,* he said in his mind, over and over. *My dear, dear love. Please, dear God, spare me – let me see her again.*

The engines of the heavy bomber aircraft roared into the night. As the crew all settled into their positions, Laurie checked and triple-checked his navigation equipment.

Over the engine noise he could hear Ron speaking into the wireless. Laurie thought of their rear gunner, Fred Howes, with whom he had shaken hands only minutes ago, at his post in the lonely gun turret behind them. Joe Riley, the bomb aimer, was in his position. Out of sight, Wallace Paine, pilot for this trip, and second pilot Angus MacPherson were in the cockpit. All of them, for that night, were obliged to trust each other more than any other people on earth.

They began to taxi, and the roar of the engines filled Laurie's head. He breathed deeply from his oxygen mask, determined that nerves would not get the better of him. After that, it was a relief to be absorbed in the tasks before him during their lurching progress towards the runway. He checked and rechecked his navigation charts. The accurate plotting of the journey was his responsibility. It made him feel both afraid and electrically alive and alert.

As the aircraft lifted into the darkening sky, he thought of the massive assembly of planes combining around them for this enterprise. Wave after wave of heavy bombers were leaving airfields all over the eastern region. Their own bombers were to be among the early groups of planes to reach Cologne, carrying ordnance that was mostly incendiaries. Behind them were more waves of bombers carrying heavy explosives. Home was below them now, their distance from it increasing with every second. They were in this strange, abstract country called air space, where all their houses and streets, beloved villages and fields were laid out in miniature like a model, invisible now in the gloom. He thought of Birmingham, of turning the plane towards his home city and flying over it, knowing that she – the woman he loved – was there below him. And then he allowed himself no thought other than his work of navigating the plane. There were key points he had to head towards: the Dutch coast, the mission over Cologne, followed by a swift south-westerly turn towards Euskirchen, then west again and home.

An intense silence had overcome the crew and there was only the engine throb and the rushing force of the wind against the aircraft. The next time a voice was heard, it was Laurie's own, speaking through the intercom to the pilot: 'Enemy coast ahead.' No more black sea below. They were flying over land, heading towards Ouddorp, in Holland.

Forty-Eight

As soon as she got home from work that terrible afternoon Sylvia knew something was wrong. The house felt unnaturally quiet. A terrible thought came to her: the baby! Was he all right? She hung her cap up, telling herself not to be so ridiculous, and was about to run upstairs to see him and Audrey when her mother appeared in the doorway of the front room.

'Oh,' Sylvia said. 'You made me jump.' Behind Mom was Marjorie Gould. Someone else was sitting in the room. She could see legs: Audrey's. Where was the baby? The look on Mom's and Marjorie's faces turned her stomach to lead.

'Come and sit down, Sylvia,' Mom said. Her voice was tight and restrained, but Marjorie put her hands over her face and began to moan.

'Oh, God!' Sylvia said. Her legs almost gave way before she reached a chair. Audrey immediately leaned over and reached out, gripping her arm.

'No . . .' Words fell from Sylvia's lips. 'No . . . no!' She had no clear thought, just an appalling dread. She looked round at all of them. Of the three, Audrey looked the most in command of herself, so it couldn't be the baby.

'It's all right, sis,' Audrey said in a desperate voice. 'We're all here.'

Marjorie Gould was sobbing, still standing halfway across the room.

'No!' Sylvia cried again. 'Don't tell me! Not . . .' But she couldn't say Laurie's name.

'Give it to her, Mom,' Audrey breathed.

Pauline's hands were trembling so much she could hardly pass her the sheet of telegraph paper. 'Oh, I don't want –' she said. 'Oh, if I could only—'

Sylvia read out:

MRS S. GOULD REGRET TO INFORM YOU THAT YOUR SON LAURIE GOULD IS MISSING AS THE RESULT OF AIR OPERATION NIGHT OF 30/31 MAY 42 STOP LETTER FOLLOWS STOP ANY FURTHER INFORMATION BE IMMEDIATELY COMMUNICATED TO YOU.

'Missing!' She looked up desperately at Marjorie. 'That means they don't know?' She could feel her eyes stretching wide, like a little child trying to take in a new and dreadful sight.

'Sis, come and sit down . . .' Audrey's tired face was full of such tender sympathy that Sylvia knew immediately they did not hold out any hope.

'I feel ever so queer,' Sylvia said. There were lights at the edge of her vision.

'She's fainting, Mom!' she heard Audrey say. She felt her sister's arm round her, and her mother telling her to put her head between her knees. As the blood pumped to her dizzy head, she heard Marjorie's agonized cries.

'My boys, my lovely boys,' she wailed. 'Oh, why did I have boys, for them to go like this? It's wicked, *wicked* – oh, my beloved little babies . . .'

Gradually Sylvia's consciousness came back to the room. She couldn't stop her teeth chattering. She felt clammy and sick. Audrey was gripping her hand and

Mom, holding Marjorie in her arms, was looking back at her, torn by the need to comfort both of them at once. Marjorie was emitting wrenching sobs.

'Something *can't* have happened to him.' Sylvia looked up at Audrey, who was sitting on the arm of her chair. 'I love him and he loves me. We're going to get married!'

'Oh, Sylv . . .' Audrey put her arm round Sylvia's shoulders and held her tightly. 'Oh my poor, poor sis.'

'I knew it,' Sylvia's voice was very small, without force. 'I was so happy. I knew it couldn't really be true. Oh,' she looked across the room at the awful distress of Laurie's mother, 'Oh my God, poor, poor Marjorie.'

A letter arrived the next day. Once again Marjorie brought it round to them. They all knew that Stanley Gould, while cut to the core by the loss of his sons, could not speak of the things he felt and would not be any help to Marjorie. They would have to provide whatever comfort they could. It was awful to see her: in twenty-four hours she had shrunk and withered. She walked bent forward, as if her body was wrapped around her pain, and the flesh on her face sagged with grief. Her once-bright hair looked faded and lifeless.

The letter was from Laurie's wing commander. Sylvia read it out:

Dear Mr and Mrs Gould,

It is with the greatest regret that I have to write confirming the news given in my telegram of earlier today that your son, First Class Aircraftman Laurie Gould, has been reported missing from an operational sortie against Cologne on the night of 30/31st May 1942.

The aircraft in which your son was navigator took off at 20.41 hrs on 30th May, since when nothing further has been heard. There is of course a possibility that the crew have landed safely, but it is still too early to expect news of such an eventuality. Should I hear anything, I will communicate with you immediately.

It was the next paragraph of the letter that made her weep:

Your son's personal effects are being collected together and will be forwarded to the Standing Committee of Adjustment, Colnbrook, Slough, for onward transmission to you in due course.

May I, on behalf of myself and the Squadron as a whole, extend to you our sincere sympathy and understanding at this anxious time.

As soon as Sylvia read the first line, the thin thread of hope against the odds – which had kept her breathing, moving, going through the motions of life for the past day – was stretched almost to breaking point. But she could not let it snap, not yet. Not while there was any chance . . .

She handed the letter back to Marjorie in silence, tears running down her cheeks. They could not look each other in the eye, not then. Each of them was too weighed down by her own grief to be able to take on the other's.

'How's Stanley?' Pauline asked gently.

'Oh, well, you know Stanley,' Marjorie said, thrusting the letter into her pocket. She was not tearful today. She seemed brittle and angry. Her eyes – so like Laurie's – kept moving round the room as if unable to settle. 'I don't know what to do with myself,' she burst out at last.

'Stanley's as silent as the grave, and Paul – well, what does Paul understand? I don't know. Raymond's not coming back. Now Laurie's not coming back, and Paul keeps asking for them. Oh!' She gave a sound of pent-up rage and tore at her hair. 'Two sons. Two sons I've given up for all this, this rotten, hellish war. And for what? Is it over? Has anything been saved by it, or the world made a better place for my two boys dying? No – it *damn* well *hasn't*.

'I used to look down on those men who were conchees, but my God, if I had my time again, I'd stop my lads joining up and throwing their lives away.' With her hands still pushed into her hair, she closed her eyes and for a moment Sylvia thought she was going to faint. But she had just run out of words. More quietly, lowering her arms, she said, 'For what? That stinking Kraut, Hitler, is still winning. Women's sons are dying – sons from everywhere.' She looked at them, bewildered. 'None of it makes any sense. I feel as if . . .' Her voice broke then, lowered to a whisper. 'Everything I've lived for has been taken away.'

Audrey appeared downstairs then, with the baby in a shawl in her arms. She looked at her mother, who shook her head faintly. This did not feel like the right moment to offer Marjorie the little lad to hold.

'I must get back to Paul,' Marjorie said. Even though there were no tears, she wiped her face with the backs of her large hands. 'At least I've got one son who they won't throw away as cannon-fodder.'

'Marjorie,' Pauline touched her arm as she passed, 'I'll be round – a bit later.'

'There's nothing to do, is there?' Marjorie said hopelessly. 'What can we do?' She stopped, looking down at the sleeping baby in passing. 'Just make sure,' she said to

Audrey, 'that you don't *ever* send him off to war. You keep him by you, love. If every mother does that, the world'll be a better place.'

It was the last time they saw her in good health and on her feet for a very long time. The next day Stanley came round and told Pauline that Marjorie had taken to her bed. There was nothing he could do to persuade her to get up.

Forty-Nine

Sylvia insisted on going to the yard to work every day. All she could think of was keeping so busy that she would not have time to think. She could not bear the thought of sitting still, even though Bill Jones kindly said that she could probably ask for a couple of days off.

'Compassionate leave, like,' he said. 'It'd be all right, love.'

Sylvia gave a wan smile. 'Thanks, Mr Jones, but I'm better keeping busy. Sitting around with too much time to think is the worst thing.'

'Well, I'm sure you're right,' Bill said. 'But if you change your mind, I'd put in a word for you.'

The others girls were sweet and sympathetic. Madge was the softest Sylvia had ever seen her. 'Oh my God, Sylv,' she said. 'That's the worst. You poor, poor thing.' Sylvia was touched by this, and by how upset the others were.

'Oh, Sylv,' Elsie said, 'your lovely Laurie.' All the girls had fallen for Laurie when he came into the yard. 'I'm ever so sorry. It seems pointless trying to say anything.'

'No, it's okay. Thanks,' Sylvia looked round, dry-eyed, at her friends, Elsie, Gina and the others. 'I suppose I can't really take it in, not yet.' Even the letter from the wing commander had not fully made it sink in. She was going through life in a numb state, as if she was not really there, as if she had slipped into a dream. Her father had come home the day they received the news and had silently taken her in his arms, something he would never normally do. The thought of that – of her cheek pressed against Dad's shirt button and his bony ribcage, of his comforting smell and the look in his eyes – could most make her weep when she thought about it. So she tried not to, except at night when she was alone in her room.

Whatever the RAF said or what other people thought, she could not believe that Laurie was dead. She didn't say this to anyone, because she didn't want to see their pitying looks. But Laurie not coming back was just impossible. Laurie was part of life. He had always been there, full of beans, his lovely fresh face grinning at her, running across the yard to her at Hockley to take her in his arms. One day he would come back and do that again – she just could not let herself believe that it was over and he was gone. It was too unbearable. Every night she lay and sobbed herself into an exhausted sleep.

'You know, Sylv,' Elsie said hesitantly one day, 'even before all this we said we ought to get out more, do a few things together – especially now the summer's coming. Maybe we should meet up, go to the flicks or summat. I don't s'pose you feel like it now,' she was gabbling, afraid she had been tactless. 'But sometime maybe, when you're ready?'

'Thanks, Else,' Sylvia said, busying herself with sorting out her things in the mess room. She had hardly even heard what Elsie said. 'That's nice of you. Now, we'd best get out there and get weaving, hadn't we?'

Audrey's baby was one of the few things Sylvia found comforting. He was so tiny and fragile, he had no idea what was going on and could not try and say kind, well-meaning things. She could just hold him and rock him, soothing herself in the process.

Pauline was trying to divide herself between comforting Marjorie and Sylvia, both of whom were left with this agony at losing the same beloved boy. Laurie was so like his mother that now, instead of sweetly reminding Sylvia of her absent love, the sight of Marjorie represented all that she had lost. But she did not run into Marjorie, because she had taken to her bed. Paul spent a lot of time at the Whitehouses' now, with Pauline looking after him.

'Is Mrs Gould ill, Mom?' Audrey asked as Pauline came back from visiting one afternoon, a few days after they received the news.

'She looks poorly,' Pauline said, sinking wearily onto a chair in the kitchen. She rested her chin on her hands at the table. 'She says she just hasn't the will to get up. I s'pose she just needs to come to terms with it, but I've never seen her bad like this before.'

It made things feel even more desolate, without Marjorie coming in and out. Sylvia could hardly bear to think of her lying alone in her bedroom, grieving silently all day long. She wondered if she should go and see her, but she didn't have the strength.

Audrey was the person Sylvia felt closest to, in a way they had never been close before. Although Audrey's own problems had been rather pushed aside by the news that Laurie was missing, Sylvia knew that she was suffering as well.

In all that was happening, they had forgotten to keep pressing Audrey as to what she was going to call her son. But on one of those early summer evenings, Sylvia and

Audrey were out in the garden while Jack was seeing to the animals. Audrey squatted down on the blue brick path, holding the little boy in front of her to watch LaVerne, Maxene, Patty and the remaining 'royal ladies' being chased into the coop for the night. Sylvia gave a wan smile.

'He's taking it all in – he is!' she said. 'Look, his eyes have gone wider, as if he's surprised.'

Audrey laughed. 'He does look a bit startled,' she said, standing up and cradling him again. Jack dashed past, trying to catch two of the rabbits that had been enjoying the spring dandelions by the air-raid shelter.

'It's a funny thing, isn't it?' Audrey said. 'I never asked for him or wanted him. I don't know how on earth I'm going to get by, really. But I can't seem to help wanting him, now he's here. We sort of came through it together.'

'It's natural, I suppose,' Sylvia said, the ache that was always present inside her sharpening into a stab of desolation. Would she ever have the chance for a husband and child herself now? She struggled to rally herself. There was still hope. He would come back. He *would*. And she didn't want to sink into feeling sorry for herself. Raymond and countless others had lost their lives, and here she was, still breathing, still standing in the sun. She must not be so ungrateful as to despair, although at times it was so hard not to. It was missing him that was the worst. It was not knowing whether now Laurie was ever going to walk into a room and smile at her again, or turn up at the yard and call her name . . . The longer it went on without any word from him, the harder it became to cling to hope.

'D'you know who called round today?' Audrey said. 'I forgot to tell you. That bloke who took us to Selly Oak Hospital.'

'What, the ambulance man?'

'That's the one. Colin something.'

'What on earth did he come round for?' Sylvia asked.

'Just to find out if I was all right. And to see this one, I think.' She nodded down at the baby.

'Well, that was nice. I don't think they normally do that.'

'No,' Audrey said. 'That's what I thought. Nice feller, though.' There was something in her sister's voice that made Sylvia look round, but all Audrey said was, 'Kind of him. They must wonder, sometimes, what's happened to people. In fact he asked if he could come again.'

'Oh *did* he?' Was that a blush on Audrey's cheeks?

'Anyway, I've decided what to call this one. In fact I've had him baptized.'

'*What?* How d'you mean?' Audrey was dropping one surprise after another. 'What about Mom, and christening robes, and everything?'

'You don't need all that. I went to see the vicar and explained the situation and he said, if I wanted, he could baptize him there and then. So we went into the church, and that's what we did. All you need is a drop of water and a vicar – well, he said you don't even need one of them, if it's an emergency. You can do it yourself.'

'Oh,' Sylvia said. She felt strangely let-down, but saw that this made complete sense. A public ceremony for a child everyone knew was born out of wedlock? No, Mom wouldn't have had it. 'So what's his name?'

'Dorian Raymond,' Audrey said.

'*Dorian?*' she said, bewildered. 'Well, that's unusual.'

Audrey spoke, looking down into the baby's sleeping face. 'It's just . . . When I was in the WAAF I knew a girl called Dorrie. It was short for Dorothea, but I liked the name Dorrie.'

'Was she the one who sent you the postcard when you'd only been away for a day or something?' Sylvia teased.

'Yes,' Audrey said lightly. 'That's the one. We've lost touch now, of course, because I moved on to another site . . . Doesn't matter, anyway. But I liked that name and I thought: what boy's name could I give him that would sound the same?'

'*The Picture of Dorian Gray*,' Sylvia said. 'That's the only Dorian I've ever heard of.' She wasn't sure about the name, but there was no point arguing. 'It's – nice. Dorrie. Little Dorrie. Have you told Mom?'

'Not yet. I was hoping you'd come with me.'

The sisters' eyes met in understanding.

'All right,' Sylvia said. 'Best go and get it over then.'

Fifty

June 1942

Audrey laid little Dorian in the pram and covered him with a soft blanket. He looked up at her, wide-eyed, sucking on one of his fingers.

'Your job is to go to sleep, young man,' she said softly.

It was a warm Saturday afternoon and she wanted to go out. At that moment it felt like the most important thing ever: to be out on her own, to get away from Mom – from all of it. Tiptoeing, she pushed the pram along the hall and was opening the front door when she heard feet on the stairs and turned in dread. It was Jack.

'Aud, are you off out?' He hesitated. 'Can I come?'

She looked up at him, surprised. 'If you like.'

Jack helped her ease the pram outside and, with Audrey pushing it, they set off down the shady side of the street. Jack loped along beside her in his grey flannels, his shirt-sleeves rolled up. He was a tall, athletic lad. In the nearly six weeks since Dorrie was born, Jack had, at first awkwardly, come to terms with the changes in the house and the fact that they were not as ideal as they might be. Laurie's disappearance had also hit him very hard. He seemed to have grown up a lot in those weeks and even to have gained a couple of inches in height.

Audrey was just beginning to relax in the sunshine

when they reached a gaggle of children playing on the pavement. Seeing the pram coming, some of them stood up from the chalk game they had drawn and began to pull each other out of the way.

'Thanks,' Audrey said, smiling at the mixed group of boys and girls, most of whom were familiar.

But as they walked on past there was an outbreak of whispers and giggles behind them. One voice half-chanted, 'Little bastard ba-by! Little bastard ba-by!' A few of the others joined in, in low voices.

Jack slammed his hand onto the handle of the pram and Audrey grabbed his arm. 'No, Jack! Ignore them. Just take no notice!'

His face was red with fury. 'Does that always happen – every time you go out?'

'No, of course not. Just now and then.' She forced him to walk on slowly. 'If you play up to it, they'll get worse. They're only kids.'

'Little sods!' Jack fumed.

'They're just repeating what they've heard the grown-ups saying.' Audrey tried not to let him see how hurt and angry she was. 'They'll only do it more if you take any notice.'

'I don't know how you can stand going out,' Jack said.

'I'm not going to miss the sunshine for those little squirts,' she replied. But it was terrible, having such things shouted at you in the street. It made her feel dirty and ashamed – but she damned well wasn't going to let them see that.

Once they were through the park gates Audrey said, 'Thanks for coming out with me. It's nice to have some company.'

'That's okay,' Jack said. After a moment he looked round at her. 'Are you all right, sis?'

'Yes, I'm okay.' She smiled to try and reassure him.

Once the baby arrived, Jack had gradually been won over by him. Audrey was very touched to see how attached he was now to her little boy and how interested he was in him. But they still mostly related to each other through the baby. This was the nearest Jack had ever come to talking to Audrey about how she felt. What had happened with the children in the street had helped open things up. She gave a small sigh.

'But . . .' Jack began. He looked down at the path in confusion.

'But?' Audrey said gently. 'But it's not okay? I'm not married, and my baby's a . . . is illegitimate?'

Jack was red in the face now. 'It's not that I—' He broke off. 'I mean, I'm not blaming you. I just think it must be very hard for you, that's all. Things like what just happened back there . . .'

'It is, in some ways.' Audrey thought about it. She was constantly surprised by the strength of her own feelings. She had felt so at odds with things, before Dorian was born. Life had cheated her. She loved the WAAF and all her friends, loved her freedom and independence, and now she was stuck at home, disgraced and under Mom's thumb. Yet Mom had stood by her and, now that Dorian was here, even though she had not loved his father, she loved him with a depth of feeling that took her quite by surprise. All the confusion she had felt while she was in the WAAF had disappeared in the daily round of caring for this tiny child. It made things easier, even though it was hard work. Dorian had become her world and she didn't have to decide anything else. She had in some way surrendered herself to nature – to being a woman – almost in the way that a log surrenders to the flow of a river. But she could not say any of this to Jack.

'At least Mom and Dad didn't put me out on the street.'

'They wouldn't have done that!'

'There's a lot would have done.'

They walked on, into the sunlight. Audrey felt the warmth of the sun sink into her, relaxing her. But she could sense that Jack was full of tension. He was breathing heavily and clenching and unclenching his hands. Suddenly, in an urgent rush he said, 'I just wish I could do something – about *anything*!'

His face was red and he seemed close to tears.

'Hey,' she said. 'What's the matter?'

Jack spoke, looking down at the ground. 'I just feel so useless. I'm too young to fight. I don't go to work – I'm just at school. Which I want, of course, but all the same . . . And everyone's having such an abysmal time. And Laurie . . .' Jack wept then. He couldn't help himself.

Audrey drew him onto a bench and put her arm round his shoulders. She could see how bad he was feeling, because he would never normally let anyone see him cry. Now he didn't seem to care whether or not passers-by saw. He had adored Laurie. While everyone was feeling sorry for Sylvia, Jack was feeling Laurie's absence almost as much.

'How can he be dead?' Jack said. He sat leaning his elbows on his thighs, hands over his face. Audrey could feel him shaking. His manly voice seemed at odds with the upset little boy who was crying beside her. Silently she wept beside him. The thought of the Gould boys, both of them, made her heart ache almost unbearably.

'I just can't believe he's gone,' Jack went on, 'that he'll never . . .' He looked up at her with wet eyes. 'We're just never going to see him again. He's not *in this world* any more.'

She looked back at him, her own eyes streaming. 'I know. I can't take it in, either.'

'Sometimes I think Mrs Gould is always going to look at us – at me especially – and hate us for still being alive.'

'No, Jack. It's not like—'

'It *is*! It's different for you – you're a girl. And Sylvia would rather Laurie was alive than me, as well. I know she would.' He put his head down again and stared mutinously between his knees. Audrey looked at him, appalled to think he had been torturing himself with these thoughts.

'Jack,' she said as calmly as she could. 'I really don't think you're right. Of course Marjorie's in a terrible state. Stanley's had the doctor in more than once. And Sylvia's trying not to show it, but I don't think she's coming to terms with it at all. I don't know what to do for either of them. The way Sylvia just ploughs on is – well, it's how she manages, but underneath . . . To tell you the truth, though . . .' She stopped, hesitating to burden her brother with any more troubling thoughts.

Jack sat up. 'What?' He raised his voice. 'Don't keep things from me, Aud – stop treating me like a child!'

'Sorry,' Audrey said, jiggling the pram in case Jack's outburst had disturbed Dorian. 'It's Mom I'm worried about, as well. I know everyone's feeling terrible for Marjorie and Sylvia, but Mom's having to carry it for all of us. The other day I went into the kitchen and she was standing there, leaning on the table and just . . .'

'What – crying?' They both knew how rare it was for their mother to cry.

'Well, no. She was just sort of breathing. Hard. She looked bad, as if something was happening. I thought she'd been taken ill for a moment, but then she saw me and just stood up straight and carried on. It's the strain of it all, I think.'

Jack wiped his eyes. 'I'll try and help more.'

'We'll all try. Don't be hard on yourself, Jack. We all know how much Laurie meant to you – and Raymond, too. Everyone's trying to bear something. In a way I'm luckier – I've got him.' She half-stood up and looked, smiling, down at the baby. His eyes were closed, the lashes tiny dark crescents against his skin, but he was stirring. 'It's a funny thing,' she said quietly. 'I had no idea how it would be.'

She indicated to Jack that they should walk again. They waited for an elderly couple to pass slowly, arm-in-arm.

'Aud,' Jack said. 'That bloke who comes to see you. D'you like him?'

'Colin?' Audrey felt a pang of mixed emotions inside her. 'He's all right. He's a nice man.' Colin had come round three times now. The first time the excuse had been that he wanted to make sure Audrey was all right, and to see the baby. But he had come back twice more.

'He's in love with you, isn't he?'

Audrey blushed. 'Is he?' she said lightly. 'Maybe.'

She knew Colin was keen on her. Why would he keep coming otherwise? He was such a gentle, kind man. He was a good number of years older than she was, but she knew that if she felt anything for him, that would not matter. He had told her he was not married. He seemed besotted by her. In fact she thought about Colin far more than she was going to let on to Jack. What if Colin was the answer to all her problems? Here was a good man who might marry her, take on her child, and take her off Mom and Dad's hands – make a respectable woman out of her in fact. It seemed too good to be true. Colin was genuinely sweet, and what right did she have to expect anything even half as good as that now?

'He's mad about you,' Jack said. 'It's written all over his face.' When she didn't answer, Jack leaned closer. 'Aud, he *is* nice, isn't he?'

'Yes,' she agreed, hearing the note of desperate hope in her brother's voice. 'He's very nice.'

Later that afternoon Sylvia came home from work, her jacket slung over one shoulder in the warmth. She ambled along from the bus stop on the Alcester Road, in no hurry to get home. She was seldom in a hurry to get anywhere these days. In the three weeks since she had heard that Laurie was missing there had been nowhere that offered a refuge from the gnawing misery inside her. The harshness of work was eased by the warm weather and everyone's kindness to her. Even Froggy seemed gentler than usual. She had started to go out with her friends, when she could face it, to the pictures or visiting Elsie and her mother in Handsworth – anything to try and distract herself. In her own home everything was so strained and sad. The one spark of new life was little Dorian, but even he came at the price of Audrey's shame and as a reminder of her own losses. At the moment Sylvia would rather be almost anywhere else than at home.

She reached the house and was just about to go inside when next door's front door opened. Marjorie Gould stepped out, as if she had been waiting for her. Sylvia managed not to gasp. She had not seen Marjorie at all since the day they heard the terrible news. She was shocked to see the gaunt boniness of the woman's face. But at least Marjorie was up and breathing the air outside.

'Sylvia, come in a minute, will you, love?' she said in her thin voice. 'I've got something I want to show you.'

The house was quiet for a Saturday, Sylvia thought, then realized with a deep pang that this house, from now on, was always going to be quiet.

'Stanley's gone out for a ride on his bike with your father, as it's nice out,' Marjorie said as they went through to the back.

The house was much the same as their own in layout. Every inch of it screamed memories of the young, lively family that had once rollicked through it. The bleakness of Marjorie's loss washed over Sylvia again, almost dwarfing her own. She struggled to think what to say. Questions like 'How are you?' seemed so pointless.

'I'm very thankful he and Ted are friends, the way they are,' Marjorie was saying. She had the kettle on ready. 'It takes Stanley out of himself a bit. He's no good with all this . . .' She swept her hand across her, as if to take in their family's entire situation. As she brewed tea, she nodded towards the garden, where Sylvia could see Paul kicking a ball around in his dreamy way. 'He'll be busy for a bit. Come and sit with me.'

They went into the back room with the tea and Marjorie produced a dark-red photograph album.

'I wanted to show you,' she said. 'Stanley was quite keen on taking pictures, as you might remember. You're in quite a few of them as well.' Her gaunt features attempted a smile as she sat down, setting the book on her lap.

Sylvia felt dread filling her. Marjorie wanted to show her pictures of them all as children: of Laurie, of that precious, sunlit past. She desperately didn't want to sit here and be made to give way to emotion. But she could not refuse Laurie's mother the one thing she wanted. In a way, painful though it was, she was longing to see them too. Marjorie seemed calm, at least for the moment.

'Oh, look,' Marjorie turned the black sugar-paper pages. 'There's the lot of you, before Paul, anyway – and Jack. D'you remember that?'

The four of them were lined up along the garden wall in – typically of Stanley Gould – age order. Audrey, long, skinny and determined-looking sat beside slender, dark-eyed Raymond. Sylvia saw herself, unmistakable with her round, smiling face and wayward coils of hair. And there was Laurie, with his big eyes and chubby cheeks, caught somewhere between anxiety and a smile. Love and longing filled her.

'Oh,' she breathed. The grief welled up in her. 'How lovely! Oh, it was all so lovely.' She turned tearfully to Marjorie. 'I'm sorry I haven't been to see you before,' she began. 'I couldn't . . .'

'It's all right, love,' Marjorie said. 'I understand.' She looked down at the album to speak the words she needed to say next. 'Sylvia, don't wait for him. I did it with Raymond, for a time. I never said, but I kept thinking they must be wrong, that he was out there somewhere and one day he'd just come home and there he'd be, same as ever.' She swallowed. 'If Laurie was alive, he'd have been in touch somehow. He or the Red Cross – someone. I know my boy. It can't be, love. Don't spend your young life waiting for someone who can't be here any more. I thought I could say it to you, if no one else can . . .'

For a moment they both kept their eyes on the photograph, then turned to each other. Marjorie opened her arms and drew Sylvia into them. Sylvia felt all the grief in her rise up and overflow.

'You and Audrey are like my daughters,' Marjorie said as they held each other. 'Whatever else, you always will be.'

Without saying any more, they both wept together.

Fifty-One

July 1942

'Honestly,' Sylvia said to Elsie as they walked to the bus stop among the crowd pouring out from the cinema, 'I thought we'd gone to see something cheerful!'

Most of the audience emerged looking tearful. When Elsie had suggested a trip to the pictures after an early shift, she tactfully suggested they go and see something light and enjoyable. So she had suggested a picture house that was showing Disney's *Fantasia*, since neither of them had seen it.

'It was fabulous, wasn't it – but it really set me off,' Sylvia said as they sat, still tearstained, in the gloom of the bus. She had been entranced by the picture with all the music and colours and fairies and at first she was completely lost in watching it. By the end, though, when they were playing *Ave Maria*, the beauty and soulfulness of it tapped into all her grief; her feelings welling up so that she had to control her sobs.

'I know,' Elsie said, blowing her nose. She was all emotional, as well. 'I thought it was going to be cheerful – I didn't think this was how we were going to end up. Look at the state of us!'

'Well, that's having a good time for you!' Sylvia said.

394

Seeing each other's blotchy cheeks, they ended up in rather soggy laughter.

They were heading back to Handsworth, where Sylvia occasionally stayed over now. Elsie had been very kind to her, trying to take her mind off things, and it was easier for Sylvia not to have to make her way home alone. Elsie lived with her mother, who was a widow, a cheerful but nervous lady, and they always went back to stay with her, so that she wasn't left by herself. Sylvia found she could keep the worst depths of her despair at bay when she was away from home. She was afraid of imposing, but Elsie assured her that her mother loved to have new company.

'She likes you,' she told Sylvia. 'She looks forward to you coming.' They had a little put-me-up bed, which they could just fit into the sitting room for Sylvia.

Mrs Phipps greeted them enthusiastically. She was in her mid-forties and Elsie resembled her in almost every way. Both were very thin and frail-looking and both had prominent teeth and watery blue eyes, which gave off a lively friendliness. The main difference was in their hair. Mrs Phipps's, in colour a faded version of Elsie's mousy rats' tails, was plaited on each side and worn pinned in a little coil over each ear in the old-fashioned way. Elsie did the best with her thin hair, curling the ends with the help of nightly hairpins and pinning it back out of the way.

'Ooh, I'm glad you're home,' Mrs Phipps exclaimed as they walked into the house in Rookery Road where Elsie and her mother had rooms on the first floor. 'I've just put the kettle on. Did you hear they bombed the Rover this morning? That's not where your father is, is it, Sylvia?'

'Hello, Mrs Phipps,' Sylvia said. 'No, thank goodness – that was Solihull. Dad's at the shadow factory.'

There had been a few sporadic raids, even though

most of the German attention was fixed on Russia these days.

'Well, it's nice to see you; go and make yourselves comfy – I've got a few biscuits. Are you hungry, Sylvia? I could rake up a bit of toast for you, if you like?'

'Oh no, I'm all right thanks, Mrs Phipps,' Sylvia said, not entirely truthfully, as her stomach was gurgling with hunger. But she didn't want to eat Mrs Phipps out of house and home, and a biscuit would fill a gap.

Mrs Phipps sat with them, still with her apron over her dress, and they told her all about the picture. She sat nursing her cup and saucer, beaming as the girls tucked into their tea and arrowroot biscuits. The sight of Elsie and her mom both grinning away, with those teeth sticking out, reminded Sylvia inescapably of a pair of cheerful rabbits, which made her smile as well. She had quickly grown fond of Elsie's mom.

'There's a drop more in the pot, if you'd like it, Sylvia?' Mrs Phipps got up.

'I wouldn't say no, thanks,' she said.

As Mrs Phipps went over to the little kitchen area of their flat, there was a sudden almighty crash from outside and she jumped so violently that the cup flew off the saucer and into the sink. Sylvia felt her whole body leap with alarm, and Elsie screamed.

'Oh my Lord!' Mrs Phipps cried, rushing back in, still clutching the saucer. 'There must be a raid. That sounded close. Where're the sirens? Did you hear anything, Else?'

'No – I don't think there were any,' Elsie said breathlessly. They listened. Sylvia could feel the blood pounding round her body. They could hear it now: the familiar drone of aeroplane engines.

'Come on, out into the shelter,' Mrs Phipps urged.

'Thank heavens you got home all right . . . Go on, Elsie – take the extra blankets and the torch. I'll be out in a minute . . .'

As she spoke there were hurried footsteps climbing the stairs and someone pounded on the door.

'Mrs Phipps?' A kind, elderly Welsh couple, Mr and Mrs Jones, lived in the rooms below them and Mr Jones's deep voice came booming through the door. 'There's a raid on, I believe. Better be making our way outside.'

'We're coming!' Mrs Phipps called. 'Thank you, Mr Jones. Go on, girls.'

Sylvia cursed herself for not bringing more clothes. Although it was summer, it was still cold in the middle of the night, squeezed into an air-raid shelter. Visions of her nice cosy night on Mrs Phipps's folding bed evaporated swiftly.

She and Elsie seized hold of everything they could, in the way of extra coverings, and hurried down the dark stairs. Mr Jones was helping his infirm wife along the hall towards the back door.

'You go first, girls,' he said. 'We're a bit slow, as you know. Switch the fire on for us when you get there,' he quipped.

'Oh, we will, Mr Jones – and the floodlights,' Elsie said fondly. She always said that the Joneses had been like an uncle and aunt to her, as she was growing up.

As soon as they got outside it became clear that things were worse than they thought. The muffled thuds they had barely heard while they were busy getting ready were becoming closer, and the planes seemed to be right overhead.

'I'm going to tell Mom to hurry!' Elsie cried, running back into the house. Sylvia stood out at the back, and within seconds she was completely terrified. The sky was

397

already glowing an ominous orange from the fires, and the noise was loud and horribly close. Mr and Mrs Jones were hobbling along the garden.

'Elsie!' she shouted, torn between running to the house and heading for the shelter.

There was a massive crash. All she remembered was a rushing sensation, as if she was being pushed and flattened against the wall, and there was hardness, jagged edges, a stabbing pain along her left side and then . . . nothing.

Fifty-Two

Someone was lifting her, causing agony in her body. She could hear whimpering, like an animal. Then there was only blackness. When she opened her eyes at last, she saw a nurse.

'It's all right,' the nurse said. 'You're safe in Dudley Road Hospital. Just sleep, dear.' A sharp sensation arrived in her left arm. Her lids were heavy and her eyes slid closed again – for how long, she did not know.

The next time she opened her eyes she saw Elsie looking down at her.

'Sylv? Oh, thank God!' Elsie was crying. 'No, don't try and move – it'll hurt you.'

Sylvia moaned. Any attempt to move gave her pain in almost every part of her body, but most especially the left side of her chest.

'You're all right. They say you've got a few broken bones: your collarbone and some ribs. And you had – what d'you call it? – concussion. But you're going to be all right.'

Sylvia felt Elsie stroking her right hand, which lay outside the bedcovers. Memories started to crowd back to her: standing at the back of Elsie's house; the noise; Mr Jones with his hobbling wife leaning on his arm.

'What day is it?' she asked.

'It's Wednesday. They say you've been asleep most of . . . Your mother's coming in later . . .'

'Elsie, your mom?'

'She's all right.' Elsie had tears running down her cheeks. She was crying as if she just couldn't stop. 'Mom was coming down when I went back in, and when we heard – well, it was so close. We just threw ourselves into the cubbyhole under the stairs. If we hadn't . . . The house is wrecked. We've had to go to one of the churches. And Mr and Mrs Jones were both . . . They didn't —' She really broke down now. 'We found them in the garden; they were still holding hands.'

'Oh, Elsie,' Sylvia whispered, feeling tears rising in her as well. She was too weak to cry properly.

'Thank God you're all right, Sylv. When we went out, afterwards, and you were lying there, I thought: Oh, if we'd had to go and tell your mom! I couldn't bear to think about it.'

'What're you going to do?' Sylvia whispered.

'We're trying to find somewhere to go,' Elsie said. 'Gina says she knows someone who might have a room. It doesn't matter – we'll find something. But we're alive, and so are you.' She wiped her eyes and then squeezed Sylvia's hand again, managing a watery smile. 'Your job now is to get better – d'you hear?'

Later, Mom and Dad came. Their eyes were very wide, as if they were afraid of what they might see. Sylvia pushed her features into a smile. Parts of her face hurt, especially the left side.

'It's all right,' she said, keeping her breathing shallow because it hurt to do anything else. 'Broken bones, they say.'

'You were lucky,' one of the nurses had told her. 'You've certainly been bashed about, but it'll all heal, given time.' That was what people said about everything. Time. Compared to Laurie, this was nothing – just scratches and a few bones.

Mom sat on the chair by the bed and Dad stayed standing, holding his hat. Even lying down, Sylvia could see that they seemed cowed by the regime of the ward. Her mother was frightened of hospitals – she remembered people going in and never coming out. Hospitals and workhouses were all the same to her. They meant powerlessness and death.

Pauline leaned forward, looking round as if someone might tell her off for moving.

'We've been so worried, love. They say you're going to be all right. What happened?'

'You know what happened,' Dad said, shuffling his feet. 'It was a bomb, Pauline.'

'Elsie and her mom are all right,' Sylvia said.

'Oh, they came to see us, straight away – as soon as you'd been brought in here. They were ever so kind. Poor souls, their house is all gone.'

'They had a lucky escape,' Dad said. 'Rookery Road's a terrible mess.'

Mom had her hand on Sylvia's, and she could feel her mother twitching. Mom looked very pale and strained.

'I'm all right,' Sylvia told them. 'But I don't know how long I'll be in here.'

'The sooner you're home, the better. It's that collarbone – that's going to take some healing up.' Pauline's hands twitched restlessly again. 'Audrey and Jack send their love; and Marjorie and Stanley, of course.'

'How's little Dorrie?' Sylvia saw Dad look away down the ward at the mention of the baby's name, as if uneasy at him being mentioned here. Then he must have realized that no one had any idea who they were, or of the circumstances of his birth, and he relaxed and looked back at her.

'Oh, he's bonny,' Pauline said with a faint smile. They were all in love with the little boy. 'Eating well. Sleeping better too.' She paused. 'Weather's nice.'

'That's good,' Sylvia said. She started to feel drowsy, her eyelids drooping. 'Sorry, I just . . .'

When she woke again, there was no one there.

She stayed in hospital for two weeks. The early days were spent in a daze of shock and pain and she slept a lot. Eventually she was able to look round and take more notice of the other patients and chat to the ones nearby. She had a lot of time to rest and think – something she had tried to avoid doing these past weeks. At last she allowed herself to travel into her memories of Laurie. She would lie picturing their brief golden months together. And she thought about their past as children. An agony of sadness filled her as she let the pictures roll through her mind: of Laurie at every age as she had known him. The terrible grief that seemed to press on her like a weight was for herself, for the future they hoped to share together. But just as much of it was for him, for the simple fact of his not being here any more. She thought of all the young men who had died in the last war, and now in this one, and of all the people who loved them. When her mind dwelt on this it made the world feel a dark, bitter, pointless place. She remembered standing in Laurie's arms, seeing his good-natured face looking into hers. His eyes had been full of love for her, and her heart cried out for him with need and loss.

But she also remembered Marjorie's words to her the day they were together – a mother's truth that had to be faced.

And Sylvia knew this was what she was trying to do as she lay in her hard, white bed, grateful to be alive herself. She wept many times that week, quietly letting the tears flow. The idea of accepting that a young man whom she loved, who had left full of life and only twenty-one years of age, was never coming back, felt an impossible feat. She was grateful to Marjorie for being strong and brave enough to spell it out to her: *He's not coming back. Don't cripple your life with waiting.*

One afternoon, as the sunlight slanted in across the ward, she lay drifting in and out of sleep. A picture came to her of Laurie in his flying jacket, getting into a plane on a bright afternoon. The propellers were turning and she could see him smiling at her from the side-window of the cockpit. As the plane began to taxi he blew her a kiss. Soon the plane was speeding along, lifting off the ground, taking him further away every second. Before it moved too far away over the horizon and out of sight, she imagined that she saw him turn to her with a smile, a wave. And then he was gone.

Fifty-Three

August 1942

After two weeks Sylvia left hospital. Her arm was in a
sling and she was still in pain from her collarbone. Her
ribs, the doctor told her, would heal themselves in time.
It hurt her to breathe deeply, and she knew it was going
to be weeks before she could do anything really active
again. Work, for now, was out of the question. The cuts
on her face were healing, though there was one on the
left side that was going to leave a long scar.

But she knew she was lucky to be alive, and it was
lovely to be home! The house smelled different now, of
warm, baby smells. Audrey came hurrying down as soon
as she heard them come in.

'Hello, sis!' Audrey greeted her with a kiss, seeming
delighted to see her. 'You're back sooner than I expected.' She had been to the hospital once, but had left
most of the visiting to Mom and Dad as she needed to be
at home with Dorian.

'They couldn't wait to get rid of me,' Sylvia said.
'Careful, don't squeeze me. And for God's sake don't
make me laugh! Come on, let me see little 'un. I've
missed him.'

Dorian was lying in his cot in a state of sleepy rapture,

a dribble of milk running down his plump cheek and his arms flung out at the sides.

'Oh, look at him,' she breathed. She couldn't take her eyes off him. 'Lying there like a little prince. He's grown, Audrey – he's much bigger than when I left.'

'Is he?' Audrey said, leaning over to look as well. 'He's a proper guzzler.'

Sylvia turned to her. 'You look ever so thin.'

'He's taking everything I've got.' Audrey's eyes were serious. She looked closely at Sylvia, who was struck by how much gentler her sister was these days. 'Your poor face. But it is looking better than it was.'

Sylvia touched the worst scar on her left cheek. 'It's going to show, but . . .' She shrugged. 'I know I'm lucky to be here – and Elsie and her mom are. It was a miracle, really.' She looked down at her arm. 'This still hurts. I'll be stuck at home for a bit.'

'Never mind,' Audrey said, sinking down onto the bed. She seemed exhausted. 'You can keep me company. It'll be nice.'

The girls' eyes met and Sylvia smiled. 'Yes. It will.'

Everyone greeted her with great enthusiasm now that she was home and, even in her grief, Sylvia had a warm feeling of how lucky she was to have her family.

Sylvia was amazed at how much sleep she needed. She would get up feeling a little bit better every morning, and ready to help her mother and go out for walks with Audrey and the baby. But by eleven in the morning, and certainly during the afternoon, she found herself falling asleep even if she was standing up.

'Sleep's a healer,' her mother said, when she complained about it. 'Best thing for you.'

Everyone was being so kind. Dad and Jack were all consideration and helpfulness. Everyone knew how easily she might have been killed that night in Handsworth. Thinking of this gave her an intense appreciation of simply being alive. Pauline moved a comfy chair close to the window in the back room, and Sylvia sat for long periods looking out at the clouds moving across the sky and at the leaves of the apple tree at the bottom of the garden moving in the breeze.

'I feel as if I'm in hibernation – like a hedgehog,' she said to Audrey one afternoon as they were sitting together. Audrey was feeding Dorian, a muslin cloth draped over her shoulder for modesty's sake. 'Or a bird waiting to hatch out.'

'I should make the most of it,' Audrey said, looking up from concentrating on her son. She gave a wry smile. 'Look at us: old maids together.'

Sylvia shifted her position in the chair, wincing and watching her sister's gaunt face. She didn't often ask Audrey how she was feeling about things. There seemed no point. Things were as they were. Terrible things were happening in the world every day, and Audrey just had to get on with life. But she was surprised at her sister's calmness, considering how stormy and impatient she had always been previously.

'D'you miss the WAAF?' she dared to ask.

Audrey gave a faint smile. 'It all seems a long time ago now. A lot of the girls I knew will have moved on to other places.' She shrugged. 'No point in thinking about it, is there? I've made my bed . . . You know what they say.'

'But – his father?' Sylvia nodded at Dorian.

'So far as Dorrie's concerned, his dad was a fighter

pilot who was killed. Nick wasn't a pilot, and it's not that likely he'll get killed. But that's all he needs to know, isn't it? He's never going to see him, so he might as well be dead.'

Sylvia looked at her, troubled. 'It's not true, though.'

'I'm not sure the truth is any better.' Audrey sat up to transfer Dorrie to her other breast. She gave Sylvia the direct, challenging look that in the past would have quelled her sister into silence. But this time she held Audrey's gaze.

'So what is the truth then, exactly?'

'That his mother . . .' Audrey held out her spare arm, palm up, as if to declare something. She brought it back down to her lap again in a defeated way. 'Oh, I don't know.'

There was a silence, then Sylvia said, 'And . . . what about Colin?'

Audrey looked up with a strange half-smile. 'Colin?'

Audrey had been out walking with Colin a number of times in the afternoon, with the pram. Each time he called at the house he had come in specially to ask after Sylvia, and she liked his concerned, thoughtful manner.

'Oh, come on – stop pretending!' she said. 'He's ever so nice.'

'Yes,' Audrey agreed. 'He *is* nice.'

'Just nice?'

'Nice will do for a start,' Audrey said, with a tart edge to her voice. 'If you like him so much, why don't *you* go out with him?'

'It's not me he's keen on – he's crazy about you, Aud!'

'He likes you too. I can see that he does.'

Sylvia waved her hand dismissively. 'Oh, not me. I don't want anyone. But you . . .' Seeing the forbidding

407

expression on her sister's face, Sylvia didn't dare ask any more.

It was the day after the disastrous raid on Dieppe, an afternoon of August warmth that made Sylvia feel even more dopey than usual. She had just woken from a long doze in the chair and was cautiously stretching herself when there was a knock at the front door.

'I'll get it!' Audrey called, running down the stairs. Mom was next door with Marjorie.

Sylvia, getting slowly out of her chair, wondered if it was Colin again. She smiled to herself. He was certainly persistent and she could see that he was very keen on Audrey, though her welcome towards him was polite rather than enthusiastic. As she crossed the room she heard Audrey exclaim loudly, 'My God, you've got a nerve – what the hell do *you* want?'

Sylvia was horrified. Who on earth was Audrey talking to like that? She peered into the hall and it was only then that she took in the voice and saw the figure on the front step: a familiar, tall man in a brown suit. But it took a moment to recognize him, because he was now wearing spectacles. It was Ian Westley.

'My mother heard what happened,' he was saying. 'I'm so sorry. I thought I must come round and see if—'

He stopped talking as he caught sight of Sylvia coming along the hall.

'Oh, did you now?' Audrey said bitterly. 'God knows how you've got the cheek to turn up here.'

Sylvia moved closer.

'I just wanted to ask after her, talk to her for a moment, that's all. Sylvia?' He appealed to her over Audrey's shoulder.

Sylvia felt a deep, cold calm come over her. 'It's all right,' she said. 'Let him in. Can you make some tea, Aud?'

Audrey gave her an outraged look, as if to say: You want *me* to make tea for *him*? But she went into the kitchen.

'Come through,' Sylvia said. 'I was sitting in the back.'

It seemed both familiar and uneasily strange, having Ian in the house again. As he followed her, she was acutely conscious of him. At her first sighting of him in so long, she was shocked by how he looked. He was definitely thinner and worn-looking, and the spectacles aged him. When she turned round she saw that he looked very tired, and his skin was dry and pale. She felt conscious of the ugly red welts on her own face.

'Sit down,' she said, going to her comfortable chair and leaving him to bring one from the table.

Ian obeyed, flicking away the flaps of his jacket as he sat in the way she remembered. He settled in an uncomfortable, temporary manner on the edge of the chair.

'How are you?' he asked with cautious politeness.

'I'm all right.' Glancing down at the sling, she said, 'My collarbone's mending. I have some broken ribs – they're getting better, too. Otherwise it was cuts and bruises.' She fingered the scar. 'I was outside, you see. I got blown against the garden wall.'

Ian nodded, frowning in concern. 'Ma heard from – I don't know, someone. I just wanted to come and . . .'

'That was kind,' Sylvia said. She found herself looking at him dispassionately, as if he was a stranger. Her feelings towards him really had closed off completely. She saw a worn, rather stiff, fussy sort of a man who looked older than his years. I could be married to this man now, she thought. The idea seemed absurd, and this recognition strengthened her.

Ian made various attempts to speak, with such hand-wringing and shifting in his seat and staring at the floor that Sylvia almost wanted to giggle. Eventually, still rubbing his hands together, he burst out with, 'She left me, you know.'

Sylvia stared at him, stunned. To her own surprise, she found she was laughing. 'Of course! Well, she would, wouldn't she?' The words just slipped out, and she suddenly found it all so amusing that it was a struggle to get to grips with the hysteria rising within her. She was shocked – of course she was. But with all that she knew about Kitty Barratt, it did not seem surprising in the least.

Ian looked down, as if she had completely knocked the wind out of his sails.

'I didn't think you were a vindictive person, Sylvia.' He looked up with a hurt expression. 'I know I didn't behave very well, but I thought you might . . . The thing is, she – Kitty, I mean – I don't know what came over me. She sort of bewitched me. That way she had, with her.' He shook his head, appealing for her understanding. 'I suppose I'd have to admit that I've not had as much experience with women as might have been useful, in the circumstances. We did *get* married – I suppose you heard?'

Sylvia nodded, solemnly. What an idiot Ian was! She wondered if Audrey was listening outside the door and hoped that she was.

'Well, we set up home and she . . . she changed. Almost immediately. She was a different woman: cold, sullen. I just couldn't understand it. And one day I came home from work and she'd gone – everything, not a stitch of anything left. Just like that! I've no idea where she went. We only lasted three months, barely even that.' He was shaking his head again. 'It was terrible, Sylvia. She's not normal. I don't know what you'd call it. She's a . . . a . . .'

'Two-faced, cold-hearted bitch?' Sylvia suggested.

Ian stared at her as if he'd never seen her before. The Sylvia he had known would never have said such a thing.

'Didn't you think, Ian, that when she left this house – where we'd put her up, free of charge, for months – without a word of thanks to my mother, and ran off with someone else's fiancé, that she might not be a very nice person? Did it never even cross your mind?'

'Well, yes, but – well, no. I mean, she was so sweet and pretty – so *feminine*. I'd never have dreamed that she could even . . . I mean, we were in *love*. It was going to be the one and only time either of us ever did such a thing. We were just carried away by it all – or I was.' He stopped, seeing the forbidding expression on Sylvia's face. 'Of course I treated you disgracefully.' He stared down between his knees at the floor. 'I know that. I behaved like a worm.'

Sylvia didn't disagree. She sat quietly, wondering dispassionately how on earth and why on earth she had ever come to be engaged to this droopy-looking specimen who was sitting opposite her. Laurie! Oh God, Laurie. Her heart hurt inside her.

'The thing is,' he went on, seeming to be working up to something, 'We're both in a fix now. You've had a spot of trouble, and so have I . . .'

'*A spot of trouble?*' She almost laughed again. 'Look, what d'you want, Ian? Why don't you just spit it out?'

Again he looked startled, then sighed and gave her a fond, almost amorous look. 'Sylvia, you were the best thing that ever happened to me. I was a complete fool, throwing it all away like that. We were so right together as a couple, and I chucked it all away. But can't we – you know – water under the bridge. With the war on, you have to value certain things, be grateful for every day and . . . I'm not free from her yet, obviously, but eventually – I mean, a fresh start. Perhaps you and I . . . ?

'Ian.' Sylvia cut into this intolerable stream of platitudes. 'I don't suppose you know that I was engaged to someone else?' It didn't matter that she and Laurie had never been formally engaged; she knew this was the truth. 'I was going to marry Laurie Gould. And three months – less than three months – ago, Laurie was—' She swallowed. 'He was killed on a night flight over Germany, fighting for his country.' She stared hard into Ian's eyes. 'I loved Laurie, Ian, *really* loved him. He was brave and kind and the best man I've ever met. And he loved me. He knew what love was. Whereas you – you haven't got the first idea.'

Ian tried to say something in response, but she cut him off.

'Please leave this house, Ian,' she said turning towards the window. 'I'm tired now. Just go away.'

She heard him get up and hesitate for a moment before going to the door. His footsteps moved along the hall and the front door opened, then banged shut. As it did so, Audrey came in carrying a tray of tea. She looked round in bewilderment.

'Where the hell's he gone?'

'I told him to get out,' Sylvia said. She turned round with a triumphant smile, though there were tears in her eyes at the same time. 'Would you believe it: he asked me to go back to him?'

Audrey put the tray down. 'What're you on about? What about *her*?'

'She left him apparently – after just a few weeks.'

Audrey sank onto the chair that Ian had just vacated. As this news began to sink in, her reaction was much like Sylvia's. She sat back and roared with laughter.

'My God,' she said, once she could speak, 'if there were ever two people who deserved each other!'

Fifty-Four

'Who's that from?' Mom asked when the post arrived a few days later. Luckily she was too preoccupied with the morning busyness to take too much notice.

'I don't know,' Audrey murmured, knowing perfectly well. As soon as she saw the letter her heart began thumping and she hurried upstairs. By the time she reached her bedroom, her hands were shaking so hard that she struggled to slit open the envelope. She sank, weak-kneed, onto the edge of the bed.

There was one sheet of cream paper inside, sparsely covered in the looped blue-black handwriting that had filled Dorrie's diary and which, until now, Audrey had not set eyes on for almost a year. She pulled it out with trembling hands, almost too scared to read it:

Dear Audrey,

It's taken me all this time to find the guts to write to you. First of all, when you left Cardington, I felt that you never wanted to see or hear from me again, the way you were then. I was so wounded and confused that I didn't know what to make of it all. Have you any idea . . . ? But I wasn't going to say these things. And it was only quite a bit later, through the grapevine (the grapevine being Cora, who I ran into in London one weekend, looking very glam as usual, and the *make-up*) – oh dear, running away with myself, as if you might be . . . well, as if we were chatting. Even now feels like a habit – sorry!

Cora told me what had happened, or some of it. I'm not sure how she knew, come to think of it. Goodness knows, you must have a child by now. I wonder how you are, and how he/she is, and – dash it, I can hardly imagine really. If you felt you could write back, no one would be more delighted than me! I'm not at Cardington any more – they moved me over to Hendon, which I was not best pleased about at first. Driving lots of top brass about. I suppose one gets used to anything after a while. There's talk of postings abroad – I might offer myself – but nothing certain at the moment.

All I really wanted to say was: no hard feelings; and to wish you well, in friendship. Best stop now. All the very best to you, Audrey. Do let me know how you are.

With love from Dorrie (Cooper)

Audrey spent much of the morning in her room with Dorian, unable to face seeing anyone else. While the baby was asleep she sat on the bed, reading the letter over and over again until she knew it by heart. She could hear Dorrie's voice in it – hurt, brave, uncertain. For a long time she stared out of the window. It was open a crack, and she could hear her mother going out to hang out the washing; the little *buk-buk* noises of the hens; and the passing clank of trains. But her mind was mostly far away, remembering, regretting.

After reading the letter for the umpteenth time, she folded it and tucked it away under her pillow.

'Oh, Dorrie,' she whispered as the tears began to run down her cheeks. 'Dorrie, Dorrie.'

It was impossible. She could not just be friends with Dorrie. Not with all this feeling inside her. She knew she was not going to write back.

At least once a week now Colin Evans came to visit her. His hours were irregular as he was working shifts, but quite often he had an afternoon off and would arrange to come on the bus from Cotteridge.

He came the afternoon after Dorrie's letter. 'I've got a whole day off today.' He beamed as Pauline opened the door to him. 'Thought I'd leave Audrey to get things done this morning, but I hope she doesn't mind me coming a bit earlier.'

'Come through, love,' Pauline said. 'Sylvia's in here, having a rest. I'll tell Audrey for you.'

'Thanks, Mrs Whitehouse,' Colin said. He always sounded cheerful.

When Audrey came down, with a wide-awake Dorian in her arms, Colin was sitting chatting to Sylvia, who looked as if she was struggling to keep awake. But she liked Colin and was pleased to see him. As soon as he saw Audrey, he jumped up eagerly.

'I hope you don't mind me coming a bit early.'

'No, don't worry – you're all right,' Audrey said. She found that Colin's almost puppyish eagerness made her turn brisk and businesslike, all the more so because he was nearly fifteen years older than she was, although it often felt as if it was the other way round.

Colin stood very politely, seeming entranced by the sight of her. 'Would you fancy a walk – maybe even some tea somewhere? It's not a bad day.'

Audrey smiled, determined to be kind. Colin was so

nice, so unremittingly pleasant. Why would anyone not want to go out for a walk and tea with him – a man who knew all about her circumstances and still adored her? It was not as if she was overwhelmed with other offers. And she had, she knew, somehow to make a life for herself.

'Looks as if we need to get this little feller to sleep,' Colin said.

'Good luck to you,' Sylvia said through a yawn. 'He looks ready for anything, that one.'

'Oh, he'll settle in the pram,' Audrey said.

Colin came to help her, and Audrey quelled a desire to ask him to leave things alone and just let her do it. He eased the pram out of the front and down the steps. Audrey looked up and down the street, hardly realizing she was doing so. It had become second nature to watch out for gossips and spiteful tongues.

As usual, she and Colin walked round the park. The day was warm, but overcast. Colin asked her eager questions about her week, about how Dorian had been, and Sylvia. She answered with every show of interest and enthusiasm. Colin was just so *nice*. He was one of the nicest people she had ever met. He was kind and considerate; he always put her wishes first, was eager to listen and be helpful – not just to her, but to the whole family. Last week he'd helped Mom put up a new washing line when the old one snapped and the post holding it was rotten. Colin had come and banged in a new post and helped tighten the line to the right height.

'He's ever such a nice lad,' Mom said afterwards. 'I wonder he's not married. That mother of his seems to have a tight hold on him.'

Audrey knew that her parents, and even Sylvia, were watching very carefully, with high hopes. Mom and Dad didn't need an unmarried daughter with an illegitimate baby on their hands forever.

As they crossed the park, trying to lull Dorian to sleep, Colin was chatting about his mother, whom Audrey thought sounded a nice, but rather helpless lady in her late sixties, a widow who relied too much on her only son. They had moved to Yardley Wood when Colin was fifteen and he still had a strong Welsh accent. He chatted about his shift the day before, telling her stories about some of the people whom he'd taken to hospital.

'It's a funny job, yours,' she said. 'Exciting really, the way you never know what you're going to get from day to day.'

'It is,' Colin laughed. 'Oh, I wouldn't exchange it for anything. Especially when,' he gave her a significant look, 'you find that one day someone really special comes along, when you're not expecting it.'

Audrey could feel his gaze on her. She turned to him for a second and smiled, acknowledging the remark, then looked away again. She felt conscious of different layers of herself when she was with Colin. There was the outside layer, which could see, like everyone else, what a good and nice man he was. She appreciated his steadfast-ness and kindness and she was grateful. But beneath that, there was the Audrey who was never fully present with him, who was bored, unengaged; who in fact would rather have been alone. She found Colin very, very dull. He lived with his mother and always had; he didn't drink or smoke or appear to have any real interests – except in her. She wondered if he had had many other women friends, but did not like to ask. He was never harsh or funny or even naughty, in ways she would have found exciting – he was pleasant, and pleasant only.

They walked alongside the expanse of grass, across

which four magpies were hopping about and chattering. They stopped to watch them.

'Lovely, aren't they?' Colin said.

'They look as if they should come from somewhere else, don't they?' Audrey said. 'Somewhere exotic. All our other birds are brown.'

'Now you mention it, they are, aren't they?' Colin turned and looked at her again. She could feel him looking and tried to stop herself blushing. 'I want to kiss you,' he said. 'For ages I've wanted to kiss you, but you're so pretty and so terrifying.'

His use of the word 'terrifying' made her like him more. She looked at him – they were roughly the same height. His earnest face looked longingly back at her. She did not want to kiss him. There was not a single spark of desire for him in her, other than enjoyment of someone desiring her. Maybe that should be enough? *Don't be so fussy*, she told herself.

The park was quiet, except for an old man sitting on a bench a good way away. Since she didn't look away, Colin moved closer. A moment later his arm was round her, his lips pressed to hers and his tongue searching into her mouth. Audrey was taken aback. She had expected something more timid, and there was an excitement in the force of him. He closed his eyes and supped her like a delicious drink and, when he pulled away, he seemed almost in a trance.

'Oh,' he said, 'you're lovely. So very lovely.' His Welsh accent made this sound poetic. He was so happy. It felt nice to make someone this happy. Watching his enraptured face, Audrey thought about Hamish and Nick and the other RAF men she had been with. There was always this sense they had found something in her that she could not possibly find in them. She thought of

Dorrie for a moment, with an anguished pang. A sad anger filled her. Why did she feel like this? There was nothing she could say to Dorrie now – what was the point in thinking about that summer they had spent together? This was real life, not WAAF high jinks. She had a child, and a child needed respectability – and a father. She must kiss Colin back and she must try to love him!

But the thought of being with Colin for more than an hour or two filled her with desperation. Easing herself away from him, she touched his hand.

'Shall we walk on?' she suggested. 'Otherwise little 'un will wake up.'

Fifty-Five

October 1942

Just before Sylvia at last went back to work at the end of October, Elsie called to see her, to tell her that she and her mother had at last found a place to live – in Leamington.

'The GWR have said I can transfer to Leamington station,' Elsie told her. 'They've been ever so good about it.'

'Oh, Else!' Sylvia said. 'It's good news for you, but we'll all miss you. It won't be the same without you.'

Elsie looked even thinner, though that hardly seemed possible, and it was clear that she and her mother were under strain. Not only had they endured the terror of that night and of losing their home, but since then they had been crammed into one room in someone else's house and the resentment had started to build up. The couple had children who were not only very noisy, but kept barging in on Mrs Phipps without invitation, and it was making life very difficult.

'I know,' Elsie said sadly. 'But it'll be good for Mom and me to have a fresh start. It's not been easy. We've got the upstairs to ourselves there – not too far from the station. It's very small, but it'll be much better than all the mayhem where we are now. It's a real stroke of luck for us. I don't think Mom's nerves would have stood much more.' She smiled her rabbity smile. 'I'll miss you like mad, Sylv – keep in touch, will you? Come out and see us, now you're better. It's only a few stops away, and it'll make the place feel more like home, having a pal round.'

Sylvia promised that she would. She was very fond of both Elsie and her mother. They hugged each other fondly as Elsie left.

'There'll be plenty to do at the yard, with you gone,' Sylvia said. 'I'd better get myself back straight away.'

However, when she presented herself at Hockley Goods Yard on Monday, it was not quite as she had expected. As she walked in across the yard, looking forward to seeing everyone, a couple of people who were busy with their work waved, and she saw Bill Jones the checker, who called out, 'Hello, Sylv – nice to see yer back!' But there was a remoteness to them. She had been away for three months and things had moved on.

And she was in for another shock. The efficient-looking woman in the offices with tightly pinned hair looked through a file and said, 'I'm afraid we've had to fill your position here. Just at the moment we don't have a place for you. We've taken on a number of new porters.'

Sylvia's spirits sank even further. She was close to tears.

'Having said that,' the woman reached over for a file, 'I'm fairly certain they'll have a vacancy or two at Snow Hill.' She thumbed through a couple of pages, saying, 'Hmmm' every so often. Then she looked up over her spectacles, reaching for the telephone receiver. 'I'll telephone them, if you wait a few moments.' She hesitated. 'Why have you been absent?' Sylvia explained and the woman's face softened a fraction. 'This is heavy work, when you've had injuries like that. We'll see if we can get you in as a luggage porter – should be a bit lighter.'

'Should it?' Sylvia asked glumly.

The woman, who was in the process of dialling, glanced up with a wry look. 'Well, we can live in hope.'

Within five minutes Sylvia was walking round to Hockley passenger station to board a train into Snow Hill and take up a new job. Sitting on the train, she realized that before all her troubles she would have been more upset about this. Now, especially as she had been away from the yard for so long, it felt just like another change among many. Elsie wouldn't be there anyway. And nothing in the way of change was as bad as losing Laurie. It was simply another job. It would be good to go out to work again. She'd been helping Mom, hanging the washing and doing things in the garden to get her strength back. She stared out of the window now at all the factories and smoking chimneys, at the soot-blackened, hard-working city, and felt resigned and calm. What did it matter where she worked?

'Hey, look at you!' Audrey said. 'Let's see the back.'

Sylvia twirled around. She had decided to treat herself, before starting work, and had her hair cut in the new Vingle style – trimmed shorter, parted into four Victory Vs at the back, the four sections of hair rolled neatly and pinned.

'That looks lovely on you!' Audrey said. 'Very stylish.'

'Well, it certainly keeps this mop under control,'

Sylvia said. She was pleased with it. Somehow having her hair done was like a new start – in a small way.

In fact she enjoyed getting to know Snow Hill. The damage from the bombing had been patched up for the moment and everything was working as usual for wartime – no frills, but efficiently. She enjoyed being busy, trying to take her mind off things. She moved from platform to platform, barrowing piles of luggage and other strange items: baskets of pigeons or chickens at times, and laden milk churns from the special milk wagons known as 'syphons'. She got to know the parcels yard, the pearly light from its glazed brick walls, the horses and trucks coming and going. She loved the busy-ness of it all and it was a comfort.

Her back and arms ached terribly for the first few days, but she was back in harness again and it felt good to be out among people on the bustling platforms, with the engines sweeping in, pouring smoke and steam up to the arched steel girders spanning the roof, with their churning pistons, the hiss of the steam and shriek of their whistles. Gradually she started getting to know people who worked around the station. Every afternoon there was the newspaper-seller yelling, 'Get yer *Spatchy Mail*!' She remembered dreaming of working at Snow Hill and feeling important. And, she had to admit, she did rather like the feel of moving briskly along the busy platforms in her uniform calling out, ''Scuse me!' or 'Mind your backs, please!' as she struggled through the crowds.

The only thing she found hard to bear was the sight of the station clocks, which filled her with an aching sadness. All those happy meetings that had taken place 'under the clock' – all those loved ones catching sight of each other's faces among the crowds and breaking into happy smiles of anticipation – made her feel lost and lonely. She tried to avoid looking at them. What was the point of making herself even more unhappy?

All that first week, as she got used to the work and the other staff at Snow Hill, everyone was full of excitement about the progress of the desert war and was listening out eagerly for news. After all these months of struggle, the Allies were at last breaking through and had set the German Afrika Korps on the run. One night in November all the family sat round the wireless in the front room as the sober voice of the news broadcaster at last announced a victory. El Alamein had been recaptured.

'We've done it – we beaten Rommel!' Jack was so excited he got up and ran round the room. 'We've beaten them, sent them packing.' He tripped over his mother's basket of knitting and sprawled flat on his face, almost knocking himself out on the fender.

'Jack, for heaven's sake!' Mom protested. But no one could really be cross. Jack got up, groaning.

'So,' Dad said. 'Those bastards . . . And they haven't got Stalingrad yet, either.' He was looking quite emotional. 'This calls for a celebration, Pauline – have we still got that bottle of port wine?'

'Barely more than the dregs,' she said. 'But I'll look.'

Mom went out to the pantry and, after a short kerfuffle as she and Sylvia searched the sideboard for an odd assortment of glasses, they were all sipping a thimbleful of the pungent, sweet wine. Audrey and Sylvia sat side-by-side, taking it in turns to hold little Dorian, who smiled and gurgled, happy that they were all happy.

The port made Jack even more excited, and he kept talking loudly about tanks and Monty and Rommel, and Mom had to ask him to quieten down. She sounded a bit tipsy after even a few sips, and her cheeks and the tip of her nose had gone pink. She and Dad sat in a cloud of smoke, puffing away in celebration. Audrey and Sylvia exchanged a smile. Mom usually looked so careworn these days and it was nice to see her looking mellow and cheerful.

'Well,' Pauline said raising her glass, 'let's hope this is the start of a better run. We could do with some good news, we really could.'

A few days later, a misty, grey Friday morning that seemed utterly dull and unremarkable became one that, for Sylvia, was stamped upon her memory forever.

She was on an early shift at Snow Hill, having started work in the freezing darkness before dawn, unloading milk churns. There was the usual morning bustle, with the trains getting up steam, whistling and chugging away along the platforms, and people in a rush to get to work crowding up and down the staircases amid the echoing blare of announcements.

Things calmed down a little after nine o'clock and she went off for a break and a welcome cup of tea with another of the porters, whom she chatted to sometimes. Refreshed, she then went back to work. She was pushing a barrow laden with heavy boxes over the cobbles of the parcels yard, her arms straining, when she met one of the foremen she hardly knew, hurrying the other way.

He came straight up to her, suddenly wrenching off

his cap to speak to her, which Sylvia found instinctively alarming, as if he was about to break bad news. The cap left his grey hair sticking up boyishly.

'You're Sylvia Whitehouse, ain't yer?'

She righted her barrow, nodding.

'There's someone to see yer – in the booking hall. Leave that.' He indicated the barrow that she had automatically been about to start pushing again. 'You can come back for it.' Seeing her stricken face, he touched her arm for a moment with a concerned expression. 'I hope it ain't bad news, bab.'

In turmoil, Sylvia ran through the station and tore up the stairs, scarcely able to breathe. What on earth could be wrong? Who would be waiting for her? The only person she could think of was Audrey.

For a second she couldn't see anyone in the booking hall that she recognized. She was looking around, feeling so full of panic that she couldn't see straight. Once her eyes had focused, she saw them – two utterly familiar people, standing together under the big clock, arm-in-arm: her mother and Marjorie Gould. How small they looked, these two mothers, arm-in-arm in this big echoing place, in their winter coats and hats, dwarfed by the grand building and by all the crowds. They looked as if they were propping each other up. Their faces were deadly serious. Sylvia's whole body went weak. The hope that the news might not be bad left her entirely. What had happened? Was it Dad? Or the baby? As she moved towards them, her legs were so shaky she could hardly get there.

The pair of them seemed anxious and uneasy, looking round to try and see her. When she was quite near they suddenly spotted her. What Sylvia noticed then was

Marjorie Gould's face, which was overcome by an odd, pent-up expression, quite different from the way she usually looked these days. It was she who first spotted Sylvia and came tearing over to her, her face crumpling. She was trembling all over and crying or laughing – it was hard to say which – but in such a state that she could scarcely speak.

'Sylv, look – take it: read it!' Whereupon she burst into tears and couldn't do anything except thrust the piece of paper into Sylvia's hand.

Sylvia stared at her in complete bewilderment.

'Read it, love,' Pauline said. She took Sylvia's arm.

Her hands shaking, Sylvia unfolded the paper. She was in such a hurry to devour the words that she had to look again and again to make sense of them. The letter was headed 'AIR MINISTRY (Casualty Branch)': '. . . to advise you that information has now been received' – Laurie's name jumped out at her – 'your son Laurie Gould, Royal Air Force, has arrived in a neutral country'.

If Mom had not been holding her, Sylvia would have fallen straight to the floor. Her knees buckled and she sank, her fall broken by her mother's arm as her legs gave way. She sat looking up at them, shaking all over and holding in her other hand – she would believe it eventually – this letter about the man she loved.

Pauline knelt on the hard floor beside her, openly weeping now, and put her arm round Sylvia's shoulders. Marjorie also knelt down beside them, crying with joy. They were oblivious to all the people passing through the ticket hall, these mothers who would normally never have dreamed of making an exhibition of themselves. At this moment no one else existed.

Sylvia, her face a ghostly white, looked up, searching her mother's face and Marjorie's. 'So it means – does it mean . . . ?'

'He's alive, my sweet, that's what it means.' The tears coursed down Marjorie's cheeks, 'He's alive, our boy is – and he's coming back to us.'

Fifty-Six

November 1942, Miranda del Ebro
Concentration Camp, Spain

Laurie squatted on the rocky ground, his left hand
shading his eyes against the low-angled sunlight of a
winter afternoon. Rows of barrack-like huts stretched
into the distance on each side of him. Around them
moved swarms of men dressed, like him, in rough cotton
uniforms.

He had just returned from the latrines and felt limp
and sick, his guts still griping. Even when you couldn't
see the latrines, the stench of them seemed to remain in
your nostrils. They stood near the main entrance,
suspended on a platform over the bed of the Ebro river,
so that the effluent could be washed away downstream.
A path led along the middle of the rows of huts, which
at certain times of the day served as a meeting place for
the camp inmates to stand around or sprawl on the
ground. Around him groups of men of mixed national-
ities were chatting, some playing cards or jackstones.
Once the sun went down, the nights were bitter. The
huts were overcrowded to bursting point, the only thing
to warm the inmates being the heat of all the other
verminous bodies.

Laurie sat quietly, trying to think of anything except

the cramp in his belly. He fingered the leather mitten that he wore at all times on his right hand, one of the pair they had made for him before he left Belgium. The edges of it chafed and itched. He leaned forward, bent almost double, rubbing his left hand back and forth over his scabby, shaven head. Then, out of a habit he was barely aware of, his fingers felt their way along the raw scar on the right side of his jaw.

He tried never to dwell on the past months. His thoughts were all of the future. The letter he had written might have reached his mother by now. British diplomatic officials would get them out of here, somehow. One day, he would go home. This was the essence of everything, he had discovered – to have hope. And until hope was killed, you had to let it burn hard within you.

'I say, are you English?' These comprehensible words emerged out of the mixed torrent of French, Spanish, Polish and other languages in the camp.

Laurie looked up to see who was speaking, shielding his eyes again. He winced as his guts griped.

'Sorry, old chap. Like that, is it? Look – I'll come down.' The man squatted. Laurie saw a gaunt, dark-haired man, his hair shaven like the rest of them. He examined Laurie closely, a mix of curiosity and amused pity in his brown eyes. 'Back-door trots, eh?' He peered more closely. 'You *are* English?'

Laurie smiled faintly. 'How did you know?'

'Oh, something about you. You could just about pass as a Frog . . .'

'Has been known,' Laurie said.

'I dare say.'

There was a silence. Laurie could feel the man's intent gaze on him and looked down at the ground, searching for something to say. 'Don't suppose you've got any grub?'

'Ah, well now, let's see. I could rustle up a steak-and-kidney pudding with heaps of mash and gravy – followed by suet pudding and custard. Or maybe you're more of a fish man?'

Laurie chuckled. 'A good roast beef would suit me best, to tell you the truth. Not sure my innards could take it at the moment, though.' He raised his head again and the two of them looked into each other's half-starved faces. The food was completely inadequate in the over-crowded camp. Quietly the other man asked, 'What happened: kite come down?'

Laurie nodded. 'The big one over Cologne. Made it over . . .' Weakness made him gasp for breath. 'Must have caught flak coming back. Not that I remember much.'

'Hurt yourself?' He eyed the mitten.

'Smashed up my leg. Singed the hands.' He held up his muffled right hand. 'This one especially. I was lucky.' He couldn't go over it, not again. 'How about you, chum?'

'Bremen. We parachuted out – the pilot was killed, and the arse-end Charlie, poor lad. Not sure what happened to all of them, but three of us made it, and two of us are here. I'm Bob Stevens, flight engineer, by the—' He held out his right hand to shake Laurie's, then withdrew it. 'Hell – sorry, pal.'

'It's okay – it's not as bad as you might think. I've still got my fingers. They gave me the mitts to hide the worst of the burns; would have looked very fishy. I just keep this one on – it's my . . .' He shrugged, searching for the word.

'Mascot?'

'Sort of. I'll take it off when – if – I get back to Blighty. Anyway, this one's operational.' He held out his less-scarred left hand and they shook. 'Laurie Gould, navigator.' He named his squadron.

'The rest of them?' Bob asked.

'I don't know.' Laurie looked away. He watched two Spaniards a few yards away, apparently about to break into a fight. They looked like a pair of angry bulls, though emaciated ones. The camp still contained Spaniards who opposed Franco – that was what it had been here for, since the Civil War. Though Spain was neutral in this war, its sympathies lay largely with Germany and its camps were packed to overflowing with enemies of the Nazis.

Bob nodded, with understanding. 'With any luck we *will* be out of here soon, and on the way to Gib. You got a girl – waiting, I mean?'

'Yes. Hope so. She's called Sylvia.'

'Pretty name for a pretty woman.'

'Oh, she is.' It was lovely to talk like this, about a proper life, true and kind.

'Keeps you going, doesn't it? My lady's called Jenny. She's a real good 'un. She's promised to marry me as soon as it's all over.'

'Mine too,' Laurie said, though for a moment he felt a chill of doubt. In all this time, for the length of his silence – she was so lovely – would she have found someone else? He was appalled by the thought of the distress he must have caused.

'It can't come a moment too soon for me,' Bob went on. 'I've been mouldering in that hellhole prison in Figueras for the last three months.' He stopped for a moment, shaking his head. 'God knows what the Consulate was doing – took its damn time. Still, all you can do is be thankful no one put a bullet through your head.' He looked at Laurie. 'I didn't see you there.'

433

'No, I was banged up in Zaragoza. We were tripped up by a patrol, once we'd come over the border. But I was only there three weeks – well, I say only . . .'

'Yes. Bloody. Not long now, though, with any luck.' Bob Stevens stood up. 'Going to see if I can scrounge a smoke from somewhere. Fancy a puff, if I can get it?'

'You bet,' Laurie said, raising his left thumb.

'Right, you stay there. I'll be back.'

1943–5

Fifty-Seven

January 1943

Rain fell and fell that morning, the wind driving it against the houses in forceful gusts. Sylvia waited all morning by the front window. He was coming. She knew he was in England – his flight from Gibraltar had come in yesterday and the telegram said he was coming home. She sat glued to the window as the water streamed down it.

'Hey, dreamboat – want a cuppa?' Audrey asked, looking in round the door, with Dorian balanced on her hip. She looked happy and excited, and he was full of beans as well.

'Oh, please! And can you pop and spend a penny for me? I don't want to miss a second.'

Audrey laughed. 'He's not going to walk on past when he arrives, is he? You won't miss him.'

'No, but I want to see him coming.'

'Still, no can do, dearie. Only you can do that. But I'll get the tea – not that that'll help, in the circumstances!' She put her head back round the door and said, 'I'll watch for you for a couple of minutes while you go, after I've made it.'

Sylvia smiled as her sister went off. The news that Laurie was alive, that he was out there in the world, instead of lying in an unknown grave, had transformed both families. Marjorie and Stanley were like people reborn; and, for her, life was once again full of love and hope, of a sense of the future.

Soon after the letter from the Air Ministry, which left them wondering where on earth he could be, a note arrived from Laurie himself. It was written on rough paper and in strange, cramped handwriting that deteriorated as it went down the page and didn't look like Laurie's at all. His signature was barely a scrawl. At the top, above '*Dear Mum and Dad*', was written, '*Miranda del Ebro, Spain*'.

'Spain?' Sylvia looked up at Marjorie, who had brought the letter round, in utter bewilderment.

'I know,' she said. 'Heaven only knows how he got all the way down there.'

Laurie wrote:

> So sorry for silence, for worry – could not contact. I am all right, but injured, so difficult to write. Long journey here. Long story. Was arrested this side of the border – await release from camp, hope within week or two will be on way home. Please tell Sylvia. I am all right. Longing to see you all.
>
> All my love – Laurie

How long they would have to wait hardly mattered. He was alive and he was coming back to them! During those weeks, after the first shock of surprise, they had had time to adjust. It took Sylvia some time before she believed it – really believed it. Once again she had to alter her whole view of her life, of how the future might be. Laurie, her best friend, her love, was alive. He was safe in Spain, and one day he would come home.

It felt like tempting fate to believe it, but it was all she could think about. Everyone at work was agog to hear what had happened. Each morning she woke and her first thought was: Is it true? He's really alive? And when she realized that it was, the whole day was flooded with light.

Ever since the letter arrived there had been an air of celebration across both houses. And now he was really coming home! Marjorie and Mom had made a banner, with Paul's help. They had fashioned it out of an old sheet, but it was far too wet to put it out today, so Marjorie said that 'WELCOME HOME LAURIE!' would be displayed along the hall instead, even though it wasn't quite the same.

'It's lovely to see the change in Marjorie,' Mom said emotionally, soon after they all heard the news. 'I really thought it was going to be the death of her.'

Instead of death, they had all been given new life.

The smell of soup was wafting along the hall and Mom was making noises about laying the table when, through the streaming windowpane, Sylvia saw a thin, blurred figure along the street. Her body began to pulse. Could it be? She leaned closer. There was something odd and lurching about the way the man was walking. For a second she thought she was mistaken. But the next moment she was tearing to the front door.

'He's here! Oh, he's here!'

He was a few yards away. As she ran, she heard little sounds coming from her throat and the rain poured down, icy cold on her face. Seeing her, he stopped, flung his bag down and held his arms out. Just for a second she slowed, hesitating: the shorn head, the thin face. It was almost the face of a stranger. But then she saw his smile, his eyes as hers met his.

'My girl,' he said. And as she threw herself into his arms, they just held each other close, completely oblivious to the rain as it lashed down on them. For long moments they were silent.

'I thought you were dead . . .' Her sobs came then, cries of relief and joy from deep inside her. She kissed and kissed his face, his chest, his shoulders, any part of him that she could reach. 'We all thought . . . Oh, Laurie, oh my lovely Laurie, you're here – you're really here! Don't ever go away again.'

And he murmured her name over and over again, saying, 'My love, oh my love' into her soaked hair.

After a few moments they drew back to look at each other, and again she saw those eyes – Laurie's gentle, kind, humorous eyes, which she had known all her life, gazing hungrily back at her. She drank in the sight of him. Both of them at the same time noticed the changes. She reached up and ran a finger along the deep mauve cut on his jaw, and he frowned, seeing the scattered scars on her face. Tenderly he touched the biggest one, in front of her left ear.

'What happened to you?' he said, appalled.

She took his hand and kissed his fingers. 'You should see the other feller,' she said. 'Never mind that—'

'Sylv.' For a moment his face was anxious. 'Just tell me . . . there's no one else?'

She shook her head solemnly. 'No, my love. Not even for a minute.'

He leaned to her, about to kiss her again, but she took his hand.

'Come inside,' she said. 'Your mother needs you.'

As she led him to his house the door was flung open and Paul came hurtling out into the wet.

'Laurie!' he bawled. 'Laurie, Laurie!'

And Marjorie followed, at a run in her apron, her face lit by utter joy as she caught the first sight of her beloved son.

Fifty-Eight

Sylvia was longing to spend every moment with Laurie, but she knew she must let him have some time with his family. Though overjoyed to be home, he looked ill and exhausted and needed sleep. But, come the evening, the two families gathered at the Goulds' house. As Sylvia and the others trooped in – Mom and Dad, Jack and Audrey with little Dorian – Stanley Gould was cracking open bottles in the front room.

'Come in – come and sit down!' He waved a hand across the table, where there was an array of drinks and glasses. 'A few tipples I've kept, in case of emergency,' he said.

'You old hoarder!' Ted accused him, picking up a bottle of Scotch and gazing lovingly at it. There was a bottle of sherry as well and some ale. 'Have you had this lot put away all this time? If I'd known, I'd've been round a hell of a lot sooner!'

Sylvia and Audrey exchanged smiles. There was an atmosphere of fizzing joy emanating from everyone in the room. Dad and Stanley were slapping each other on the back, Mom and Marjorie chatting excitedly. Paul kept clapping and making happy noises. It was longer than they could remember since they had heard such a joyous tone in everyone's voice.

Laurie came down dressed in his own clothes now and looking more like his old self, except for his very short hair and the limp, which was very obvious as he came over to Sylvia. And he was so painfully thin. But, seeing him, her whole being leapt with happiness. They walked into each other's arms and she drank in the feel of him holding her so tightly and kissing the top of her head.

'You're here,' she said yet again, looking hungrily up into his face. It was still astonishing, and hard to take in. 'You're really, really home.'

Laurie grinned. 'At last – it's taken long enough.'

'I just keep thinking I'm going to wake up.' Tears came again and she wiped them away impatiently. Laurie stroked her shoulders. She pulled back and looked down at him. 'What's wrong with your leg?'

'Oh, it got pretty smashed up. That's why I couldn't get out sooner. I had to wait until I could walk – after a fashion, anyway. They say I'll have to have an operation on it soon; it's set wrong.' He looked at her concerned face and reached up to stroke her cheek. 'Never mind – it's just a leg. Could've been an awful lot worse.' He leaned to look at her left cheek. 'Mom told me: about the night you got caught in the raid. My God, if I'd known.'

'That could've been a lot worse too,' she said.

Laurie squeezed her arm. 'They all want to hear everything about it. Come and sit next to me.'

They gathered round him in the front room, the blackouts drawn closed, the lights on and the fire lit, their glasses clinking. Sylvia looked round at everyone, choked with happiness. All she wanted was to sit here and capture this moment, gazing at Laurie next to her. He was so lovely, so familiar and now very grown-up. And for such a long time she had not expected to see him ever again. She felt an overwhelming tilt of emotion each time she looked at him. Every so often he turned to her, just as hungry for the sight of her, and they reached for

443

each other. But when she held his left hand she could feel there was something wrong. It felt hard and stiff and slightly curled. She turned it over and looked at the tight, shiny skin.

To her questioning eyes he said quietly, 'I picked up the fire extinguisher – in the plane. It was red-hot.' He looked at his crabbed right hand. 'This one's worse.'

'Oh, my goodness . . .' She stroked his scarred palm. There was no point asking more now – he was going to tell them all.

Audrey sat holding Dorian on her lap. He was a beautiful little boy, with dark hair like Audrey's and delicate features. When he first saw Laurie he gazed up at him with huge eyes.

'He's marvellous, Audrey,' Laurie had said, rather shyly, and Audrey blushed with pleasure.

Now she tried to keep Dorian still, but he was so excited by being at the heart of this gathering that he fidgeted to get down and made frustrated attempts to move. Paul was fascinated by him and sat close by, making faces at the baby and laughing at his reactions, so that both were soon laughing at each other.

'Quieten down a bit, Pauly,' Marjorie squeezed his shoulder as she came to sit down, a glass in one hand. 'He's going to be off crawling soon, isn't he?' she said to Audrey, leaning down to stroke Dorian's face with the side of her finger. Her eyes glowed with joy.

Stanley was pouring drinks for everyone. He passed Sylvia a glass of sherry. Sylvia sipped the sherry and began to feel warm and, if it were possible, even more contented.

'I want to drink to my son.' Stanley stood in the middle of the room, looking across at Laurie. Sylvia had never seen him so openly emotional.

'Here, here!' Ted added, raising his own glass. 'Here's to you, lad.'

They all drank to Laurie.

'I won't pretend to you, son,' Stanley went on, as he took a seat. 'We all thought you weren't coming back. That you were . . . Well, that you'd gone the same way as your brother. And your mother . . .' He looked at Marjorie, who was welling over with tears, but managed overjoyed smiles at the same time. 'Your mother and I . . . well, I don't know what to say. All I can say is that having you back, sitting here, is – I'm not one for talking about these things – but it's the answer to a prayer all right.' He raised his glass again. 'There's never been a better day. Welcome home, son.'

Laurie's eyes were shining with tears as well. 'Thanks, Dad,' he said, his cheeks flaming red. 'I'm just sorry I put you and Mom through so much worry. It was, well . . . it was how it was. There wasn't anything I could do. But being home again with you, all of you,' he pressed Sylvia's hand, 'it feels like a miracle. It's the best ever.'

Marjorie got out of her chair and bent over him, laying her hands on each of her sons' cheeks. 'I just need to make sure I'm not dreaming,' she said, laughing and crying at once. Paul was bouncing on his seat making excited noises, and she went back to her place and took his hand.

'Here's to you, son,' Stanley couldn't seem to stop raising his glass, and they all toasted Laurie yet again. 'Now – let's hear it. What took you so long, eh?'

They were kept spellbound for the next few hours. Apart from brief pauses while Audrey crept upstairs to put a sleepy Dorian down on Raymond's old bed, for thirsts to be assuaged, bladders relieved or the fire stoked, they all sat listening, their eyes fixed on Laurie at the centre of it all, in the brown leather armchair. He sat forward, full of animation, and told them how he had made the journey from occupied Belgium after the crash, all the way to Gibraltar. Later on, as he confided more details to her, Sylvia realized that Laurie had spared them all a lot in the telling, that there were things he did not want his parents to dwell on. But he gave them the essence of it, and the essence was this.

'The raid itself went off as planned, from our point of view,' Laurie said. 'The navigation went like clockwork. It was an awesome feeling, knowing there were so many bombers going that time.' That raid on Cologne had been the first thousand-bomber raid on any German city.

'When we were over Cologne, we could already see fires dotted about. The strange thing is, when you're up there, you can't hear a thing except your own engines and the air rush. You just see the fires and the flak and the searchlights, but it doesn't feel real. Terrible, really, when a city's burning down there . . . Anyway, we had turned back south-west and left Cologne behind. I didn't see exactly what happened. It was either flak or, more likely, one of their night fighters had got us from below, but we were on fire: the port engine was burning. Our pilot, Wallace, radioed through that he was going to dive – sometimes that'll put a fire out – and we raced right down, but it was still burning, so he did it again. We were down to about ten thousand feet by then. For a minute every-thing seemed to be all right, but as we levelled up, suddenly it was everywhere, the whole thing full of flames – everyone shouting . . . I caught hold of the fire extin-guisher, thinking I could do something. I didn't see the state of my hands until much later – didn't even notice.

'Wallace insisted that we get out ahead of him while he tried to land. We got our landing packs on. Ron, the wireless operator next to me, got out – I saw him jump ahead of me. Sam Masters, the flight engineer, was behind me somewhere, I think. But I never . . .' For a moment his voice cracked. 'I didn't see any of them after that. I was in the air. My parachute was on fire as I came down, and I remember panicking – it would mean I could be seen, like a blasted beacon, coming down. I remember hitting the ground, hard. That's when I smashed up my leg. And I blacked out.'

Sylvia took a deep breath. She realized that her body had grown more and more tense as he talked. Glancing round the room, she saw her mother's expression, tight-lipped and solemn. All of them were there with Laurie in their minds. Marjorie had her hands over her mouth, almost as if she was trying to stop herself crying out.

'Where were you, son?' Stanley asked quietly. He seemed in awe of Laurie since he had come home.

'We came down somewhere outside Liège in Belgium. I came to in the dark sometime. My leg was in agony and I must've passed out again. Next thing I know, there's a bloke leaning over me with a great big bushy beard. He went off and came back with another bloke and a ladder. They carried me on it – not far, just to a barn nearby. The two blokes were very decent, only I just couldn't make out the lingo. They brought me a blanket, some bread and a hard-boiled egg and a bottle of wine. They kept saying something to me, and in the end I got it: I'd stay there till dark. God knows how I got through that day. I suppose the last thing I needed really was a bottle of wine, but I kept swigging on it, and most of the day I was out for the count! Which was for the best – except that when I woke up, I had a head on me like you wouldn't believe!'

That night the men moved Laurie across the fields to the attic of a house in the nearby village. They delivered him onto a big, hard bed. The reasons for this house being chosen soon became apparent. It was a family home, and he often heard the sound of children downstairs and out in the garden at the back. There was a small, high window in the attic, facing over the garden. Once, he said, when he managed to stand on the chair to look out, he saw two little boys wrestling and tumbling on the grass. At that moment, though, the householder – a thin, worried-looking man in his thirties – came into the attic and rushed over to Laurie, pulling him furiously away from the window.

'*Non!*' he cried, adding a torrent of furious instruction: *Laurie must not let his face be seen at the window, at any cost.*

He knew what a risk this family was taking for him. The father of the family was called Maurice. He indicated to Laurie that his wife was aware of their guest in the attic, and the maid had to know as well, but that he had not told the children.

Maurice's old mother lay mortally sick in the room below the attic. Each day one of the nuns from the local convent came to the house to help nurse the elderly lady. Occasionally, as these duties were performed, Laurie heard a low moan rise through the hefty floorboards, and sometimes he heard her making sounds in the night. The nun, a young woman with anxious brown eyes below a white veil, took the opportunity on these visits to play her part in the resistance by ministering to the fallen British airman. She and Maurice did their best to set Laurie's mangled leg, rigging it up with wooden splints.

'She dressed all my cuts. I had blood all over the top part of me, when I got there, from this.' Laurie tipped his head to show the scar on his jaw. 'Luckily, the position I'd been lying in, and the collar of my jacket, must have helped push the wound closed. I would have lost a lot more blood otherwise. But she patched me up.'

'What wonderful people,' Marjorie said, her eyes filling. 'Oh, I want to go and thank them, bless them all!'

Laurie nodded. 'Everyone was marvellous. And there were a lot of others to be even more grateful to, further down the line – there was a line, literally: an escape line. It was incredibly dangerous for all of them. Maurice's family wasn't part of it officially; they were just keen to do anything that meant going against the Germans. But I knew that every day I spent there I was putting them in danger. For the time being, though, it was no good me trying to go anywhere, with my leg in the state it was in.'

'You should see it,' Marjorie said to the others. 'It looks terrible. I don't know how you managed to walk all that way . . .'

'It wasn't easy, but I would have done anything to get back home,' Laurie said. He looked at Sylvia again and reached for her hand. She felt as if she was overflowing with happiness.

'I stayed there for the best part of three months. The leg healed up gradually, though we could all see it wasn't right. Eventually I started to hobble around. Maurice would come up after dark and take me down into the garden. It was wonderful to be outside, although walking was pretty grim at first because I was lurching all over the place, but I had to get started. I just had to get out of there – for their sake as much as mine.

'The main thing was, I had to be able to walk, and by the time it had stitched itself together, I could, after a fashion. They got me some local clothes and country boots, like they wear. I still don't know how they made the arrangements. All I do know is that one day Maurice announced that he had my papers, and that we were going to Brussels. If anyone challenged me, I was to pretend to be deaf and look to him to answer. I was dressed as a farmhand, and my hair had grown by then. They gave it a rough cut, like a farmhand's, and what with my limp and my deafness, I was supposed to look a bit simple. It seemed very risky to me, but I was so glad to be off.'

Laurie leaned forward, picking up his glass with difficulty. He looked round at them all. 'I'll never forget those people. I know their surname was Lambert, but to this day I don't know the names of all the family. I saw the wife just as I left. She looked very happy that I was going! It was better that I didn't know any of them.' He took a sip and sat looking thoughtful.

'The bravery of all those people was incredible. They hated the Germans so much, loathed having them in their country. They saw helping airmen like me as getting back to the fight. One of them, who I met in the safe house in Brussels, spoke English. He said there were signs up in the city saying that men who helped Allied airmen would be shot. The women would be sent to camps in Germany.' He looked round the room again. 'I owe them my life. I don't know how many of them have lost theirs, helping blokes like me.'

Fifty-Nine

'But how did they get hold of all these different papers for you?' Stanley asked, as Laurie began to describe the complex, dangerous journey home that he had made. He explained that he was helped by an escape route called *La Comète*.

'They had people forging them – using papers of people who'd died. And we had to learn not to stand out as foreigners. It wasn't just the clothes. They'd say, "Don't march about like a serviceman, slouch a bit!" But of course I was lurching about like a cripple anyway. They said, "Always carry your knapsack just on one shoulder, not two." They'd given me an ancient, worn out thing to carry. It was a strange thing really. All the while normal life was going on, farmers milking cows and carts of stuff going about the place. You could kid yourself that there was nothing to worry about. And then you'd see them: Germans, or one of their signs up on the walls; "AVIS," it would say – a public warning to everyone. And it hit you: if you were to get caught . . .

'The first leg was Brussels to Valenciennes. I had a Belgian passport – then a French one. And then, to cross the line – the *Démarcation* into the Vichy part of France – there's a permit called an *Ausweis* . . .'

'Well, how the hell did they do all that?' Stanley asked. He was sitting right forward on his chair, completely gripped by everything Laurie had to say. Sylvia found the whole account nerve-racking in the extreme, and even though Laurie was here now, safe, it was fraught with imaginings of all the catastrophes that might have been.

'I was in a sweat all the way across France, because I'd been given papers from a bloke who was years older than me. I was scared stiff someone would take a close look. When we left Paris, this German came along the train checking, and I was – well, brown-trouser job almost . . .'

'Oh my Lord!' Marjorie breathed again.

'He was just asking for my papers when the whistle went and he had to get off the train. The other snag was the passengers. They would keep trying to talk to you and, with my French being as bad as it was, I spent most of the journey across France pretending to be asleep! We went to Bordeaux and then headed south. You have to cross the mountains near the coast – they're too high in the middle. So we went to Bayonne and crossed from there.'

'You walked over the mountains!' Marjorie said. Her face was constantly stretched in surprise.

'Most of the guides were smugglers before, I was told,' Laurie said. 'And they frogmarched us over so fast we could hardly keep up.'

'But your leg?' Sylvia asked.

'It wasn't easy, I'll say that. Even that part of the mountains is covered in snow. There was a group of us. One bloke, a Londoner, was already pretty sick, but he was adamant that he could make it. He collapsed and died in the middle of the night . . .' Laurie looked down for a moment to indicate that he didn't want to go into too much detail. 'We walked non-stop for about fourteen hours. The best moment was when the sun came up. It was beautiful – I'll never forget it. We'd just got across the river close to the Spanish border: it was an amazing feeling. We got well inside Spain, ten miles at least, and thought we were safe – and then we ran into the Spanish police.'

'I thought Spain was supposed to be neutral?' Marjorie said indignantly.

'The Gestapo are there, even so. And the Spanish are still rounding up enemies of Franco. There were a lot in the prison in Zaragoza – and in the camp.' Only much later did Laurie tell Sylvia about the terrible conditions in Zaragoza prison, the daily sounds of torment and shootings. For now, he spared everyone the details.

From there he had been transferred eventually to the squalid camp at Miranda del Ebro, where the British Consul had arranged for his release and that of three others. They were driven in a diplomatic car to Seville and hidden in a Norwegian boat, which was leaving the port for Gibraltar. From there they were flown home.

'Ten hours sitting on the floor in a Dakota,' Laurie said. 'It was about the most uncomfortable part of the whole journey! Did we care, though? Couldn't have cared less!'

There was almost too much to take in. But the main thing to absorb that night was that he was home and alive. That was all that really mattered now.

It was well into the small hours when everyone got up to go. Paul had fallen asleep and had to be woken, grumpy, to go up to bed.

Sylvia stayed behind, and everyone understood that she and Laurie needed to be alone.

'You've got an early shift tomorrow, haven't you, love?' Pauline asked as she went, but she was teasing.

'I don't care,' Sylvia said. 'I don't need to sleep!'

The Goulds said their goodnights, both his parents hugging Laurie close before they went up to bed, which brought tears to Sylvia's eyes. They were not often a demonstrative family – especially Stanley.

'Good to have you back, son,' he said, releasing Laurie and clapping him on the shoulder.

'It's good to be here, Dad.'

The women exchanged smiles at the understatement of this.

After all the goodnights, Sylvia and Laurie were left alone. Silently they moved into each other's arms and stood for a long time, holding each other without speaking. Sylvia drank in the feeling of him, the wonder of his body – strong, but very thin at the moment – and the familiar smell of him, this man she had believed she would never see again. Laurie stroked her back and shoulders, also as if reassuring himself that this was real. When she turned her face up to look at him, their eyes met, then their lips. She closed her eyes, losing herself in a long kiss, finding the taste of him again after all this time – here, alive, the man she had believed she would never hold or kiss again.

After a time Laurie drew back and took her hand.

'Come and sit down,' he said and they settled by the fire on the hearthrug, their arms around each other.

'Let me see your leg,' she said.

'It's not very pretty.' Laurie seemed almost embarrassed. Rolling up his trouser leg, he showed her where the shinbone had been broken in two places. It did look a mess, neither joint being set evenly.

'What will they do?' she said, running her hand down the misshapen limb. It felt very strange, with bits protruding where they should not be, the flesh scarred and raw over it.

'I've got to go into hospital in a couple of days, down at RAF Halton. They'll reset it – straighten it out, I hope. They might be able to sort out my hands a bit, too.'

'Oh, love.' She took his hands and kissed the scarred palms. 'That looks agony.'

'It wasn't too nice. But they'll want to get me sorted out.'

She sat up abruptly, staring at him as the realization hit her. 'My God!' Horror filled her. 'They won't want you to go back, will they? No, they can't make you!'

Until that moment it had not occurred to her. Now that Laurie was here, it felt as if it was over – he was home, and out of it. Surely they couldn't make him go back and start it all over again? The thought was unbearable.

'I'm afraid so. I'm not out of it yet. But it'll be a while. The leg will take a few months, and who knows? Things are turning, from what I hear. Maybe it'll all be over.'

'No – oh God, no!' She leaned against him, her arms tightly around him. 'I can't let you go again. Oh, if only it would just stop,' she said, tearfully. 'It's like a machine, grinding everyone up.'

Laurie held her tenderly, unable to say the reassuring words that she most wanted to hear. Sylvia wiped her eyes, not wanting to give way to her feelings at the thought of Laurie leaving again. They sat in each other's arms, quiet for a few moments, looking into the remnants of the fire.

'You're what's kept me going, all the way through,' Laurie said. 'I just thought about you all the time, and about how much I love you. I'm just sorry for what I've put you through – you thinking I was a goner . . .'

455

'We did think so,' she said. She couldn't bear to recall it. 'Anyway, you're here now. You're a miracle! We're the lucky ones.'

'The thing is, Sylv.' Laurie hesitated, gazing into her eyes. 'I'd like to say – I mean, all I want is to ask you to marry me, for us to be together forever. But I feel I shouldn't, just in case. For us to get married, then for something to happen . . .'

'Oh, my love,' she said, full of clashing emotions of joy, relief and dread. She kissed his cheek, his loving, familiar face. 'You're all I want. Of course I want to be with you forever.'

'It feels like tempting fate, to make promises. To hope we'll have the future. So many of the lads . . .' He didn't finish the sentence.

Quietly she said, 'The thing is: I'm yours. Whatever happens.'

'You've always been the best,' he said. 'D'you know that? I've never met anyone who was a patch on you.'

'Oh.' Sylvia laughed, leaning her head against him. 'Don't be daft.'

'I'm not,' he said. 'You're the best.' Laurie kissed the top of her head and they sat quietly, her shoulder against his chest. Faintly she could feel the beat of his heart. And Sylvia always felt this was the moment when they really made their promise to each other.

Sixty

August 1943

After his return home Laurie spent six months invalided out of the RAF, at first in hospital while his leg was operated on and reset, then at home. The doctors also managed to make some repairs to his scarred hands. It was a very happy period for Sylvia, knowing that he was home and safe, and she was able to visit him from time to time. When at last he came home to finish recuperating, they had a blissful few weeks together.

At that time Audrey was talking about going back to work. She was loath to leave her little boy, but was restless sitting at home when there was work to be done. Pauline, who also felt guilty that she was not doing enough, seemed relieved to have a grandson to mind, as her contribution to war work. Sylvia and Laurie also sometimes helped out with looking after Dorian. Sylvia knew, when they sat together playing with the little lad, that they were playing at families. Perhaps it was this, along with the pressure of knowing that he would soon have to go back, that gradually made Laurie change his mind about marriage.

'I want you as my wife more than anything,' he said. 'I just don't want to make a widow of you.'

'If anything happens, I want it to be with me as your

wife,' Sylvia told him, 'not just waiting to be married to you.'

Laurie was recalled to his squadron in Lincolnshire at the end of August 1943, and Sylvia thought she had never dreaded the dawning of a day so much. As in the old days, they had to say their farewells before she went to work, at five in the morning when it was barely light, in the hall of the Goulds' house. Sylvia had barely slept the night before, and got up feeling sick and exhausted. Laurie quietly let her into the house.

'I couldn't sleep,' she said, as they stood with their arms round each other.

'Me neither.'

There seemed nothing else to say. She didn't want to pour out her choking fear and dread. Everything there was to say had either been said already or would be of no help this morning. She wanted him to remember her smiling, not weeping and complaining.

They held each other close, as if memorizing every line of each other's bodies, then she drew back and looked up at him. 'I'll have to go.' She was determined not to cry. Forcing a brave smile, she took his face gently in her hands. 'I love you so much. I'll be here, always.'

She saw the emotion in Laurie's eyes. He leaned over and kissed her, lingering for a few seconds, as if he could not bear to move his lips away from her cheek. 'That's all I need to know. That's everything.'

She stepped out into the mild darkness, feeling as if she was being torn apart.

That evening she wept to Audrey, 'I know that his being alive is everything. That's all that matters. But now that he's flying again, I'm so frightened that our luck won't last.'

'I wish I could just say it'll be all right, Sylv,' Audrey

said sadly. 'Let's hope and pray it will, even if it is all in the lap of the gods.'

Sylvia never knew how she got through the weeks after Laurie was wrenched away from her again. All she could do was hold herself strong and find something to look forward to. But during Laurie's first leave in September they decided to get married as soon as possible. The next six weeks were a flurry of arrangements and excitement. They were also a time more full of dread for Sylvia than any other time. Was it tempting fate – could she ever truly be married to Laurie? Every day of those six weeks she lived in terror of receiving a telegram and of all her hope and joy being snatched from her again.

They tried to be in touch every day. She would go to the telephone box along the street and dial the number at the base, trembling until she heard his voice, especially if it was the day after she knew he had been flying at night. She was a bag of nerves, and felt badly about the fact that her loving someone in Bomber Command affected the whole family. Mom and Dad could see that she was living on a knife-edge. The whole family loved Laurie and, after all he and Sylvia had already been through, it was unbearable to think that it could all so easily happen again.

One night in October little Dorian was restless with a cold and fever. Audrey gave up trying to pacify him in her room and carried him downstairs to make him a drink. When she took him, snivelling, into the back room and turned on the light, she found that she was not alone.

'Oh my God, Sylv!' she laid a hand over her pounding heart. 'You frightened the life out of me. I came down with this one – he's a bit poorly . . . Sis, are you all right?'

Sylvia was sitting bolt upright at the table, her hands resting on the cloth. Audrey took in the look of her, pale and so very still. Her hair was tied back, rather austerely, from her face.

Audrey went and sat beside her. Dorrie quietened a little at the sight of his auntie and reached his hand out.

'Sylv?'

'He's flying tonight,' Sylvia said in a barely controlled voice. 'I know he is. He's out there somewhere. I can't sleep – I don't know where to put myself. Every time I just think: *There's another chance gone* . . . I can't believe we'll ever really get married. Something will happen – I think I'm cursed.' She turned to Audrey, her eyes wide with fear. 'I can't stand it. I feel as if I'm going to . . .' She lowered her head. 'I don't know.' She spoke in scarcely more than a whisper. 'I feel as if I'm going mad thinking about it.'

'Oh, sis.' Audrey reached over and laid her hands over Sylvia's, clasped on the table. They were icy cold. There was nothing she could say. Nothing that was sure to be true. Sylvia curled a finger round one of Audrey's, as if for comfort.

'Do you come down here like this often?' she asked. 'You should wake me, not sit here on your own.'

Sylvia shook her head. 'Sometimes. No point in anyone else losing sleep, is there?'

She sat staring ahead of her, and Audrey knew her thoughts were far away, flying out into the night sky as if she could be like an angel, keeping Laurie safe. Audrey's heart ached for her.

By the time Laurie finally came home on leave in November, Sylvia had lost weight and looked hollow around the eyes. She had been close to the edge, so convinced that she would never see him again that, when she did, she went to pieces and wept in his arms.

'I thought you'd be taken away from me,' she sobbed, unable to help herself, once they were alone in her room. 'I thought you were going to leave me again. I thought we'd never get married, and I want . . .' Her words were lost in a storm of crying.

Even in her distraught state she could see that Laurie was disturbed by the sight of her looking so thin and haunted. He held her close, murmuring reassuring words.

'I'm here now, my love. Oh, Sylvia, it's all right. I love you so much and we're going to be married – in two days' time.'

She pulled back and looked up into his face, her eyes swollen with tears. 'Are we? Is it really going to happen? I can't believe anything any more.'

'It is,' he whispered, drawing her close again. 'You and I. Nothing can happen now. We're going to be together.'

She sank into his arms, feeling the breath going in and out of his body and the warmth of him. At last she began to trust that it was really true.

Sylvia and Laurie married at All Saints' Church in Kings Heath on a sunny November afternoon. Sylvia managed to get Elsie to come and be her bridesmaid. She stood beside Laurie in the church, in the beautiful, simple white dress that Marjorie had kept for her, with Laurie in his uniform. They looked into each other's eyes and she knew that she had come home, and that she had never been so sure of anything before. The sight of Sylvia, now so radiant, reduced both mothers to tears. They knew everyone was thinking how easily this day of joy might never have arrived.

Sylvia had leave from work for two days, and she and Laurie went away for a night to an inn in the Warwickshire countryside. Although food was in short supply, the place was an oasis of peace.

They stood side-by-side in the old timbered room late that afternoon, looking out at the view of fields and copper-leafed trees in the gathering dusk. Sylvia snuggled close to Laurie and he put his arm round her.

'It's so lovely,' he said, moved. 'God, when I think of Belgium and France, with those bastards crawling all over them . . .' He turned and looked down at her. Sylvia was struck then by how much Laurie had aged. He looked content at that moment, full of love and joy, but she could see that he was no longer the happy-go-lucky boy she had once known.

'While we're here,' he said, 'let's just try and forget about it: the war, flying, everything. We won't talk about it or think of it again. Let's just be us, here and now.'

She turned to face him and kissed him. 'It might be just a bit easier to pretend out here. The fields and trees don't change all that much, do they?'

Laurie gently touched one of the scars on her cheek, first with his fingers, then his lips. His other hand found its way to the buttons of her blouse and she felt her breasts tingle with longing for him to touch her. She helped him, unfastening her brassiere, so that his warm hands found her all the sooner.

'You've changed a bit,' Laurie murmured, kissing her nipples. She could hear the smile in his voice. They had not seen each other fully naked since they were about four years old.

'I should hope so,' she said and heard him laugh with pure happiness.

Sixty-One

January 1944

One evening during the dark of the New Year days of 1944 Ted Whitehouse arrived home from work through the back door with urgent speed. Sylvia was upstairs, and the first she knew of anything going on was a yell from Jack.

'Sylv – Audrey! Come and see this, quick!'

Audrey was bathing Dorian by the fire in the back room. As Sylvia ran downstairs she heard her calling, 'I can't just come, you idiot! D'you want him to drown? You come here, if you want me.'

Sylvia went into the kitchen to find Mom and Dad bent over the kitchen table, staring intently at a copy of the *Daily Sketch*.

'I don't know,' Mom was saying, squinting at a photograph on one of the inside pages. 'Is it? How can you be sure? I'm no good with faces.'

'It is. *Look!*' Ted jabbed his finger at it. 'Shape of the face – everything . . .' He caught sight of Sylvia. 'Look, that's that wench who was living here. You can tell a mile off.'

'You mean Kitty?' Sylvia felt her heartbeat begin to pick up speed. The thought of Kitty Barratt always filled her with a sickening dread and they seldom mentioned her name. What on earth could Dad be talking about?

She leaned over the paper. Beside headlines about the Allies fighting at Monte Cassino she read the words: BARONET KILLED IN NIGHTCLUB SHOOTING. Alongside it was a poor-quality photograph. Her eyes dashed through the story: love-rivalry in a Soho house of hospitality between a baronet, Sir Rawsthorne Chalmers, and Donald Benson, 24, a white US airman. Both men were besotted with the same woman, who offered 'hospitality' in a private house in the area, one Kitten Amador, 22. Sir Chalmers – 'Rawty' to his friends – was found in a pool of blood, having been shot through the heart by Benson in a love-feud.

Even as she was devouring the words, Sylvia could feel her attention drawn as if magnetically by the photograph. A chill wrapped itself tightly around her heart. A woman with pale hair was seated at a table on which there were drinks, beside a man with a long face and soulful, hooded eyes: Rawsthorne Chalmers, in happier times. Each had a glass in their hand and was smiling at the camera. The hollows of their faces were heavily shadowed. In a second, before Sylvia had even taken in the details, the shape of the face leapt out at her, instantly familiar. She knew from a glance – and from a gut recognition that preceded her more conscious thoughts – that, despite the exotic name, this was Kitty Barratt. That smile, even from the grainy, slightly blurred picture, could not be that of anyone else.

'It is! It's her.' She had to remind herself to draw breath, amazed that even the sight of Kitty, a mere outline of her, could affect her so strongly. She stared at the picture with rage and horror, but also with an absurd pang of longing. How she had loved it when that smile was directed at her! And that poor Irishman, Joe Whelan, had become besotted with it. Ian had fallen for it, too. And now a titled man with sad eyes had been drawn into Kitty's spell, plus an American far from home, who, the report said, was now in gaol at Shepton Mallet awaiting trial.

'God!' she said. No other words would seem to come. She felt sick.

'So, she's been one of them Yankees Bags now,' Ted observed. 'Doesn't stop at anything, that one.'

'A murder!' Jack was relishing this. 'Will she go to prison?'

'What's going on?' Audrey came in with Dorian trotting beside her, wrapped in a pale-blue towel.

Pauline handed her the paper.

'D'you know who it is?' Jack couldn't resist quizzing Audrey.

Her eyes moved over the page. They saw her horrified realization. 'That's *her*, isn't it? Is it, Sylv?'

Sylvia nodded. 'That's her all right.'

'My God!' Audrey breathed, trying to take it in as well. 'Look what she's done now! What a . . . She's like a poison tree: everything she touches . . .' She was reading on further. 'Oh, it says here she's expecting a child!'

'Whose?' Pauline asked.

Audrey shrugged. 'They wouldn't say, would they – even if she knows.'

'Poor little bugger,' Ted said, finally taking off his coat. 'With a mother like that, what chance has he got?'

'They won't send her to prison, will they?' Sylvia asked. Dear God, she was even feeling protective now, after all this!

'It wasn't her who pulled the trigger,' Audrey said. 'It's that poor Yank's going to swing for her.'

466

Sylvia sat staring across the table, trying to take in the life that Kitty had been leading far away in London. And, despite her bitterness at the way Kitty had betrayed her and lied to her, and in the face of all the horror Kitty had caused, she felt an overwhelming sadness at the memory of the girl she thought was a friend. The girl who had once seemed sweet, who had cooked and chatted and laughed with them in this very kitchen.

To mark Sylvia and Laurie's married life, Marjorie Gould had given the two of them Raymond's old room at the front of the house, as it was the biggest. Sylvia and Laurie were very touched by this. In the brief times he was at home it became their cosy nest.

Sylvia imagined that, because she was married, she would have a baby at once. Instead, life continued as usual. She was still living at home the rest of the time and working at Snow Hill. Laurie was away, and once again it was her lot to spend her time fretting. Even though the agonizing, superstitious terror she had felt before their wedding was never repeated, the fear and worry were forever acute. Usually she knew whether he was flying or not. If so, she lay sleepless, imagining the dark swarms of aircraft taking off from the east coast. During the spring of 1944 the papers reported raid after raid, casualty list after casualty list. She felt as if her whole existence was strung between one communication from Laurie and another, letting her know that he was still there, still alive. They wrote to each other as well as speaking on the telephone. She loved letters – they often said so much more than a telephone call. The raids were now focused on France, on preparations for what would become known as D-Day. All she knew was that

467

everything Laurie did was terrifyingly dangerous, and that each day he was alive was a bonus.

She was so caught up in her own feelings and fears over Laurie during this time that she scarcely noticed the changes in Audrey and what was happening to her. That was something they all had to come to terms with later on.

Sixty-Two

September 1944

Audrey never knew exactly what made her write the letter.

By the autumn of 1944 she had been back at work for a few months doing secretarial work in a firm in Balsall Heath. She was doing her bit, she told herself. And she did not want to be too far from home, so that she could get back to her little one all the sooner. Two-year-old Dorian was the centre of her life.

All the same, Audrey was feeling restless. Perhaps that's all it was. Though Sylvia was still at home, all her attention was fixed on her concern for Laurie. Audrey was happy for her sister, though she also worried about them. She knew Sylvia and Laurie were right for each other.

As for herself, she had shelved any thoughts of marriage or even romance. She was ashamed of the way she had strung Colin Evans along, giving him reason to hope that he had a chance with her. Colin had really been in love with her, she knew that. He was a good, kind man, but try as she might she could not love him back. In the end, to the family's bewilderment, she had broken things off with him and had said it would be better if they did not see each other again. She knew she had hurt him badly. Since then there had not been anyone.

One mellow afternoon she was walking to the bus stop on the Moseley Road after work. She was wearing an old skirt that she had had for years, in a dark-green colour, but the skirt was quite full and swinging, for these austere, utility-clothing days, and she knew it hung well on her slim figure. She wore a cream short-sleeved blouse and had a black cardigan draped over her shoulders. Away from the clack of typewriters and office bustle, she felt suddenly very alone. Stopping at the end of the line of other office and factory workers waiting for the bus, she had a sad, sinking feeling. Looking along the queue, she thought: If only one of those faces was familiar! If only she could look and see someone whose presence would fill her with happiness and enthusiasm. Instead there were all these tired, grey-faced people, worn down by years of war, work and rationing, and she didn't know any of them.

I suppose I'm lonely, she admitted to herself. Audrey never found it easy to admit her own weaknesses to anyone. But the ache persisted. Oh, to have someone she longed to see, who made her laugh and feel excited!

When she got home it was easy to forget this feeling because life was all busyness again. As she came in at the door, she heard her mother say, 'Who's that? Who's come home, Dorrie?'

Audrey waited in the hall, a smile growing on her face. There was a pause as her mother helped Dorian down from his high chair, then the sound of his feet and his eager face appeared at the kitchen door.

'Hello, little man!' She squatted down, her arms out-stretched.

'Ma-ma!' His dark eyes alight with happiness, he came charging along and into her arms.

'Oh! There's my boy!' She held him tight, kissing his

round cheeks, his soft arms, overwhelmed with love for him. Every time she saw him, her son seemed more beautiful.

'You're back soon,' Pauline said, at the kitchen door.

'I was lucky with the bus. Everything all right?'

'Yes, he's been a good boy, haven't you, Dorrie? He was just finishing his tea. Come on, I've boiled the kettle.'

It felt very reassuring to sit with Mom and her little boy as they caught up on the day over a cup of tea. The evening was taken up with playing with Dorian, tea with the rest of the family and getting her son off to sleep.

Once it was bedtime and she was alone in her room, Audrey sat for a time with the lights off and the curtains open, looking out at the trees in the fading light. Her loneliness surfaced again, and the memories that she tried to keep from her mind of the one person who had ever made her feel completely happy, excited, loved. Dorrie's face blazed vividly in the forefront of her mind. Dorrie waving from a service jeep, or bent in concentration over her writing; Dorrie smiling at her, full of love and fun.

Audrey was washed in a sense of shame at how she had treated her friend. With increasing distance from the situation, and now that she was not in a panic, she felt angry and disappointed in herself. So Dorrie was a woman who preferred women (Audrey didn't like the word 'lesbian', which made her cringe). Was that really so bad? And she, who had been supposed to be Dorrie's friend, had turned against her and betrayed her, instead of standing by her and being able to accept her for what she was. But hadn't that been because . . . ? Audrey still could not let her mind admit that there was a *because*.

She got up to close the curtains and, after draping a cover over the top of the cot so that Dorian would not wake, she turned on the light and went to her chest of drawers. A few weeks ago she had paid for a studio picture of Dorian, and she had some small prints of it. The photographer in the High Street had sat the little boy on a low stool with a white fleecy cover on it. Audrey had dressed him in white and, with his dark hair and solemn eyes, he had sat staring intently at the camera. Despite all their efforts, they had not persuaded him to smile, but he looked lovely: alert, intelligent and sweet.

She selected a small print and sat down on the bed with the remains of a pad of writing paper and a pencil. There were a hundred ways she could begin, and she was not happy with any of them. In the end, sitting with her legs tucked under her on the bed, she chose to be direct. 'Dear Dorrie,' she wrote, 'I thought you might like to see a picture of my little boy. His name is Dorian and we all call him "little Dorrie".'

She stopped and stared at the page. Only now, seeing the words written down, did she wonder what on earth Dorrie was going to make of this. How stupid could she have been, all this time? She knew really that she had named her son after the person she truly loved. It was because she wanted to hear that name on her own lips, and other people's. And it was because that was all she had left of Dorrie. The family had thought the name strange at first but by now everyone was used to it – 'Little Dorrie' was just her son's familiar name. But seeing this statement written down to send to Dorrie herself, the force of what she felt truly hit Audrey. She thought about tearing up the letter and not sending it. But now, she realized, whatever anyone thought – and whether or not Dorrie was happy, had found a new love, or several – she wanted to put her side of things straight.

'I owe you an apology,' she went on. 'I feel stupid and

ashamed of how I behaved at Cardington, and for not answering your letter.' Again she ground to a halt. *I miss you so much*, she wanted to go on. *You're the only person who's ever . . .*

In the end she told Dorrie a few things about her life, about her son, and the fact that she was working again now. She wanted to say so many things, but simply put, 'I wish I hadn't messed everything up so badly.' She signed off, 'Love, Audrey'.

She didn't keep reading it over and over. If she did, she would end up rewriting it dozens of times, and how could she ever be sure of the right thing to say? The envelope was her last one. She had no idea whether Dorrie was still at RAF Hendon. But Dorrie's home address in High Wycombe was still burned into Audrey's memory. She addressed it there, and the next day bought a stamp and slipped it into the post before she could change her mind.

On the Friday she came home to find a telegram waiting for her. She looked in bewilderment as her mother handed it to her.

'We thought it was for Sylvia,' Mom said. 'It nearly gave us both a seizure.'

It's all right if it's for me, Audrey thought rather sadly. There was no one out there for her to dread hearing bad news about.

'Who on earth's it from?' Jack asked. Everyone was crowding round, curious.

'No idea.' She frowned.

CAN YOU MEET ME TOMORROW AT FOUR PM STOP
SNOW HILL STATION STOP DORRIE

Audrey thought her heart was going to escape from her chest. 'Oh!' she exclaimed. Then, realizing that Mom, Sylvia and Jack were all staring curiously at her, she said, 'Well, what a surprise! D'you remember Dorrie, the girl I was in the WAAF with? She's taken it into her head to get in touch.'

'Oh yes, her,' Pauline said, turning away. 'Well, tell her not to send a flaming telegram next time.'

'All right, I will,' Audrey said. She was trying to sound measured and only slightly excited. Her body was standing soberly in the kitchen, while her mind was turning crazed cartwheels outside and along the street, and all the way to Snow Hill, in a fizzing ecstasy of happiness. 'I suppose I'd better go and see what she wants.'

Sixty-Three

Four o'clock, Dorrie's telegram had said. Audrey had arrived at Snow Hill far too early and, by the time it was nearly four, she had been standing for what felt like an eternity looking back and forth across the booking hall. She was such a bag of nerves that she could hardly stand still, shivering in her cotton frock, even though it was a hot day. She kept looking up at the huge clock face. Surely the hands were not moving? Wasn't that exactly what they had said the last time she looked up? The time between ten to four and five to four seemed to pass with the slowness of an entire year.

What if Dorrie did not come? she kept thinking. But what if she did? She felt on the brink of something so important, yet so frightening, that she could hardly bear being inside her own skin. For days now her thoughts had been chasing round and round. The truth that she had been running away from for so long was now breathing down her neck.

And this truth was that, of everyone she had met in her life, the person she loved – and could not stop loving – was Dorrie Cooper. If this meant that she was one of *those* women who loved women (or at least loved Dorrie), then surely now she was going to have to accept it. What sort of dull, dark, loveless life would she continue to lead with no Dorrie in it? Instead there might be a string of men who, even if they were as nice as pie, meant nothing to her. She'd already had a son out of wedlock. People judged and condemned and poked their noses in, but they were never the people that really mattered. What was more important: people approving of you because you did everything the way they thought you should, or finding a way to be happy?

But there was another agonizing route that her mind kept chasing along. Maybe Dorrie was coming to see her to tell her something. Perhaps she had changed her mind about how she felt and had found a man. Maybe she was getting married? Or she was emotionally tied to another woman and had just come to see Audrey as a courtesy. Audrey told herself she was mad to have hopes of anything – and she was not even sure what 'anything' might be, in any case. What did such women do in this situation? She didn't know any.

Gazing across at all the people moving in and out of the booking hall, she was constantly trying to pick out a familiar face among them. By the time she did, the face was so close that she did not have time to prepare herself. There was Dorrie almost upon her, in her WAAF uniform, her honey-coloured hair gathered under the cap, a bright, expectant look on her face.

'Audrey!' Dorrie said loudly. She was showing no signs of nerves, though Audrey knew her well enough to realize this did not mean she was as calm as she looked. She came striding up and then stopped, at a loss. Audrey looked into her clear, blue eyes and Dorrie suddenly glanced down for a second, overtaken by uncertainty. But she gathered herself quickly and looked up again, smiling.

'Well, where's my namesake? Didn't you bring him with you?'

'No, he's with Mom,' Audrey said. The crowds ebbed and flowed about them, but for her, in that moment, no one else mattered or even existed. 'Oh, Dorrie, it's so nice to see you again.'

'And you, you daft baggage.' Dorrie put her holdall down and held out her arms. For a moment the two of them hugged each other in a tight embrace.

'Mom says you're welcome to stay,' Audrey said.

'That'd be nice,' Dorrie said hesitantly. 'I mean, I could go back down tonight, but . . .'

'You've only just got here!' Audrey tried to sound relaxed, though her heart was thudding like mad. 'Let's go and have a cup of char somewhere, shall we, before we get the bus?'

'The refreshment room I saw looked rather swish,' Dorrie said.

They found a space to sit down in the gracious refreshment room, with a cup of tea each. Suddenly they were facing each other across a small table. Dorrie appeared rounder in the face, Audrey thought, and looked very healthy.

'You're looking skinny,' Dorrie said as they took each other in. Her eyes moved over Audrey's face. 'Is that young man taking it out of you?'

'You could say,' Audrey said. 'What with feeding him and running about after him.'

'Gosh!' Dorrie said, sounding awed. 'Motherhood.'

That seemed to stop the conversation for a moment, but then Dorrie started talking fast, as if she was afraid that any silence would make them both seize up and be unable to start again. She kept her eyes lowered, fiddling with a teaspoon as she talked.

'I came straight away, because I wanted to see you –

after your letter. The thing is, I shan't be around much longer. It looks as if I'm going to get an overseas posting.'

Audrey felt a sinking, devastating sensation inside. What had she expected? Dorrie, being the person she was, had wanted to make things right, and had come before she was sent abroad for who knew how long. But none of this meant anything else.

'Gosh,' Audrey said. She could feel the WAAF lingo coming back to her; she had lost it while she was at home. 'So, where are you going?'

'Ceylon, by the look of things. We'll hear soon whether we're going, and when. It's rather exciting actually. By all accounts it's a very beautiful place – paradise on earth, some say.' She was chattering away fast. Her voice, Audrey noticed, had become slightly more clipped over the past two years. She put it down to WAAF life – unless it was because she was nervous.

'That sounds like an adventure.' Audrey found, to her alarm, that she was very close to tears. Above all, she suddenly wanted Dorrie to leave again. She had seen her, she had apologized, but now they inhabited quite different worlds and Dorrie was about to depart for yet another one, not even realizing that she was taking Audrey's heart with her. What could they possibly have in common now?

'If I go, I'm going to write about it like mad,' Dorrie went on. 'I'm even more sure now that's what I want – when we get peace, finally. I want to write about things – report on them. So I might as well get into practice.' She paused, suddenly sober, looking down at the tabletop with its rings of wet. 'I thought I might as well. Go, I mean.'

'It'll be very interesting,' Audrey said carefully.

Dorrie looked at her suddenly, a frank, rather sad

look. 'I just meant, I thought I'd go, because there didn't seem to be much on offer for me here.'

A host of questions hung in the air amid the buzz of other people's conversations. An atmosphere grew between them, more tense and expectant by the second, until it was unbearable. They sat looking at each other over their half-drunk cups of tea. Audrey felt she barely knew where to begin. What was Dorrie saying? Did she mean . . . ? She had found the courage to come here, and Audrey now knew it was up to her to say something that would let them talk properly. She owed Dorrie that. Her heart was beating so fast that she could hardly breathe.

'Oh.' She laid a hand on her chest, struggling to take a deep breath. 'I feel . . . Sorry. It's silly. I feel ever so nervous and wound-up.'

Dorrie put her head on one side. 'Why?' She looked sweet, vulnerable, when she could have been forgiven for looking bitter and closed.

'Because . . .' Audrey gazed at Dorrie, afraid to speak. At last she managed to bring out the words, 'Do you have anyone, Dorrie? Anyone else?'

A flicker of pain passed over Dorrie's face. 'No. It's not easy, as you can imagine. It's not that I haven't tried. But the thing is . . .' She looked away for a moment, her cheeks flushing pink. Bravely she turned to Audrey again. 'No one else is you.'

Her words made Audrey's already-hammering heart beat even harder, filling her with pulses of fear and confusion, but also with a growing, amazed joy. She reached out and, for a moment, wrapped her hand over Dorrie's on the table. In a low voice she said, 'No one else is you, either.'

*

On the bus to Kings Heath they sat holding hands, under cover of Dorrie's bag. Audrey had a heady, defiant feeling of being on a crazed, adventurous voyage into the unknown and being overjoyed to be there, if the journey felt as loving and right as this. At the same time, this embarkation felt like coming home and putting your slippers on.

At home Dorrie was welcomed as Audrey's friend, and everyone was pleased to have a guest. Sylvia was looking more relaxed than she had in many months because, after D-Day in June, Laurie had been put on a tour of instruction duty for six months. For the moment he was as safe as he could be. She greeted Dorrie warmly. Dorrie was enchanted with little Dorian and sat with him on her lap in the back room as she chatted away to Sylvia and Jack, and to their parents, about the WAAF and her imminent posting.

'We haven't heard about any of Audrey's Air Force friends for a long time,' Pauline said to her. She was watching them both with a slight air of puzzlement. Audrey considered whether Mom was wondering exactly why her grandson had been named after this young woman. Audrey could see that her father was rather curious about Dorrie, too. Dorrie's forthright, energetic southern ways were not what they were used to, but they seemed to have taken a shine to her. Jack hung around too, shy and silent for once, but obviously fascinated.

'No, I've been dreadful about keeping in touch,' Dorrie said. Audrey looked at her, as if to say: *You shouldn't be the one taking the blame*.

'I expect you've been busy,' Sylvia said. 'The time flies by, doesn't it?'

'It certainly does,' Dorrie said. 'But I thought, as

I'm about to go overseas, I should go and look up some old friends. After all, Audrey came to stay with my people once, didn't you? They still ask after you. And I hadn't met this little fellow, either. She leaned round and kissed Dorian's cheek. Audrey felt a thrill of delight on seeing this. 'And you're so old, aren't you already, little man?'

Dorian kept turning round and staring at her with big eyes, seemingly fascinated. He wanted to fiddle with her bright, polished buttons, and Dorrie gave him her cap to play with as well.

'I don't know where you're going to sleep,' Mom fretted. Jack, you could come and sleep downstairs.'

'No,' Audrey said firmly, before Jack had a chance to agree. 'No need. Dorrie can have my bed, and I'll sleep on the floor.'

'I suppose you girls want to chatter half the night,' Ted remarked.

'Yes,' Audrey said. 'I expect we do!'

'Won't it wake the lad?'

'Oh no,' Audrey replied. 'He'd sleep through an earthquake, once he's gone off.'

When they were finally alone in Audrey's room, with Dorian tucked up in his cot, they had the chance to catch up on all the time since they last met. They lay in Audrey's bed, huddled together, their arms round each other, and stopped talking every now and then just to gaze on each other and exchange kisses.

'Tell me about everything,' Dorrie said. 'How it's been, having a child, being here – all of it?'

Audrey told her all she could think of. The main thing she kept coming back to was, 'I've missed you, Dorrie. I was so stupid and cowardly, the way I behaved. I was

481

so terrified at the thought that I might be different. Of what people would think and say.'

'What about now? How do you feel?'

'Terrified,' she confessed. She felt a pulse of laughter go through Dorrie. 'Aren't you?'

'Oh yes. I think you have to get used to it.'

Audrey lifted her head and looked at her. 'Is this real? Are we real? I don't know anyone else like this . . . Do you?'

'There were two teachers at my school. Everyone called them Mr and Mrs Knowles. They were really Miss Knowles and Miss MacIntosh, but Miss Knowles dressed in a very mannish way.'

'Were they nice?'

Dorrie giggled. 'Not very, no. Miss Knowles had a drink problem as well, and used to rave at times. And Miss MacIntosh tiptoed around her like a terrified mouse.'

Audrey put her head down on the pillow again. She felt Dorrie's soft hair with her cheek. 'Does it have to be like that?'

'I hope not.' Dorrie turned to her, very serious now. 'I truly hope not. Look, I've probably got to go away now . . .'

'I know – I wish you hadn't.'

'But it'll give us time to think, to get used to the idea again. Because, I don't know about you, but I'm in this for the long run. I don't want to lose you again, Audrey, my dearest. I know we might seem a strangely assorted pair on the face of it, but, crazy as it may be, I love you and that's how it is.'

Audrey pressed her lips against Dorrie's cheek. Closing her eyes, she experienced another moment of bliss, of sweet homecoming. 'I love you too. You're the only one for me – I know that now. Thank God you came back. Thank *you* for coming back.'

'And I'll come back again.'

'Write to me?'

'Of *course* I'll write to you. That's one thing I can actually do! And you've got to write back.'

'I will. Pages and pages, just telling you how much I love you.'

'We can worry about what everyone else thinks later on.' Dorrie slid her hand inside Audrey's nightdress. Their eyes met in delicious understanding. 'But tonight no one is any the wiser, except us.'

Sixty-Four

February 1945

'Here we are, love – look, it's finally finished.'

Marjorie Gould opened the door of Raymond's old bedroom, which had become Sylvia and Laurie's married quarters. Sylvia knew that Marjorie loved it when they were both there, whenever Laurie was on leave, and having the house full of life again. Stanley had moved Laurie's bed in there and had pushed it side-by-side with Raymond's. Now, spread across both beds, was a colourful patchwork quilt that Marjorie had been stitching for months.

'Oh, it's beautiful!' Sylvia exclaimed. She had seen some of it in the making, Marjorie sewing sections of it, little hexagons of colours and flowers. Now it was all fastened together, each section fitting into the others in coloured patterns. Sylvia kissed her mother-in-law affectionately. 'It looks so nice! Oh, thank you.' She went and stroked it, staring at it in wonder.

'It's a late wedding present,' Marjorie said. Half the neighbourhood had contributed scraps of material to it. 'I'm glad you like it, love.'

'I *love* it,' Sylvia said. As she leaned over the bed, running her hand over it, a surge of nausea passed through her and she closed her eyes for a moment.

'Are you all right?' Marjorie asked.

'Yes, I'm fine.' Sylvia was longing to share the news with Marjorie that she would soon be giving her a grand-child to keep Dorian company, but first she must tell Laurie. It was only right that he should know, before his family. The past three months had been a more peaceful time, with him working as an instructor. On his last home leave at the end of December, when they had made love in this room – and unknown yet to him – he had left behind a tiny piece of the future!

She straightened up groggily and managed a smile. 'Thank you, Marjorie – I think that's the nicest present I've ever had. It's absolutely beautiful.'

Marjorie beamed at her. 'I've enjoyed doing it. I'm going to miss it. In fact, with the bits I've got left I think, I'd better make one for little Dorrie – although he's getting a bit big for a baby-quilt now.'

'Well, perhaps you could start on one,' Sylvia said, not meeting her eye. 'After all – you never know.'

The next night she and Laurie were snuggled up under the blankets and colourful quilt when she told him. They had already made love and were warm and relaxed, relishing being able to lie together in peace, to love one another and talk. Sylvia snuggled against Laurie's shoulder, one hand on his warm belly. When the moment felt right, she raised herself onto one elbow and looked into his eyes. She had thought Laurie seemed a bit distant, as if lost in thought, and now she wanted to claim his full attention.

'I've got news for you.'

She could see that he could tell it was good news. Had he guessed? For a moment, once again she saw a flicker of something in his eyes – worry, fear? Then he started to smile. 'Go on then.'

A grin spread over her face. 'You're going to be a dad.'

'Oh!' he gave an overjoyed cry and pulled her into his arms. 'Oh, Sylv – are you sure?'

'Quite sure,' she said, cuddling up happily again. 'I've been feeling really sick – in the mornings mainly. I'd missed my monthly and . . . Anyway, I asked Mom in the end, because I wasn't sure, and she said I'd better go to the doctor.' She looked up at him again. 'I haven't told your mom and dad yet – or Audrey and the others. I swore Mom to secrecy because I thought you ought to know first.'

Laurie was laughing with happiness. 'I can hardly believe it! Are you really sure, Sylv?'

'Sure as I can be – I feel funny. I've never felt like this before.'

'What about work?' he asked, with concern.

'I'm managing, just. But I'll have to give up before too long.'

He stroked her hair. 'I can't wait to see you as a mother. You'll be so lovely – the best mom ever.'

'Maybe it's something I can be good at, for once!'

'Don't be daft. You're good at lots of things. And I'm going to be a father,' he said in wonder. But a moment later she heard him give a deep sigh. He turned his face away for a moment.

'What?' she said, pushing herself up in the bed again. 'What's the matter? Tell me!'

He turned back to her, his face troubled. 'This isn't the moment to say this, but I'm going to have to. I've been dreading it.'

She stared at him. Fear clutched at her. 'They're not . . . Tell me they're not—'

'They are – I've got to go back on ops.'

A chill spread through her. She could see the pain and dread in his eyes. 'I knew there was something – you seemed . . . As soon as you get back?'

Laurie nodded. For a moment they gazed at each other in silence.

'Right,' she said. She drew in a deep breath. More nights of waiting, in terror. She *would not* cry. Determinedly she resorted again to the only way she could think of surviving. 'Let's not talk about it, or think about it, because I don't think I can stand it.'

'Come here.' He wrapped his arms tightly around her. 'We're here now. That's all. And that's all that matters. Here and now. I love you, Sylvia – more than anything.'

It was a week of celebration. When they broke the news to Mr and Mrs Gould, Marjorie wept with happiness and Stanley suddenly became very jumpy around Sylvia and solicitous, as if she might break.

'It's all right,' she laughed, as he took a jug of water from her in case it was too heavy. 'I am still working as a porter, you know!'

'Well, it's time you stopped,' he said. 'That's no job for a woman in your condition.'

'I will, as soon as I can,' she promised. 'I'm off for the next few days anyway.'

When she told the family, her father grinned bashfully and said, 'Well, that's nice news, wench.' Jack made gruff noises about a football team, and Audrey was especially happy. 'I thought you might be!' she laughed. 'I heard you heaving in the mornings. Thought I'd better not say anything, though. Dorrie!' She called her little boy to her. 'Auntie Sylvia's going to give you someone to play with.'

Sylvia basked in the excitement, determinedly blocking out all thoughts beyond that week, as they celebrated and lived and loved as thoroughly and happily as possible.

A month later Sylvia had got over the sickness and was feeling better. She had told her employers at Snow Hill that she was expecting, and they kept her on duties that were as light as possible. Dealing with pregnant porters was not something they were used to.

She was so glad still to be at work, to be kept busy and not sit at home thinking unbearable thoughts about what Laurie might be doing. Surely now it would be all right, she prayed. They were winning the war – the Allies were pushing forward on so many fronts. Surely it would be over soon and her lovely Laurie could come home, safe and sound? But the work of Bomber Command was far from over. She knew that, but kept trying to push it to the back of her mind.

'If anything happens,' she begged Pauline, 'come into work and tell me – like you did before. Don't wait, please.'

'I don't think I could stand waiting anyway,' her mother said.

Every day that went by without bad news was another victory, another day closer to peace, when they could all sleep properly, knowing that Laurie was safe, for the time being.

They got through one day, then another and another. One March afternoon, the air heavy with cold, Sylvia walked wearily back from the bus stop after work. As she reached the house, she saw the net curtain at the front drop, as if someone had been standing looking out. She only registered this with half her mind. But as she pushed the front door open, something already felt different. Almost immediately her mother and Marjorie appeared from the parlour, Mom in front, their faces very solemn. This again . . . No . . . no . . . ! Sylvia's legs buckled. She was too busy screaming to notice the pain as her knees hit the hall floor.

'No!' Her arms flailed at them. 'No – go away! Don't look like that. Stop it, go away. Don't!' She was shrieking, completely distraught now. 'Don't speak to me!'

'It's all right, bab.' Her mother rushed to her, as well as Marjorie, both putting their arms round her and pulling her to her feet. 'It's all right,' Mom kept saying, frantic with distress. 'There's been an accident, but it's all right . . .'

They were helping her, limp as an empty sack, into the front room.

'He's alive,' Marjorie said. Sudden, pent-up tears rushed from her eyes.

Sylvia sat looking up at them groggily. These were, for now, the only words she needed to hear.

'What's happened?' she whispered. 'He's alive? Tell me he's alive.'

Through her tears, Marjorie said, 'He's alive. But they haven't said much else. They say he's to be invalided out.'

It was only quite some time later that they got the full picture. Laurie's squadron had been performing training flights that day, over the North Sea. As they were on their way back, the plane Laurie was navigating developed engine trouble; they reached the Norfolk coast, but the pilot mishandled the landing and crashed the plane. The crew were all injured – though none killed – and Laurie less seriously than the others. He suffered only cuts and bad bruising, but (and this was something he could never make sense of, to his own satisfaction) that day something broke in him. The rescue party found him some distance from the smashed fuselage, sitting in a field of frostbitten parsnips, rocking back and forth, sobbing.

'One of the lads, a Canadian who was on the base by then, just came up to me and put his arms round me,' Laurie told Sylvia later. 'I think he could see that I'd had it.'

The months that followed were full of anxiety. As their child grew inside Sylvia, Laurie was invalided out to recover. Though he was no longer in physical danger, Sylvia almost found it worse now than when he was on operations. At least then he had been himself. But after his breakdown it was as if he disappeared into a deep, black place, where she could not reach him and did not know how to give help or comfort. Even after he was allowed home from hospital, Laurie was in a very fragile state. No one had flung at him the accusation of LMF – lack of moral fibre, or cowardice in not being able to fly – but he certainly flung it at himself.

Even though he eventually recovered enough to go back – not to an air crew, but at least to the RAF, as an instructor again – she knew that Laurie suffered terrible remorse. The chance of any airman surviving another tour of duty of thirty sorties was horrifyingly low. But now he was safe, and out of it, unlike the rest of them. However much she told him that all this was understandable, he could not shake off the feelings of guilt and failure. Every one of his original air crew was dead. He was the only one, so far as they knew, who had come out of Belgium alive. Some blokes had done so much more, had paid the ultimate price, while all he had done was go to pieces. That was how he saw it, and Sylvia knew it was something he would never fully get over.

1953

Sixty-Five

May 1953

Sylvia sat staring at her cooling mug of coffee. The custard creams she had thought she was so hungry for, as she dashed inside for a break, lay forgotten on the plate, lit up by a slanting sunbeam, on the tablecloth's embroidered hollyhocks.

The letter, folded into three by the sender, was lying half-open so that she could just see the handwriting, a rounded, childish hand in blue ink. Abruptly Sylvia slammed her hand down on it, pressing it closed so that she couldn't see the writing any more. She rested her elbows on the table and her head in her hands, threading her fingers through her dark, springy hair. Sylvia was in her early thirties now and a mother; in the emotions that raged in her this morning, though – the tight, terrible surge that almost stifled her breath – she was twenty again. Twenty and full of rage and anguish. She eased herself a little more upright on the old kitchen chair, took a deep breath and, shakily, let it out again.

'You all right, love?'

She hadn't even heard Laurie come in for his own break. Her coffee had a puckered skin on the top now.

'Feeling a bit weary?' He went to the stove. 'Not to worry – I'll get my coffee.'

'There are biscuits here,' she told him, indicating the plate as she quickly gathered up the letter with its envelope and pushed it into her skirt pocket.

'Who was that letter from?' he said, his back to her, as he relit the gas under the pan of milky coffee.

'Oh.' Sylvia hated not being truthful with him, but she wasn't ready to talk, not yet. 'It was a girl I was at school with years ago. I can barely remember her. Heaven knows why she wanted to write; she'd got nothing much to say.'

'Oh, I see.' Laurie showed no further interest. Sylvia stared at his back for a moment, tall and slender in his stationmaster's uniform, looking so tender and true. With all her heart she wanted to protect him, and all that they had. For a moment she saw all her life with fresh eyes and loved it all fiercely – and him. Why did she suddenly feel so threatened and unsettled?

'I'll go out and water the baskets, while it's quiet,' she said.

'Right-o.' He was settling at the table in the cosy kitchen, eyeing the newspaper and looking forward to his break.

Sylvia stepped out into the warm May morning and paused on the path, breathing in the scents. The garden of Station Cottage was full of blossom, lilac and laburnum, roses in bud and clematis trailing up the black drainpipe at the front of the house and spreading out its tendrils across the warm bricks. The marigolds, petunias and white alyssum in her flowerbeds had all opened their faces to the sun, and there was a low murmur from bees busily knocking against the flower heads.

Normally it was her quiet, serene time of day. The children were at school and no train was due in for another half-hour. She loved titivating the little station:

two platforms only, and the sidings that ran off to the Maltings and for the Co-op milk trains. She kept it looking pretty with flowerbeds and hanging baskets. At this time of year it was at its brightest and best, and it was the time she loved it the most.

She went to the tap at the end of the house to fill a watering can and carried it round through the wicket gate into the station, hoping for a few quiet minutes while the other station staff were having a break between trains. She put the can of water down and sank onto the bench on platform one. The opposite platform was in deep shade, but this side was bathed in sunlight and she felt the warmth sink into her. The rails reached away into the countryside. She liked the way, even in this back-woods part of the railway, it made her feel connected to everywhere else. And she was proud of their home, their work. She had kept a clipping of an article that the local paper had published about them, when she was taken on again by the railway: 'The stationmaster and lady-porter's marriage!' It was all she could have asked for, in this lovely little station, right at the end of a GWR branch line. 'Wallingbury,' the sign said in big white letters on black, the paint flaking in the heat.

A plane rumbled overhead, high and distant. As on so many occasions, she gave thanks for her life. But today the warm contentment that often rose within her on such a lovely morning was ruined by the cold turmoil inside. She pulled the letter from her pocket, looking round to check that she was truly alone.

The now-crumpled envelope was addressed to 'Sylvia W.' *Couldn't she even remember my name?* Sylvia thought bitterly. The first attempt at an address, in the blue hand-writing, simply said, 'C/o British Rail (Great Western Region)'. Above that, it said, 'Please forward'. There had obviously been some official passing-round of the letter, which had been rubber-stamped by various railway offices, until at last someone had addressed it to 'Railway Cottage, Wallingbury, Berkshire'. Perhaps she was the only Sylvia left working in the entire western network? If only they hadn't found her, she thought. How much further can you go than the end of the line, for a quiet life?

Forcing herself, she opened the letter again: one sheet of white paper. At the top there was an address in Kent, mercifully far away. The date was more than a fortnight before. 'Dear Sylv' (*Sylv!*), it said:

> I thought I'd send this to the good old GWR and
> see if anyone can track you down, after all this time.
> It would be so jolly to see you again and talk over all
> the old days. I've missed you. I can hardly believe how
> it was during the war now – it all seems like a dream,
> and such an age ago.
>
> I hope you're happily settled. I have a son of nine
> and am trying to become a sober matron at this time
> in my life! Not much in the way of family, though.
> I've had quite an eventful time of it. I do wonder how
> you're getting along. We didn't part on the best of
> terms, but I hope we can let bygones be bygones.
> I'd so love to come and look you up. I do hope your
> family are all well, especially the lovely Jack, who
> must be a big grown man by now.
>
> Do write back, don't be a stranger!
> From your old pal,
> Kitty

Sylvia folded the letter again, sickened by its contents. She did not even reread the address. She had never been to Kent and certainly had no intention of replying. Why on earth should Kitty suddenly be thinking of looking her up?

But she knew. Kitty's loneliness echoed through the letter. Kitty was always alone in the world – always would be. What 'family' did she have? The parents of the dead father of her child? Was that how it was? And, in her loneliness, had she thought back to someone who had been a friend to her? God knew, but the very thought of Kitty filled her with horror.

She remembered the grainy photograph in the newspaper, Kitty's smiling face beside the man of whose death she would shortly be the cause. And here was this letter – so jolly, as if nothing had ever happened. Had she no shame, no idea, even now, of what she caused, the effect she had on people? The American airman who had shot Kitty's rival had been hanged by the American authorities at Shepton Mallet prison. How could Kitty imagine ever again facing anyone who had known her?

What if she turned up here? Sylvia was filled with an icy, primitive fear. No – Kitty would have to go to a great deal of trouble to find out where they were. It was probably just one of her impulses, Sylvia told herself, a passing mood to write, but not meaning it.

But she walked back into the house feeling very shaken. After tucking the letter into the bottom of one of the kitchen drawers, she pulled the kitchen window shut, despite the warmth, as if to keep something out. And she felt a powerful urge to cleanse the house, as if Kitty Barratt had bodily invaded it; to scrub and clean until there was nothing left of her, anywhere.

*

Even after long years of peace Sylvia had not lost the habit of looking at her husband, the lovely and at the time same fragile man she had married, and seeing it as a miracle that they were here. Now she knew more about the massive losses there had been among Bomber Command crews, it seemed even more of a miracle.

'I don't know why I came through and so many didn't,' Laurie would say sometimes. The guilt that he had survived, when so many had not, played on his mind. However much she tried to reassure him that he'd done his share, that he was only human, Sylvia knew it would always haunt him.

Their son Jonny was born in September 1945 in a nursing home in Kings Heath. Sylvia had never been happier, seeing Laurie's delight at his first sighting of his son, hoping and praying that this little child would give her husband new light in his place of despair. Even his joy at the birth was tempered by the shades of all the dead air crew who would never see the faces of a growing family.

Gradually he recovered, though. While Laurie was still away, Sylvia lived at home with her family. Little Dorian and Jonny grew up as brothers. The man who came home – though loving and still devotedly her husband – was a more fragile, angry man than the fresh-faced innocent who had left in 1940. He was even more resistant now to his father's views about 'making something of yourself' and advancement in a good job. It was as if the well-trodden paths of professional careers that Stanley envisaged meant even less to Laurie. And he resisted being under certain sorts of authority – or 'knuckling down', as his father put it. They fell out about it often at that time, and Laurie would grow explosively angry. The two men were better kept apart. Stanley saw the end of the war as time for a fresh start – which of course it was – but for Laurie it meant something quite different. His father had not been through his experiences; he could not seem to grasp how Laurie felt. Marjorie, as ever, was quite different.

'At least Mom understands,' Laurie said to Sylvia, 'All I want is a quiet life, not to be in some dead-end job with a retired major bossing me about. I want to be able to think my own thoughts, not what some other bugger thinks I should.'

It was she who suggested the railways. By then all the factories and railways were turfing women out of the jobs that they had been doing for the past five years. Some went gladly, others with reluctance. Sylvia had already had to make that break because of having little Jonny.

When Laurie had applied to the GWR, his first job had been – to his father's disgust – in a clerical role at Shirley station. Sylvia wondered whether he would settle, but he did, and was promoted to assistant stationmaster. They rented rooms nearby for the year he did that job. But then the offer came up of the stationmaster's post at Wallingbury. Both of them knew he could have done a job requiring more brain power, but he had wanted an occupation that was not hard on his nerves – something that left him time to think, that was steady, but peaceful.

Sylvia found it a wrench leaving Birmingham, but Audrey had gone by then and she knew it was time to branch out and have a fresh start. It was only a good while later, when the station needed a new porter, that she applied for the job and they had become a stationmaster-porter team. By then their other child, little Barbara, was starting school and Sylvia knew she could manage.

She loved the job: being back on the railway, working with the station staff and seeing Laurie content in the work as well. The town was small, a beautiful old place on the Thames, and they took lovely walks along the river when they had some spare time. Laurie discovered that he loved drawing. Even with his stiff hands, he could manage very well, and when he had the time he would sit for hours sketching the willows and boats. He liked to read books on philosophy, to try and think things out for himself. Between them they had built a life. She tried never to mention the war. All she wanted was for Laurie's memories and his sense of self-reproach to fade. And, whatever he felt, he was glad enough to be alive and to know that it was no good dwelling in the past. They had a life together – and a good one.

During the days after she had received Kitty's letter, Sylvia could not get it out of her mind. She went about her daily routines of cleaning and cooking, taking her children to school. Jonny, who was eight now, liked to ride along on his bike, with Sylvia keeping him in sight. He was a sturdy, blond boy, very like Laurie, but with more confidence. Little Barbara, or Baba as they always called her, who was six, still liked to walk holding her mother's hand, chattering away. When Sylvia got home again, the house always felt almost eerily quiet.

But that week all that had happened with Kitty came rushing back, and she had to let it force its way through her mind. It was as if a boulder had come crashing into these quiet waters, stirring up memories like stinking pond mud. One afternoon she was sitting with a pile of mending in her lap, to which she was paying no real attention, lost in thoughts that had rolled her back to 1941. For her, that year had been full of pain and betrayal. After having pushed those events from her mind for years, now they came back, ugly and bitter.

'Sylv? Sylvia?' Laurie was suddenly in front of her and she took in the loud chuffing of a train drawing slowly alongside the platform behind.

'Heavens!' She jumped up. 'The four-thirty, already!'

But Laurie stopped her with a hand on her shoulder. His face was troubled. 'Sylv, is everything okay?'

'Yes – course.' She pushed her face into a smile. The train's brakes were squealing as it halted. 'Come on!'

Much later that evening, when the children were already in bed, she felt Laurie's gaze on her across their cosy sitting room with its flowery chairs and bright cushions that she had made. Her eyes met his.

'What's the matter, love?' he asked gently. 'I know there's something. You've been miles away for a couple of days now. And this afternoon in the garden – you looked like thunder. Don't say it's nothing, because I can see that it isn't.'

She took a breath. She didn't want to breathe Kitty's name, but even more she didn't want any secrets leaching like poison into her household. Kitty had already done enough of that.

'I'm sorry,' she said. 'It just all knocked me for six a bit. You know that letter?'

'From your school pal?'

'It wasn't exactly someone I was at school with.' She looked down at her lap. 'It was from Kitty.'

There was a silence. 'You mean . . . *That* Kitty?'

'Yes. *That* Kitty.'

'Oh,' he said. 'I see.' Laurie looked troubled, but also

puzzled. 'Does she matter now? What did she want?'

Sylvia got up, wanting to talk, to be close to him.

'Come here,' Laurie said.

She hesitated. 'Sure your leg'll be okay?' Though the surgery had much improved his leg, he still walked with a slight limp and it was weaker than the other one.

'I'll let you know if not.'

She snuggled up on his lap, her face close to his, feeling the itchy woolliness of the knitted blanket that was over the back of the chair.

'No, Kitty doesn't matter, in answer to your question,' Sylvia said, kissing his cheek. He still had freckles, just a few. 'Of course she doesn't. It's just brought it back – what she did, and all of that time.' She leaned round and looked into his face. 'D'you think about it much now?'

'The war? Not if I can help it. I think about a few people – the ones in France and Belgium mainly. Apart from that, it was a complete flaming waste of—' He stopped himself. 'No, I try not to think about it. I'd rather just get on with my life – since I've got one,' he added. She felt sad at the bitterness in his voice.

She sank back beside him. The last thing she wanted was to bring his mood down. Her mind showed her a door, and her shoving Kitty out of it and slamming it for good. The past – away with it, she thought. Back to where it belonged.

'Did Baba show you the gold star she got at school today? She said it was her best drawing ever.'

Laurie smiled. 'No – I'll get her to show me tomorrow.' And he kissed her neck and nuzzled against her cheek. 'Shall we go up soon?'

*

504

The next afternoon, when things were quiet, she took Kitty's letter out of the kitchen drawer and went to the bottom of the garden. There was a little charred patch where they had a bonfire.

'Dear Sylv . . .' She read Kitty's letter through one more time, then slowly tore it into tiny pieces.

'I don't need anyone like you in my life,' she said quietly. 'You can go to hell.'

Laying the pieces on the bonfire patch, she took a box of matches from her pocket and set them to burn, watching as they curled quickly into soft grey ash, sending a few thin threads of smoke into the air.

When it was quiet, later on, she walked round to find Laurie in the station. Smiling, she took his hand. 'Come with me,' she said.

Laurie looked puzzled, but pleased by the sight of her light-heartedness.

She led him to the big clock on platform one and, standing underneath it, turned to him. 'Remember when I said "Meet me under the clock and I'll be there?"' She saw a glow begin in his eyes and his face lightened. 'I love you, Laurie,' she said, putting her arms around his neck. 'Like nothing and no one. Give us a kiss, my love.'

A smile spread over his face until his eyes shone. Tenderly, he touched her cheek, then kissed her and held her close as if she was the most precious thing in the world. 'I've always said you were the best,' he said.

Sixty-Six

A few days later another letter arrived – a happy one.

'It's from Audrey,' she told Laurie, holding it in one hand and handing out toast to the children with the other.

'Auntie Audrey!' Baba said happily. She was a rosy child with a cloud of dark hair like her mother's.

'She says she's coming on Saturday.'

'With Auntie Dorrie? And Little Dorrie?'

'Yes,' Sylvia laughed, thinking how children accepted such situations long ahead of the grown-ups, who had to struggle. 'They said they'll come down and see us for the day.'

Baba jigged with excitement and Jonny grinned.

'Oh, look – she's sent me their meat coupons! What shall I cook?' Sylvia said. 'We must have something really nice!'

They heard the 'parp!' of the car's horn outside, and Jonny and Baba rushed down the garden path yelling, 'They're here!'

'Ah,' Laurie said. 'The two sirens have arrived.'

Sylvia gave him a look. 'Now, now – none of your jokes.'

She followed the children outside in time to see Dorrie climbing out of the driver's seat of the old, black Austin

10 Tourer. The roof was down and all of the car's occu-
pants were looking windswept and pink-cheeked. The
car had once belonged to Dorrie's father. Though he still
barely managed to acknowledge Dorrie's existence in
other ways, he had arranged to hand it on to her when
he got a new one.

'Ah – death obviously pays well,' Laurie remarked the
first time he saw it.

'Well, it's a steady and certain business, that's for sure,'
Dorrie replied with a grin.

Audrey called out, 'Hello, we got here quickly today!'

She was urging Dorian out of the back seat. He had
just had his eleventh birthday and Sylvia had a football
to give him. He looked a little sheepish, as his hair was
standing almost vertical after the journey and there was
always a bit of initial shyness between the cousins when
they first met.

Everyone hugged and greeted each other.

'You're looking very glamorous,' Sylvia told Audrey,
linking arms with her to go up the path. Audrey was
dressed in a full red skirt, a white blouse with red spots
and red shoes. She wore her hair in a swinging ponytail.
'You make me feel quite a frump in this old dress.'

'You?' Audrey laughed. 'Never!'

'You do look ever so well, sis.'

'I am,' Audrey said. She was glowing. 'I've got some
good news.' She turned. 'Have you got the basket,
Dorrie? We made some cakes for the feast.'

'Yep – coming!' Dorrie was hauling something out of
the car. She was dressed in tapering, calf-length navy
trousers and a white short-sleeved blouse.

'Let's have a cuppa,' Sylvia said. She had managed to
give Dorian a kiss before the children all rushed out to
play at the back.

'Ooh, something's good in here – is that beef I can smell?' Audrey said.

'Yes; thanks for the coupons!'

When Dorrie came in they all kissed in greeting. Sylvia filled the teapot and the four of them sat round the table. 'What's this news then?' she asked Audrey. 'Don't keep us in suspense.'

Dorrie smiled. 'Audrey's been given a column to write as well!'

Dorrie was gradually achieving her dream of working as a journalist. After starting off writing for various local London papers, she was now getting articles published in a range of magazines. She had a humorous style, which went down well in the women's magazines, but she had also had a couple of pieces accepted by *The Times* and two reviews for *The Listener*. It was she who had encouraged Audrey.

'Well, you always were good at writing, Aud,' Sylvia said. 'Not like me!'

'She tried a piece for *Time & Tide* – about bringing a child up without his father. They don't actually know she's not a widow, of course. And now they want her to do something else.'

'That's good,' Laurie said. 'Bully for you, Aud!'

'I've always wondered if I could earn money in a different way,' Audrey said. Dorrie had been the main breadwinner, and Audrey had done some typing work at home. 'This is much more of a challenge than just typing up papers for other people. I'm surprised to find I've got things I want to say.'

'Oh, you always had that,' Sylvia said.

'All right, all right!' Audrey made a face at her.

'We're not saying our Audrey is opinionated, are we?' Dorrie teased. Through their laughter she added,

'Talking of which – young Dr Jack came round the other night.'

'Oh, how lovely,' Sylvia said. Jack, who had not yet in fact earned the title 'Doctor', was at medical school in London. To everyone's surprise, he had hardly batted an eyelid about Audrey and Dorrie. He just seemed glad that Audrey was happy. 'It's so nice that you're both down there together. How is he?'

'Thriving,' Dorrie said.

'There's talk of a girl.' Audrey winked and she and Dorrie grinned. 'Called Margaret – we think.'

'Yes,' Dorrie said. 'After all, he only mentioned her name every other word.'

Sylvia saw how happy and alive Audrey looked. After the war, when Dorrie came back from Ceylon and the storm of Audrey's and Dorrie's love for each other broke over their family, things had been a terrible struggle for them both. Throughout the upheaval of it all, Marjorie Gould had once again been the saviour of the situation, by pointing out that having children who were alive was the main thing, whatever else they might choose to do with themselves. And, she had said to Pauline, you can't accuse Audrey of not giving you a grandchild, can you? The two fathers, Ted and Stanley, seemed to have a bemused notion that any relationship with no men involved did not quite count, so they tried to pretend that Audrey and Dorrie lived like sisters or maiden aunts. But what about Audrey's son growing up with two women? *What about all those boys growing up with widowed mothers?* Audrey pointed out. Pauline was both anxious and embarrassed.

'I'm not going to cast you off – you know that,' she said to Audrey. 'And I've nothing against your . . . your friend. But I can't say I like it. It's not right.'

509

Having them both living a distance away in London seemed to make things easier, though it was a great wrench when Pauline had to part with her grandson. But things settled down. They had to, one way or another.

They all enjoyed a happy lunch together, with roast beef and heaps of crispy potatoes, and the children all squeezed round the table with them. Sylvia had made pies with some early rhubarb and they drowned them in custard.

'Oh,' Audrey groaned afterwards. 'I'll have to walk this off. Shall we go down to the river in a bit?'

In the mellow late afternoon they wandered through the old town and went to the meadow by the bridge where the children could run about. It was even warm enough to paddle, in a spot where the bank slipped gently into the water, forming a little muddy beach. There was a big house on the other side, its garden stretching down to the river and, further along, willow trees hung dipping into the water's wide flank.

Sylvia and Audrey sank back on the grass together, watching the children splashing and screaming amid the sunlit ripples. Laurie stood nearby, chatting with Dorrie. The sun was warm on their faces, gnats jittered in the air and it felt as if summer had truly arrived.

Audrey watched the three children with amused eyes. 'He loves seeing your two,' she said, smiling as Dorian chased the younger ones in the shallows.

'Does he get comments – at school?' Sylvia said anxiously.

Audrey turned. 'You mean about his mother and mother! I don't know – he's never said. I think they think

510

Dorrie's his auntie. Half the kids in his class have no dads about, for one reason or another.'

Sylvia nodded, reassured.

'It'll all be different for them,' Audrey said, watching the children again.

'What?'

'Everything. Attitudes – things are changing.'

'That's what Laurie says. Things can't stay stuck as they were – everyone knowing their place, and all that.'

'No.' Audrey looked thoughtful. Then, with her usual spirit, she said, 'I want to know new places, not be stuck eternally in the old ones.'

Sylvia laughed happily. 'Trust you,' she said. Then she added softly. 'It's good to see you so happy, Aud.'

Audrey smiled joyfully at her. 'You too. Hey – come in for a paddle?'

She held her hand out to pull Sylvia up and the sisters waded in, holding up their skirts and giggling like little girls, up to their shins in the cool, shining water.

Acknowledgements

Stories like this contain a huge number of researched details, ranging from breeds of chicken to the names of bomber aircraft, and it would be impossible as well as tedious to record them all. However, some sources I have used deserve particular acknowledgement.

A great deal has been written about the mechanics and the awe-inspiring machines of the steam railways; rather less about the people who worked on them. I am particularly indebted to Helena Wojtczak's recent book, *Railway Women: Exploitation, Betrayal and Triumph in the Workplace*, and to Rose Matheson's *Women and the Great Western Railway*. Also to Frank Popplewell's excellent series of articles on Hockley Goods Yard in the *Great Western Railway Journal*, nos 15–19. My thanks also go to Derek Harrison for his two books, *Birmingham Snow Hill: A First Class Return* and *Salute to Snow Hill: The Rise and Fall of Birmingham's Snow Hill Railway Station 1852–1977*; to Tom Quinn for *Tales of the Old Railwaymen*; Bob Brueton for *All Change* and Pete Waterman for *Rail Around Birmingham*. Thanks also to the Museum of the Great Western Railway at Swindon and the Tyseley Locomotive Works Visitor Centre in Tyseley, Birmingham.

For details about the WAAF I drew on John Frayn Turner's *The WAAF at War*, Beryl E. Escott's *Our Wartime Days: The WAAF in World War II* and Joan Rice's *WAAF Diary: Sand in my Shoes*.

Details about the Second World War, and the war in Birmingham in particular, come from many sources, but especially *How We Lived Then* by Norman Longmate, and Angus Calder's *The People's War*, as well as Mark Arnold-Forster's *The World at War* and *Nella Last's War: The Second World War Diaries of Housewife 49*, edited by Richard Broad and Suzie Fleming. Carl Chinn's book *Brum Un-daunted: Birmingham During the Blitz* was helpful, as was the website www.bhamb14.co.uk/index_files/WW2.htm, about the bombing in Kings Heath. The Birmingham online History Forum is always a rich resource for local details.

The BBC online oral-history archive is invaluable for insights into people's varied wartime experiences. I was able to supplement these, with reference to Bomber Command, with help from the Imperial War Museum's DVD, *Journey Together*, and Max Hastings's *Bomber Command*. There were also various websites containing details about escape routes out of occupied Europe during and the Second World War, in particular www.ww2escapelines.co.uk/escapelines/comete. I was also able to build up a fuller picture by reading Kenneth Skidmore's *Follow the Man with the Pitcher* and Herman Bodson's *Downed Allied Airmen and Evasion of Capture: The Role of Local Resistance Networks in World War II*.

My Daughter, My Mother

BY ANNIE MURRAY

Two daughters. Two mothers.
The secrets of two lifetimes.

In 1984 two young mothers meet at a toddler group in Birmingham. As their friendship grows, they share with each other the difficulties and secrets in their lives.

Joanne, a sweet, shy girl, is increasingly afraid of her husband. The lively, promising man she married has become hostile and violent and she is too ashamed to tell anyone. When her mother, Margaret, is suddenly rushed into hospital, the bewildered family find that there are things about their mother of which they had no idea. Margaret was evacuated from Birmingham as a child and has spent years avoiding the pain of her childhood – but finds that you can't run from the past forever.

Sooky, kind and good-natured, has already been through one disastrous marriage and is back at home living with her parents. But being 'disgraced' is not easy. Her mother, Meena, refuses to speak to Sooky. At first her silence seems like a punishment, but Sooky gradually realizes it contains emotions that are far more complicated, and that her mother may need her help. Meena has spent twenty years trying to fit in with life in Birmingham and to deal with the conflicts within her between East and West, old ways and new.

This is the story of two young women discovering the heartbreak of their mothers' lives, and of how mothers create daughters – and learn from them.

ISBN: 978-0-330-53520-5

The Women of Lilac Street

BY ANNIE MURRAY

Troubles in life.
Strength in friendship.

Birmingham, almost a decade after the end of the Great War, and the women of Lilac Street have had more than their fair share of troubles . . .

Rose Southgate is trapped in a loveless marriage. Shy and isolated, she makes the best of life, until she meets a man who changes everything.

Jen Green is struggling to make ends meet, with a sick husband and five children to support. Aggie, her eldest daughter, is twelve years old and longs for excitement. But prying into the adult world shows her more than she had bargained for.

And Phyllis Taylor is a widow who has managed to put a dark and traumatic past behind her. But the return of her daughter Dolly threatens all that . . .

These women find strength in friendship, as they discover that the best way to solve their problems is to face them together.

ISBN: 978-0-330-53521-2

FOR MORE ON

ANNIE
MURRAY

sign up to receive our

SAGA NEWSLETTER

Packed with **features, competitions, authors'
and readers' letters** and **news of exclusive events**,
it's a must-read for every Annie Murray fan!

Simply fill in your details below and tick to confirm that you would
like to receive saga-related news and promotions and return to us at
Pan Macmillan, Saga Newsletter, 20 New Wharf Road, London, NI 9RR.

NAME _____

ADDRESS _____

_____

_____ POSTCODE _____

EMAIL _____

☐ *I would like to receive saga-related news and promotions (please tick)*

*You can unsubscribe at any time in writing or through our website where you can also see
our privacy policy which explains how we will store and use your data.*

Bello:
hidden talent rediscovered

Bello is a digital-only imprint of Pan Macmillan,
established to breathe new life into previously
published, classic books.

At Bello we believe in the timeless power
of the imagination, of good story, narrative and
entertainment and we want to use digital technology
to ensure that many more readers can enjoy
these books into the future.

Our available books include:
Margaret Pemberton's *The Londoners* trilogy;
Brenda Jagger's *Barforth Family* saga; and
Janet Tanner's *Hillsbridge Trilogy*.

For more information,
and to sign-up for regular updates, visit:

www.panmacmillan.com/bellonews